Love on a Half Shell

By

Elvy Howard

Edward Allen Publishing, LLC
Hampton, Virginia

Edward Allen

E A

PUBLISHING, LLC

For information about our authors and/or their availability for live events, contact our marketing team at info@edwardallenpublishing.com

Cover Art Design by Katherine Basey
Book Design by David Price

Manufactured in the United States of America

10 9 8 7 6 5 4 3 2 1

Edward Allen Publishing, LLC
PO Box 7769
Hampton, Virginia 23666
www.EdwardAllenPublishing.com

ISBN print 978-0-9853123-3-6
ISBN eBook 978-0-9853123-2-9

My attention is snagged by a woman coming from the other side of the marina. She seems familiar. She's wearing a baseball cap and has a long brown ponytail sticking out the back. About my height and weight. What is it about her?

Chip! It's Chip.

Is it?

I haven't seen her since I was sixteen or so and stopped coming to the beach house. Is it really her? I'm squinting, trying to be sure. I think it is! I think I'd recognize her peculiar loping stride anywhere.

I shout Chip's name and grab the now wet Melissa from her game with the boys. She protests when she has to drop the hose she just got control of, but I carry her sideways, bouncing across my hip, to the dock opposite us. Melissa continues to holler for me to put her down, but I'm not listening.

I run until I'm right in front of the woman. "Hey there, Chip Madsen?" She looks at me. I can tell she has no idea who I am. I turn Melissa upright and drape her on my hip. She puts a thumb in her mouth and pouts around it. "Rae Green. Remember me, the summer kid?" I grin.

Chip's brown eyes light up with her smile. She cocks her head to one side. "Rae? Is that really you?"

"Yes. I'm so glad to see you." Gladness bordering on hysteria. I need to calm down.

Acknowledgments

I have to thank the people, past and present in my critique group. Our group has been meeting for many years and a more generous bunch of diverse characters couldn't be found. They are, Sara Rupnik, Barbara Pedrotti, Jim Cotter and Sylvia May. I also have to thank my great friend, publisher and cheerleader, Leah Price of Edward Allen Publishing.

The author acknowledges the trademarked status and trademark owners of the following wordmarks used in this work of fiction:

Boston Whaler
Chuck E. Cheese's
CorningWare
Evinrude
Knorr
Kool-Aid
Play-Doh
RITZ crackers

DEDICATION

To Michael, of course.

I started making this dessert in high school, mostly for pajama parties. It became one of the stars of the catering business I started to get me though college and graduate school.

It was originally my mother's recipe, with the racy name, "Better Than Sex Cake."

I hadn't made it in years, but when I got the girls, I renamed it "Better than Anything Cake" and made it a lot the first six months or so. All the bad-for-you ingredients and empty calories meant nothing by then. I'd do anything to get them to behave. But in my head I called it what it was:

Crap Cake

- 9 x 12 rectangular cake pan
- one box chocolate cake mix, any type: German, fudge, devil's food
- one jar caramel ice-cream topping
- one jar fudge ice-cream topping
- one can sweetened condensed milk
- whipped cream style topping
- cherries, optional

Make cake according to package directions. When done and with a wooden skewer, poke lots of holes in the top of the cake, and while still warm, pour over the condensed milk and half of each jar of ice-cream topping, cover with foil and let toppings soak into the cake. Plate squares of cake, add whipped topping and, using the rest of the ice-cream toppings, stripe cake, cream and plate with the fudge going one way and the caramel at a 45-degree angle, creating a design over the cream and plate. Top with cherry.

September

Nine Months Ago

The girls fell into my lap late one rainy night, like giant bombs from thin air.

The last time I saw her, the youngest had been a crawling, drooling baby, so I wasn't prepared for the four-year-old, sprawled asleep on my sister's couch with bunged-up legs hanging over the couch's arm. Her head, angling towards the floor with long, blond hair cascading over the couch's faded striped cloth, was another surprise.

The reality of Melissa struck me silent, a sad memory of wispy, sticky-outy hair and a toothless grin washing through me.

My niece's perfect pink lips had a thumb inserted dead center. She looked more like the front-page model for "American Child Magazine" rather than the youngest daughter of a woman arrested earlier that night.

No one had noticed me yet, a woman still on the youngish side of middle age, with curly brown hair pulled back in a rubber band, wearing jeans, sneakers, and a trench coat to go along with a probably blank expression.

There were plenty of people around though, determinedly heading in different directions—outside, back towards the bedrooms, or behind me towards the kitchen.

Some had clipboards; others, boxes; and others, nothing at all. Laughter came from a group in the brightly lit kitchen, but the living room was dim. Only light that spilled from the kitchen and from police cars outside, whirling through the night and rain, allowed me to see the child in all her four-year-old glory.

The swirling police lights announced, *This is where the action is,* for all the forensic, county, state, and federal employees assigned to my sister's case.

I hadn't expected the light show any more than I had Melissa. I'd noticed a glow in the night sky as I drove towards their house and hadn't grasped what it was about until I got close.

As I pulled onto my sister's street of small, dilapidated houses with lights and vehicles jamming her front yard, the first part of my new reality began to sink in. Vicky was in jail, and I had to get her girls.

Somehow, I made it inside.

A woman, probably the one who called me from Family and Children's Services, was asleep too, in an over-stuffed chair nearer the TV. At least that's who I thought it was. She'd said her name was Mona Stumples.

What a horrible name. Who in the hell would name their kid Mona Stumples? Mona didn't wear a wedding ring, but maybe it was her married name and no one person was fully responsible for it. She was the only adult, outside of me, not in some kind of uniform.

I stood there, numb, trying to feel anything but the coldness seeping into my skin.

Mona had called me two and a half hours earlier, saying she would wait at the scene until I arrived.

Wait at the scene. I couldn't process the line. It sounded too much like something from TV.

I looked around, attempting to piece together some memory of the house — *the scene.*

The lamps, end tables, and couch were from Momma's. Thankfully, the lamps hadn't been broken, but so many things were, with the toys trampled underfoot and stuff scattered everywhere. But how much of it was from her arrest and how much of it was the way they lived? I didn't know.

My impression was that everything was damaged in some irreparable way, everything destroyed.

I looked on Melissa's peaceful form. She was oblivious to the activity and noise, and a cold, clear understanding dawned on me. I was a complete stranger to that child.

I let her sleep and cursed my sister for creating the scenario, for never letting me get to know Melissa and then dumping her into my life.

My heart raced while I resisted the urge to bolt and leave both Melissa and Mona Stumples in their sleep, and everyone in that place. Leave before they woke up. Drive back to Richmond, my condo, and my sane job and life.

Back to a world that made sense. It wasn't my fault—let North Carolina take care of its own problems. But that would mean leaving Torey behind, too, and that wasn't an option.

The uniforms still hadn't taken notice of me. They were focused on their varying tasks. One uniform, on a cell phone near the front door, nodded and smiled sympathetically towards me.

I nodded back, thinking I must look like another social worker, called out on that miserable night.

Roars of laughter came from the kitchen—loud, soft, then loud again—police officers and detectives joking with FBI people. The scent of coffee spilled into the room where I stood.

I wondered, since I also worked in justice, if maybe I threw out those same kinds of vibes, like someone from their side of the blue line.

After all, people from the outside were usually easy to spot. They came in hysterical and acquiescing to anyone in a uniform. Or alternately, they might be one of those geniuses who snarled and cursed out someone with the authority to lock them up. I'd seen it many times.

The thought of joining the group in the kitchen, getting caffeine zinging through my blood, possessed me.

Once I got going I could trot out my best jokes. I wasn't in Virginia; no one in that room had heard my jokes. I could pull out the best, splurge and go for broke.

All the macho uniforms would laugh and accept me,

think I was cool. That was, until they found out I was the perp's sister. How to avoid that part I couldn't figure out, and realizing I was actually considering doing something so insane made me back up and rethink the moment.

Backing up and rethinking a moment was something I had recently gotten a lot of practice at.

I wondered where Torey was.

Something inside said it was time. I had to start the thing. Quickly, before panic or insanity got their grip on me again. I crossed the room and gently shook Mona on her shoulder.

She woke up clear as a bell, knowing exactly where she was, and without ever meeting me, knowing exactly who I was too. I was grateful; the night was already hard enough.

"You must be Rae." She sat up, smiling like we were old friends.

The North Carolina twang was jarring, but I smiled back. "Yes, that's me." I adopted a friendly, professional tone and tamped down the fires of fear trying to rage in me.

Mona glanced at her watch. "Wow, you made good time, especially in this weather."

I saw gray roots in the woman's faded red hair. "I probably drove too fast. Where's Torey?"

"She'd better be around here somewhere." Mona stretched, and looked around. "Maybe back in their room."

During the long drive I'd hashed and rehashed our phone conversation.

Mona had history with Torey. She'd interviewed her last spring after a report of suspected neglect from her school. The school's complaint stated Torey had been wearing dirty clothes, and was unwashed. Torey's explanation was the lousy county had turned off their water. It wasn't her mother's fault.

Mona had monitored the situation since, checking on Torey at school monthly, after first visiting my sister and making sure she got the water turned back on.

Torey was a chronic truant who'd worked the system to the point of expulsion but never beyond it. Because of the truancy, Mona had been to the house several times, yet had never found Vicky or Torey "amenable to services." Vicky had been only interested in whatever financial assistance

Mona could scrape together, and Torey had as little to do with her as possible.

I looked at Melissa, still asleep and oblivious. She was adorable, and she terrified me, but Mona, returning, distracted my fears.

She was breathing heavily and dragging a large box that had clothes and ragged stuffed animals sticking out from its top. "Torey's still packing their things. I think this stuff is mostly Melissa's." She poked around the open box. "I'd better get her up."

Mona reached out to tap Melissa on the shoulder, casually, easily, and I had to consciously restrain my hand from stopping hers.

There was no way I was ready to meet that child. But Melissa didn't wake; she rolled over, sucking her thumb louder, and moaned softly.

Mona sighed and straightened up.

The notion of Mona being the person who tipped off the police, the one who initiated this nightmare, filled my mind. It hadn't occurred to me until then, and it threw me. I wasn't sure how to feel towards the frizzy redhead bent over a briefcase; family loyalty and my career collided and I didn't know whose side I was on.

"Torey!" Mona shouted, going back down the hall while I shuddered, gripped by a strong desire to keep Melissa sleeping, keep Torey in her room a little longer, not begin yet. I sat, nervously, and stroked Melissa's silky blond hair, so like her mother's.

A sound made me look up and see Torey, stumbling towards us and dragging a large suitcase that once belonged to her grandmother, my mother. I recognized the blue designer fabric and leather edges, and I flashed on my mother's smiling face going off with Daddy somewhere wonderful.

That memory of my mother in happier times vanished, replaced by a keening in my head. *No longer a child.*

Torey approached—a woman, complete with breasts and hips, everything about her rounded and set off by a gold ring glinting from the dusky skin of her exposed belly button. The same belly button I kissed when drying her off after a bath or changing her diapers.

The actual loss of the past four years hit in a newer, sharper way, and I was glad to be sitting.

My eyes searched for traces of the child I once knew and found nothing.

Because I was stuck there, hanging on for dear life to a long dead couch, I didn't do any of the things I should have.

I didn't rush up to help her with the suitcase or welcome her back into my life. I didn't even smile or speak. I was rooted where I was and attempting to absorb who'd she'd become.

Tears slid down my face as I mourned the loss of a skinny little girl with a fuzzy halo of black hair. Torey would be petite like Vicky, her tiny woman's form not blocking Mona, who came up behind, dragging another large box.

Torey's hair was long like Melissa's, only in beautiful black waves past her waist, and she glared at me as she entered the room.

But she's only twelve, I argued with no one.

"From what I gather, it's been a while," Mona said, looking at my niece with a horribly fake smile. "So Torey, this is your Aunt Rae. Do you remember her?"

Torey ducked her head, instantly hiding her face. "Yeah." Her voice was muffled by the hair and the angle of her face.

"Well, that's great. Give me the keys to your car and Torey and I can take these things out. Then we'll come back for Melissa. In the meantime, Rae, I need you to sign the forms on this clipboard." Mona picked up a stack of papers and snapped them to the board before handing it to me. A pen was attached to the board's clip.

I could have screamed the sadness overtaking me, but I pulled the keys from the trench coat instead, and handed them to Mona like a trade for the clipboard. My insides were empty, a void made of shock and the crumpled lies I'd been telling myself about how much I'd missed them.

If Vicky had been in the room I could have saved the state the expense of her upcoming trial, I would have killed her with my bare hands.

I sensed myself more alone than I had been in a long, long time. I hadn't expected that either. "It's the Mitsubishi parked next to the mailboxes," I said to Mona.

"No need to wake her up until it's time to leave. Melissa can be...." The certainty Mona had been operating with evaporated, her face turning red as she searched for a word. "Excitable. I have a child carrier for her in my car." Mona began dragging the cardboard box towards the front door. After a moment's hesitation, Torey followed. She seemed to be as unsure of what to do next as I was.

I shook my head, trying to clear it, and looked at the first form on the clipboard. I could make out nothing. It was the same with the next and the next.

I stroked Melissa's hair and waited for Mona to get back. She did in record time, still dragging the now damp box and looking very angry. Torey trailed behind.

"What in the world were you thinking?"

Having no idea what I'd been thinking, I wasn't able to say. I must have looked as blank as a snow-covered beach.

"You have a two-seater convertible out there that won't even hold this luggage."

Luggage? I tried to comprehend the angry woman standing over a damp cardboard box.

"I told you when I called there were two girls here; you have two nieces."

She was shouting. Somehow I had stumbled outside the blue line and the aloneness I'd been coping with all but engulfed me.

Panic, and the question of how to create a suitable automobile in the next five minutes, became my world. I sat like something stupid; yet a small flame ignited in my chest, something like a pilot light flaring up. I welcomed it because the fire spreading through me woke up my brains as well. I took a deep breath and shook my head again, slowly gaining momentum. Mona was breathing heavily, waiting for an answer.

I stood up, and as if speaking to some inept secretary said, "You are correct, Ms. Stumples." I saw my tone wake something up in Mona as well.

I could see the wheels turning in her head, trying to recall my position in Virginia and calculating how much of an impact I could have on hers in North Carolina. She hesitated. Big mistake.

"I'm sorry I wasn't thinking clearly when you telephoned me *at one a.m.* to come get these girls." I walked towards her, towering over the shorter, dumpier woman and looking down with all the condescension I could muster. I paused to give Mona a moment to absorb the situation. From the corner of my eye, I noticed Torey looking at me with interest.

Mona began to say something but I interrupted with an impatient sigh, "Let me finish, please, if that's okay with you." My glare said a lot more.

I handed her the clipboard. "Show me what I have to sign tonight so that I can leave immediately with these girls. I don't have time to go through this entire thing right now."

"But what about…?"

"Don't worry, I'll get a new car first thing in the morning. Let's get these girls to a nearby motel. You can drive them."

She tried to say something, but I stopped her with another look that said, *Go ahead, screw with me and see what happens.* No civil servant was safe in a look like that.

"The girls are too tired to deal with anything else tonight." I'd perfected the note of finality in my voice. "I'm sure you agree."

Mona sagged like sails collapsing. She nodded absently, going through the pages, pointing out various lines for me to sign. Then she headed back outside, dragging the box. "I'll need to see you tomorrow before you leave the state." She shook the clipboard in her free hand. "All these forms will have to be signed, transfer of custody, all that."

"I'll come by your office right after I get another car," I promised again.

Mona sighed and dragged the box out the front door.

I took my mother's suitcase from Torey. "Can you carry your sister?" I asked to be polite. Torey has been carrying Melissa since Melissa was born.

She nodded and I was secretly overjoyed by the respect I saw in those beautiful green eyes of hers. Finally something I remembered, something left from all those years ago.

The flame in me grew and my spirit soared. I fully

believed I could do it, take on those girls and make a good life for them until I got Vicky straightened out. They wouldn't have to live at the mercy of their mother's addictions anymore, and neither would I.

I put down the suitcase and took off my trench coat. After Torey expertly slung the still-sleeping child onto her hip, I draped it over them.

I picked up my mother's old suitcase, and we went out in the rain together.

Emergency Meal #7

- English muffins
- bottled spaghetti sauce
- any cheese you prefer
- any cooked ground meat or sausage

Split muffins and spread with sauce, sprinkle meat, grate cheese over top and broil.

June

Nine Months Later

Whoever built our beach cottage must have scavenged all its parts because absolutely nothing matches. Windows are different widths and heights and no two doors are the same. The bathroom door is a solid wood contraption, probably from some previous century, and so heavy, iron straps secure it to the wall.

It makes a hell of a noise when slammed open by Torey, who's framed in the doorway and screaming, "What do you mean leaving us alone until eight o'clock at night? What the hell was I supposed to do all day? I left messages at your job and on your cell. Where were you?"

"Do you see me sitting here?" There are so many things wrong with this moment I can't find a starting place. Torey's dark curls quiver with fury, her fists clench and relax, then clench again while her nostrils flare. She looks like some character from TV.

"So? What about me? I'm almost a teenager! I'm supposed to be hanging out with friends, but no, I don't get to do that. You move us out here in the middle of Bum Fuck Egypt where there's nothing—not even cable! You're holding us prisoners, Rae. I'm calling Social Services. This is neglect."

"Watch your mouth, and please do call Social Services.

The number's on the refrigerator. Maybe they'll take you and I'll finally get some privacy around here. Now get out. I mean it. Shut the door and leave."

"You can't do this. Melissa is as bored as me…"

I'm stuck, so tune out Torey's latest rant. There's no reason to listen anyway; she's been saying the same damned thing since we moved—and that's been what? Only two weeks?

For the lack of anything better to do, I stare at Melissa, standing behind Torey and sucking her thumb. She nods vacantly as if in complete agreement with everything her sister spews.

I know a stranger would never guess the adorable-looking child is as disturbed as the monster continuing her earsplitting and foul soliloquy in the doorway.

Torey smacks one fist into the palm of her hand, making a sound like she's punching someone. I know she wishes it was me. She does this to emphasize her point, which is always the same—how I had screwed up her life.

Last week, when Melissa turned five, I took them to Chuck E. Cheese's in Williamsburg, to celebrate. I thought it would be fun for them, with tokens for video games and prizes. At first it was, but Melissa's idea of a good time was to notch up her usual unpleasantness to a point where no one could take it and then notch it up some more.

I ended up half-carrying her, half-dragging her, kicking and screaming from the place. It was one of the worst nights of my life and I swore they weren't going out in public again until they learned to behave themselves.

Melissa is a baby-acting, wannabe bimbo with a princess fixation, and I hate her only a little less than her sister Torey, the Drama Queen from Planet Teenzilla.

Melissa notices me noticing her, and the cloudy, unfocused look in her eyes clears. Alarm takes its place.

"Take that damned thumb out of your mouth, right now." I growl and don't have one clue as to why. I wish I hadn't and am immediately sorry—but to show it would be beyond stupid. It would be the same as going with open bloody wounds into a pool of sharks in the middle of a feeding frenzy.

Melissa's large, blue eyes puddle with tears. "Why are you hollering at me, Arae? I didn't do nothing."

Torey named me Arae when she was two. I used to love it. "You didn't do *anything*," I counter, as if improving her grammar was a possibility. I can't believe I'm picking on a five-year-old.

I look at my nemesis Torey and say in a tone that contains enough finality to stop the madness, if even for only a moment, "If you don't get the hell out of this bathroom, right this second, you can count on not even having a phone tomorrow."

"You can't do that!" Torey screams an octave higher.

For once, the lack of neighbors is a blessing. "You watch me." I can't go higher, but I can go louder and angrier.

Torey, always with the last word, "I hate you, Rae. You are such a bitch. I hate you, hate you, hate you!" They stomp down the hall.

"Watch your mouth," I whisper to myself. The sliding glass door leading to the screened-in porch squeals like something insane when they open it, and I guess they go out, because it squeals again when they close it.

The bathroom door, of course, is left wide open, and since I have no desire to get up, it stays that way.

I'm too exhausted to distract myself with laundry, cleaning, picking up, yelling at them to take showers—*with soap*—brush their teeth—*with toothpaste*—and all the other crap that goes along with having kids in your house.

I'm in over my head and know it. All the signs are there—upset stomachs, headaches, a wobbly memory, not sleeping, and the worst part is a growing sense of terror that threatens to overtake me.

I don't know what I'm going to do. Staring at the chipped green and white tiles on the floor, I do some deep breathing. For us, the last three remnants of my family, the situation is becoming desperate. We're like shipwrecked sailors washed up on some sandy shore and going nowhere.

When my sister was incarcerated, my heart broke for her and the kids; the agony of their separation broke my heart.

Now, the thought of being chained to her kids for a minimum of another eight years and three months is making an anxiety in me that scrapes away at whatever used to cushion my nerves.

It's like we all are incarcerated—me, Vicky, Torey and Melissa—each trapped in our own piece of hell, and I don't know what to do to get us out. We have the rest of the summer to get through and then the next eight years. The way things are going, I don't see how.

I crank open the window next to me, and a sweet Virginia breeze comes in the stuffy room. The day has been a complete nightmare, now capped off by Torey's latest outburst. But there isn't anything new about that, and I can't figure out why the day has been so hard.

My new job wasn't worse than usual, just longer because of the list of home visits I had to complete so my caseload didn't get out of compliance.

It's the last day of June, ergo the need for all the home visits before July arrived, but there's something about today suddenly striking me for a different reason. It was exactly a year ago, on this exact day, when I broke it off with the rat-bastard that is Dennis. Had it been only a year since I called off that doomed affair? With all the shit from the girls and everything else, it seemed a lot longer.

But only one single year had passed since I had woken up. A flash of myself a year ago, my complete naiveté, presents itself, and I shake my head in disbelief. How could I have not seen, even then, the cold evil in the man? And how did one person go through so many changes in just one year?

Finally, I peel myself off the toilet seat. I should go and see about the girls but dawdle in the bathroom instead. I wash my face and, for no particular reason, brush my teeth. New worry lines are on my forehead, and my hair seems to have lost whatever shine it once had.

Hiding out in the bathroom all night isn't an option, and there aren't too many other places to go. Two bedrooms, one bath, a kitchen/family room and the screened-in porch make up the entire cottage.

I go to my room and change into shorts and a T-shirt.

It's an ugly room, painted a depressing green selected by my mother, probably thirty years ago. The hall isn't much better. Why she picked mustard for the hall I'll never know. Probably she thought it went with the horrible green and white asbestos tiles she covered the floors with.

The kitchen is in its usual state—milk left out with the remnants of everything they'd eaten. I place the milk back in the refrigerator and notice it's warm. I used to yell about things like that but can't get worked up over petty things anymore.

They're still out on the porch. We'd had an unusually cold and rainy spring, but now that it's warmed up, they'd claimed the screened-in area of the cottage as their own. I'm glad; it gives us all a little breathing room.

The sounds of giggling, the slamming of the battered, old wooden swing against the side of the house, and their radio playing some horrible rap music way louder than it's supposed to be, come through the wall.

I'm not ready for any more confrontations, so I pick up the clothes and pillows left on the couch and floor and take them back to their room. Dennis's face, red with anger because he can't talk me out of leaving him, flashes in my head.

I go back to the living room and, sighing, gather up what's left of my reserves, or strength, or whatever you call it, and push open the damned, not-sliding-but-sticking glass door.

I honestly don't know how Torey gets it open. With all my strength, I can barely manage it. They immediately get quiet, and Torey stops the swing. Resentment locks on her face, and Melissa puts a thumb in her mouth. I snap off the radio. The only sound, outside of small waves hitting against the pier, is Melissa's rhythmic sucking of her thumb.

The same picnic table my family used to sit at is here on the porch now. I moved it in years ago so it wouldn't melt into the sand outside. The wood is silver-colored and so silky, smoothed down by the salt air and wind, it's become an art form all its own.

I used to put bouquets of wildflowers on this table, in one of my mother's collection of antique vases. But that was part of my old life, not this one. Now those vases are stored in the attic where they can't be destroyed, and the table sits empty.

Along with the picnic table, the porch has a large, white-painted wooden swing, an antique wicker chair, and some falling-apart folding chairs with half their webbing missing. In a corner, an ugly wood cabinet with peeling, yellowed paint resides with some rusting TV tables leaning next to it.

I sit at the picnic table in a broken aluminum chair and look at them, the weird fruit of my sister's loins. "I am so sick of this."

The resentment my nieces generate when I speak curdles the air. I could have predicted it, so why say anything? I don't know. But then words I never intended come from my mouth. "I quit," I hear myself say, and instantly feel better. A whole lot better. I say it again. "I quit."

"Go ahead. We don't care," Torey mumbles.

"I bet you don't." That's what the parenting research tells you to say. Instead of saying, "You are a piece of shit," or "You ungrateful, horrible brat," you say, "You sound upset," or "You must be having a difficult time today," or some other dishonest thing.

A delicious, cool breeze stirs, and I look out over the Chesapeake Bay to a suspension bridge carrying cars with people in them, people going places. My heart aches to be among them again, going places I want to go. Still staring at the lights on those cars, I ask Torey, "Why were you calling me? What did you want?"

"Nothing now."

"Just tell me," is what I say, but what I'm really thinking is, I could strip naked, run down the pier and jump off the end. The girls can swim but are terrified of the bay with things like crabs and fish in it. They only swim in cement pools where the bottoms and occupants are clearly visible. I wouldn't have to worry about them following me, and it was too early for jellyfish. I could float around out there forever. Maybe the tide would carry me out to sea.

"We wanted to know when you were coming home."

I look at her in disbelief. "That's what all the screaming

was about, because you wanted to know when I was coming home?"

They don't say anything.

I don't either. I go back to watching the tiny car lights moving through blackness. "I had a bunch of home visits to make. Remember I told you last night?"

No response.

"Then I had to stop at the grocery store which you also knew about because you said we were out of cereal, remember?"

Still no response.

"And then, of course, it takes a while to get here. I never heard my cell ring. I guess it needs to be charged. Did something else happen? Did you need something?"

"No," Torey mutters.

"You just wanted to know when I was going to get here?"

"Um, yeah."

Now I'm the one who doesn't know what to say, and that's pretty much the way I always end up when I try to talk to them. "You guys know we didn't ask for this, don't you?"

"What are you saying? It's my mom's fault?"

Torey's ability to take affront and get all worked up is exhausting me. I'm only thirty-six and feel ninety-sixed. "I'm not saying that, Torey." Although I'd like to know who else is to blame. "It's just the three of us are stuck here and I'm sick of carrying the load."

"It's not our fault you moved us out here, that's for sure. Why couldn't we have stayed in Richmond? At least there we'd have a normal life with cable and a mall."

"Do I need to review the last six months with you guys?"

"Oh, God, Rae, not again." Torey puts her hands on her head. Melissa copies her, like I'm giving them both headaches.

"Yeah, I guess I have to. Evidently you all don't remember." Then—and where this is coming from I can't say—my voice takes on story-book theatrics. "Think back, girls, into the mists of time. I lost my job, my condo wasn't big enough for all of us, plus it was too expensive. And then, when I couldn't find work anywhere near Richmond, I began looking for something around here."

I wait. No response.

"So I was lucky enough to get something in Williamsburg, and we got to move here."

"Are you done yet?" Torey has perfected her own voice — the bored and condescending teenager.

"No, I'm not, Torey. Your Social Security checks got screwed up." I look at Melissa, "And your dad disappeared, so no money from him." Back to Torey. "And your momma is in prison."

They glare but I am not backing down. "Yes, prison. Your mother is in prison, which is still not my fault, but after paying for her lawyer, there's nothing left. So here we are and I'm broke and we are barely getting by on what I'm making."

They don't budge. Melissa continues to suck her thumb and Torey continues to glare.

"Moving here was our last option. I already told you. At least this place is paid for and we can have a roof over our heads. It's the best I can do, but it looks like it's just not enough."

Torey slumps over in the swing, landing in a pile of pillows like she's dead and can't hear me. Melissa, of course, does the same. If only they'd stay that way.

"I quit," I say, again without intending to. It's strange, but every time I do, I feel a whole lot better. My head is clearer, the uneasiness lessening.

Melissa sits up and pulls her thumb from her mouth long enough to speak. "Arae, we don't like it here."

"Where else do you want to be?"

"With Mommy," she says and begins crying.

Torey sits up and puts her arm around Melissa, proving she isn't completely insensitive to every human on the planet. Her more intense glare tells me what a jerk I am to hurt "the baby."

Maybe she has a point. I don't know. "I told you we could go see her this fall." Melissa doesn't respond. It's like I'm not here, or am a ghost or something. She keeps crying.

"I won't have any vacation time until then. Going to Ohio and back will take a few days."

Nothing. Melissa only keeps up the tinny-sounding wail.

"Every time one of you gets sick or has an appointment, I have to take off. Saving up vacation time will take a while." My voice is taking on the hysterical plaintive note I know is dangerous, so I shut up.

I look at the creatures destroying me. I'm tired of cajoling them, of being sensitive to the pain they have to be in. Sympathy isn't working. Structure is a joke. Any kindness I've shown them becomes an instant victim to their greed for material items of any kind.

Consistency and rules make no difference. Everything I try only increases the horribleness of our day-to-day life, and I never even see how this is possible until I find the abyss we're residing in even deeper than before. My brain registers the reality of being completely out of ideas, and worse, out of hope.

Melissa's crying subsides. She's probably more tired than missing her mother. Among the three of us, she seems the least affected by Vicky's incarceration, but when she's tired, anything can and will make her cry.

I should give her a bath, put her to bed, but I don't have the energy.

"If I don't use any more vacation time, we can go see your mom in the fall." That is, if I don't run out of here, jump into the bay and float away.

"And I bet we don't do it then, either." I hate the sarcasm in Torey's voice. I do. I hate it.

"We can, if I still have some vacation time left."

"That's not my problem, is it?" Torey is screaming again.

I don't have it in me to fight. "No, I guess not." But then I feel a spark of something still alive in me. "Wait a minute. I think it is your problem."

"What?"

"If you want to see your mom, it's your problem, not mine."

"What do you mean? You won't take us?"

"I will if I can, but I'm not the one who wants to go. It really isn't my problem." I smile, enjoying the sense of relief washing over me.

Torey looks at me with an expression I'm used to, a mix

of frustration and confusion, with real hatred mixed in. "Shit, Rae, you are so weird."

"Watch your mouth." I glare at her. Being thrown together like this has been more than just a shock. We live with the stress of constantly clashing values, beliefs, and customs, grating against each other like sandpaper in a wound.

I find it hard, at times, to believe Vicky and I were ever kids in the same house, much less raised by the same people. I know Torey doesn't understand a thing I do, either.

There's nothing left to say, so I get up and leave. The kitchen is in darkness, but I can see well enough to get myself a glass of water. I know I should eat something or get the groceries from the car, but I stand there, next to the kitchen sink.

Some perverse sense of liberation continues to build in me, but why? Nothing has changed. Still, I'm afraid to leave this spot. I'm afraid to jinx it.

I let water splash into the sink, filling it, then put dishes and pans in to soak. I drink another glass of water. I feel even better and wonder how I can live in hell yet experience this sense of freedom. What's happening? Am I cracking up?

It isn't my problem. The sentence keeps ringing in my head. But my nieces think it is. They think everything is my problem and they aren't the only ones. I guess I believed it too. Ever since I got them, I'd been wondering why everything was so damned hard, and now, unexpectedly, it is as clear as a panoramic view of the world.

A plan pops into my head, fully formed, and I consider it. Why not? At this point, I have nothing to lose. Still, I hesitate. It's a big gamble.

When I go back out on the porch, I take a deep breath. This will require guts, lots of them.

I look the girls squarely in the face. "You know what? I can't take it anymore. Working and worrying and coming home to tantrums and kids who can't even put milk back in the refrigerator. I guess I'm the worst person in the world to try and take care of you."

They give me that blank stare they use when calculating where I'm coming from. When I first got them, I would get creeped out by this look, but now I'm immune.

"You win. I'm terrible at this and have no idea what I was thinking when I took you guys on. We need to come up with a better plan."

"Like what, Arae?" Melissa looks concerned. Torey elbows her to shut up.

"Well," I say, looking at my younger niece, "maybe you could go live with your nana."

"Nana Ames?" Melissa's voice shoots up.

"Well, outside of your mom, dad, and me, she's the only relative you've got."

"Momma said Nana Ames was trash." Melissa's voice is getting higher pitched, a sign of nervousness I know only too well.

"Well, I think Nana Ames would say your momma was trash too."

"She is not!" Melissa shouts.

"I didn't say it. I think your nana might though."

Melissa is quiet. She knows I'm right. She asks in what, for her, is a quiet voice, "Would Torey come too?"

"What do you think?" I answer gently, knowing Melissa is aware of her nana's feelings about Torey.

"I don't think Nana would let her. She'd say Torey was a nigger, and niggers don't live in her house."

I'm shocked. Even I didn't know her nana used words like that. "Don't ever say that word again, Melissa. Sometimes your nana says stupid things. I don't want you being like her." I keep my voice stern.

Torey keeps her arm around Melissa but looks down at the cement floor. "And you, Torey, could go into foster care because I'm the only family you've got, outside of your momma."

Torey looks at me, her green eyes narrow and unreadable.

I go on. "It probably wouldn't be too difficult to find you a black family, so maybe you'd finally feel like you fit in somewhere."

Torey screams, "I don't want to go into foster care. Are you stupid or something?"

Melissa's eyes grow big and she takes her thumb from

her mouth.

"Are you sure?" I stand up and walk close to the swing. "Think about it. You're the one always complaining about living in a white family and how I could never understand you."

Torey's cheeks flush. She hates not being able to crush me in a verbal battle.

"Tell me something, Torey. Since your momma is white, how come she can understand you and I can't?"

"'Cause she's my momma, you stupid bitch!"

Automatically, I grab my hands behind my back so I can't slap her. It happened once, and I feel myself too near the place where it could happen again.

"You're right. I am a stupid bitch," I say through clenched teeth, "to put up with a bunch of crap from you. And you know what?"

The edges of Torey's nostrils are dead white, a signal she is afraid and liable to do anything, but I'm committed to this damn idea and can't turn back.

"I'm not doing it any more. I'm calling Social Services in the morning. I'm surprised you aren't happy. Think about it, you can finally get rid of me and be able to find out what it's like to be black."

"I'm not black. I'm mixed. I'm both!"

"Well, that's what I thought, but you always tell me I'm too stupid to understand."

I'm trouncing her and hating it. I despise getting caught up in these fights. The dead silence we usually live in is better, but Torey lives in a war zone even when there is no war, and I'm tired of losing ground.

"So that's it, I'll charge up my cell and call your nana, Melissa."

"Go there without Torey?" The horror in Melissa's voice is difficult to ignore, but I'm hanging tough. I have to, this is too important.

It's hard to hear myself think over Melissa's screams. She's able to reach a pitch that would drive anyone insane and then, unbelievably, go higher.

"And you," I say, yelling over the noise to Torey, "will go

to a nice black family who might be able to teach you how to behave like a decent person. I sure haven't been able to, so it must be someone else's turn."

I leave the porch and shut the squealing glass door. I put away containers of food and wash up the dishes in the sink. It's important to act normal I've learned. It looks like Torey heated up canned pasta and made jelly sandwiches for their dinner. What if they let me follow through?

There's no sign of them. I can't see past the closed curtains, an attempt to shut out the sun and keep the house from heating up beyond the capacity of the single air conditioner, rattling away in the window next to the TV. It's tempting to peek but I don't.

Instead, I look at my watch. It's nine o'clock. If they don't say anything, I'll have to call Melissa's grandmother by nine-thirty at the latest. Then it occurs to me, it's possible I might actually follow through.

I'm dizzy with the options suddenly before me. Not be trapped in this hell? Maybe leave Virginia, get an interesting job somewhere else?

As much as Melissa's grandmother is a redneck bigot, she also genuinely cares for her granddaughter. There is no way the constant screaming around here could be good for a barely five-year-old child, already traumatized by the neglect Vicky inflicted on her.

And, even though it terrifies her to be away from Torey, it might be a good for Melissa to come out from behind her sister's shadow, find an identity of her own.

Maybe I could get Norma to agree not to smoke around Melissa—I worry about her asthma.

Torey is another matter. Torey is an angry mess. I hate admitting it, but she is no different from any of the kids on my juvenile probation caseload, maybe even worse than some of them. If she went into Social Services, they'd probably put her in therapeutic foster care, or maybe a hospitalized setting, get her stabilized.

Maybe that's what she needs, a situation that might help her. Vicky's hatred towards me probably poisoned any chance I had with Torey anyway. Maybe, maybe, maybe, I don't know, and my damned heart starts racing again. I remember to take deep breaths.

The sliding glass door screams, but I ignore it. This is scary, but I can't make it easy. I know that for all our sakes, things have to change.

"Arae, can we talk to you?" Torey says.

She only calls me Arae now when she wants something. Forcing my voice to sound normal, I say, "I don't know." I begin making something to eat. But no, I can't even do that. The leftover chicken I'd planned to have with a salad is gone. It's going to be just a salad again because they'd never touch anything like lettuce, cucumbers or spring onions. I sense my freedom within arm's reach. I remind myself we don't have to be chained to this hell anymore.

Melissa pipes up, "We want to tell you something, Arae."

It's harder to be tough with her. "What?"

"We want to stay together."

"I don't know how that's going to happen," I say as I pick up my plate and glass of water and struggle to open the damned door with one hand. They follow me out to the porch where I sit at the picnic table. "How's that going to happen?" I ask, feigning nonchalance.

"We want to stay here, with you."

Melissa's seriousness is cute but I don't smile. "No thanks."

That surprises them. They say, in unison, "What?"

"No way. This sucks. I don't like my job, I don't like the commute, and frankly, I hate even coming home." I take a drink of water, look at them, and say, darkly, "The way things are, there are just too many things I don't like around here." That shuts them up.

I'd made some Asian salad dressing the previous weekend with ginger and garlic which made the plain salad tasty, and I get to finish eating in silence. Then I sigh and stand up. Picking up my plate and glass, I leave, not cajoling them, not begging them, or ordering them around.

I really had quit. I put my dish in the sink. The groceries I'd forgotten in the car silently call to me. I sense butter going soft and bread growing moldy in the damp, humid air. I can't afford to waste anything, so go up the hallway. Then, when I open the front door, it's suddenly all too much.

Oh, shit, screw it. Screw all of it.

Exhaustion I'm not expecting settles in and I find myself sitting on cement steps, which are gritty with sand. Something sharp is beside me and cutting into my bare leg, attracting my attention. I pick it up, an oyster shell, one of the millions making up the driveway.

Melissa has some sort of game to see how many shells she can pile on top of each other. Stacks of them are everywhere, like little totems to unknown gods.

I turn over the shell, and bright moonlight reflects from its underside. I remember my dad shoveling oyster shells from this driveway into a wheelbarrow, then dumping them off the end of the dock. He smiled when I asked him what he was doing and said new oysters would grow on those broken shells. I wonder how long the one in my hand has been out of the water.

The sound of them coming down the hall interrupts my thoughts. Turning, I see them backlit in the doorway.

"We won't yell no more," Melissa says.

There's nothing left, so I stay silent.

"Yeah, we promise. Tell her, tell her what you said," Melissa whispers to Torey.

"We want to stay here."

The side of her face is outlined from the hall light—raw pain. I hate this. I want an alternative and find none. "With me?"

"Yeah."

"No, sweetie, no thanks. I'm out of anything that would make me want to try again." A joyless chuckle escapes. "You must think I'm made of steel or something, that I could take anything you dish out. Look around." I spread my arms as if embracing the woods, the driveway, the night sounds. "Why in the world would *anyone* want to live like this, with two kids so irresponsible they can't even put the damn milk away?" I turn back look at her. "Who act like the only thing they want to do is make my life as miserable as theirs is?"

I'd only asked a question I'd asked in different ways, a

hundred times. But this time I hear it.

Make me as miserable as they were; that's *exactly* what they'd been doing. Torey's shocked expression confirms it, and I hesitate, feeling myself waver, but if I back down, we are all lost. Even sympathy is dangerous. Both girls stand behind me, still as statues.

"I can't do this anymore."

The breeze stops. It's quieter now. Tree frogs peep in nearby woods and Melissa loudly sucks her thumb. It's true, I don't have to do this, and if it's not going to get better, I shouldn't. My stomach clenches as a deeper truth I hadn't wanted to see becomes clear.

I turn so she can see my face. "I'm not feeling good about this Torey, but I'm done in. I don't have it in me to keep on trying."

It's out. A great weight lifts from me. We sit with this floating around us, ringing in our ears. Melissa is crying the helpless tears she gets into when she wants something she can't name, so I guess in some way, she understands.

The truth, even a rotten one like this, has a way of doing that, clearing the air, making us see. I know it's over. Torey is crying, too. So am I; tears are sliding down my face.

Despite the pain they are in, that I am in, I sense the rightness of this. I know as hard as it will be, we will all benefit somehow in the end. Torey comes and sits next to me. She encases the hand holding the oyster shell in both of hers. Its sharp edges cut into my palm, yet I enjoy the sensation.

"I can change." She looks and sounds older than her almost thirteen brief years. I see a hint of myself in her eyes and an unwelcome spark of hope ignites.

This is the first sign of affection I've seen since getting her from the rat hole they lived in. When we got to the motel, she'd grabbed me like I was saving her life, which I fully intended to do.

Her earnestness now, and holding onto my hand, take me back to the days before Vicky banished me. My head spins and I feel strangely shy. "How?" I ask.

"I can handle Melissa. I've been doing it forever. The only thing wrong is I've been pissed off at everything. I don't like it here."

I begin to say something but she stops me.

"Let me finish, Rae. You're right. I *have* been taking it out on you, and I don't need to. I see that now. It's not your fault we're here." She's crying, but her eyes are fixed on mine. "Please let me stay—let us stay. I know I can do better. I can!" There is urgency in her voice I want to believe.

Can I do this? Can I allow myself to get sucked back into trying with them again?

I don't know. I don't think I have the energy to stand up right now, much less commit to these two very messed-up girls. I keep my voice hard. "Do you want to? I mean really want to?"

"Yes. I've been rotten, I know it. I can do better, and I want to."

She sounds sincere, damnit. I don't think I've ever heard her sound this mature, this genuine.

"I haven't expected you to be perfect, but I expected you to try. You never tried."

"I know." Sobs erupt from her, but she continues, "I know, I got like that with Momma and I'm acting the same way with you. I see that now."

That's a surprise. Torey has never admitted to anything but sheer admiration for Vicky. Compared to the great Vicky, I was the most horrible person in the world.

"I understand you aren't Momma. You try to do right by us and you want us to do right too. I didn't understand that before."

Torey's words sound outlandish, fake, beyond the truth, even though they are accurate as hell. "I don't know. I just don't know. I'm so tired I don't think I can take care of myself right now, much less you two."

"But it won't be like it was." Through tears, Torey's voice is soft, scared and completely without hope. I sense this is it, it's all she has to offer, and she knows it isn't enough. She's given up.

Something about taking part in another defeat in her life angers me and I become unwilling to participate in creating more failure for her, no matter what the cost. Yet caution is required.

"Things have to get better around here."

The relief on her face is obvious and comes much too quickly. I keep my voice stern. "I need to see Melissa doing better, too."

"You'll see, it'll be different. I'm gonna be different. We'll be different. I promise."

I don't have a lot of hope. I'm not elated at the prospect. The idea of starting over without them, making a new life for myself sounds a lot more probable. But who knows? At least this is a shot, and I'm going to go for it. Maybe we can pull this off, get a second chance at being a family.

"I don't know. I'm not feeling optimistic about this."

"You will, you'll see."

I'm silent. I look at her and then at Melissa behind me. I can't give in too easily.

"I'm not sure."

Torey holds her breath. Melissa is zoned out in a world powered by thumb sucking.

"Arae, you've got to let me try." Torey's fierceness is in each word.

She's right, I do.

"One more time, that's it. That's all I got in me." I take a deep breath, blow it out and stand up.

I go to the car for the groceries.

They follow.

Crabby Cakes

As much picked fresh crab meat as you can get

For every two cups of crab, add:
   - one egg
   - one-half teaspoon lemon zest (the skin, not white pith, of a lemon)
   - one-quarter cup of a creamy Caesar salad dressing
   - chopped fresh parsley to taste (a lot if you like it, less if you're not a fan)
   - a tablespoon or more of grated onion
   - one-quarter cup of Italian seasoned bread crumbs

Mix all ingredients and make patties, roll in more bread crumbs. Fry in small amount of olive oil. The cakes make excellent appetizers if small, great sandwiches if larger, or are wonderful on top of a green salad dressed with a good, lemon-based vinaigrette.

July

This rotten mood consumes me. Looking at my littlest niece, who grins and holds up a piece of paper, isn't helping much either.

Assembling a smile, I wonder what the hell is wrong with me. I should be glad or at least relieved she's gotten a good report today. The day-care's director is beaming at me too, which is so weird I hardly know what to say. Scowls and complaints are what I'm used to.

"We're going to the marina now, right?"

"Right, baby." Even though it's the last place I want to go.

She doesn't make her usual complaints when I buckle her into the much-hated car seat. How her mom got away with not using one, I'll never know. The streets we drive through are devoid of life. No breeze, no traffic—just dusty, hot humid air, my despicable station wagon creaking down the road, and us. Not even a dog panting in the heat to break the monotony of this town.

I try cheering myself up. Maybe the day-care center won't kick her out after all, which would be great. Really great. The town of Cornwallis boasts one high school, one elementary school and two day-care centers, with the other day-care connected to an evangelical church. I'm not sure how well Melissa, who curses better than me, would fit into that setting, so the day-care she goes to is my only hope.

And maybe, just maybe, when kindergarten begins in two weeks, she'll be ready for it.

"Turn here!" She's excited, looking out the window and marking our progress.

"I know, I know. Keep your shirt on."

"I'm wearing a dress, Arae."

"I know you are. It's a joke."

Arae, Aunt Rae, that's me. She doesn't get my jokes, but who cares? Maybe she'll learn to get along with kids her own age.

Melissa's reward for not biting, hitting, or scratching one of her "playmates" is to come here, to the marina, to pick out her choice of fish heads. Fishermen leave not only heads, but scales, guts, the whole works, right there in the bin at the fish cleaning station, and free for the taking!

She's become an avid crabber and we will fill the plastic bags I'd brought with fish heads. When we get home, I'll take her out on our pier and she'll bait her traps. At this point I don't care what it takes. Bribery is fine with me if it gets her to behave something resembling a normal five-year-old.

Crabbing is such a weird thing for her to get excited about, but I'm relieved to find anything to motivate her. As far as I can tell, she has no use for dolls or toys. The only things she seems to enjoy are TV, irritating me, and crabbing. That's it.

I guess her first four years with my sister were so screwed up, she never learned how to play, but now, as we pull into the marina, she's scrambling out of her car seat and yelling at me to open the door. Soon she's earnestly digging around in the blood and guts, searching for the right enticement for crabs.

Oh, no. A group of women are walking towards us from the yachts docked at the end of the marina. They are beautifully dressed and assume horrified expressions as they draw near.

The incongruous click of high heels on rough boards and flashes of jewelry in the strong sunlight announce their approach. I can almost smell their expensive perfumes and shut my eyes, wishing I was anywhere but right here.

Right on cue, Little Precious holds up a fish head, bigger than the one perched on her own tiny neck, and with blood streaming down her arms, screams, "Look, Arae! This one is great!"

"It sure is, honey." The damn head is so big, I don't think it could be squashed into a trap, but I hold open one of our bags anyway and she proudly chunks it in. "This will make a great dinner," I say loudly, with a perverse need to shock the ladies even more. Melissa doesn't even look up. She knows I'm talking about the crab's dinner and not hers.

But then, old contrary me wants to say something to the group, now passing with disgust leaking from their very pores. My contrary nature wants to call out to them, explain I'm not the low-life they think.

She wants to explain I'm actually a professional person, educated, with a master's degree. Try and impress them. Get them to understand I'm actually a saint who took in my sister's screwed-up kids. But why? And what does old contrary me think she'd get out of it anyway?

My shitty mood isn't helped by any of this.

Two little boys come over. One looks older, but it's hard to tell as Melissa takes after her father and is tall for her age. She enlists their help, and soon they have filled all three bags. Since I'm no longer needed, I drag them to a nearby bench and sit, grateful for a moment alone. It's been a confusing day of dragging around plastic bags filled with one thing or another.

That morning, in my guise as a juvenile probation officer, I drove to Richmond to pick up a thirteen-year-old shoplifter named Valencia and then drove back to her home in Williamsburg. She'd been committed to the Commonwealth of Virginia for nearly three months, a fairly serious consequence for a kid so young.

Usually when children are released from Learning Centers, what used to be called reform schools, they come home by bus. I know because I've picked up a few from the station already.

This time, in typical knee-jerk reaction, my supervisor felt it best I drive to Richmond to pick up Valencia as one of our younger clients recently ran away under similar circumstances.

In a month or two, when my caseload gets so heavy it will be impossible for me to do everything, she'll forget about this policy, and all our kids will return by bus again. I'm beginning to understand how the system that has employed me my entire adult life works, or rather, doesn't work.

I wasn't around when Valencia was committed, so I'm not sure what circumstances caused it outside of chronic theft. Her folder is short on comments and only holds basic paperwork from the court.

Valencia is one of the cases I inherited from my predecessor who had the good sense to leave the underpaid, overworked and totally useless position I now occupy.

I like Valencia, though. Today was the first time we'd met. She was gregarious, engaging, and most of all, appreciative when I asked her where she'd like to go for lunch—appreciation being something I don't get much of, so that was nice.

While we were eating, I asked her about the anger management and shoplifting classes she'd had to complete. She said they were a total bore and waste of time.

I smiled to myself. She'd never know, but I designed those programs in my previous life, the one where I had prestige and a paycheck I could actually live on. I got a lot of kudos from the department when those programs were unveiled. Along with the rest of it, I guess I got that wrong, too.

Her home was in a low-income apartment complex, with plastic trash bags turning like tumbleweeds in the breeze, broken cars listing in parking spots, and paint peeling from graffiti-coated walls.

She spotted some girls she knew. Valencia rolled down the car window, waving and yelling. She wanted to see them, but I said we had to see her mother first. We pulled up in front of their apartment and she jumped out.

Her clothes and things were in plastic bags in the trunk of the agency's car, so I fetched them and brought them to where Valencia stood, still knocking and yelling for her mom.

I knocked, too, and rang the bell. Her mother knew we were coming, so why didn't she open the door? I still don't know.

At first, I was only terrified I was going to get stuck with Valencia and be late picking up Melissa.

Day-care would fine me a dollar for every minute I was late past six-thirty, something I couldn't afford, and another black mark would be made against Melissa.

Any problems Valencia faced faded before my growing panic, but then she went to the strip of grass next to the door and picked up a rock. She dug around and found a key. Holding it up, she questioned me with her eyes.

I said, "Go ahead."

She did and her mother was sitting at a table a few feet in front of us. The woman glanced up. We'd never met in person, and the eyes I looked into startled me with their emptiness.

I was struck by the situation. No wonder Valencia stole. How else was she supposed to fill the hole this woman would leave in a child's heart?

"I'm sorry, are you Mrs. Warren, Valencia's mother?" Those eyes weren't going to stop me. I was pissed.

We waited for a response. She finally said, "Yes," in her odd, deep voice and nothing else.

"We spoke on the phone, do you remember?"

Again, the strangely pitched voice made a statement. "Yes."

"I don't understand why you didn't open the door. Can you explain why you didn't?"

All she did was shrug. I glanced at Valencia to see how she was taking this. Her expression revealed fear, shame, and embarrassment. I wanted to smack the bitch that stood in for a parent.

Maybe I could have put Valencia in juvenile detention for the night, if they had a bed available, but it would have required a paperwork nightmare, and later on, what then?

Put her in foster care? Would my supervisor have supported that idea? I didn't think so. I didn't think my supervisor or the Family Preservation Team would think it was a good idea. We were supposed to be saving money, not spending it. I knew it was wrong, but I left Valencia there with the thing calling itself a mother.

Getting Social Services involved wasn't an option. They'd have laughed in my face. What happened wouldn't qualify as neglect, much less the emotional abuse I knew it was.

I pulled Valencia outside. "Is she always like this?"

Valencia looked nervously at the door. "Naw, she's just in one of her moods right now."

I went back inside and gave her mother a hard look, which didn't seem to register at all. I made the woman sign some papers and gave her instructions to come in with Valencia the following week or face the judge.

Tears were in my eyes all the way back to the office, but I couldn't cry, or stop thinking about Valencia's joy vanishing into the black hole living in their apartment. I also couldn't stop blaming myself for playing my part in the destruction of her child's spirit.

The bleakness of that encounter is still here. I'm going to have to develop a thicker skin, learn to let go, create better boundaries and all that professional crap if I'm going to make it as a juvenile probation officer.

But I don't think I'm going to be able to. I don't think thicker skin is on the menu for me, or a more professional attitude. Even though Torey has made good on her promise and they both are doing better, I'm not. I'm not at all.

I feel an albatross circling over my head. I can't see it but sense it up there, sometimes swooping so low a panic takes root and threatens to overwhelm me.

I'm terrified of failing at this job I hate. I get even more frantic watching my options shrink and shrivel to nothing, my tiny savings disappearing as fast as my optimism, and the damn car needs tires.

Melissa's screams shock me, bringing me back, but they are screams of laughter. The boy I've decided is older is squirting the other two with a hose, and he looks to see if I'll object. As long as Melissa is laughing, I don't care, so I smile to let him know it is okay.

Glancing around the marina, I notice, despite the heat, there are more people around now. Probably the fishing fleet has come in.

Hopelessness makes another grab for me, but I fight it off. After all, Melissa *did* get a good report today. I stare at the water past the marina, sparkling in the sun.

It's pretty, but my attention is snagged by a woman coming from the other side of the marina. She seems familiar. She's wearing a baseball cap and has a long brown ponytail sticking out the back. About my height and weight. What is it about her?

Chip! It's Chip.

Is it?

I haven't seen her since I was sixteen or so and stopped coming to the beach house. Is it really her? I'm squinting, trying to be sure. I think it is! I think I'd recognize her peculiar loping stride anywhere.

I shout Chip's name and grab the now wet Melissa from her game with the boys. She protests when she has to drop the hose she just got control of, but I carry her sideways, bouncing across my hip, to the dock opposite us. Melissa continues to holler for me to put her down, but I'm not listening.

I run until I'm right in front of the woman. "Hey there, Chip Madsen?" She looks at me. I can tell she has no idea who I am. I turn Melissa upright and drape her on my hip. She puts a thumb in her mouth and pouts around it. "Rae Green. Remember me, the summer kid?" I grin.

Chip's brown eyes light up with her smile. She cocks her head to one side. "Rae? Is that really you?"

"Yes. I'm so glad to see you." Gladness bordering on hysteria. I need to calm down. I'm breathing heavily from running. A little boy comes from behind Chip and shyly slips his hand into hers.

She looks down, smiling. "This is my youngest, Rae. His name is Barry. Say hello, Barry." He looks down at the wood pier, all shyness and very cute.

Her youngest. Gosh, she's only a year older than me. I know my voice sounds shocked when I ask, "How many do you have?"

"Three, three boys." She laughs like it's the funniest thing in the world, then adds softly, "You are so lucky to have a girl." Chip smiles at Melissa and gently touches her bare leg.

Melissa's struck dumb for some reason but smiles a gooey smile around the thumb and puts her other arm around my neck.

"She's adorable. Are you going somewhere? Do you have a few minutes to catch up?"

"Sure." My happiness has no bounds. Chip was my best friend during some tough adolescent times. Meeting up with her again is my great good fortune.

"Well, come on then. We can let our little ones play while we talk."

"Okay." I follow her up a hill to the playground, Melissa still on my hip, her long legs dangling and wet sneakers banging against my knee.

Eventually I will tell Chip how I got here and who Melissa is, but for right now, for the time it takes to walk up this hill, I'm pretending to be the lucky mother of this adorable little girl.

I sense that old albatross giving up, lifting high in the sky, and winging its way across the bay in search of some other unlucky soul.

Clam Dip for Chips

This is the easiest and best clam dip in the world.

- one pint of sour cream
- one package of dry Knorr Leek Recipe Mix
- one small can minced clams, drained (but not thoroughly, leave some clam juice).

Mix together and refrigerate. Add a few drops of hot sauce or more if you like a kick.

August

Racing home in the hot afternoon, I'm keeping the windows down to save on gas. I have to get our laundry because my mother's old washer, which worked just fine for the past twenty years, conked out on me just when I needed it the most.

If I hurry, I'll have some time for myself before getting the girls. Outside of my daily commute back and forth to work, I'm never alone and I want like hell to take advantage of this rare opportunity.

Every other Tuesday is laundry day. We stay in town for dinner, something the girls look forward to. They like the video games at the local Dino's Pizzeria with tokens earned for doing chores and following the rules.

But what the hell, I'm delighted to have over two hours before the girls expect me to come get them from Lucy's, wonderful, patient Lucy who Chip introduced me to, and who never fines me when I'm late. Now that school's started, Lucy's is where they stay until I get them after work.

It's like an unprecedented luxury to sit on my own porch, by myself, with a cartoon-covered glass of the wine I keep hidden in the utility room behind the oil furnace. The water reflects the sun's rays, and I rock myself in the big wooden swing I never get to sit in anymore. I wish I could stay here forever and bliss out.

The front door slams and I'm immediately on high alert.

Living in an area this remote has its good aspects and bad.

"Hullo? Anyone there?"

I relax at the sound of Torey's voice, but then wonder what the hell she's doing coming home on the bus. I quickly get up and pitch the wine into the bushes next to the back door. Substances of any kind have a tendency to upset my girls.

"What's up with this?" I say, walking into the family room/kitchen to meet her. I rinse the empty glass in the sink.

"I could say the same thing to you."

She still gets defensive at the drop of a hat, but I've learned how to pick my fights. "Here's an idea. Let's not fight. Let's just say the hell with it and be, like, friendly to each other. What do you say?"

Torey acts like she doesn't know what to say, which I'm beginning to regard as a major victory. She will turn thirteen next week, and living with an almost-thirteen-year-old gives a person a whole different perspective on life. I nonchalantly go back to the porch, body language being just as important as verbal.

I wonder if she'll follow. She does, announcing her entrance with complaints about the lack of "good" food in the house like chips and soda. "And when are you going to make that good dip again?"

"So why aren't you at Lucy's?" I ask.

"I thought we were going to be friends," she says.

Good counterpoint. "I am your friend. Don't you notice the lack of screaming?" I give her a large, obviously fake smile.

Despite her nearly adolescent state, she actually smiles back. "Yeah, I do."

"Okay, continue to notice the not screaming here. You were supposed to be at Lucy's with your sister. Why are you are here instead? I bet Lucy's beginning to get worried. What's up with that?"

"I couldn't handle being there, Arae. I was going to call her when I got home."

She calls me Arae more often now. It's her way of trying to be nice, or manipulate me. I'm never sure which.

"Well then, call Lucy and let her know where you are." As she leaves the room, I shout, "Tell her I said it was all right. Tell her I will pick Melissa up in an hour."

"Okay," she hollers back.

I lie down on the porch swing; it's full of every kind of pillow imaginable. The girls love the swing. It's huge and comfortable. I can stretch out and hold on to the strap my father nailed to the back wall and swing myself like I'm in an enormous cradle. I plump some pillows under my head and begin relaxing again.

"Lucy said okay." Torey comes back to the porch.

She's wearing the obligatory, skin-tight, bell-bottomed jeans and tight-fitting, long-sleeve knit shirt she insisted we buy for school clothes. She was right, though. She looks exactly like the rest of her class who all manage to be clones of each other. I don't know how they figure out how not to sweat to death in this heat.

"Good. She's not worried?" I ask, gently rocking myself.

"She might be worried. I don't think she believes me."

"I should call her, but this feels too good," I say with closed eyes. "I will in a minute."

Torey sits in the old wicker chair from my parents' house. I'd replaced the cushions a few years ago, but they are beginning to fray again. Our cottage definitely has that lived-in look.

"I don't think Lucy cares if I'm there."

"Don't you dare say anything bad about Lucy." Lucy is God's gift to me. Chip said Melissa wasn't ready for day-care, and found this wonderful person for us. "Besides, I thought you said she sounded worried." I feel my eyelids grow heavy.

"I'm not saying anything bad. All I mean is I can tell she likes Melissa more than me."

"Well, Melissa's only five. You know Lucy never had any kids, and she probably enjoys babying Melissa. It's no crime to enjoy cute little kids." Torey doesn't say anything so I add, "Not everyone enjoys being around teenagers as much as I do."

"Right, Arae."

"Well, I do. Why do you suppose I work in juvenile

probation? It's so I can be around teenagers, twenty-four seven."

"You work there because it's the only job you could find."

"Can't fool you, can I?"

I hate the thought of getting up and driving back to town. I'm beginning to believe a half-hour nap, right here on the swing, would do me a world of good. I'm beginning to doze when I hear, "Arae?"

"Hmm?"

"Were you popular in school?"

Something in her tone alerts me to dangerous waters ahead. I wake up, not sure how to answer, so tell the truth. "Not really. I had some good friends in boarding school, but not in public school. I was a bookworm, a nerd."

"I wish I had some friends," she says.

I look at her in surprise. Torey is crying. Not in rage behind a slammed door, not in frustration over this hated life with me, just tears. I don't remember plain, simple tears before.

I sit up. "Are you okay?"

She looks so tiny in the large chair, her long black wavy hair descending into her lap. Her hands are over her face, but her shoulders are shaking, and sobs come from the small form.

"It's as bad here as it was back home." Her voice comes out muffled behind her hands.

That's a shocker. Torey never complains about any aspect of the life she was forced to leave in North Carolina.

I surprise myself by patting the seat next to me. "Come here, sweetie." I don't think the girls know when I shock myself with things like this because I've learned to act like it's perfectly normal.

A more stupendous event—she actually does it. She crosses the room and flings herself next to me on the swing. I put my arm around her and we rock a while. Me and my tough little street kid with snot and tears running down her face. Still feeling a sense of unreality, I kiss the top of her head. "What's the deal here?" I ask gently.

She wipes her face on my shirt and looks intently at me with her beautiful big green eyes. "They all hate me, Arae." More tears dribble down.

"Are you talking about the kids at school?"

"Yeah. The black kids call me 'zebra,' and the white kids won't hang out with a black kid that acts white. Everyone thinks I'm a freak." More of her bodily fluids leak on me.

I try to be cool and not care about stuff like tears and mucous, but it bothers the hell out of me. I worry I will never be very good at this parenting stuff. "Oh, Torey, I'm so sorry," I say, trying to both hug her and not get any more contaminated than I already am.

She cries and I consider her situation. We live in a rural area of Virginia where bigotry is still rampant. I knew that coming here, but for some bizarre reason, probably due to my recent exposure to too many after-school specials on TV, thought the kids around here wouldn't be like their parents.

Also, before right now, I thought Torey's lack of friends was due to her scorn towards kids her own age. I never wondered if her contempt was a defensive move or if being biracial was a handicap.

I pat her head. It's unbelievable how stupid I can be. She always seems so self-possessed, I actually bought the act.

I try to think of something to say and feel sorry for this kid who had already survived way too much. "I am so sorry, sweetie. I didn't think the kids around here would be like that. It was like this in North Carolina, too?"

Her head nods against my chest. I can't think of anything to say. "I wish there was something I could do to help."

"I know you can't, Arae. I'm just sick of it is all."

"I don't blame you. It's got to be hard. People can be so ignorant." And then out of nowhere I say, "Do you know why your momma gave you her name?"

"We don't have the same name."

"Yes, you do. Your real name is Victoria, and so is hers. You are both named after my grandfather. His name was Victor."

"Well, she goes by Vicky and calls me Torey. That's not the same."

"I know that, Victoroonia."

She giggles slightly between heavy sighs.

"Do you know what your mom told me when you were born?"

"No."

"She told me she gave you her name so that no matter what happened, you would know she wanted you."

Torey doesn't respond, and I wonder if talking about Vicky is still off limits. Since Torey isn't putting up a fight, I give it another shot. "I think it was one of the best things your mom ever said in her entire life."

Torey starts crying again but more softly. "Oh, Arae, I miss Momma so much," she says, leaning against me.

"I miss her too, sweetie, and I know she misses you." I hug her.

"I miss Gemma and Grandpa too."

"Me too, baby, me too." This is the first time she's mentioned them. I can feel my own eyes well up with tears at the unexpected comment. "I didn't know if you remembered them."

"Of course I do."

"Good. I'm glad."

She was only five when they died. Vicky left home with Torey a year before the accident that killed them. I used to believe I'd never forgive Vicky for making our parents' last year on earth hell from missing Torey. "They were crazy nuts about you, that's for sure."

"I remember you back then too, Arae."

"You do?"

"Yep, I remember being a flower girl at your wedding, and staying with you for a week when Gemma and Grandpa died."

"You were only three when I got married."

"I know, but I remember anyway."

"Do you remember coming here? With them?"

"Yeah. Didn't Gemma and Grandpa have an old white refrigerator back then, sorta round looking?"

I laugh. "Yes, they did. It was always needing to be defrosted. You remember that antique?"

"I remember Grandpa always had Popsicles in the freezer part."

"I bet he did."

"He said they were just for me."

That sounded like him. "You remember staying with me when you were six?"

"Yeah, I remember." She looks down at the floor. They had to be confusing memories for her.

"Torey, I don't know what to tell you about school." She tenses up, but doesn't say anything. "I've been thinking maybe we might move to Williamsburg."

"Leave here?"

"Well, I could sell this place. I could get a lot of money for it."

"How much?"

"I don't know. I can find out."

"You'd sell it?"

"Maybe, I don't know. I hate the drive from here to work, and now with this stuff with your school. I'm not sure. I've been debating it for a while. What do you think?"

"Would you still have to work two jobs?"

"I don't know. Maybe not if I made enough off this place." Actually, I'd hate to quit the other job. Another benefit from meeting up with Chip is the extra paycheck I'm getting from working as a waitress with her at *The Sea Witch Saloon and Grill* on alternate weekends. My schedule is doable, even though tough at times, but I love working with Chip.

Still, maybe we should move to Williamsburg. But uproot Melissa just when she's doing better? Leave Lucy, sell this place? It's all I have left.

Torey seems to have calmed down. "Wouldn't you miss it?"

"Yeah, this place has a lot of memories for me. When I think about selling it, I'm not so sure. But maybe that's what I should do."

"Mom would miss it."

"She hasn't been here for what? For a long time."

"Yeah, ever since you turned her into Social Services."

That's a conversation stopper. I wonder how Torey

feels about it. Vicky's still pissed. She says she's grateful I'm taking care of her kids but I should never have turned her in. According to Vicky, "If you can't trust family, who can you trust?"

I tried to explain to my sister that her own kids couldn't trust her, which was why I turned her in. That got the phone slammed in my ear, which was fine because I can't afford the long distance collect calls anyway. The penitentiary won't let them make calls to a cell phone.

Torey is still sitting next to me, and I'm not sure how to respond, so ask, "How do you feel about it?"

"I dunno."

We'd wandered into taboo waters. I backstroke out. "Your mom feels the way she feels," I say lamely because I wish she didn't.

"I heard what you said to her on the phone last week."

"You did? What?"

"I heard you arguing with her about that Social Services thing."

"Eavesdropper, but you know what? I should quit arguing. It doesn't do any good anyway, and as far as turning her in, I don't know if I did the right thing or not. All that happened was your momma got so mad at me, and I didn't get to see you guys for a long, long time." I sigh, remembering the horrible year it took for me to get over the loss of all the family I had left.

Torey shifts and sits up, away from me. She looks me in the eyes. "It helped a little. Mom straightened up for a while afterwards."

This is a day of astonishing revelations.

"Momma had to attend parenting classes and things were better. Then they got worse again. I started missing school 'cause I had to watch Melissa when Mom was gone or out of it. Mom was supposed to go to court about me missing so much school."

She considers me, I guess to see how I'm taking the information. I try to act casual. "I didn't know. When your school records came, I wondered how you got away with so many absences. What happened in court?"

"We never got there. When Mom was arrested, she lost me just like I told her she would. Only different than I thought it would happen. Oh, crap." Another round of tears begins.

I'm going to seriously consider keeping some tissues out here. "You know, when we talk to your mom on the phone, she sounds like she's taking responsibility for all the stuff that happened."

"She's done that before."

"Oh." She probably had.

I feel awkward. Torey is crying even harder. So much for my comforting skills. "Shit, Torey, I don't know what to say." I pull her close and hug her. Here's an interesting fact—no resistance. "Let's just take each day as we get to it. My sister will be locked up for a long time, and you and I are gonna have to figure out how we are going to pull this off."

"Pull what off?" she says through sobs.

"Raising you and Melissa to be the best you got inside."

Torey calms down again, sighs, and wipes her face with her hands. "Melissa seems to be doing okay."

"It would help a lot if she could stop whining." I sigh dramatically, and Torey chuckles through her tears.

"Doesn't Mom get part of the money if you sell this place?"

"Your mom doesn't own it," I say without thinking.

"Didn't Mom get part of it when Gemma and Grandpa died?"

I hear anguish in her voice. I think she's plain worn out from Vicky's failures. I hesitate to tell her the truth but can't figure a way around it. "Yes, she did. But she sold me her part."

"I guess she blew that money like she did everything else." Bitterness replaces the anguish.

"Maybe, I don't know. You were still little and living with Melissa's father then. She spent some of it on the house you guys lived in, so she didn't blow it all."

"I didn't like Billy. He never liked me either. Did you know Billy?"

"Not very well. We only met a few times. I know I don't like him skipping out on Melissa's child support."

"Arae, did you know my dad?"

Ah, the big question. Now we are getting into very deep waters. I decide to be as honest as I know how. "Yes, I knew your dad."

"What do you remember about him?"

"That he was the most gorgeous human being I'd ever met."

"Really?"

"You've seen pictures of him, haven't you?"

"Yeah, but he just looks like some black guy."

"André was never just 'some black guy.'"

"Do I look like him?"

I'm tempted to fudge a little but figure the truth is still my best bet. "Torey, don't you know you look a lot like me?"

"Mom always said I did, until she got mad at you."

"Well, you do, right down to your curly hair. You're just shaded a bit darker and a whole lot prettier than me."

She seems to be considering things. "Did you like my dad?"

I think about my answer. "I can't say I did. I never really knew him very well, but that didn't stop me from being a bitch to him."

"What?" Torey's eyes are big when she looks up at me.

I smile at her. "Yeah, isn't that stupid? I didn't know him, but I was wicked mean to him. I blamed him for your mom's drug problems."

"Did he get her started?" Torey's whispering.

"I don't think so. He may have even tried to get her to stop, or at least that's what he told me the one time I talked to him."

"When was that?"

"When you were a baby. He tried to see you and Vicky, but my parents wouldn't let him, even got a restraining order against him. They threatened him with child support, rape charges, all sorts of things. There wasn't much he could do. Your mom was only fifteen and he was over eighteen. I was working then and he came by my office. He tried to get me to help, but I basically told him to go to hell."

"What did he want?"

"He wanted to see you. He said he wanted to be your father, even if Vicky didn't want him anymore. I remember feeling bad afterwards. It wasn't like me to act that way. I hurt him, I could tell. I know he thought we were all a bunch of bigots, and I guess we were."

"Did you ever see him again?"

"Nope, and when I found out he died, I knew I'd always feel guilty about the way I treated him that day, and I have, sweetie, I have."

"I know Grandpa didn't like him. He told me André was a bad man. I told Momma what Grandpa said, and they got into a big fight about it."

"I don't know if he was good or bad. He was probably both, like everybody. Maybe he had a lot more good in him than any of us really knew."

"Why?" Torey asked.

"Because he cried when he saw I wasn't going to help him see you. He must have had a good heart."

"I wish I'd met him. I wish he'd met me."

"He did. Didn't your mom tell you?"

"Momma didn't like to talk about André."

"It was after you were born. My parents threatened him with a rape charge because your momma was underage. That kept him away from the hospital." I don't know how she's taking this. I'm looking in her face but don't get a clue. "I was the one who was there when you were born."

"You were?"

I smile. "Yep. I cut the cord and everything. Your grandmother said she could barely deal with giving birth herself and didn't see how she would be able to do much, so she asked me to be there. I was the first person in our family to hold you."

"What did I look like?"

"Oh, Torey, it was the most incredible thing. I was barely an adult myself, but Vicky did okay and then you came, and it was just overwhelming, all of it, in a really, really good way. I was closer to your mother that day than I've ever been to anyone in my life, and you—you were beautiful. You still are."

"So how did my dad get to see me?"

"When your momma left the hospital with you, she lied to Gemma and Grandpa about when they were supposed to pick her up."

"She did?"

I can tell Torey is delighted with this story. "Oh, yes. Miss fifteen-year-old Vicky Green snuck you out of the hospital in a tote bag. No one saw you guys leave. She told me later she took the service elevator down to the basement and met André back behind the loading platform."

"Then what happened?"

"They ran off and stayed with some relatives of André's in Goochland. Until his aunt figured out how young your mom was, and sent her home."

"Why?"

"Because my parents could have said she was kidnapped and put André in jail, and probably his family, too. They threatened to do exactly that, so she came home."

"With me?"

"Of course with you."

"How long did we stay with André?"

"Maybe a week, I don't know for sure — I had to get back to work, so I wasn't there."

I remember the depths of my happiness to get away from the chaos. Walking into my crappy little apartment and feeling safe, insulated from all the screaming and drama, and no one able to point their finger at me or call me selfish.

I'd been so relieved, I sat in a chair by my rickety kitchen table and consciously took a giant emotional step away from them, and was grateful as hell I could.

"So he did know me. He probably did hold me."

"Of course he did."

"I'm glad. Do you think his mom is still alive?"

She'd obviously thought a lot about this. I'm ashamed it never crossed my mind. I hesitate before answering, trying to come up with the right one. "Baby, I don't know. We can look at your birth certificate and get the address where André was living then. Maybe we could go and see if we can track down someone who knows anything about that side of your family. We could go on the computer and do a name search. What about that?"

"I already tried it. I got nothing on Google. I wanted to do the online search but that costs money and Momma wouldn't let me."

Torey is staring a hole in the floor and I know better than to dig around in it. "Well, if you want, we could do it. We don't have a lot of money, but how much could it cost?"

"Really? You would?"

"Sure, I don't blame you for wanting to know about that side of your family. I'm sorry I never thought of it before."

She looks sort of sheepish. This is amazing. A bashful Torey, who knew? "That's okay, don't worry about it. Tell me more about when I was a baby."

"Where was I? Oh, yeah, later on after your momma married Richard and moved to North Carolina with you, I didn't get to see you as much then, but you were still the cutest baby in the world."

She smiles. "Did you miss me?"

"Did I miss you? Of course, we all did. It was like a funeral at my parents' house."

"They missed me."

"They missed you so bad I thought they'd go crazy. They ended up hating Richard as much as they hated your dad." I stroke her hair.

"Why did they have to hate everybody?"

"I don't know. Gemma and Grandpa were messed up."

"That's what Mom said."

"At least your mom and I agree on something," I say, laughing.

Torey sits up and stops the swing. She takes a peek at me.

"I don't think I would like it if we left here."

I smile at my little niece. It's nice being able to agree with her. "Me either, but we're going to have to figure out a way to make this work if we're gonna stay here. I'm tired of you being unhappy all the time."

"I guess I could try harder at school."

"Maybe that would work, maybe it wouldn't. Maybe it's

not your fault, I don't know. Maybe you need a better school district with a more mixed population. Maybe you'll get used to the kids around here, or they'll get used to you. We'll see."

I gaze at her. She has circles under her eyes like an old woman. "You're going to have to let me know how it's going. Will you do that?"

"Sure, Arae." She seems drained, exhausted.

I make a decision and go to the kitchen to call Lucy. I ask if Melissa can spend the night. Lucy keeps a supply of clothes for Melissa, who is delighted to stay. She doesn't even ask to speak to Torey.

I change into old shorts and a T-shirt. When coming back through the kitchen, I grab a set of keys that Daddy kept on a nail inside of the pantry door. I go back out to the porch and look at Torey. "Follow me," I say mysteriously.

Torey troops behind me to the shed where I unlock the padlock and go inside. The motor is still there. I shake the gas can; it's half full.

I show Torey how to help me turn the Boston Whaler over. It's only twelve feet long but has been sitting in the grass for so long it's difficult to pry out of the weeds. We finally get it turned over and push it into the water, next to the pier. I tie it to the cleats screwed in the wood. Getting the motor on the boat without dropping it in the water is more of a job for two adults than a skinny little teenager and me, but we manage. I pull the engine's cord to make sure it's still running, and after a few tries, it catches. I let it run a few minutes and then shut it off.

We go back in the cottage, making two trips to the boat with life jackets, a cooler, and some sandwiches. Torey changes and gets a flashlight. She seems happy. We have hours of light left. I get the old fishing poles and tackle out of the shed, then send Torey back for a shovel. I show her how to dig up sand crabs for bait.

An entire summer is nearly gone, and I haven't even tried to teach her how to fish. I think my dad would say it's about time I got around to it.

Orange-Blossom Special

This drink is perfect for hot weather. Orange blossom water can be found in the Latin section of a good grocery, usually next to the rose water.

For every drink use one-half teaspoon of the orange blossom water and fill an eight-ounce glass with ice, a good lemonade and excellent, ice-cold vodka. Stir and drink.

September

"How are the girls?" Chip asks.

"They're okay." I put my pocketbook in the locker. "I had a nice talk with Torey. We're looking for her dad's family on the Internet."

"No kidding? Any luck?"

"Not yet. We found out her grandmother passed, and that was disappointing. She must have been secretly hoping a grandparent was alive."

"I thought you said Torey was a teenage monster, straight from hell and unable to maintain affection between herself and any other living creature."

"I never said that." And then, for absolutely no reason at all, it's like a bucket of shyness gets dumped on my head, which irritates me to no end.

"Yes, you did. When she didn't like what you got her for her birthday, and now you're blushing." She hoots with laughter, which doesn't help at all.

"I am not blushing. My only problem is having a crazy person for a friend."

"Sorry, I'm always forgetting how sensitive you are."

Chip's warm brown eyes usually see past my crap. I hesitate, not sure what to say. "Well, anyway, it's like we are getting closer except for the birthday present thing."

"Sounds like it, and I told you not to get her that art set."

"She used to love to draw and paint."

"She was what? Seven?"

I nod my head.

"Every seven-year-old likes that."

Chip is a wealth of information on everything from pimples to how to handle Melissa's kindergarten teacher, a prickly individual who wasn't at all pleased with the substitutions I'd made to the list of supplies I was supposed to procure. For some reason, the things I stole from my office, like a steel-bladed ruler, mucilage glue, and sharp-pointed scissors, are verboten in her classroom.

Chip smoothed that over for me, explaining to Mrs. Prickly that it was my inexperience that caused such gargantuan gaffes.

What I end up understanding is I can't afford to be so cavalier about things like that in the future. My mistakes somehow spread shame on us all, and Melissa is challenged enough at school.

It's Thursday and the restaurant is almost full, with only a few empty tables. I'd taken over for Linda at seven. Chip and I have the eight tables on the right, actually five tables and three booths.

The restaurant is supposed to close at ten, but I rarely get out before eleven. I do this every other Thursday and Friday night. On alternate weeks I work Sundays. Tips are great and I'm lucky as hell to get the hours and days I need. I can breathe a financial sigh of relief and working with Chip is great. She is not only my parenting guru, but also the first honest-to-God girlfriend I've had in a long time.

Another bonus. After spending part of almost every year of my life in Cornwallis, I'm finally meeting a lot of the people who live here. "It's really surprising," I say to Chip during a lull.

"What do you mean?" She laughs. I seem to be a source of endless entertainment.

"I, um… I never thought I'd enjoy being a waitress, and the thing is, I like it. I keep waiting for the honeymoon to be over, you know?"

"You're waiting for reality to set in." She glances around the room.

"I guess. I mean I get tired and all. It's just that there are a lot of times when I take the girls home from Lucy's, all I want to do is go in with them and collapse, especially if it's been a bad day at work. But when I get here, it's like my batteries recharge or something. I honestly don't understand it. It's sort of relaxing, not like the other job. This one's kinda fun."

"With you around, it is."

The rest of the evening is a blur. We get slammed by the drunken contents of a late-arriving yacht and don't get out until after midnight. I drive home exhausted but happy. Tips tonight made up for the lateness, and after tomorrow, I'm off all weekend. I can look forward to that.

The first inkling of something wrong comes before I park the car—the whole cottage is pitch black. They never turn off all the lights. They are both terrified of total darkness. I go in, turning on lights and calling, "Torey? Melissa?" But the words bounce back at me, echoing the emptiness.

Their backpacks, pocketbooks, and all the other crap they carry back and forth to school is piled high on the kitchen table, obviously undisturbed since I'd brought them home earlier.

Something sad and forlorn about the tableau scares the hell out of me while my brain argues with my engulfing panic. Something else is wrong, and it takes me a moment to identify what. There's no food out on the counter. They never even opened the refrigerator. The hair on the back of my neck stands up.

I hear my rational mind arguing that they are at Lucy's, they called Lucy who came and got them. I am so scared I can barely breathe as I look at my cell for her number and punch it.

Lucy hears my panic and can offer nothing. I run back through the bedrooms, tearing off covers and looking under beds, but find zilch. The entire house is empty and untouched.

Briefly, I consider calling Chip. But what could she do outside of coming here and holding my hand? I *have* to find those kids; this is no time to worry about myself.

I go out the back porch and stumble in the dark, past the reach of our lights. I narrow my eyes, straining to see a tiny scrap of movement anywhere.

I pray they are hiding in the bushes, trying to scare me. I yell their names over and over, but get no answer. The wind blows my voice away, and I sense a loneliness I haven't felt since my parents died.

Someone's kidnapped them, maybe Melissa's father. I hope it's him. He wouldn't hurt them. I hope it isn't someone bad. Please, dear God, make it someone not bad.

Knowing how many bad people there are in the world, and the terrible things they are capable of, shakes me to my core. I know anyone could find out about two beautiful girls in this isolated place, all by themselves on alternate Thursday and Friday nights while I'm at work.

I know children like my nieces bring top dollar in many venues. Finding out they are alone wouldn't be difficult for someone wanting that kind of information.

I turn on the big arc light at the end of the dock. My eyes ache to see them. Where the hell are they?

The boat is missing.

That stupid little Boston Whaler, with one emergency oar and a nine-point-five Evinrude motor, gone, vanished. I go back to the house and get the same flashlight Torey and I used the afternoon we took the boat out. With it, I can see the ropes I used to moor the boat are now coiled on the dock, exactly the way I taught her.

The water lapping against the wood pylons takes on an ominous tone. I'm attacked by prickly sensations in my brain, hands and feet.

I can't afford to let fear possess me, so I force myself to focus and move. Like walking in a stiff leather suit, I go and check the shed.

The strap hinge with the padlock is still on the door, its key now on my key ring. But the door's other hinges have been unscrewed and hang from the side, unattached to any door. The shed looks odd with the padlock still attached, and in my haze of fear it takes a moment for me to figure out what she's done, then I drag the door open and go in.

The gas can, life jackets, and fishing poles are all gone. Torey was watching a little more closely than I realized when we went out a couple of weeks ago. At least she remembered the life jackets.

Where are they? It's nearly one a.m. I search the black water with the flashlight, empty as far as I can see. I call, scream their names, but only wind answers.

I run back inside and phone the county sheriff's office. The dispatcher taking the information is clearly unconcerned about two girls, age thirteen and five, strangers to the area, adrift somewhere in the Chesapeake Bay in a twelve-foot open boat with very little fuel. I'm sure whatever was left in the gas can is long gone by now, and they are floating around out there, helpless against the currents.

I wonder what I will tell my sister Vicky. Panic grows with the wind picking up across the bay. I can't sit and do nothing. I think about driving along the coast with my feeble flashlight and wish I had another boat or knew someone who did.

A boat, I know where a bunch of them are, back at the marina next to *The Sea Witch*. I run to the car and race back, parking in the nearly empty lot. I look out at the boats moored in the marina. None have lights on.

I run down the rough wooden planks making up the marina anyway, yelling, "Is anyone here?" Even yachts moored at the far end remain silent and dark. I battle down panic, trying to stay focused, but on what?

I look at my watch. It's almost two. I don't know what to do with the fear threatening to strangle me. I'm trying to remember how to breathe when a light flicks on at the back of the restaurant. A guy, someone I don't recognize, is standing in the doorway. He begins walking towards the parking lot. I run up the ramp to him.

"Excuse me. Do you have a boat?"

He seems taken aback. I must seem strange, my hair wild in the wind, but I don't have time to worry about it. "I need a boat. Do you have one?"

After a moment, he says, "Yes, I do."

"I need help. I have two little girls out there in a twelve-foot dinghy somewhere."

I wave towards the bay in case he doesn't know where

I'm talking about. I grab his arm and start walking/dragging him towards the ramp leading down to the marina. He allows me to pull him along.

"I don't know how long they've been gone. I've got to go look for them." I still have his arm in an iron grip and am tugging him toward the boats.

"Did you call the Coast Guard?"

"Oh, shit, I didn't think of that." I stop and look at him, "How do I do that?"

"Follow me."

I do and on the way tell him I called the sheriff, but the dispatcher didn't seem too concerned.

My rescuer has a fishing boat, the kind that charters for sport fishing. It's sleek and beautiful, and I admire how he leaps onto the deck. It takes me forever to negotiate getting onto *The Clemency*, which I decide is a good omen of a name. When I get to the cabin, he's on a ship-to-shore radio with the Coast Guard. He puts me on with them.

"Where did the children put in?" a voice wants to know.

The man shows me how to click a button on the hand-held transmitter to speak, and I'm grateful for the concern in the voice of whoever it is I'm talking to. "From our house, east of the river, where Tinker's Creek comes into the bay."

"If you're in the bay, facing the creek, are you on the right or the left of the creek?"

"The right."

"How long have they been gone?"

"I'm not sure, sometime between when I dropped them off at six-thirty and one a.m., when I got home." I feel the need to add, "I was working."

The Coast Guard guy asks a bunch more questions while the man next to me listens. The more information I give, the more embarrassed I feel. What kind of person leaves kids that young alone for so long? The man on the radio says they'd send a cutter to search for the girls. I'm thankful to my core and hand the radio hand-set back to the guy beside me. I'm dizzy from the tiny flames of relief I'm feeling.

It's a warm September night. I'm glad they won't be cold. If they stay in the boat, they'll be fine. Even if it tips over, the Whaler won't sink and they can hang on. I don't think hypothermia is an issue yet. I glance up at the man.

"John," he says.

"Excuse me?"

"My name is John, John Clements. And your name?"

I think. "Rae. Rachael Green, but I go by Rae."

"All right then, Rae Green, you sit and we'll get under way, see what we can do about finding those girls."

I steady myself against the dash. It was him saying "we" that got to me. I unexpectedly find my knees weak at not being alone in this, aloneness being the thing killing me right now.

I hate that a man, any man, could take over and I'd respond like this, but screw it. I'm so grateful I would gladly kiss his ass.

John comes back into the cabin from untying the boat and fires up the engines. They are loud and thrum beneath the floorboards.

"I'm going up top," he says. "You coming?"

He goes out the sliding glass door that, unlike mine, functions perfectly. The fishing deck is out here, and he goes up some tiny steps fastened to the outside wall of the cabin, which serve as a ladder. I look up. He's about ten feet above me on the flying bridge, a contraption on top of the cabin with a second set of gauges, throttles, steering wheel, and captain's chair, all the way up there. I'm scared of heights but feel so bad about losing my nieces I probably would have jumped out of an airplane.

"Sure," I say to myself, as if it's nothing.

I go up, glad my death-grip on the handle-rails is not visible from where he is. I dare not look down at the tiny strip of water separating us from the boat next door. One false step and I imagine the huge boat rocking next to us smashing my body into tiny pieces, grinding me into chum for the fish, which I probably deserve.

I make it to the bridge and am unable to stand, so I crawl to the captain's chair, pulling myself up. I'm too ashamed to look at the guy and hope he will pretend not to notice the crawling and the vise-like grip I have on the back of his chair. There's nothing else to hang onto.

John sits in front of me and pulls the boat out like it's a sports car. I resist the impulse to grab him around the neck and scream.

He says something, but I can't hear him over the roar of the engines. I yell, "What?" in his ear.

"You're east of Tinker's Creek, right?"

"Yeah. They aren't my kids," I yell into his ear.

This is awkward. I can tell John doesn't know how to respond. Great, now I look both inept and uncaring instead of just plain inept. He gives me a curious sideways glance.

"The kids aren't yours?"

"They're my nieces. I have custody of them. I appreciate this. Thank you very much."

I quit shouting. I sound like an idiot and feel worse. John goes faster once we are out in open water. I can see the buoys he follows to stay in the channel and mark our progress towards the cottage. My terror recedes slightly.

John is on the radio, talking to anyone up and listening. The girls get plenty of airplay, and John seems to know everyone who responds. The consensus of the various voices over the radio is the tide will take them up the bay, rather than out toward the ocean. I feel better and relax a little as I realize how many people are actively looking for them.

The Coast Guard cuts in. "The girls have been located at Pimmie's Point Campground. A deputy is on his way to pick them up and take them home."

"Whew, that's good news." John eases back on the throttle.

Pimmie's Point is upriver from our place, they weren't even out in the bay. Thank God they are okay. At least until I get my hands on them.

"Do you want to go back to the marina or be dropped off at your place?"

I stare at the back of John's head. "I don't know," I say, stupid with relief.

He tries to turn his chair around, but I'm still hanging on and unable to budge. I realize he's trying to see me and make a grab for the dash, wedging myself between him and it. I look at the guy squashed in front of me. From the glow of the lights from the gauges and stuff up here I can see him clearly. Lanky, a little rough around the edges, older than me, but he has kind eyes.

He's waiting for an answer.

All I think to say is, "I don't know," so I say it again.

He seems confused, then lifts the radio handset. "I'm taking their aunt back to her place. We'll meet the officer there in about twenty minutes."

"I'll notify the deputy the aunt's on her way." The Coast Guard signs off.

"Taking you home will be quicker than going all the way back to the marina. I can help you get your car tomorrow if you need me to."

He engages the throttle and cranks up the motors. Thank God, thank God, thank God, thank God. I try to stop the tears leaking out of my eyes.

John notices. "How about going back down to the cabin? The worst is over now."

I look at the deck, looming a thousand feet below us. "I can't." I start crying for real.

I make an awkward leap for the side of his chair and kneel on the floor, wrapping my arms around the armrest like it's a lifesaver. If that's not embarrassing enough, I'm now bawling in a completely out-of-control way that encourages my latent suicidal thoughts.

John looks at me with a concerned yet nervous expression. I understand the look and wish it wasn't me causing it. He shuts the engines off. The instant quiet is startling.

"Rae, are you all right?"

I choke out the reason. "I'm scared of heights."

"You're afraid of heights?" I can tell he has no clue what I'm talking about.

"Yeah, I don't think I can make it back down."

"You mean here? You're afraid of *this* height?"

"Yeah."

I want to find a big rock, the biggest in the world and pull it over top of me. I want to be magically transplanted back to my bedroom and never have to leave again.

He waits and lets me cry for a while.

"The girls are okay. The Coast Guard said so."

"I know." The information does nothing to alleviate this insanity.

"I've seen you before."

"You have?"

"Yeah, at the restaurant. You work there sometimes, right?"

"I was working there tonight. That's where I was when they took the boat."

I'm beginning to think it's everything—nerves, stress, the challenges of the whole past year, getting rid of the asshole that is Dennis, Vicky's arrest, problems with the girls, losing my job, my whole rotten life. Hysteria, they call it.

He's a nice guy. He pulls me up in his lap. John isn't like me. He doesn't seem to care about the tears and snot I bury in his shirt. He's a better mother than I could ever be, and it makes me cry even harder.

He starts up the engines and drives like that, with me in his lap. When we get to my dock, he puts me in his chair, climbs down and ties up the boat. Then he comes back for me.

I was worried he might.

John tells me he will start down the ladder first and instead of sliding down the rails, face outward like he'd done, he will go down facing the cabin. I'm to climb down in front of him and his body will shield mine on the trip down. He says there's no way I can fall and if I somehow begin to, he will catch me. After a bunch of extremely embarrassing false starts, I try doing it the way he says. I'm grateful for his consideration yet still, halfway down and completely against my bidding, I freeze.

I'm humiliated as hell until John pulls his body close to mine and speaks softly into my ear. "Relax, we're going to make it down alive, I promise."

Again the magic word "we," and for a moment, I forget to be embarrassed or worried about acting like a jerk. I relax against him and feel his whiskers against my cheek. It feels wonderful. I think I could spend the rest of my life right here, leaning into him.

A line from "A Streetcar Named Desire" pops into my

head. Blanche saying, "I rely on the kindness of strangers." Maybe I'm crazy like she was.

I pull myself together and we continue the downward trip without me falling apart again, or even going overboard. He gets me off the boat, up our pier, and to the cottage where he shakes hands with the deputy and continues to be in charge.

I'm silent. So are the girls. We avoid looking at each other. Both the deputy and John fill in the awkward gaps. It's obvious they know each other when they speak of mutual friends. The deputy leaves and John walks him to the door. I hear them outside, the comforting rumble of masculine voices, but not what they are saying, which is good. They are probably talking about how weird we are.

John comes back and introduces himself to the girls, smiling at them. He squats down to Melissa's level and taps her on the nose. She's too scared to speak but smiles at him anyway. He acts like we are happy to be reunited and we don't correct him.

Nothing could be further from the truth yet it helps to pretend he's right. It seems appropriate to try, but I feel made of wood when I attempt to hug them. They stand stiff and lean towards me, playing their part in this little charade.

We all hate to see him leave.

I tell the girls to go to bed. My voice is not angry, but I can't conceal the cold, empty, forlorn feeling that came over me when I discovered they were gone. It seems to traipse down the hall with them, yet it stays here with me, too. It's the only thing still connecting us.

I stand still in the silence and decide John's wife is a generous woman and doesn't mind the few minutes I borrowed him from her on the ladder. I send her a silent thank you through the night. Like someone dying of thirst, I surely needed some kindness.

"I'm buying you a drink tonight," says Chip.
I'm surprised and look her way. I didn't know she drank.

In fact, I'm fairly sure she doesn't.

"How come?" Suspicion seems to be my closest companion lately.

"I feel like being a bit wild tonight."

Chip is never wild. Even when we were kids, she was as stable as an old woman. Her idea of a wild time might consist of skinny-dipping with a bunch of girlfriends in the dead of night. Still, the idea of taking a break and having a drink is very enticing. "Well, it must be the full moon or something, but a drink sounds exactly like what I need. I'm almost done with my area. You need help?"

"Yeah, get the vacuum. Maybe our stragglers will get the idea."

It's after eleven, time to close. When I'm done vacuuming, I go to the bar to wait for Chip.

The real drinkers are filing into the bar as diners depart. Mostly men who work or play on the water. Torn T's and expensive sport shirts mingle easily here. An occasional female is mixed in, but loud masculine laughter dominates and is always relaxing to me for some odd reason.

I know a few of the faces from the restaurant. A couple of these guys hit on me before, and I hope they don't do it again just because I'm in here by myself. I don't trust my taste in men anymore. Still, it's nice to wave and smile at a few people I know.

It's been a long, long time since I went out for a drink, almost a year since I'd lost my job and all the people I thought were friends. I wish I'd known my social life was only a perk of the position I used to have because then it wouldn't have hurt so much when I found myself alone.

I'm equally sorry to report no improvement in my life since then. The minute I start to feel a little trust, believe things are going a little better, Torey smashes it to pieces. A drink would definitely help. What's keeping Chip so long?

"Long Island iced tea," I tell Jack when he nods toward me.

Jack and his wife, Marie, own *The Sea Witch*. He rules the bar and I adore him. A retired waterman, he was born and raised here and knows everyone and everything. I wish

I worked for him instead of Marie. She's the witch of *The Sea Witch*. I have a short wait before he brings back my drink.

"You drinking alone tonight?"

"I'm waiting for Chip."

"For Chip?" He's surprised too. Good. It's not my imagination.

As if on cue, she arrives and sits at the barstool next to me.

"What're you having, sweet-pea?" Jack asks her.

"I'd like some of that pink wine, and put it and this on my tab." She points to my drink.

"You got it sugar-plum." Jack goes off before I can protest.

"Let me pay for this." I don't want her paying for my expensive drink. Money is as tight for her family as it is for mine.

"Don't worry, it's not costing me a dime."

"It isn't?"

"Nope, because these drinks are on John."

I look around and don't see him. "Are you talking about John Clements, the guy I kidnapped two weeks ago?"

"One and the same."

She takes a sip of her wine, and I watch her closely. Maybe she's done this before. "I thought you didn't drink."

"I'm sacrificing my virtue so John will have an excuse to see you." She's grinning like a child and I could smack her.

"Where is he?" I whisper and look discreetly behind me.

"On his way over. I just called to let him know his plan worked. You don't have to whisper, silly." She grins evilly at me and then says, "If you tell him I told you, I will never speak to you again."

"That's rotten. You can't get away with it."

"Watch me."

I'd already asked about him. He wasn't married after all. I look at the rows of bottles on the wall behind the bar. They are backlit and glowing different shades of amber with some electric green and a deep purple mixed in. I'm scared shitless.

We wait.

"Maybe he chickened out," I say after a while.

"Maybe. How're things with the kids?"

"Horrible. I can barely speak to them."

"Kids mess up, Rae. You have to forgive them and move on."

"Your kids don't." There is no way she can compare her likable sons to my monsters.

"My boys don't have the problems..." Chip doesn't seem to know how to continue the sentence politely.

"Don't worry, you're not offending me." When she doesn't say anything, I fill in for her. "I mean it. I know my sister screwed them up. They never had a chance with her. But their problems could get them killed, and that's something I don't know how to deal with."

My drink tastes good, but for some reason it has absolutely no effect. I'm stone-cold sober and could have been drinking soda pop.

"You can't be angry with them forever." Chip is looking at me with concern.

"It's been two weeks, and I am as pissed off as if it happened yesterday." I take a swallow and continue. "Even Melissa, I'm so pissed off at her I don't know what to do."

"What's wrong with you tonight?"

"I don't know. I made a deal with Torey and she messed up again. Maybe I should let her go into foster care, I don't know. I'm just so damned angry all the time. I can't figure out how to stop feeling like this. It's wearing me out."

"Have you tried talking to them?"

"Of course. Melissa cries, says it's not her fault. She was only listening to Torey. She's only five, blah, blah, blah."

"What do you say?"

"I told her if Torey wants to jump off a cliff, she'd better have enough sense not to follow."

Chip looks thoughtful.

"What does Torey say?"

"Torey is walking on eggshells when she's around me, which is good, because if she said one wrong thing right now, I think I might hit her."

"You don't mean it."

"Yes, I do." I look at Chip so she'll know I mean it. "I

won't, but I can't stop feeling like I really would like to." We are both quiet after that admission. A while later I say, "I think she scared the shit out of herself and that's the only thing that's keeping me from following through on foster care right now."

"Torey's young, she lacks judgment."

"Lacks judgment? I can't get past what could have happened, if they'd drifted out to sea... Hey, Jack," I shout down the bar.

He looks up from his cronies. They are grouped at the other end of the bar, laughing hysterically about something. Jack wipes his eyes on a dishtowel and raises his eyebrows at me.

"Two more like these on my tab," I yell again.

He nods.

"Don't you think maybe she learned a lesson? Torey's a smart girl."

Chip is looking at me with her earnest expression. The wine has made her beautiful brown eyes go all soft. What a sweet person she is. And she has absolutely no clue what life is like outside her charmed circle.

"Yeah, she's smart." I sigh and stare at the bottles on the wall. "Unfortunately, her intelligence will probably be wasted. She'll end up a bum like her mother."

"Rae, stop being so hard on the kid."

"I'm not. I see kids like Torey all the time. Most of them end up exactly like their parents, no matter what the department does."

"Torey's not incarcerated, her mother is."

"Not yet. That's another statistic. Chances are she probably will be, too.

"You know what? It sounds like you're giving up on her for one childish prank, and that isn't like you."

Chip is disappointed in me. I can't stand it. I turn on the barstool to face her. "The problem is I was just beginning to trust her and she goes and pulls a stunt like this. I have to look at what she's really saying to me."

"The only thing being said is she's a kid who messed up."

"It says more than that. She knew she had to do well or living with me was no longer an option."

"You mean even though she has problems she has to act like she doesn't?"

"No. Well… maybe. Shit, I don't know what I mean."

"Yes, you do. What's the real problem?"

"I don't know. I've told you what it's been like with them, for over a year now. I guess I'm just scared to care about one other person who's going to end up going nowhere. I know that sounds bad. Maybe I'm just too selfish to be their guardian." Misery strikes instead of alcohol. I turn back to the bar and feel the damned helpless anger take over again.

Chip stays put, seeming to consider me. "I'm sitting here listening to you and realizing that all of the mothering things I grew into with my boys, you're facing all at once."

"What do you mean?"

"My kids were babies when I got them, and I got them one at a time. I got used to being their mother over time, Rae. You're overwhelmed is all. Anyone would be."

"I would have agreed with you awhile back, but now I'm beginning to believe Torey is unfixable."

"I don't know, Rae. You live with them and maybe you're right, but what if Torey *isn't* too messed up to be helped, and then there's Melissa to think about. I still say you've got to be feeling overwhelmed."

I don't answer. I'm tired of being upset, tired of not enjoying my life. Tired of trying to be something I'm not—a parent.

"Even for me, Rae," she continues softly, "it's a roller coaster. The emotional ups and downs of being a mother, of being any kind of involved parent, takes more out of a person than anything I know."

I spoiled our good time. Chip looks sad. "Thanks, friend." I give her a hug.

We sit in comfortable silence for a while.

"Karla's watching them tonight?" she asks. Karla is the sixteen-year-old she'd recommended.

"Yeah, you should have seen Torey's face when we picked her up."

"Was she upset?"

"I think she was more embarrassed than anything else. When she saw Karla was only a few years older and going to baby-sit them... I don't know, I almost felt sorry for her."

"You don't have to worry about Karla, she's a nice kid. She might even help Torey get situated in school."

"I hope so."

I look to see if John is here, not yet. "If John ever shows up, I'm telling him to sell the boat."

"What boat?"

"My boat. I asked him to take it somewhere where the girls couldn't get their hands on it."

Chip giggles. "He came back after you kidnapped him?"

I glare but Chip doesn't take the hint. "Yeah," I concede, "he's storing it until I can figure out what I want to do with it. I don't have a trailer for it anymore, but I just decided to sell it, as is."

"So John managed to see you last weekend, too. He sure is an enterprising guy. Speak of the devil."

Chip is looking towards the doorway. It takes all the control I didn't know I had not to turn around. My heart freezes.

She leans over and whispers, "I'm not kidding about not letting on. You better play this like it's a big surprise."

I look and see she means it. Sweet Chip has some steel hidden somewhere inside. Then she stands up and waves at John. He's pretending to talk to some guys and then pretends to notice her. Then he sort of, unnaturally, ambles in our direction.

"How're you ladies tonight?"

"John, I bet you remember Rae here? You saved her from drowning herself, looking for those girls."

She's giggling like a teenager. I swear she's drunk and hasn't even touched the wine I'd gotten her.

"Hi, John," I say. "I owe you a drink."

"You don't owe me a thing. I was happy to help."

John waves to Jack, who nods back at him. Jack comes over with a bottle of beer, and John sits down on the other side of Chip, away from me. A smooth move. He's too chicken to sit next to me.

"Put that on my tab, Jack. I owe him," I say.

"Sure thing, sweet-pea," Jack replies.

"Thanks, Rae. How are the girls?" John leans in around Chip, looking at me.

"Still alive." I know I sound brusque. Damn, I hate it when I cop an attitude.

No one seems to know what to say. Chip stands up.

"Where are you going?" I ask in a shaky voice. She picks up her pocketbook. I stare in disbelief.

"I'm going home to my kids and my husband. Besides, you're in good hands."

She smiles her evil smile again. Her back is to John so he can't see. Since she's blocking him, I give the evil look back. But she only laughs.

"Good night, John," she says, turning around. "It was real nice running into you." Then she turns and gives me a warning glare. "Good night, Rae."

"Goodbye, traitor," I whisper.

John says, "Good night, Chip." Then there's a moment of distinct discomfort, us sitting with our drinks and Chip's barstool screaming its glaring emptiness between us.

I decide to try and fill the gap. "I really do feel like I owe you a lot. I mean, you've been great."

"Don't worry about it. I'm just glad it all turned out okay."

"Not only with the kids, but it was really nice, you coming back and taking me to get my car, and then it was really nice you coming back for the boat. I don't know how to thank you for everything." Not knowing how many more times I'd work the phrase "really nice" into a sentence, I decide to shut up.

John looks irritated. "Quit worrying about it. Can I get you another drink?"

I glance down and am surprised to see my glass is empty. "Sure." Why not? I still didn't feel a thing.

John smiles and moves into Chip's vacated seat.

"Well, anyway, thanks for coming by." I feel as uncomfortable as if I had a third elbow growing from the middle of my chest.

"It's quite all right. How are you doing?"

"I'm managing." Again the screaming silence, then I think of something to ask. "I've been wondering about something."

"What?"

"Why were you here that night?"

"You mean when I met you?"

"Yeah, when I saw you come out of the back of the restaurant. It was late."

"I stay here." He has an odd expression I can't decipher.

"You stay here? At the restaurant?"

He's embarrassed, his face flushing. "Sometimes. Have you ever been upstairs?"

"Yeah, to get stuff like napkins and things."

"Didn't you notice it's like an apartment up there?"

"No."

"Well, it was once, and I have the bedroom, bath and kitchen in the back. Jack's my uncle."

"Really?"

John chuckles. I must be acting like the fan I am. "Yeah, he's really my uncle." He smiles and takes a long pull from his bottle.

"Why were you leaving right then?"

"When you ambushed me?" He's smiling.

"Yeah." Usually I don't like being teased, but the way John did it, it was okay somehow.

"I heard someone hollering out in the parking lot." He grins. "No, that's not true. I needed to get some things ready for a charter."

"That early?"

"Yeah, Gulf Stream trips leave at four a.m. usually."

"So I must have been real lucky to run into you when I did, I guess."

"I guess."

We talk about the girls. He wants to know how they ended up with me and how we ended up here. I tell him and talk for over an hour. In the process, he gets me another drink, and it's absolutely wonderful to sit and tell someone as nice as the guy sitting next to me, the entire story of the past year.

I begin to understand what Chip meant when she said I was overwhelmed. Explaining all that went on in the past year allowed me to appreciate how much it has been, for me and for them.

As I tell John about my adventures with my nieces, another conversation is taking place inside me. I see it's my old nemesis *trust*, causing some of my problems with the girls. That one always trips me up, that and my inability to admit to fear. Usually I'd rather walk into a lion's den than admit I'm scared to go.

For some reason, though, right now, I understand it's okay to be scared. I'm scared because I care about them. It's easier to see it all laid out this way. I feel myself finally relax and John gets us another round.

"Sounds like you sure got your hands full with those two."

"Yeah, I do." I smile, remembering the other night. "We were crabbing out on my pier—that's Melissa's big thrill, crabbing—and she pulls this huge crab from a trap before I can get to her. He pinched her and I could tell it hurt, but she didn't drop him or cry out until she got him in the bucket. When I asked her if she was okay, she burst into tears, saying, 'He weren't going to get no rematch from me.'"

"Is she a wrestling fan?"

"Sort of. She watches those stupid shows with Torey. Why they like them I don't know."

"Oh, they have stories to them, like soap operas. Most of the kids around here are fans."

"Those girls were real curious about you when you came for the boat." I smile at him, grateful to be relaxed.

"They were? They never said one word to me. They must be as difficult to get next to as their aunt."

He's smiling, too, but I can't tell if he's teasing me or means it. Either way, I'm glad.

"I'm not difficult." Then I laugh. But I notice a hysterical ring to it that alarms me. I take a deep breath and calm down.

It looks like he's going to say something else but I beat him to it. "Excuse me for a second." I get down from the barstool and grab my purse. I need to pee, badly.

On the way to the bathroom, somewhere between the bar and the toilet, a Long Island iced tea bomb hits my brain dead center. In some distant part of my awareness, a thought is generated — it's so odd I could be getting this drunk and have no warning. The rest of me is hijacked by the panic squad.

I make it to the bathroom and look in the mirror. It's bad, very bad. Whatever hopes I had my looks had not followed me down this horrible, slippery slope, die a terrible death.

There's more. I get into the stall and in my attempt to pull down my jeans, knock myself over and fall sideways onto the toilet seat. Hoping nothing is getting wet, I half-sit, half-crouch over the seat and pee, wondering what my next move will be.

Resurfacing next to the sink, I try to get my act together by splashing cold water on my face. I almost get sick but can't pull that off either. Finally, I stagger out and go straight through the front door. I figure I'm better off not exposing myself in this state. I almost make to my car where I plan to pass out when…

"Rae, where are you going?"

Shit, shit, shit, shit. "Oh," I say, turning and attempting to adopt a casual attitude. "I thought I'd go home."

John walks closer, the gravel crunching under his feet. As he gets nearer, I notice a sort of lopsided grin on his face. He doesn't say anything but is looking at me with raised eyebrows. I figure my act may not be fooling him. "But I wasn't planning on driving anytime soon," I add with as much dignity as I can unearth.

"Rae," he says softly, like talking to a two-year-old, "how are you planning to get home without driving?"

It's definitely getting to be fall. We are having our first cold snap and it feels great out here; the restaurant was way stuffy. Trees rustle with leaves that haven't dropped but are thinking about it. I look among them, hoping to find an answer. How was I planning to get home?

I love these great nights you have only out in the country, a sky so inky black stars dazzle against it. A piece of moon seems tangled in the branches of the enormous oak tree rising up from the parking lot.

I get a little dizzy taking it all in and accidentally stumble. Probably the drinks didn't help, but I think it was just sheer unluckiness. John tries to grab my arm, but I snatch it back too quickly and then go down. It's a good one. Arms flailing, I take a good while before making it to the ground. I conduct a quick inventory of body parts, all reporting in cheerfully. *Nothing broken!*

"Actually, I thought I'd sit until I was sober enough to drive home."

He stands there, looking down and finally asks, "Do you plan to do your sitting in a car or here in the middle of a parking lot?"

It seems a fair question. I think about it. "I guess my car would be better."

"I'd really like to drive you home," he says, pulling me to my feet.

I suppose he sees fear in my eyes.

"If I didn't know better, I'd think you didn't like me."

Before I can stop them, words tumble out of my mouth. "How did you know I liked you?"

"Chip told me."

"Chip told me you set this up." He wasn't the only one who knew things.

"She wasn't supposed to."

"I know. Don't let her know I told you," I whisper guiltily. I can't afford to piss off my one and only friend.

"Are you going to let me take you home?"

I guess I still look uncertain. John says, "I've never been in prison or even jail since I turned twenty-one."

"What'd you do when you were twenty-one?" It seems important.

"I tried to drive in the same condition you're in right now."

I have to admit, it's a good argument, but I'm wavering inside and out. I don't want him to see me like this, but on the other hand, he doesn't seem overly disgusted either. Plus I'm tired and won't be in any condition to drive for a long time.

I guess he takes my silence as the inability to talk which it sort of is. John smiles and takes my arm again. This time I don't pull away. He leads me to his battered and scarred pick-up truck, the one he drove when we were getting my car, and I'd been so happy to be next to him I was ashamed to admit it to myself. When he helps me into the front passenger seat, I feel like a princess being handed into a carriage.

I know he knows the way, so I can relax and let him take over. Rolling down the window I lean back into the creaky seat. We drive out the highway again, towards the bay, while cold, clean air washes over me.

"Are you doing okay?" John smiles and turns towards me. I look at him. He isn't movie-star handsome or anything, but if you were describing him to a girlfriend you'd have to say he was nice-looking.

"How old are you?" I ask, something I'm not planning to say, and I'm surprised when it slips out. I don't know what I'd planned to say when I opened my mouth. Confused, I shut up and pretend I know what's going on. I can see he's a little thrown, but I act like everything is normal as can be.

Then he laughs and says, "Forty-one."

"Ever married?" Again with the unexpected questions. I wonder if I'm experiencing an alternate personality taking over my mind. Maybe I've developed a multiple personality disorder from all the stress I've been coping with.

"Are you a detective or lawyer or something?"

"I'm a probation officer." I'm proudly back in control of my voice and can say what I intend.

"I can tell you're in some sort of law enforcement." He takes a deep breath. "I give up. I've been married twice and divorced from my second wife about six years ago. How about you?"

"I already know. I asked Chip." I laugh and hiccup simultaneously, a weird sensation.

"Then why'd you ask?"

"I don't know."

"How old are you? Some of us don't go prying around like others of us."

I need to think before I answer. Something's wrong here. "You're not supposed to ask a woman that."

"I asked anyway."

Silence ensues. I give in. "I'm thirty-six."

"Thirty-six?"

"Yeah. What's wrong, too old for you?"

"Not at all. In fact, maybe a little too young."

"No, I'm not. I'm just right. Chip said so."

He doesn't seem to know what to say. Maybe my alternate personality has driven him off with her lack of tact. Of course, that would never shut her up. "So do you like me or what?"

"You are the most direct woman I ever met."

"I'm not usually this direct. I think the booze is loosening up my mouth or something."

Then I hiccup, really loud. Great, what a dainty creature he's going to think I am. "Sooo…"

John glances over. "I'm available, if that's what you're asking."

"That's good."

"It is?"

"Yep, 'cause I…" I have to think.

"You what?"

"Because you are the kindness of strangers." Somewhere it makes sense. "And I like the way you get me out of trouble."

"Are you planning on getting into any more trouble tonight?" he asks as we pull onto the dirt road leading to my cottage. I think I detect a hopeful note in his voice.

"You never can tell about those things. I'd be careful if I was you." The voice is mine, but the teasing tone isn't. I can't remember ever speaking to anyone like that. It's way beyond flirting. I sound like the girl who used to live in my dorm the first year of college. We called her "Susie Slut." There was something wrong with her. Had I caught what she had? Did I care?

We pull up beside my place. I can tell the house is sleeping. It seems to breathe in and out with the dreamers inside. We sit in the truck after he turns off the motor, and I feel excited and happy and finally in a really good mood for the first time in months, or years, or maybe my whole life.

I want to sit next to him for an undetermined amount of time. Here beside my sleeping house. He takes my hand and kisses it. I love how things are progressing. He unhooks his seatbelt and scoots next to me. I like first kisses better than anything and snuggle into his chest to savor our first.

John puts his index finger under my chin and turns my face towards his. He bends and kisses me gently, right on the lips, exactly perfect. He smells of saltwater, wood smoke and male. His whiskers are rough and I remember the first time I felt them on my face, how he comforted me then.

John's sweet kisses grow deeper and I'm pushing up against him with all my newly developed muscles from working at the restaurant. In a very little while, we are both breathless.

I catch mine first. "I'd ask you in, but I've got a teen-age babysitter spending the night for the first time, and I don't want to wake her up." Or give her any wrong ideas about me to take home to her mother either.

"Oh, well." John looks out the windshield. "I guess maybe here's the part where I'm supposed to ask you out."

I smile inside. "Yep, that's the point we've gotten to."

"How about tomorrow night?"

Suddenly it hits—the logistics involved in an honest-to-God date. I'd never considered what single mothers went through to date. Being asked out had gotten lost somewhere in the nightmare year I'd had the kids, and now that someone was, it was—well, it was just awful. I'd never even given birth, and here I was, stuck, stuck, stuck.

I guess I was staring at my own personal wall of futility a bit longer than I realized when John nudges me and asks, "Well?"

"I don't think I can," I wail and probably scare the crap out of him. This is a disaster. My nieces are not only destroying my life, but also any potential I'll ever have for happiness. "I've got the girls and babysitter costs. I can't afford to go out. I don't believe this." I stare hopelessly at the house holding my jailers.

"Kids aren't the end of the world." John laughs. "We can take them with us, go to dinner or something."

I stare at him and wonder if he is the stupidest man in the world, or if all men are stupid. "Oh, right, that would be *loads* of fun. You haven't met my nieces, have you?"

"Of course I did, remember? You told me they were curious about me."

"That wasn't them. They were still afraid I was going to kill them so they were behaving. Things are beginning to get back to normal now. You haven't met Teenzilla and her five-year-old accomplice, the whiner from hell. Thirteen-year-old girls can kill a good evening without even breaking a sweat. How long has it been since you've been around a thirteen-year-old girl?"

"Not since I was fourteen," John says with a sigh. "We'll figure something out."

We both sigh. I don't want him to leave. "Want to walk down to the dock?"

"Sure."

We go around the cottage towards the water. I'm more confident in my walking abilities now but hold his hand anyway. It's warm and comforting.

With the wind coming off the bay, it's colder on this side. My pier reaches out in the water about forty feet and has a floating dock attached to the end that goes up and down with the tides.

We sit on a metal bench my father screwed on the weathered wood with lug bolts a long time ago. John puts his arm around me, and I happily anticipate his next move.

Then I kiss him. Or at least someone wearing my skin is kissing him. That person puts her arms around his neck, pulls his head down to hers, and kisses him right on the mouth.

Then I freak out because I'm becoming a crazy person and it's not like me to pull dumb stunts like this. I don't want him to think I'm like Susie, ready to go at it the first time we're alone together. Still, when he leans down to kiss me back, it doesn't seem like he minds all that much. He kisses the way I like, intense and focused. I feel that old deep-down wiggle, the one I thought I'd lost forever. I forget to worry and start to enjoy this guy, a lot.

The thing wearing my skin doesn't seem to care about the cold. She wants his skin too much and his warm hands. She takes off my deep-red, *Sea Witch* T-shirt with such grace

I silently marvel. She's right, his warm hands and the cold wind on my back feel great.

This wild thing becomes unhinged from earth and escapes gravity. I hang on with all I've got and watch as she straddles his lap, facing him and trying to lose her tongue in his mouth. His hands are greedy, and I like that, too. I like the sounds he makes and that he feels beautiful to me.

That's new. He's beautiful in ways I'd never imagined a man could be. I like everything—his rough whiskers, his clean starched shirt, the smell of the sea about him.

Filled with admiration, I note John is a master at one-handed bra unhooks. By the time his mouth finds my nipple, we are both moaning as loud as the wind.

Someone looking a lot like me rips open the front of his shirt and buttons fly like fish scales. The satisfaction of skin on skin demands more. I stand up and begin to peel off my jeans when he stops me.

"Rae, I'd like nothing better than to continue this, but I'm freezing."

I'm stopped in mid-zip. For a waterman out in all sorts of weather, he sure is a wimp. He's breathing heavy. So am I.

My real personality kicks in. Things are moving too fast. My head is swimming. What the hell am I doing?

Then way down deep inside, I hear another voice answering very distinctly, *Having a great time, don't mess it up.* This is unnerving. I'm not used to internal voices responding to rhetorical questions. I'm definitely going back to the real me. The unreal one is getting a little too scary.

"Hey, look. Before you go…" I say, but he pulls me into his lap and kisses me so intently I forget what I'm going to say and start believing all shirts should be banned forever.

"Rae." His voice is husky from lust. How wonderful he sounds. I begin to attack him with my tongue. "Wait a minute!"

I feel ashamed. I've never had a guy stop me and don't know what etiquette is involved. "Sorry, John, I need to tell you that I don't usually…"

"You don't usually go this far on a first date, right?"

"Yeah, how did you know what I was going to say?"

"I don't know. Listen, do you want to do this? I'm not trying to push you or anything, but let me know because I'm freezing here. We gotta make some plans."

I look in his face. It's inches from my own. He's so handsome in the moonlight and all. I trust the kindness in his eyes.

"I want you," says someone with my voice. Before I can say anything else, he smiles so big and gets such a happy look on his face I forget to talk.

"I want you to know that I don't usually take advantage of someone who's…"

I can see him searching for the right word. "Of someone who's drunk." I say it for him.

"Yeah, but this time, I'm willing to make an exception. Rae, we've got to get inside somewhere. Aren't you cold?"

I look down. I have no idea what I expect to see. Icicles forming on my nipples? "Not really." But I guess he is. He's beginning to shiver.

"I can get us a room somewhere, or we can go back to my boat if you want."

"Your boat?"

"Back at the marina."

"Or your room back at *The Sea Witch*?"

"Naw, not with Marie around. She'd have my head if she found out I had a woman up there."

Damn, the marina is thirty minutes away. By the time we get there and back, it will be morning.

Karla's asleep in my bed, the girls in theirs. We could go into the living room, but it would be my bad luck for someone to come out at the worst possible moment. Then I remember a room with a good sturdy lock on its door.

"I have an idea," I say and grab his hand. We make our way back to the house.

We are quiet. I get the pillow and comforter off the couch where I'm supposed to sleep and lead him back to the bathroom.

"How romantic," he whispers. We are both giggling in the light of the nightlight. He fixes a bed on the floor while I lock the beautiful brass deadbolt I'd installed, all by myself, not very long ago.

The bathroom, along with the rest of the world, falls away so fast my head is spinning again. We discover tiny motions made slowly. Time leaves. Keeping unintelligible noises quiet requires more and more effort. We are lost in a mutual blur of the same ragged lust I heard in his voice, when a knocking at the door gets louder. Someone I don't know is saying something I can't decipher.

"Arae?"

Shit, it's Melissa, calling my name. I freeze. We both freeze and wait, hoping with everything sacred to anyone anywhere, she'd go away.

"Arae?"

Silence

"Arae?" Melissa says, louder now, and getting panicky.

"Umm, yes, Melissa?"

"Arae, can't you hear me? Can I come in?"

"Ahh, no, you can't because I'm…" I desperately search my mind for any other reason than the one that comes to me. "Because I'm sort of stuck on the toilet right now."

I can feel John start silently laughing. It makes him jerk around in a weird way.

"Oh, Arae, do you have squirty-poo?" she asks.

John's attempts to laugh quietly are no longer working. He's making strange huff-huff sorts of noises. I elbow him in the ribs. All he does is fall over and start making louder sounds.

"Yes, Melissa. I'm sick, and I need to be left alone. Go on back to bed now."

I glare at John in the gloom of the nightlight. He's still laughing.

"But, Arae," she wails, "I have to go now!"

I hear Melissa's own personal siren crank up behind the words. She's building up to the super-whine. I know the signs.

Damn it, damn it, damn it. By now, I'm also realizing the battle is lost. I'm pulling on clothes and trying to get the blanket and pillow picked up. John is worse than useless. He's laughing into the pillow and ignoring my attempts to direct him into his jeans.

"Hang in there, Melissa. I'll be out in a minute." I lean down and hiss into John's ear, "Get dressed, damn it."

"I gotta go now!" She's in stage two. I have thirty seconds, maybe fifteen, before she loses it for real.

John finally gets into his jeans. I push him next to the door and hand him the pillow, blanket and the rest of our clothes. I open the door and squash him as hard as I can behind it. I hear a muffled "uumph."

Poor Melissa is so sleepy she's unsteady and looks so tiny in her sister's Hard Rock Café T-shirt that falls to her ankles. She's dragging beloved Night-Night, the baby blanket, behind her.

She toddles in. "Thanks," she whispers.

She pulls up her shirt and sits on the toilet. I squat in front and let her lean on me while she pees. I act nicer to her than I hardly ever do, and she puts her arms around my neck. Hoping I can keep her in her in this sleepy, semi-conscious state, I pick her up when she is finished.

I almost get her out, but I see John's reflection grinning at me in the mirror, and I glare back at him to shut him up. Melissa sees me looking at something and looks, too.

In the dim light of the nightlight, Melissa sees a shape of something reflecting in the mirror, something big and lurking in the shadows behind the door. She drops Night-Night and lets out a blood-curdling scream that sets dogs howling many miles away. I put her down.

Torey comes tearing down the hallway exactly like I knew she would. Melissa rushes to her side, tears streaming down her face.

Torey glares at me and holds Melissa.

"What did you do?" Torey demands.

"It's not Arae, it's him!" screams Melissa, pointing to the bathroom door.

But from where they stand in the hall, Torey can't see anything. She looks at me with a puzzled expression.

Karla sticks her head out of my room. "Everything all right?" she asks.

"Fine, Karla, go on back to sleep. I'm home now is all."

She nods and withdraws. I'm leaning out in the hall, trying to herd the girls away from the bathroom and back to their room.

But they aren't budging. Torey is trying to figure out what I'm up to. All my trying to act normal isn't working.

I consider trying to convince Melissa she'd had a bad dream, but then I think about how rotten I'd feel if I tricked a little kid that way. I guess I get to thinking about the whole damned thing for so long Torey figures something is up for sure.

"Arae, whose shoes are those?" she asks, pointing at John's size giant tennis shoes in the corner of the bathroom.

She flicks on the light and elbows her way past me. I slump against the door frame. Melissa is still clinging to her sister's side.

"There he is." Melissa shakes Torey and points at John behind the door, still holding the bundle of blankets, pillow and miscellaneous pieces of clothing, shirtless and grinning.

Torey jumps like he's a snake. Melissa screams again.

"Hey, it's just me, the guy from the boat. I brought your aunt home, remember me?"

"That's that guy that was here last week, isn't it?" Torey says, looking at me with those narrowed green eyes.

I sigh, trying to think of a good answer and can't. I try to think of any kind of explanation and can't. "Yeah, that's the guy that was here last week."

Torey regains her composure and looks back at John, then at me and stomps out of the room with Melissa.

I'm going to be paying for this for a long damn time. I look at John who is still smiling, the idiot. He doesn't know what I do. When a thirteen-year-old finds out she is morally superior to you, you just might as well go shoot yourself.

Chicken Spaghetti

There are no exact ingredients to this recipe. You can use a roaster, a fryer or a Cornish hen (or many Cornish hens), depending on the number of guests. Split whatever fowl you choose on the breast side and open it like a book. Turn it over and flatten the back by pressing down.

In a jelly-roll pan (or any pan large enough to hold the ingredients and having a lip), place any of the following that appeal to you and your taste buds:

- peeled, cut-up carrots
- onion quarters
- artichoke hearts (fresh, canned or frozen; if using the kind that comes in a marinade, dump in the marinade)
- jumbo olives
- green or red peppers
- a few cloves of minced garlic
- fresh or dry rosemary, oregano and thyme
- some olive oil and a small amount of balsamic vinegar.

Mix vegetables with hands until covered by oil, seasonings and vinegar.

Place fowl on top and bake in a 350-degree oven until fowl is done. (Check to make sure juices run clear when thigh area is pricked.)

Remove fowl and let rest, tented in foil.

Turn the oven up to 400 degrees. Stir remaining vegetables and any juices from fowl and return to oven for fifteen minutes to a half-hour.

You want them to begin to char. Stir every ten minutes or so.

Boil large quantity of salted water for spaghetti. I use the extra-thick kind, but any variety will do. Make enough spaghetti to be a good counterpart to the rest of the ingredients.

When spaghetti is cooked (al dente), drain and put in bowl or platter large enough to hold everything.

Grate Romano, and/or Asiago, and/or Parmesan cheeses into a separate bowl.

Cut up fowl into serving pieces — the wings from the breast, the breast into two parts, the leg from the thigh, the thigh into two parts. Remove and discard backbone.

Remove vegetables from oven and do not drain. Dump entire contents over spaghetti and mix, pour cheeses over top and mix. Check for enough seasonings and adjust if needed. Place chicken parts on top and serve.

Your guests will want this recipe.

OCTOBER

I pick up the phone. "Hello?"

"Hey there, girlfriend, I thought I'd call and see how you're doing."

"Chip?"

"Yeah."

"I'm a nervous wreck and could use some hand-holding. Can't you come over?" I'm sitting on my bed, biting off the fingernail polish I put on earlier and trying to talk myself out of an anxiety attack. I want a drink, but considering the last time I attempted that as a cure for my issues, I decided it was probably better to forego the pleasure.

"You know I can't. How long before he gets there?"

"He's supposed to be here in an hour and a half. I'm losing my mind and don't think I will make it that long."

Chip's laughing. "How come?"

"I just figured it out. I feel exactly like I did when I was fifteen and going out on my first official date, a blind date. I was scared exactly this way."

"Gosh, I can't even remember the last time I had first-date jitters. I kind of miss those days."

"I'll trade you."

"You'd take sitting at home, watching action-adventure movies with three boys—no, make that four boys, my husband's a bigger kid than the other three—over a romantic evening with John? I don't believe it."

"Believe it. What you're doing sounds like heaven. I want the whole damned thing over with. First dates suck." It's true, they do. Even if I scrubbed, creamed, and perfumed every inch of my skin, and every orifice, to get ready for it.

"Poor John, I'm going to have to fix him up with someone who can appreciate him if you're going to be like this."

"I didn't say I didn't like him. You know how I feel about him."

"That's right. I almost forgot you're attracted to the guy."

"What's he going to think, Chip? I almost raped him. He's got to think I'm desperate and easy."

"You're being hard on yourself. You don't have to be so embarrassed. Besides, you are desperate and easy."

"Oh, thanks. What a friend. You know what else I figured out? There's nothing worse than going out on a first date with someone you nearly had sex with. I've created for myself the worst possible scenario ever."

"That was the funniest story I ever heard." Chip begins laughing again. She was laughing so hard at work last night, after I finally blurted out the sordid details, she'd ended up going outside to get away from me. "I can't believe you thought you could get away with it. Don't you know kids have radar when it comes to sex?"

"I do now," I say sadly. "You know, that was the first time in my life I came on to someone like that. What's he going to think?"

"Didn't you ever like anyone before?"

"Yeah, but I ... shit." I hate it when words dry up in my brain and leave me speechless. "I don't know. I never did, is all."

"You mean you were too cool to put the moves on anyone before?"

"Maybe," I admit. "Or maybe it was all the alcohol, and now I'll have to become an alcoholic to be that free again. Plus you didn't answer my question—what's he expecting tonight? Is he going to assume all I want to do is get laid? I mean, we don't even know each other. This is nuts. I'm nuts. What if he expects me to jump his bones tonight?"

Chip is laughing the same helpless sort of laughter she'd

gotten into last night. I guess it is funny, if you aren't living it. "Rae, meet Rae. You had a tiger in your tank the whole time and didn't even know it. You're lucky to find it. I was married a long time before I found my tiger. If it's any help to you, I know for a fact that John is just as scared as you are."

"He is?" The conversation suddenly gets very interesting.

"Yep. Randy got home a little bit ago. He was John's bait boy today. John had a rockfish charter, did you know?"

"Yeah, that's why he's coming over so late, but what about Randy?" I ask.

"To hear my boy tell it, John almost worked him to death."

I'm confused. What did that have to do with being scared? "Did they catch a lot of fish or something?"

"Nope, Randy was worked to death getting the boat cleaned up to Captain Romance's satisfaction after they got in. It was hard to keep a straight face listening to him complain about how uptight John was all day and that he couldn't get the boat cleaned up enough to suit him.

"Randy got so disgusted by the way John was acting, he left when John's back was turned. As far as I know, Randy has never left a job without getting paid before. He said he'd go back for it after John calms down from whatever has got him all worked up. That's a direct quote, 'from whatever has got him all worked up.'"

"So John is freaked out?"

"Sure sounds that way."

"Okay, even if John doesn't expect me to be a whore, what if I find out I don't like him?"

"You think you don't like him?" Chuckling comes from the phone.

"I don't know! I mean, what happens if I get to talking to him and find out he's, like, a member of the KKK? Really Chip, I could never date someone in the KKK. I'm half-Jewish!"

I wasn't trying to be funny but have to wait while Chip howls. Finally she catches her breath. "I'm sorry, I don't know anyone who's a member of the KKK, so I'm pretty sure John isn't." She's laughing again. "I do think you like him. I hope he gets there soon so you can be put out of your misery."

"Me too."

The girls come in as I'm hanging up. They are curious, wondering what I'm up to.

Torey always begins their inquisitions. "Who was that?"

"Chip."

"So how's she doing?"

"Okay." I don't know why I don't want to tell her I have a date.

She sits on the bed, considering my attire—a robe, curlers and makeup. "So what're you getting all fixed up for?"

Melissa is shadowing Torey, as usual, dragging Night-Night across the floor, then sitting on my bed and sucking her thumb. I can tell she's getting tired. She used to get so horribly cranky this time of day, I dreaded the setting sun, but now all she is, is sleepy. Again I silently thank God for Lucy and the miracles she's working in this child.

I'm at my grandmother's old dressing table. It's a dark brown wooden relic from the '30s and has a huge, round mirror attached to the back of a tiny table. The bench I'm sitting on matches. It's from my other grandmother's house. My mom brought it here when her momma died.

I remember watching her in the evenings, putting on makeup before going out with Daddy.

She seemed like a movie star then. That was when she most looked the way I felt about her—glamorous, distant, and aloof with some sort of sparkle I could never capture but always wanted to.

I turn around on the bench. "I have a date." The oversized curlers in my hair nod in agreement. I feel intensely embarrassed for absolutely no reason, and the more I try to kick it out, the stronger it gets. Luckily, Torey doesn't seem to notice.

"With that dude in the *bathroom*?"

"Yeah, that one," as if there were so many.

"So where's the babysitter?" Torey's voice is sarcastic. Even though she knows I can't trust her, she resents the hell out of having to have one.

"You. You're going to be in charge tonight, and you'd better do a better job than last time."

That surprises her. "You mean you're leaving me alone with Melissa?"

She's so shocked and hopeful I can't tell her the exact truth. Instead I smile and say, "Sort of."

"Are we coming with you?"

"No, you're staying here."

"So this guy is coming here? What in the hell are we supposed to do? Stay in our room all night?"

"No, me and John aren't staying here. We're going out. I promise you'll have the place to yourself. It's like a riddle. See if you can figure it out."

"You figure it out." Torey stomps off to her room. I wait for her door to slam and then sigh when it does. I should have just told her the truth. Even gentle teasing is beyond what she can handle.

I stand up and am surprised to see Melissa still sitting on the bed, still sucking her thumb and doing the Linus thing with Night-Night, but there in my room without Torey. I'm fairly sure it's the first time she's ever been voluntarily alone with me.

I smile at her tentatively. She pulls the thumb out of her mouth and smiles a gooey smile back. The little bedraggled kid sitting on my bed seems almost adorable. I sit next to her. She doesn't appear the slightest bit alarmed, so I put my arm around her. Melissa snuggles up like we'd been doing this for years, and it feels nice to be there in my mother's old robe and my arm around my baby niece. Torey and I had been close like this once. When she was tiny, I was "Arae the Wonder Aunt," her rescuer. The one who made Play-Doh worlds with her on the kitchen table while my parents and her mother fought about who got to live Vicky's life.

When Torey was older and living with Vicky in North Carolina, I could tell by the tone in her voice when she needed me to come get her and take her home with me for a long weekend. Super-Aunt also planned fabulous vacations in the summer for just the two of us, like Disney Cruises designed to make up for the rest of her life.

Melissa smells dirty. "Would you like a bubble bath?" She nods enthusiastically, and I decide to give her a bath with the good-smelling stuff I'd used earlier.

We go into the bathroom, plug the tub and turn on the old-fashioned spigots. I make a mental note to get her some bath toys. I bet she'd play with them. She likes the water. I'd never thought about it before because she usually takes a shower with Torey before going to bed at night.

I get some pans and wooden spoons from the kitchen and soon she's splashing and enjoying herself. I'm glad for the distraction. Anything is better than waiting for this date to begin.

Torey comes out to see what we are up to. She stands in the doorway not saying anything, but I know she's there. For some reason, I'm proud of being able to make Melissa happy and think Torey will be proud of me too. I'm kneeling next to the old-fashioned footed tub, washing Melissa's hair, and I grin at Torey in the doorway.

Melissa is splashing away, laughing and yelling out, "Look! I'm getting a bubble bath! I have a bubble beard."

Torey doesn't respond except to glare and go back to their room, slamming their door yet again.

It's like our fun leaves with her, like we both feel guilty or something. Melissa looks at me with a worried face.

This is so stupid. Melissa needs to branch out, have relationships with people other than her sister. I didn't want her fun to stop. She has so few things she enjoys.

I bend down, smiling, and put my face close to hers. "Guess what?"

"What, Arae?"

"Tomorrow, we are going to go shopping, just you and me, and we are going to buy you some bubble bath of your very own and some toys just for the bath."

It's so easy to make her smile, I'm ashamed I rarely attempt it. I get Melissa in the warm pajamas I bought last week, and she sits on my bed talking about nothing and everything while I dress in jeans and a sweater.

Torey figures out how I planned to go out on a date yet not leave them alone when John pulls his boat up to our dock. I'd already turned on the arc light, and we see him tie up. Torey acts like she's in a permanent grump tonight.

"Your dinner is in the oven and dessert in the fridge. Make sure Melissa gets to bed by nine. You know how she gets if she's sleepy tomorrow."

She won't even look me in the eye, only grunts so I'll know she's heard. Oh, well, I'll get her straightened out in the morning.

I put our dinner in a large plastic container. For some reason I don't want to leave the kitchen and stand by the counter, watching them watch one of the videos we'd gotten for tonight, some ridiculous story about dogs in a hotel.

Torey looks up from the couch, surprised to still see me. "Isn't he waiting for you?" she snarls.

"Yeah, I guess so." I know I have a stupid look on my face. Torey must have figured out I was stalling. Disgusted with me, she snorts and turns back to the TV.

Here goes nothing. I pick up the storage container and go out the door.

The walk to my pier reminds me of death row, but I play my part, smiling at John when I reach his boat. He grabs the container and helps me aboard. "This is great," I say, looking around. It is getting dark earlier now, and colder too, but the main cabin is cozy and warm. John had placed lanterns and candles around and, if you ignored the smell of diesel, his boat had become a romantic haven. I like the jazzy music pouring out of speakers hidden somewhere.

My multiple personality disorder continues to develop well. I met a few more of them today. There's a fifteen-year-old girl who's as eager for this date as any fifteen-year-old. She'd primped and hogged the bathroom for over an hour and told Torey to go pee in the woods when she attempted to invade my space. The fifteen-year-old is terrified John doesn't like her very much.

Then there's a middle-aged spinster. This is the personality that's supposed to be thinking about our future. Making sure I didn't do anything stupid to mess it up. She's been horrified for so long I keep her locked up where I don't have to hear the screaming.

Somewhere, lurking in the skin I'm wearing, is Wild Wanda, a creature who wants to strip naked and take him right here on the cabin's floor. She's the one who stole Torey's thong out of the clean clothes basket this morning, the thong in danger of bisecting me this very minute. I'm fairly sure I need to protect myself from her, too.

So while I'm looking around and saying, "This is great," I'm actually doing a lot more than making small talk. I'm wrestling with a bunch of people inside, and no one's coming out a clear winner. I look at John.

He's put some sort of crap in his hair and tried to slick it back. Big mistake. I think he knows it, too, because he looks miserable. Between us, we make quite a pair. I'm afraid it's going to be a long night.

I look out the window to see the cottage. It's set back from the water, so it's only an outline of house and lit windows. I'd told the girls unless it's an emergency, defined as immediately life-threatening circumstances, they are to stay inside. If they leave the premises on a non-emergency basis, they will never see a mall again. I'm fairly sure Torey believes me.

Now this man with greased-back hair and I are stuck here for the next few hours. I figure there's nothing much I can do to make the situation worse and find the thought oddly comforting. I begin pulling food out of the container and putting it on the counter.

The boat has all the amenities, a gleaming wood bar where we can sit on bar stools, a tiny galley with a range and a box-like refrigerator. He even has stereo, video, couches, and carpeting. Fishing boats have changed a lot since my dad took me out on a Gulf Stream charter over twenty years ago. Down some steps must have been the forward cabin and probably his stateroom since he lives here part-time. I blush for absolutely no damn reason.

John gets something out of a cooler. "I couldn't find anywhere to plug in, but if you need me to turn on the microwave I could start up the generator."

"Plug in?"

"Yeah, you know, electricity?"

"Oh, right."

"Next time, I'll bring a longer extension cord; we can run it up to the house." The "next time" rings out like cannon shot and his brow furrows. There is a long silence. "The range and oven are on propane." He says this in a whispery voice.

I probably have the same stupid look on my face Torey had sneered at earlier. It takes me a while to respond. "Propane?"

"Yeah." He clears his throat and his voice returns to normal. "It's how I keep the cabin warm without electricity. You can use the range or oven to heat up anything if you want, or I could turn on the generator for the microwave. The cooler is full of ice." He's beginning to sound desperate. "You look real nice tonight."

If only he knew what I'd been through before deciding on this outfit. Something attractive, but not too flirty. Not too dowdy either. Not this, not that. Along with all the voices in my head, I was lucky to not be standing in front of him stark raving naked. "Thanks." God, this is awful. I feel stress piling up on the back of my neck, probably making me look like a hunchback.

John turns and stumbles on his way to the bar. I feel sorry for him. It looks exactly like something I would do. He's carrying a bottle.

"Sit down, take a load off," he says, slaying me with his witty remarks. But the barstools are actually comfortable with padded leather seats and backs, and I like the rails to hook my feet onto. "I didn't know if I should get white or red, so I got pink."

"Pink?" What the hell is he talking about?

His face falls. "Yeah, I didn't know what to get, red wine or white, so I got pink. Is that okay?" He's holding up the bottle of wine he'd pulled from the cooler.

"Oh, wine." I'd made chicken spaghetti, a fairly basic meal most people liked. A good, crisp chardonnay would have been nice, but at least he wasn't holding up a box. "Pink is fine. How about pouring me some?"

John perks up and hands me a plastic wine glass full of some kind of pink stuff. It's the kind of wine glass you get at the grocery store. So much for amenities. I wonder if we'll be eating off of paper plates. I wait for him to pick up his own wine glass so that we could, well, not clink them together, but maybe do a romantic plastic tap or something. Maybe we could lighten up the graveyard tone of this evening.

"Where's your wine glass?" I ask.

John's happy look falls away, and after an incredibly long, difficult pause with lots of throat-clearing, he says, "Well, I've been meaning to tell you something."

"Yeah? What is it?" Maybe he only drinks beer or something. "I don't drink alcohol anymore."

I have no idea how to respond. "What do you mean, you don't drink alcohol? You drank beer with me last weekend, didn't you?"

"Yeah, but it was the non-alcoholic kind."

"Oh," I say, not sure what else to say.

"I used to drink alcohol. Sort of the reason I don't anymore." John's face is turning an uncomfortable-looking shade of red under the slicked back hair.

I get it. He's a recovering something. "How long have you been sober?" I sound like a drill sergeant.

"Six years."

"Are you in a program?" I should consider a career in the military.

"Yeah, AA."

"Your only problem is booze?"

"Yeah."

"Anything else?" I'd had it with the drug-addicted. I know that the substance someone is addicted to isn't supposed to matter, because if you're recovering from something, you're recovering. But for me, there's a big difference. I hold my breath while waiting for an answer.

"Isn't booze enough?"

"I need to know. Anything else?"

"No. How come?"

"I needed to know, was all." He looks embarrassed and I feel like a bitch. I'd been wrong. It actually was possible to make things worse. I try to make a joke. "Oh, well, maybe with my track record, it's a good idea one of us is sober."

"Maybe." He agrees, yet seems puzzled, like I'm weird, which I am. He doesn't understand I have every reason to be. My dad was an alcoholic but he at least had some limitations on his behavior that Vicky never had.

Plus, literally every man I've ever been attracted to turned out to have some sort of fatal flaw. Booze, drugs, other women, gambling, or like my ex-husband, the pathetic loser, an addiction to online porn. I'm shook up by my own ability to attract yet another addicted boyfriend. But how did his recovery fit into the equation?

He smiles a hopeful-looking smile. "You hungry? I've got some chips or pretzels if you'd like."

"I brought dinner, remember?" I'm angry, disappointed, and unable to pretend to be otherwise.

"Yeah, I do. It smells great. What is it?" He seems determined to make the best of this, no matter how rude I am.

Why couldn't I just once get to date a normal guy? How come they never turn out the way you think they're going to?

But John stands there, still holding the wine bottle and wondering if we are going to go any further. It's in his eyes, the wondering, the hurt.

"It's something I invented," I say, which must have been a mistake. Shyness implodes in me and I can barely breathe from the impact.

"Invented?" He comes close to see what I'm pulling out.

The casserole dish is one I love, one I'd spent way too much money on even when I could afford it. Oval, white porcelain with low sides topped in intricate designs of vines and berries.

"Oh, man that smells good." He leans over when I pull off the aluminum wrap and steam escapes. But I'm taking in his scent and remembering the night on my dock. Torey's thong rides up a little higher.

But he's already turned away to get his inevitable paper plates.

I squirm a bit and begin dishing up chicken spaghetti.

I have to admit I'm an excellent cook. I take after my Grandma Green, my dad's mother, a tiny Jewish dumpling who knocked grown men off their feet with her cooking. Gabriella Green's dinners were legend in the small Ohio town where my parents grew up. John is now sitting across the bar from me. I wait smugly for his reaction.

He stands, pushing on the bar with his hands, leaning over to kiss the top of my head. "Thank you."

It could have been for the dinner I made, but I didn't think so. The "thank you" was for accepting him. He stood there so open, so clearly there, I felt rotten for having ever been rough on him.

He leans in and kisses me on the lips. It was an unexpected gesture making me flush with pleasure. So what if he's in recovery. At least this time I won't have to try and figure out what his deal is.

I notice how nice the place looks with red carnations in shot glasses on the bar. Between the flowers, lanterns and candlelight, along with the sheer luxury of the boat, I'm reminded to relax and be glad I made the effort to slog through my personal minefields of crap to get here.

I fill a paper plate for myself as John begins to eat. In one of Chip's many lectures on the phone today, she told me there was nothing wrong in just being nice to each other tonight. We could have dinner, talk, get to know each other, and I could quit putting so much pressure on myself. She said she'd known John all her life. He'd been one of her older brother's friends, a guy she looked up to. He'd been the kind of teenager who was never too cool to be nice to kids like her. She never told me he was in recovery. I wonder why?

I get the salad, rolls, butter and dessert out of my bin and create sort of a salad plate/bread plate combo for each of us. I scoot John's combo plate next to the one he's attacking. I come around and sit next to him, watching him shovel in salad, spaghetti, a bite of roll, a swallow from his water bottle, a sigh, and repeat.

He says nothing, shoveling food so fast, I don't know how he finds the time to breathe. His plate disintegrates under the onslaught, so he stacks a few together and attacks again.

After a while, I wave a basket of rolls under his nose to see if I can distract him. He grabs two and begins using one to mop up his plate.

"Whoa there, cowboy."

"What?" He knows what. The embarrassed expression on his face gives him away.

"Take it easy. I promise we aren't in a race."

"Sorry, this is really good."

"I'm glad you like it. I'm just worried you might get sick."

He grins and slows down, but still manages to empty the entire contents of the casserole dish and five rolls. I'd cooked two chickens, the girls had gotten one-half of one of them, and I'd had maybe a quarter, which means he'd just eaten over a whole chicken by himself. Along with that he'd had approximately a pound of spaghetti with roasted tomatoes, artichokes, black olives, with Asiago and Parmesan cheese melted over it all.

"Oh, Rae," he says, leaning back. "Oh, my God, Rae."

Not quite the setting where I'd anticipated him issuing those words. He sits back and rubs his stomach, looking exactly like someone who had just eaten one and one-quarter chickens and groans again. I wait and begin to wonder if our "date" is over. Finally he speaks. "Did you cook that?"

Did I cook it? Who the hell else could have? Torey? There sure wasn't any place in our rural burg making food like this, so I couldn't have gotten take-out. My look must have said he was insulting me.

"Oh, I'm sorry, I don't mean anything. Excuse me a minute, I got to go outside."

John quickly gets up and goes out on the deck. I hear an enormous belch, peeing, followed by more groaning. Then he comes back in, grinning and rubbing his stomach. I wonder what strange or unusual thing he was going to do next.

"That was wonderful."

"The salad was good, too."

"Yeah, it was." He looks at the bar, smiling nostalgically. Then he laughs as if we were sharing some great, good joke.

"John, are you all right?"

"Yeah, I'm terrific. That was wonderful, Rae, thank you. I think it was the best stuff I've ever eaten."

"You're kidding."

"I don't think so." John stops and considers for a moment. "Yeah, I think that's the best meal I ever ate." He sits next to me, hooking his sneakers on the bottom rung of his bar stool, and begins to relate the food highlights of his life. Each year he looks forward to the Brunswick stew in the fall at the Catholic church, his momma's oyster-stuffed wild turkey at Thanksgiving, the baby bluefish he smokes in the spring in an old refrigerator he's converted into a smoker. He says his smoked fish usually do well at the fair; evidently there's a lot of competition. He swears his fish will knock my socks off, along with the char-grilled oysters on a half shell he's famous for.

John says his daddy made a mean hoecake before he got sick. John describes it as sweet biscuit dough fried in oil and dabbed with jelly. He says he'll make it for me and the girls some morning and they will probably like it. He wraps up the food commentary. "The guy that owns Pimmie's Point has a pig roast every spring, and it's pretty good. Still not this good, but pretty damned good. You cook like this all the time?" The question seems sincere.

My head's spinning, and not from the unfinished cup of wine. I wonder if it's because the evening turned out so entirely different from anything I'd anticipated, but whatever is happening, I'm going to continue to behave as if this evening is as normal as normal can be.

"No. The girls hate decent food, and I'm too tired to make a separate dinner for myself every night, so we eat junk most of the time. Stuff like hamburgers, sandwiches and breakfast."

"They like breakfast for dinner?"

"Yep. If I get home in time, I make them blueberry pancakes or fried eggs on toast. Sometimes I make them my grandmother's coffee cake. They love it. Evening is the only time their mom cooked breakfast, so they like it at night."

"Oh." His voice is tired, but happy. "Would you make me your grandmother's coffee cake sometime? I bet it's good."

He sounds like a little boy. I giggle. "Sure."

"Good. Thanks. Would you like some more wine?"

"Yeah, that would be great." I'm feeling a little let down. I'd hoped to be the main topic of the evening, not my food.

John pours me another plastic cup full of pink wine.

While his back is turned, I hop off the barstool and try to

surreptitiously dig the thong from my insides.

I think he senses my mood and crosses the room to sit on the larger couch. He pats the seat next to him. "Come over here and sit next to me for a while."

"There's dessert," I offer.

"Oh, God, no! Woman, back off. I can't take any more. Mercy please." He's laughing again.

I sit and John puts his arm around me, kissing the top of my head again. I really like that kiss. "Thank you, Rae. I don't think I've felt this good in a long, long time."

"John?"

"Hmmm?"

"You need to recycle more."

"I know, but the paper plates are recyclable."

"You could buy some plastic cups that aren't disposable, and they make great plastic dishes or even Corning Ware dishes that won't break. I got some when I got the kids. They are great and they don't break, trust me. You could use regular silverware. Stuff you can wash and reuse."

"You're right. I've been lazy, and there's no reason. I'd save money in the end. I'm gonna do that, Rae. And at least a real plate won't shred to pieces when you put real food on it."

I feel better. Recycling is becoming an almost religious quest for me. I argue constantly with the girls about reusing containers, never microwaving anything in plastic, and using the clearly labeled recycle boxes I keep on the porch. I even got the office to begin recycling our shredded paper and arranged to have it picked up weekly. Maybe I go overboard with trying to save the planet, maybe I don't do enough. I don't know.

It's warm and cozy in the cabin, the boat is rocking, and I'm relaxing and thinking about getting kissed again when I hear a snore. He's sound asleep. I feel insult and anger rise up inside. But then I stop, rethink the moment, and ask, why?

It had been a nice enough evening. True, I'd never actually seen anyone eat that much before, but it was an obvious compliment to the meal. Besides, I am tired too. Between the full-time job, the part-time job, the kids, and today's nervous energy, it's been a long week. I put the empty wine glass on the floor and my head in his lap.

The next thing I know I'm in the middle of a dream about swimming naked with dolphins. We communicate telepathically yet only discuss mundane things like the price of gasoline and ingredients for German chocolate cake. In my dream, the water gets very cold and I wonder why my dolphin friends seem not to notice, but I hesitate to say anything because it seems bad manners to denigrate the water's temperature. I want to continue in the dream and resist waking up, yet when I do I realize the coldness is reality. The cabin is freezing and saved from complete darkness by only one lonely candle, sputtering on the bar. John is gently trying to disentangle himself from me and stand up.

"What time is it?" I mumble, my voice groggy and sharing my discontent.

For some reason, he's whispering. "It's three."

"Why is it so cold?" I sit up, grumpy and miserable to be separated from the freedom of endless oceans.

"I think the propane tank is empty," he says.

"Propane?"

"For the stove. Remember? It's how I heat the cabin when there's no power. Give me a minute to start the generator. The cabin will warm up in a second."

"Oh." I shiver. Damp cold like this goes right through me. He's heading toward the steps. "Don't go," I call after him. He comes back and sits, putting his arms around me.

"Aren't you freezing?"

"Yeah, but I think it's time for me to go. It's late. You need to get home, too." I stand up to get my things together.

"Don't go," he says, grabbing my hand, with an underlying urgency not present before. "Please."

I know what he's asking. In the clear, cold air of the cabin, I consider my options.

Everything I'd said to Chip on the phone came back to haunt me. I don't know this guy. What would I be getting into? All I know is he's a two-time loser in the marriage department, recovering from an addiction to alcohol, and basically raised by wolves, as evidenced by the meal we shared.

Still, the hand holding mine in the dark is warm and

inviting. In the glow from the single candle, I see the faint outline of him. I sense his hunger for me.

And am instantly aroused.

My luck with men is abysmal, beyond abysmal. What the hell am I getting myself into?

I'm still holding his hand, asking myself how I'm going to feel later on. I like that he waits for me, giving me this time.

In the sputtering darkness, I feel a thing connecting us — we need each other. It's need, pure and simple. We are both dog-tired of being autonomous, independent, responsible, hard-working and so damned fucking alone. There's no shame in this, none at all.

Life knocked us around some, and we are old enough to know what we're doing. I know he isn't some jerk only trying to get in my pants. John lacks Dennis's ability to be ruthless and vicious. He isn't like my ex either. John at least has a personality, and if he's a sex addict, at least he wants to do it with me and not some damned computer. I don't know how I know, but I know I can trust John and me to do whatever we want to. I put my arms around him and stay right where I am.

I sit next to his warm self. I feel his arms wrap around me again and lose myself in lovely, lovely anticipation. Wild Wanda is thrilled.

"Let's get in bed. I've got a lot of blankets." He nuzzles my neck and reaches to kiss my mouth.

"Okay."

He takes my hand and leads me down the steps, through a narrow hall and back to his stateroom, complete with a double bed. Some sort of skylight thing overhead allows the moon, stars, and my arc light to filter in enough brightness to barely see.

I feel cocooned, safe, and snuggle down under what seems like ten blankets/quilts/comforters. I watch John stripping off his sweater, polo shirt, and jeans. His chest is pale compared to his tan arms, neck and face — a fisherman's tan. Teeth chattering, he hops in beside me wearing only boxers.

"Are you warm?"

"Not yet." I laugh.

"Let's give it a minute."

But it doesn't take a minute for time to leave us again, for him to become beautiful to me again, and this time–thank God–there are no knockings on any doors, no little girls around, no wise-ass teenagers to ruin it for us.

The sheer expansiveness of the moment is nearly overwhelming. I feel a sense of freedom with this guy that's deeper, more delightful, more wonderful and delicious than anything I've known.

My nieces, my job, my responsibilities all fade into the background and I'm left with fun. Just fun to kiss each other, take off my clothes, feel each other's bodies, and when Wanda can't take it anymore, she straddles him.

We mutually groan when he enters me. So wonderful to slide myself down him. He grabs my hips to keep me still.

His husky voice says, "Give me a second here."

But Wanda wants what she wants and I can't stop her. It only takes a few moments for each of us, and I'm so glad the girls can't hear the sounds we make.

"Oh my God," he says, when I tumble off and fall into bed beside him.

We are breathing heavy. I'm flooded with contentment, an ingredient long missing from my life, and I welcome it back.

I'm too excited, too happy to sleep. John wraps his arms around me and kisses the side of my face. "That was incredible."

I agree but smugly say nothing. I stretch out and feel our nakedness under the mound of blankets. It has been so long since I've had this.

John half sits up, still breathing heavy. "You know, if you gave me about ten minutes I could probably do that again."

I hear his smile in his voice. "I'm game." I'm smiling too.

The sun can't get through the blackout window shades in my room, so I have no idea what time it is. Cracking one eye open to check the clock, I discover it's only nine-thirty and I desperately need more sleep. What the hell is waking me up?

The tapping continues on my bedroom door while Melissa repeats my name over and over. This is a precursor to full-blown madness.

"Come in." I sigh and listen to the sound of a doorknob opening. Melissa pads across the room in bare feet. I can hear the slap, slap, slapping sounds they make on the tile floor. I pick up the covers for her to crawl in. Once I'd actually lured her back to sleep this way. Maybe I can do it again. Her little feet are like blocks of ice on my shins as she snuggles under my raised arm. Her whole body is cold and she's shivering some. Why is she so cold?

"What's wrong, baby?" I mumble, trying to not wake up too much. I feel relaxed in places that haven't been relaxed in a long damn time, and want to put a "Do Not Disturb" sign on the door to my life right now. Marvin Gaye is right about how good sexual healing is for me.

"What time is it, Arae?"

I crack an eye again and look at the clock next to my head on the nightstand. "Nine-thirty."

"Is that late?"

"It's late if you have to go to school, but it's early for the weekend. I'd sure like to sleep some more. How about taking care of yourself until Torey wakes up? There are some of those breakfast bars you like the cabinet." Even though she's still shaking, her little body is warming up.

Melissa doesn't answer. I'm almost back into dreamland when I realize she's crying.

"What's wrong, honey?" I wrap my arms around her.

"I don't know where Torey is."

"She's asleep in the bed next to yours."

"No, she isn't."

I'm waking up fast. "What do you mean?" Melissa's crying intensifies, and I understand her shaking is fear set in motion, not cold.

"Torey set the clock for me to go to bed last night. I was supposed to go to bed when it rang, and I did. Torey said she'd be home before I woke up, but I've been awake a long time, Arae, and she's not home!"

The last part is barely intelligible. Melissa's becoming hysterical. I try to get up, but she turns around and wraps herself around me so tightly I'm forced to carry her with me. Getting out of bed like this isn't easy.

I go into the girls' room. Torey is in her bed. I see the outlines of her body under the covers even in this morning's gloom.

I pull back the bedspread. An old comforter I recognize from my childhood is where Torey should have been. My sleepy self wonders where it had been hiding, this lumpy old cotton comforter with tiny faded roses printed on its fabric.

The same cold fear possessing Melissa now invades me.

I grab the comforter and make my way to the family room with Melissa clinging to me like a monkey. The green and orange asbestos tile underfoot is like ice. Mom and Dad had blanketed the whole cottage with this crap, and I hated it even then. When I'd tried to talk them into classier black and white, they didn't listen. They never listened, and now it's too late. We are stuck with crappy orange and green forever.

I call the sheriff's office for the second time in my life, and both times because of Torey. At least this time Melissa is safe with me and not drifting out in the bay with her fucked-up sister.

I sit on the couch with Melissa wrapped around me like a vine. I cover us both with my old comforter, but there is no comfort to be had anywhere, not anywhere at all.

Vicky calls at seven most Wednesday nights. It's Wednesday again and dark outside. I've been dreading her call the entire, horrible, rainy day. It had been raining since Torey left, the sky matching the total gloom I live in now.

I have no freaking idea what I'm going to say to my sister when she calls, but one thing is sure—she won't be talking to either of her daughters tonight.

It's six-thirty and I've got a little while. I'm on the phone now, with Roger Peterson, the detective who'd taken the report on Torey. He'd grown up with John, who I suspect arranged for him to take the case.

"Any leads?" I keep my voice low, standing in the doorway to the bathroom while monitoring Melissa splashing in the tub.

"Sorry, nothing specific, but I'd be willing to bet she went with a local boy named Fisher. No one can seem to find him, either."

I can tell there's more to it than that. "So what's the scoop on Fisher?"

Roger hesitates. "We think he has drug connections in Norfolk, probably Virginia Beach too, but he doesn't seem to have any violent tendencies. Look, I know this doesn't sound good, but I'm feeling like it's going to end up being no big deal."

Hadn't I been just as nonchalant with some freaked-out mom whose kid was missing? Never again would I ever be so careless. "Are people in Norfolk and Virginia Beach aware she might be in the area?" I hate being pushy but can't help it.

"Yeah, I spoke to a buddy of mine in Norfolk and faxed him her photo with the details. She doesn't qualify for Amber Alert so…"

"Why not?" I interrupt.

"Because it looks like she went willingly."

"With Fisher?"

"That's what it looks like."

Which pisses me off, even though it's probably true. I stay quiet, not wanting to anger our detective with what was likely to come out of my mouth.

I guess he senses my feelings and continues. "Amber Alert is for abductions, and we can't honestly say she was abducted, can we? But she is registered with the National Center for Missing and Exploited Children, so her photo is actually everywhere."

"And that's it?"

"I know it doesn't sound like much, but for now that's all we can do. I visited Fisher's grandmother today and told her he'd be helping himself if he gets her back home right away. The grandmother seems worried, so if he calls, I think she'll say the right thing. Sorry it isn't more."

"Thanks, Roger, I appreciate it."

"I'll let you know if anything else pops up on our radar."

"Okay, thanks again." I stand in the doorway with a death grip on the phone. The waiting is killing me. I think of throwing Melissa in the car and driving to Virginia Beach to see if I could turn up something. But the idea is hopeless and stupid. I have to go to work tomorrow and take care of other people's screwed-up kids.

"Fisher, fisher, fisher." Melissa is singing to her plastic whales in the bathtub. "I'm a fisher, Arae."

"You're a clean fisher, Melissa. Time to get out."

"Awww…"

But she complies and I towel her off. Her pajamas are hanging behind the door. I'd prepared for tonight with two videos! A bonanza and usually a weekend activity, but not tonight. Tonight we are having a movie night and Melissa is delighted.

Around six forty-five I plug her up to it. She hasn't quite gotten the hang of the days of the week, so hopefully isn't expecting a call from good old mom. I don't want her telling Mommy that Torey isn't here. If Melissa knew her mom was on the phone, she'd pitch a fit to talk to her, so hopefully my distractions will work.

Maybe she won't even call this week. It happens sometimes. Rarely, but sometimes. When the damned phone rings, I jump and feel my skin grow cold. Melissa looks up from the TV expectantly. I pick it up.

"Hello?"

"Hey there, sis, what's happening?"

"Hey there, how are you?" I shake my head at Melissa, letting her know it isn't her mom.

Vicky laughs. "Surviving. Had a little problem with my level this week. They didn't want to give it to me even though I earned it."

"I hope you get that straightened out soon." She's always having problems with her levels. I wish earning privileges was the major focus of my life. I wish I could remember how to breathe normally.

"Don't worry, I will. These bastards can't keep me down. How're the kids?"

"Fine, everyone's fine," I say, carrying the portable phone to my room and partially shut the door. As long as I can hear Melissa laughing at her video, I'll know she's alive.

"Listen, Vicky, the girls are grounded tonight, and I can't let you talk to them." I hear her intake of breath. "Sorry," I add lamely.

"What do you mean?"

I laugh, trying to sound casual, "Nothing big, they didn't do their chores and I warned them, but you know how they can get."

"Punish them some other way. This is the only thing I look forward to all week. Do you have any idea what I go through to make this call? Let me talk to my kids." She sounds confident I will hand the phone over to her phantom daughter.

Vicky had always been the more determined sister, the one who had to have her way, and would fight with our parents or anyone else to get it. I was glad a phone line separated us.

But my voice trails off when I say, "It's just not a good night, Vicky. They've been acting up, and I told them if they continued this is what would happen. I can't change the rules now." Even I wasn't buying it. I could tell she wasn't either.

"What the fuck is going on? I'm talking to my kids!"

I feel sick about the fear in her voice, but there's no way I'm telling her the truth. That would be harsher where she is. Better to wait until I knew exactly what needed to be said.

"God damn you, Rae, put Torey on the phone. You can't keep her from me, it's against the rules. It's important we maintain contact. You said so yourself. What the hell's going on?"

Like you would know a rule if you met it. "I told you, they're grounded."

"Grounded? From their mother? What the fuck is wrong with you? Or are you just being your usual high-and-mighty self?"

"Probably just high and mighty." The sound of the

phone's slamming is followed by a dial tone. I sit on my bed listening to it for a long time, feeling like I should be the one locked up.

The video is still playing when I rejoin Melissa on the couch. I clutch a big fuzzy pillow for warmth and watch cartoon animals with voices I recognize from TV. They are doing inane things I can't follow. Melissa, in the warm pajamas, robe, and slippers I'd gotten her, doesn't seem to notice my absence or return. She bought the story I told her about Torey visiting friends. Melissa is much easier to fool than her mother.

An hour later, four days after she'd left us, Torey slips back into our lives.

I see her first, standing in the doorway, looking worn and used up, like an old woman in a child's body. Torey's glorious hair is dull and matted. I didn't know it was capable of looking dead.

Her left wrist is wrapped in a homemade tattoo. Maybe it's supposed to look like a bracelet, I don't know. What I see is more like a manacle, the skin around it inflamed and raw.

She must have walked the dirt road from the highway because the bottoms of her jeans are covered in mud, and deep red clay is dripping on the floor like blood. I stare at the puddle growing on the pitted green and orange tiles.

"Torey!" Melissa shouts, startling me, and jumps up, running to her. She wraps herself around Torey the same way she'd wrapped around me when Torey left us. Melissa doesn't see the mud, vacant eyes, dirt—the things that made her sister now.

In the tableau before me, two sisters cling to each other. Melissa is cast in a light that somehow eludes Torey. I wonder how? The fluorescent light in the kitchen and the lamp next to me make the room bright enough. Why is Torey cast in shadow? The video rattles on by itself. Torey pats Melissa on the back. Melissa's joy seemed disjointed and odd in the room filling with the smell of despair.

"Are you okay?" It's an empty, hollow-sounding thing, and I know it. Bent down with her head buried in Melissa's hair, Torey nods yes.

"Where have you been?"

She shrugs.

"Who were you with?"

Silence, then, muffled from Melissa's hair, "I can't tell you."

"What do you mean you can't tell me? You better fucking tell me!"

"Arae, she was with her friends, remember?"

What I didn't remember was Melissa. She already knows something is up, and me losing it is a sure-fire way to get her back into old behavior.

I damn sure don't need both of them there. Obviously Torey isn't planning to tell me what happened, so why bother with it tonight?

We are waiting for something. Someone is supposed to do something, but I don't know who it is or what they are supposed to do.

"Are you hungry?" I finally think to ask. The hollow sound doesn't go away. I'm frightened by her appearance and don't remember runaways I worked with looking quite this bad, but maybe they had and I simply didn't notice.

Torey looks up from Melissa and our eyes meet. She nods again, but her eyes are lost in some nightmare I don't want to know. Still, it wakes me up. I turn away from those eyes and go to the refrigerator, refusing to answer them. Whatever happened is not my business. A cold sensation clamps down. This is what people like Torey and my sister end up with. People who run off and do whatever the hell they want to. Who don't give one shit about the ones they leave behind.

Anger is a relief from the aching fear that consumed me the past four days. I fix a plate to heat up in the microwave. With Melissa still attached, Torey shuffles over to the table and sits down.

Melissa is crying now. She can tell something is wrong, just not what. I guess she's scared. She's asking Torey where was she. But Torey doesn't answer. She only pats Melissa and whispers, "I'm sorry."

I want to pull open the drawer under the stove where the cast iron skillets are and pull out the biggest one, the huge one my mom used to fry an entire chicken in. It's so heavy it takes two hands to pull it out from underneath the others, but right now, I could get it easily and bash Torey's skull in.

How could she do this? How could she put me, Melissa, and herself, through this? I very much need to keep the sadness that's calling to me as far away as possible.

I push numbers into the microwave and hit *Start*. I watch the plate begin to spin and try to figure out what I should do next. But the more I think, the angrier I get. I hate Torey in so many ways it overpowers me. I can't fit that much anger in a sentence, and there's nowhere to begin, so I leave and go to bed. Melissa's tears are Torey's problem. She caused them. She can deal with them.

I don't turn on the light, just let my clothes drop to the floor, and get in bed. My entire body quivers with emotions I'm unable to decipher. Eventually I understand I'm suspended somewhere between rage and fear. I hadn't been able to consider the possibility she might be dead.

That was the elephant I'd been avoiding all week. That and all the other horrible possibilities I'd held at bay are now free to run rampant since I know she's finally home. My frozen fears are thawing out and invading the numb place I'd been residing in.

I see my unwillingness to tell Vicky the truth for what it was—an attempt to protect me, not her. Vicky might have broken my resolve not to feel.

How come? I ask the ceiling of my bedroom. And does it matter anyway? Even if I wasn't such an asshole, being open to my fears wouldn't have changed one damn thing. Maybe I would have told Vicky what was going on, but Torey would still be sitting at the kitchen table, dripping blood-colored mud on the floor. I guess this is it. I guess she'll go into foster care. On some level, she's asking for it, whether she's aware of it or not.

Rage and fear, fear and rage. I know I'm hooked again, and there's nothing I can do about it right now.

When was I taken captive again? All my life I'd been caught up in the dramas of others. It was unfair, but since adulthood I'd learned to detach, to let go. It took a lot of effort, but I finally succeeded. So how come I was back in this hell of caring for someone who had no ability or desire to care for themselves?

"She didn't die," says some voice in my head. Some tight area in my chest relaxes a bit, and I breathe the first deep breath since she'd left.

She didn't die, she didn't die, she didn't die. I stare into the darkness feeling fear fade.

Like Melissa, I cry to see a thing go. I know by morning all I'll have left is cold rage, and it's no compensation for all that is lost.

It's still raining when I call work to tell the receptionist my niece is sick. Connie, my supervisor, calls me back. "You've got court today, don't you?"

"Yeah, but there's no way I can make it. The files are up to date, and it's only a review to see if the Causewells are complying. The school report's in there. You've got all you need."

"You know, missing court, this just doesn't look very good." Connie's slogged through bosses as horrible as she is to finally achieve a position where she doesn't have to do much for a living. She resents the hell out of anything resembling work. Fuck her.

"Sorry, Connie." But she knows I'm not.

I call the girls' pediatrician. Torey will need an exam, maybe a morning-after pill to prevent pregnancy. I'm not sure how those things work, or if it would be an option after four days.

When the receptionist wants the reason for Torey's appointment, I hesitate, then say it's a private matter, and I need to speak to Dr. Qureshi prior to him examining Torey.

I need to make sure she gets an AIDS test along with everything else for sexually transmitted diseases. I wonder how many AIDS tests Dr. Qureshi gives thirteen-year-old girls. I get an appointment for later on.

I phone Lucy, to let her know Torey is back.

Lucy speaks first to God, "Thank you, Lord." Then to me, "Rae, I'm so glad." Despite the religious stuff, I like Lucy. She's one of those rare people who uses their religion as a vehicle to become a better person, rather than a superior one.

"Will you call Chip for me and let her know?"

"Of course. Is Melissa in school?"

"No, I'm letting them both sleep in. I'm hoping I can bring Melissa to you before I take Torey to the doctor. Would that be all right?"

"Is Torey hurt?"

"No, it's just a precaution."

"Sure you can. What time?"

"Around ten?"

"That would be fine."

I call Roger—rather, Detective Peterson—and am glad when he answers the phone. "I guess you were right. Torey is back from her adventures, even though she isn't telling me who she went with or what happened."

"Bring her in. I'll make her talk."

Roger speaks in a way I've never heard—flat, rough, scary—and I'm startled by it. For some, unknown reason I answer apologetically. "She looks bad, Roger. I think I'd better get her to the pediatrician this morning. I made an appointment."

He softens, becomes the Roger I know. "Okay, bring her in afterwards. Call me on my cell when you're done and we'll work out a time."

I make myself some coffee and take it out to the porch. We are having an Indian summer, and despite the rain, it's warm and muggy and doesn't feel at all like the Halloween almost upon us.

Melissa is excited about going trick-or-treating for the first time in her life. She is going to go in town with Chip's youngest and a pack of their relatives. She's almost worn out the fairy costume we bought, trying it on and prancing around with her wand.

I sit on the swing and look out over the gray, misty morning. Everything is damp, even the pillows and pad on the swing. I need to bring them in before they mildew in this weather.

I'd gotten out of the habit of morning coffee, but want something to fortify myself this morning. I remember my parents had used that same expression, *fortify themselves*. I'd always thought it was a stupid thing to say, but now I can't think of anything else that fits.

In my previous life, I'd go for early morning runs with a group of people from my building. We'd end up at a coffee bar near the converted tobacco warehouses where our condos were. I learned to drink coffee with my running group. Those same people I used to laugh and run with melted into the background of my old life and disappeared, just like my old life.

"Arae?"

I turn to see Melissa coming out on the porch, dragging Night-Night. "Yep, that's me."

"Whatcha doing?"

"Watching the rain."

Melissa observes me. She's not sure if I'm teasing.

"Can I watch it with you?"

"Sure." I stop the swing and wait for her. Even though warm, it's still damp and the cement floor's cold. I put my coffee on the floor and her in my lap. We resume swinging, and I wrap my arms around her and stick her feet under my legs, warming them up.

After a while, she says, "Arae, is this fun?"

My gloominess must be catching. "Not really. It's just something to do while waiting for you guys to wake up."

"Torey's still sleeping."

"I know. I guess she's real tired." Melissa's hair is silky on my cheek. She has some sort of unique body chemistry making her smell like sandalwood and honey. Smelling her is comforting.

"Am I going to kindergarten today?"

I wonder what it's like for her to never know what to expect any given day. She seems concerned about school, though.

"No, not today. The bus already came and went."

"Will my teacher be mad with me?"

"Why would she be mad at you?"

"'Cause I didn't come."

"Sometimes kids don't go to school, if they're sick or on a trip or something like that."

"But I'm not sick and I'm here. Is it 'cause of Torey?"

"No, it's because of me, Melissa. I decided to keep you here with me this morning."

She's quiet, thinking this over.

"Arae, why?"

"Melissa, because I want to rock you on the swing."

This is a game between us. I haven't any idea how it started. Every sentence has to begin with the other's name, and we keep it up until someone messes up.

"Arae, you are silly."

"Melissa, I am your aunt, Arae. My name is not Silly. You are silly." I tickle her ribs. "See, only silly people laugh like you."

"Arae, I make you laugh, too." Melissa jams her fist in my neck, as she believes this is my tickle spot. I make laughing sounds. "See, you're silly, too!" she says.

Suddenly Torey's in the doorway, startling us.

I freeze, not knowing what to do. But Melissa does. It's the real reason she's home right now.

"Torey!" She jumps and runs across the porch. Melissa makes her usual flying leap, but Torey doesn't make any attempt to catch her. Melissa slides down and ends up a bewildered heap on the floor. We are back to three strangers.

I look at my watch. It's time to get them dressed and fed.

"Come on, everybody, let's get ready."

Torey turns without saying a word and goes back towards their bedroom.

Melissa looks at me. I can tell she wants me to explain what's going on, make it all okay. I don't have any idea how to make it all okay again.

"Let's go get ready, Melissa." I pick her up and carry her on my hip back towards their bedroom, her feet dangling below my knees.

Torey's standing next to her bed, putting on a bra. Her back is to me and a large bruise covers her left side. I must have made some sort of sound because Torey's head whips around and she glares at me.

"Wha-what happened?" I feel like an intruder, awkward and unwanted. "Your back, it's hurt," I sound like an idiot. Of course she knows she's hurt, knows where she's hurt.

I put Melissa down. Torey stands, unmoving, and continues to glare at me as if I'm the one who caused the marks on her body. Melissa stands between us, looking at Torey, then me, confusion showing on her face.

I pull out some clothes for Melissa and wait to help her with her shoes and socks, the only part of dressing herself she can't accomplish on her own. I keep glancing at Torey. "You know, Torey, sooner or later you're going to have to tell me what happened. The police are involved. It's more than just me."

She doesn't respond. Melissa jams her thumb in her mouth and looks tense. It was a mistake to blurt out the police's interest; this is getting us nowhere.

"Breakfast will be ready in ten minutes. I've got an appointment for you with Dr. Qureshi." I turn and leave. Whatever happened while she was gone isn't my fault. Damn her, damn her, damn her to hell anyway.

Melissa is delighted to find she's spending the day with Lucy, who, when we arrive at her house, comes out toting a big umbrella. It looks like rain intends to be a permanent fixture in our lives, which is fine with me as the gloom perfectly matches my emotional state.

Melissa is unfazed by the rain or moods filling the car. She loves Lucy and is probably glad to get away from me, Torey, and all the unfathomable things we involve ourselves in.

Torey usually rides in the front seat but today opted to sit in the back with her sister. When Lucy opens the rear door, Melissa scrambles over her. Torey winces, bends over, and makes a sound as if she's in pain. Lucy notices and our eyes meet over Torey's bent head, silently telegraphing alarm.

"Thanks for taking Melissa today. Torey is going to the doctor, and I know Melissa would be bored to death."

"No problem. I'm glad to see you, Torey girl." Lucy says softly as she reaches in to pat Torey on the cheek. Torey flinches and turns away. Once again my eyes meet Lucy's and I'm grateful to not be alone with my concern.

My voice shakes as I say, "I don't know what time I'll be able to come back for Melissa."

"It doesn't matter. I'm not doing a thing but checking up on my mom later on. Give us a call here or there, whenever you're ready to pick up Miss Baby," Lucy says, using her pet name for Melissa. She closes the door and takes Melissa's hand. They began walking back toward the house. Melissa is skipping by her side, obviously engrossed in their conversation.

With Melissa around, Torey and I attempted to keep up appearances. Now, with no reason to put on an act, we fall into separate worlds of gloom. I drive the few blocks to Dr. Qureshi's office.

I try to think of something to say and can't. I'm glad she didn't put up any resistance to this appointment, and after seeing the bruises and her reaction to Melissa climbing over her, I'm glad I made it.

When we get there, I say, "Stay there, I've got an umbrella," but she's already out of the car and halfway to the front door. She seems impervious to the rain and me.

I follow, register her, and then hesitate. I want to tell the receptionist I need to speak to Dr. Qureshi alone before Torey's exam, but don't want the entire waiting room to hear me, or embarrass Torey any more than I have to.

Small towns are full of snoops, so I decide to write the request on the back of another form and hold it out to the woman sitting behind the open glass window. I wait for her to take it from my hand, but she seems unable to respond to anything but her usual routines. Finally, I shake the paper in her face a few times, and she gets the idea, takes the note and reads it.

"I'll see what I can do."

We have to wait over an hour. I've been immune to stares

forever, but today the curious glances at the white woman with the biracial kid seem too much, way too much.

Torey doesn't read a magazine or speak. She sits, looking at the floor the entire time. I try and fail to decipher her emotions. Finally the nurse calls, "Torey? Torey Green?"

We both stand up, which I guess Torey didn't expect. She looks at me with a hate so intense it startles me. I almost obey the look and sit back down, but then she shrugs like it doesn't matter at all what I do, and we both follow the nurse back toward the examination rooms.

She puts Torey in one of them and tells her to wait until the doctor comes. Then she says, "Doctor Qureshi will see you in his office, Ms. Green."

I glance at Torey and say apologetically, "I need to tell him why we're here, Torey."

She shrugs again, like caring about anything is beyond her, so I leave.

"Sit down, Ms. Green," says Dr. Qureshi when I enter his office. He speaks with a heavy accent, so I listen carefully.

"Dr. Qureshi, I appreciate this."

"What exactly is the problem with your niece?"

"She ran away four days ago and came back last night. I'm concerned about a number of things like pregnancy, sexually transmitted diseases—including AIDS." I pause. "She also has an ugly bruise on her back and her wrist looks infected from a tattoo."

"These are grave concerns for such a young girl."

"Yes, they are." Tears well in my eyes, but I'm damned if I'm going to cry.

"Has she told you what happened to her in the time she was gone?"

"No, she hasn't."

"Perhaps she wasn't even sexually active?"

"Somehow I think she was."

Dr. Qureshi sits back and stares at me thoughtfully. We'd only met once, when the girls had their back-to-school physicals. About my age, small and delicate-looking, he has coal-black hair and skin the same color as Torey's. At the appointment, he'd compared his forearm to hers and joked she could be his child. I liked him and felt fortunate to have this gentle man as our pediatrician.

"You are all the family she has, you know, and you must talk to her." His eyes through his glasses are serious and concerned.

"It isn't easy to talk to Torey sometimes." My voice sounds nervous, not the way I want to present myself.

"Certainly it may not be, yet the talking must occur."

I can't think of a response and look down.

"For now, I will make an examination of the child and speak to you afterwards. This is all right?"

"Yes, thank you." I'm grateful to get out of the office. For such a gentle person, he doesn't pull any punches when it comes to telling me how to handle my niece.

It seems a short time later when a nurse is calling me back from the waiting room. She shows me to the examination room that holds Torey.

Dr. Qureshi is pacing the small room. "This child has been beaten and raped. She has anal tearing and must be taken to the emergency room immediately."

Torey is sitting up with a paper gown on. She is crying and a nurse is handing her tissues. I stand there, dumbfounded.

"Ms. Green!" Dr. Qureshi says sharply.

I jump and look at him.

"The emergency room must perform tests on this child, rape tests. I do not have the proper materials here. I will call them now and arrange this. Please take this child to the emergency room. Go there immediately."

Dr. Qureshi speaks directly to my face, and when I nod, letting him know I understand, he leaves and shuts the door behind him. I stand in the middle of the small room, not sure what to do and trying desperately to process the doctor's words.

I look at Torey while the nurse hands her clothing to her. I feel worse than useless, a mute observer; yet when Torey stands up to put her panties on, she leaves a smear of blood on the paper sheet that makes me gasp.

"I'll get you a pad," says the nurse, leaving us alone.

"What happened to you?" No anger now, only confusion,

fear, and a very deep, intense sadness.

She doesn't respond, only shakes her head as tears fly out of her eyes. I try to go to her, hug her or something, but she puts her arm out like police stopping traffic. My arms fall helplessly by my sides.

The nurse returns with a sanitary napkin, and I look away, giving her some privacy.

When the paper gown comes off, I look back and see two more bruises, both on her abdomen. Large, ugly-looking things making my heart break; her beautiful skin, her beautiful body, desecrated this way.

Dr. Qureshi knocks on the door. "May I come in?'

The nurse looks at Torey who is now dressed and says, "It's okay, Doc. Come on in."

"Torey, take these pills." He hands her two paper cups, one small one with pills and a larger one with water. She does as he asks. "These will help your pain to go away and may make you sleepy. I am giving your aunt prescriptions for more of these and other medications I will be wanting you to take when you get home."

Torey nods and he pats her shoulder. "You are a good girl, Torey. I will see you in the hospital and make sure you are healing in the right way. Okay?"

She nods again.

Dr. Qureshi looks at me and says, "I will talk to you at the hospital." He looks back at her. "And Torey, you must ask me about any worries you may have. I promise you, you will be made well again."

"Okay," she says in a small voice.

Dr. Qureshi sighs, pats Torey's arm again, then he and the nurse leave. I feel immediately awkward. I think Torey does too until I say softly, "I guess we better go."

The hospital is right across the street, but for some reason, I drive us there. I suppose my brain still isn't working very well. The emergency room doors whoosh open, and I tell the receptionist who we are. A few moments later, Torey is whisked off in a wheelchair.

I'm directed to an office where I'm given a clipboard with forms to fill out. I sit in the lobby and attempt to focus on the pages in front of me over the "beaten and raped" mantra ringing in my ears. She's only thirteen. Who would beat and rape a thirteen-year-old? Anal tearing? What sort of world did we live in? I'd worked with a lot of kids who'd had terrible things done to them and had studied cases even worse than this, but somehow they all paled in comparison. I thought about the families of those kids, and finding out loving a child is suddenly a dangerous activity.

Sometime later I look up to see a large, square-built, middle-aged woman in an ugly brown, polyester pantsuit striding towards me, carrying a battered leather briefcase. In a loud voice she asks, "Are you Rachael Green?"

When I respond affirmatively, she sits down in the seat next to me. "I'm Detective Bullock from the Cornwallis Sheriff's Department." Her eyes are dead.

Something in my stomach is fiercely repelled by the woman. "Where's Roger? We had an appointment to see him later on." I sound defensive as hell.

The detective tightens her lips before responding. "Detective Peterson does not take rape statements. It's believed a female officer is better suited to handle these things than a male." People seated nearby take more interest in our conversation.

I stare at Detective Bullock and wonder if there is a female creature in the world less feminine-looking than the person in front of me. I sigh and blow out my breath. "How can I help you, detective?"

"You have legal custody of your nieces?"

"Yes." I figure she already knows this and wonder why she needs to ask.

"Her mother is where?" Detective Bullock pulls a yellow legal pad from her briefcase.

I glare at the people trying to appear as if they are not following every word. "Banesville Federal Detention Center. It's in Ohio," I respond as quietly as possible.

"Your sister is there on drug-related charges?"

"Yes." Obviously she knows this as well, and she's speaking too loudly. Why the interrogation here in front of everyone?

"Has your sister been in contact with your niece?"

"Of course. She calls every week and writes them, too. What does that have to do with... wait a minute, my sister doesn't have anything to do with what happened to Torey."

"How do you know?"

"Because I do. My sister is a rotten mother at times, but she has limits as to what she'd involve her kids in. You're welcome to see the letters they get. They're in a basket at the house." I'm going from dislike to outright hatred and no longer care what other people hear.

"Are you aware that your niece was probably raped?"

"Probably? The pediatrician said she'd definitely been raped, and beaten, too." I'm glad to see our curious neighbors called by a nurse in the doorway. They reluctantly get up.

Officer Bullock licks her ugly purple lips. "We won't know that for sure unless Torey talks to me, which so far, she has refused to do."

I look intently at this unpleasant woman. She'd already tried to talk to Torey? Without her guardian? Suddenly I understand it isn't Torey's welfare concerning the person in front of me. Officer Bullock's agenda is about getting the goods on us all, adding another notch to her gun, maybe getting info for the feds. What a bitch. I'm glad my obstinate niece is finally putting her skills to good use.

"Well, I don't know what to tell you, Ms. Bullock. She isn't talking to me either." Waiting around and putting up with anything and everything that comes my way is no longer an option.

I stand and go to the receptionist. I rap on the glass window to get her attention. When she opens it, I hand her the clipboard and say, "I'd like to see my niece, Torey Green."

The receptionist's smile is kind. "I think she's been admitted. Let me look." She punches something into her computer and stares at the screen.

I glance back at the detective in absolute disgust. She is still sitting next to the chair I vacated, her mouth open in surprise. Evidently she's not used to women like me and my niece who are unwilling to be her pawns. As far as I'm concerned, she'd better get used to it. Hell will freeze before I speak to that creature again.

The woman behind the glass says, "Dr. Qureshi admitted her. She's in room 203."

"Thank you." I go to the elevators.

The hospital is old and looks it, with its sad, almost broken chairs and scuffed carpets. The elevator walls are padded with some sort of turquoise stuff that shows small rips and tears in its vinyl fabric where stuffing leaks through. It makes its painful ascent and the door creaks open. I find Torey's room and go in. Someone made a futile effort to spruce it up. A sad, faded flower border is pasted above gray walls. Torey is asleep, hooked up to a bag suspended next to the bed. A nurse comes in behind me.

"Hi there," she says softly.

"Oh, hi," I whisper back.

"We probably don't have to whisper. She's heavily sedated right now."

"What's she hooked up to?"

"The ER doc ordered some I.V. antibiotics along with tranqs. They want to keep her overnight and make sure she's okay. I'll have him talk to you, but first you need to go to admissions. There are some additional forms that need to be filled out. Can you take care of that?"

"Sure, where is it?"

"I'll show you."

"Let me have five minutes first." I walk over to the bed.

The nurse smiles at me. "I'll be at the nurse's station when you're ready."

Torey's hair is tangled. I will go home and get her nightgown, comb and brush, and some clean clothes to wear home when she's released. I'm sure Lucy can keep Melissa tonight. I will get her Night-Night and stuff too and drop them off. I will call my supervisor before she leaves for the day and let her know I'm not coming in tomorrow.

I brush some stray hairs off Torey's forehead. There's something broken in my niece and I need to find out what it is. I look intently at her child's face.

I hadn't wanted to see that before. She's still only a child. Vicky was right. I *was* Miss High and Mighty, seeing what I wanted to see and not what was in front of me. I pull up the sheet and get a blanket from the closet in case she's cold. I put the blanket over her. She's a beautiful girl. I'll never leave her alone again. There is nothing she can do to keep me away. After all, she's only a child.

I will stay here tonight, and when she wakes up, I will be here. We will talk and decide what to do. Not me, not her. Us. And since she's asleep and can't stop me, I kiss her face, over and over.

Nana Green's Twice-Baked Potatoes

Get some large russet potatoes (preferably organic), scrub them, stick them with a fork and bake them unpeeled at 400 degrees until soft when pricked with a fork or knife.

Cut an oval in the top of the potatoes and scoop the insides into a bowl while still hot.

Add:
   - some grated extra-sharp cheddar, Parmesan and/or Asiago cheeses
   - butter
   - sour cream if you like it
   - seasoning salt
   - some unsalted herb seasoning blend or chopped fresh herbs (parsley, chives, dill, oregano) to taste.

Mash together with a fork or electric mixer.

Put potato/cheese mixture back into shells (discard the tops) and return to oven for 10 minutes or so to brown tops. Great with steak and a salad.

November

"Arae?"

"What?"

"Didn't you say Tabasco was good with cheese?"

I look over my shoulder. Torey is engrossed with a large, steaming bowl of potatoes, cheeses, sour cream, and an herb mix. I see where she's going with this. I'd never thought of adding Tabasco to twice-baked potatoes, but why not? It might be good.

"Go ahead. Just don't use a whole lot this time. See if we like it." I turn back to the salad and smile. These are the moments that allow me to keep it together. Torey is mostly remote and silent, yet when she does come out of her shell, the bond between us is almost palpable. I'm holding her heart with all I've got.

She has problems with nightmares, kids talking about her in school, and interviews with police here and in Norfolk which always stir up gloomier moods. At least I was able to get rid of Officer Bullock and get Roger assigned back to the case.

Torey had gone off with Fisher, just as Roger had thought. But he'd left her with some dealer friends in Norfolk, telling her she could stay until he figured out their next move.

There was a party and she remembered a girl giving her the tattoo but didn't remember much of anything else until waking up in Fisher's car shortly before being dropped off on the highway by our road. She'd been given date rape drugs, which would account for why she couldn't identify where she'd been or what kind of car Fisher drove her home in. They'd left on his moped. Imagine going to Norfolk on a moped. No one has seen Fisher since. There were five samples of semen in her and on her clothing.

We have to see Judge Merrill next Wednesday, something we are both apprehensive about. A social worker, Sarah Davis, from Cornwallis Social Services, was here yesterday for a home study. She looked around the cottage and told me I needed to get smoke alarms and where to put them.

The last thing in the world that concerned me was smoke alarms in a cinder block house. What a surreal afternoon. Torey and I were interviewed separately and then together. That night, we watched videos as if nothing unusual happened. It's hard to figure out what is the right thing to do. Maybe I should have tried to talk to her, but it felt like we both needed a break from everything.

Sarah Social Worker spoke to Melissa and Lucy, too. Torey asked me what the judge might do. I've told her that he will decide if she needs services.

She asked what kind of services, but I didn't have a clue. I'd checked out Merrill's reputation and learned he is new, fairly young, and takes his court seriously. This tells me nothing. I have no idea what to expect, or what to tell Torey.

I wonder if new mothers feel this same sort of sharp fierce love. I wonder if they crave, like a drug, answers to their family's problems or hurt at their own limitations and inabilities the way I do every waking moment.

I try and explain to John how fragile I sense Torey is right now, and how I can't leave her. I want to annihilate the men that hurt her. I think I could. I think I could single-handedly extinguish them. I wake up at night with clenched fists, and my arms ache during the day, like I've spent the night fighting and impaling bad men on sharp objects.

I also want to annihilate the kids at school who talk about her and the people in town who are curious about the black girl who was raped.

The idea of moving away is beginning to sound better

and better. I'm starting to hate this town, except for Lucy, Chip, and John. The other exception is John's mother, who I've never actually met, bringing over a casserole and leaving it by the front door with a get-well card for Torey.

It was a good casserole, a chicken, broccoli, and cheese dish the girls enjoyed too. I look at the clean casserole dish sitting on the counter with a thank you note inside, waiting for John to take it back to her.

He'll be here soon and I'm sort of nervous about it. It feels like our first step back to normality, and I'm not sure we are ready. It's only been a little over a month since our world blew up. Tonight is supposed to be a sort of a substitute for the Thanksgiving dinner we forgot to have.

Torey is earnestly engaged in grating cheddar cheese. When she concentrates, she sticks her tongue out a tiny bit. It's something she's done since she was a baby and she's doing it now.

I won't believe she's better until I see her give into a first-class temper tantrum. What a surprise to find myself in the position of eagerly awaiting the next Torey Green tantrum, and as far as I'm concerned, the bigger the better.

I hear a knock on the front door. John's being formal for some unknown reason. He must have moored his boat and walked clear around. I laugh as I open the door. "Hello there, stranger," I begin, but stop when I see the large bouquet of lavender roses he holds.

He's nervous. I can see it in the shaky smile he gives me before the quick kiss on my cheek. He makes his way around me. Torey, still working on her potatoes, looks up at the same moment he extends the bouquet over the counter.

I carry snapshots in my head. There's one of Torey as a toddler in a plastic blow-up pool. Vicky had somehow coerced me into watching her so she could go to the store by herself.

Torey's in a tiny purple bathing suit with a large pink flower stitched on the front, splashing and jumping in her pool and laughing. There was something about the color of the air that morning, the water falling around her, and the slant of the sun on her black curls. Purple was the exact right color for her, and somehow reflected around her like an aura.

I remember being mesmerized by the laughing baby and purple light dancing on that beautiful summer morning. It's probably the moment Torey first stole my heart completely.

This is another Torey snapshot—John with his lavender roses extending over the countertop, taking up the right side of the frame. Torey—her mouth open in surprise, her eyes filled with wonder and her arms reaching up, almost touching the flowers—takes up the rest of the picture.

John says, "I'm glad to finally see you."

"Thank you." Then holding her bouquet, she looks at me with such surprise, delight, and shyness, that I have another snapshot to treasure.

I put John to work grilling the steaks I'd marinated. When I go out back to see how he is coming with them, I see he's brought a surprise for me too.

Pulling a flask from inside his heavy coat, he says, "I bet you could use a shot."

I'm in shock. It's the last thing I'd expect. "What is it?"

"Some good booze my last charter left behind."

"Did you have some?" I ask, more sharp than I intended.

John's bemused expression speaks volumes, and I'm ashamed.

"No, Rae, I didn't. I didn't have a drink today and I'm not planning to either."

"But should you be around it?"

"Lord woman, I live over a bar. I'm around it all the time. I bartend for Jack when he's under the weather."

"At *The Sea Witch*?"

He smiles like I'm a child. "Yes, at *The Sea Witch*."

"Aren't you ever tempted to drink?"

"No, not at all, not since I quit. I think I experienced something like grace from my Higher Power, or God, or whatever you want to call it."

"You did?"

"I guess so. Do you want some or not?"

I look at the flask. It sounds terrific.

"Go ahead, have a swig. I won't tell." I love his grin.

I take the leather-covered glass flask and upend it. Good whiskey, warmed by John's body, courses through me. It is exactly what I needed.

"Oysters, right?" I ask, peering at the grill.

"Exactamundo," he says, shucking one and placing it on the grill with its siblings. He sprinkles something out of a jar on it and splashes it and the others with what looks like butter melting in a small pan.

"What's that you're putting on them?"

"You aren't the only one with cooking secrets, young woman."

I like it when he calls me "young woman." I reach for the jar and open the lid. It looks like Parmesan, the kind you get in a can, and probably dried parsley and maybe some garlic powder with other stuff mixed in. The oysters smell wonderful.

"Any of these done?" My mouth is watering.

"Yeah, here, let me fix it for you." John takes a roll from a pan I hadn't noticed on the old rusted TV table next to the grill. He knocks an oyster shell off the fire and then scoops up its insides with the roll. Handing it to me, he says, "Careful, it's hot."

I cautiously eat the edges of the roll. "It's wonderful. Where'd you get the oysters?"

"Off of your dock."

"You're kidding. When?"

"Little bit ago when I got here. Don't you know you got a whole bed out there?"

"I do now." Man, these are good. I snag myself another. "Did your momma make these rolls?"

"Yes, she did."

"They are great. Tell her I said thanks."

The girls won't try the oysters, but make up for it with steak. John compliments Torey on the potatoes, which makes her blush. Imagine that. I want to write Vicky, since she's no longer speaking to me, and tell her Torey blushed.

Melissa sits so close to John she's practically in his lap. I can't wait to get him away from all this competition.

When I was a kid, on rare occasions, my parents would play a game with me and Vicky at the dinner table. One of them would place an index finger on the side of their nose and whoever saw it would stop eating and put their finger on the side of their nose too. Eventually the whole table would be quiet except for the last unfortunate person, who was too busy eating to notice. That person was pointed at by everyone else and called "pig" in unison. I'd forgotten the game but evidently Vicky hadn't.

I immediately recognized the game when a chubby little finger began sliding alongside Melissa's upturned nose. She's such a character. Melissa is trying to laugh and be quiet at the same time so ends up with her head bobbing up and down, hunched over with her finger all over her face.

Torey and I are quick to follow Melissa, and John is, of course, the one most interested in his dinner so ends up the "pig."

Once he figures out the joke, he smiles at me and says, "Your aunt knows it's the truth." He retaliates by teaching the girls how to balance spoons off the end of their noses. I do it too and laugh so hard I nearly fall on the floor.

The girls have videos to watch, and as much as I'm itching to be alone with John, I feel self-conscious about leaving them. I think John does too. We stand awkwardly in the kitchen after washing up.

Torey looks over the back of the couch and says, "You guys can go. It's okay. I promise I'm not going anywhere."

"We didn't think you were, sugar." John looks at me and cocks his head toward the door with a question in his eyes.

I'm surprised by the kindness in Torey's voice so it takes me a minute to reply. I'm staring at the back of her head as she's already turned back around to the TV. I look into John's eyes and smile all the surprise and happiness I'm feeling. I say, "All right, let's go." We grab our coats and leave out the back door.

"Torey seems to be doing great."

"Yeah, well you were great. I was really surprised when you gave her those flowers. What made you do that?"

"I don't know." He seems embarrassed. "I want her to know not every man is a vicious animal, I guess. How's the investigation going?"

"Nothing new to report," I answer softly.

He helps me aboard and without even asking, pours me a glass of wine. It's the first time we've been alone together in over a month if I don't count the midnight quickie after my shift last weekend. The boat rocks gently as wavelets lap against its side.

I don't know how single parents date. Even though I can see the cottage, I feel anxiety gathering. Damn it, why can't I just relax and have a nice time? I look between the boat's railings, torn between wanting to stay here and wanting to make sure they are okay.

"You want to check on them, don't you?"

"Yeah, how'd you know?" I guess it's obvious and I feel guilty. This guy puts up with a lot, especially lately. I wonder if he's getting tired of all the crap that goes along with dating me.

"Go ahead. By the time you get back, I'll have the cabin warmed up."

"You sure you don't mind?"

"Mind? Hell, no. Go on so you can get back here."

He'd put away our coats, so I grab a blanket off the couch and wrap it around me. Outside is bitter cold. Still, it's a gorgeous night. The light of the moon illuminates the dock better than the arc light my father installed a hundred years ago.

I follow John's orange extension cord up the grassy slope to the cottage, and something stops me before I get to the porch. I see light pouring from the side of the house and decide to walk around there.

I'm not actually worried that Torey will do anything wrong. I don't know what I'm feeling anxious about. Torey and Melissa are still on the couch.

At only five years old, Melissa is already a big kid. She takes after her daddy, one of those good ol', blond boys, well over six feet tall. By the time she gets to be Torey's age, she'll probably tower over her petite, exotic-looking older sister. Melissa's straight blond hair, blue eyes, fair complexion and sturdy limbs couldn't be more opposite from her sister's, yet there's a family resemblance between them somehow.

I frown, trying to see how that could be. Maybe something

about their posture or focus on the TV, or maybe it's just the invisible bond of sisters.

Melissa is leaning against Torey, sucking her thumb. They have my old comforter over them. The cottage is leaky, and on nights like this, you feel it. I thought about Vicky leaning up against me on that same couch. She'd been a thumb-sucker too. Something tight around my chest snaps open and I breathe again. I was worried they wouldn't be okay without me, but they are fine. I don't have to worry. I don't even have to let them know I was here.

I run back to John's boat, anchored at the end of our dock, blanket flapping out behind me like a cape. The cabin is warm and I'm glad to get inside.

"You're back. Good," he says, smiling. "Are they all right?"

I grin back. "Yep, and so am I, thanks."

It's a night for blues music, and he'd dimmed the lights. "I need to take care of something. I'll be right back." He goes out on the deck. A few minutes later, he comes back in with a rush of cold air. "I'm glad you looked in on them. I was worried, too." He falls onto the couch next to me and pushes back the brim of the red baseball cap he always wears.

It has a logo on it that's barely legible, "Pimmie's Point Family Reunion." I asked him once why he always wore it and he said it was because he wore the same cap until it blew off into the ocean. In three years, this one hasn't, some sort of personal record or something.

"Alone at last. This is great." He puts his arm around me. "So how are you doing?"

I relax against him. "I'm worried about court, which is stupid."

"I don't think it's stupid."

"You don't understand. I've been going to family court for a while now, it's part of my job."

"Yeah, but this time you're on the other side of the fence. What sort of things could happen?"

"Worst case scenario? They could take Torey from me. Actually, they could take both girls."

"That sounds like something to be worried about."

"Not really. I don't think there's chance in hell it would happen. I'm a responsible adult. The courts don't take kids away from family, even ones who aren't so responsible. They sure aren't going to take them away from a drug-free aunt with a job and insurance."

"So what's the problem?"

"I don't know. That's what's so stupid." I feel ashamed of something I can't put my finger on. Shit, it's that damned fragileness again. I can't seem to shake it. You'd think I was the one that got raped. When did I turn into such a baby?

"It'll probably be fine."

We hit a quiet spot. I always get uncomfortable when this happens. I take a big gulp of wine, knowing it won't help, but unable to think of anything else to do.

"I know how to relax you. You need the cure." John laughs and kisses my neck.

"The cure" is sex. He'd said it before and I told him then it was the most unromantic line I'd ever heard. I narrow my eyes and give him a baleful look over my shoulder, but damn, I love looking at him, sitting there with his red baseball cap cocked back and grinning at me. It's hard to stay gloomy.

"How's Torey handling everything?"

"Not well."

"Is there anything I can do?"

"I don't know. I mean, I worry about her all the time." I haven't told him yet about the nightmares, or how difficult school is. "You know what? Giving her those flowers did a lot of good, I think. Thank you."

"Come here." He puts his arm around me and pulls me close. I relax and try to let go of my worries. They will still be there when John casts off and I stand on the dock, shivering and waving goodbye.

"I've missed you," he says, kissing the top of my head. Mentally I put all the damned concerns in a box and kick them overboard. I can count on them finding me later.

"What're you crying about?" he says, peering into my face.

"I'm grateful as hell for right now, for right this minute with you."

"Oh." I can tell he's not sure what to say. "Well, don't go crying about it." But he smiles that nice smile of his, like he's relaxed and happy to be here too.

He smells like salt water, wood-smoke and aftershave. I turn, wrap my arms around his neck, and breathe him in.

"Man, I've been waiting a long time for this," he says, hugging me back. "Let's get married."

The temperature in the cabin seems to drop about a thousand degrees. John freezes too. We are like statues. I sit up and get eyeball to eyeball with him. "Where the hell did that come from?"

"I don't know," he says, and I notice his eyes are looking scared—wild around the edges.

"Did you mean to say it?" Now I'm more curious than freaked.

"I don't think so."

I don't know where to go from here so I shut up for once. Tension in the cabin is through the ceiling. So much for relaxing. I wait for something to happen, but nothing does. When it gets to the point I begin fearing for my sanity, I say, "You better tell me what's going on."

John gets up and sort of bounces around the cabin. "I have no fucking idea where that came from, Rae." His voice holds a desperate tone, like facing death or something just as awful. "I have no intention of getting married again, ever. I embarrassed myself to no end." He goes towards the captain's chair and sits down.

"Well, why'd you say it?" I'm so tired of not understanding the things happening around me.

"I don't know." He swivels to face me.

"You don't have to look like the world came to an end." This is beginning to get insulting. After all, it's not like I made him say it. Some part of him must think it's a good idea.

John looks up from his floor-watching. "Oh, Christ, Rae, if there was anyone I'd like to spend the rest of my foreseeable future with, it's you. I'm sorry, it's just when I'm around you, sometimes I don't even know myself." He looks miserable.

I know that look intimately. I take pity on him. "That's all right," I say, or rather someone a lot nicer than me says.

"Since meeting you, I seem to be somebody I don't know very well either."

"Is there something going on around here?" he asks as he walks towards me. Squatting down, he cups my face in his hands. If he had any idea what this particular look does to my insides, he could use it to have me whenever he wanted.

"Maybe." I'm grinning again. John is getting the soft look he gets before kissing me, but as he looms closer I stop him. "Wait a minute."

"What?" He leans back.

"I think we should talk about the marriage thing."

"Oh, no." He groans and moves away.

"What?"

"I don't want to talk about the marriage thing."

"Why not?"

"I just don't want to. Is that okay?"

He's shouting and it's pissing me off. "No," I say a little louder than I intended.

John stands in the middle of the rocking boat and appears to be considering something. It might be me. "All right, all right, let's talk about it. You know where I stand. How about you?"

"I don't want to get married either."

"Good."

"You didn't need to say it so quickly."

"Okay." He waits a bit. "Good."

"You'd know I wasn't big on getting married if we ever talked about anything, knew each other better."

"I know you pretty good, and the more I know, the better I like." John leans over, putting one hand on the back of the couch and the other on my face. He kisses me. I almost forget what I'm saying.

But I remember and pull back. This is important. "The thing is, we really don't know much about each other. The reason I don't want to get married again is that I went through a bad time, and not just with the jerk I was married to, either."

"Rae." John put a finger on my lips. "Shhh, you don't need to tell me about your past. I don't want to know."

"You know I'm divorced, but I haven't told you much

about that or…."

"Oh, no," John says, pushing himself away from the couch and me. "Shit, is this the place where we have to talk about all the crappy things that ever happened to us?" He stands in front of me, glaring.

I'm surprised to find myself instantly furious. No more Ms. Nice Person for him. I'm more than angry, I'm outraged. "Oh, I'm sorry, I wouldn't want to inflict my past on you or anything. I guess I'm just along for the ride, since you're calling all the shots."

"Oh, for crying out loud, Rae, I just don't see the logic in talking about all the bad things we've done or have been done to us."

"What the hell are you saying? People shouldn't communicate?" The nice thing about being on a boat is there are no neighbors to hear you really scream. I kind of enjoy letting loose but can tell he doesn't. Typical dude reaction.

He's looking at me, maybe waiting for me to calm down. He can wait all night as far as I'm concerned.

He takes a deep breath. "The way I see it, there's no point to it. I'm not going to know you any better even if you tell me in exact detail about the lousy bastard you used to be married to. I don't even like thinking about you married to someone else. Why isn't what we know about each other enough?" His face is getting red. "Why do you females think it's a good idea to talk every damn thing to death?"

That took me back. He'd never attacked the feminine front before. Not only are the gloves off, the brass knuckles are on. "You know, fuck you. I am so sick of crap like that. If it weren't for females trying to get things straight… Oh, screw you." I get up to get my coat.

"Where are you going?"

"This date is over."

"Why, because you can't handle anyone thinking differently from you?"

I wasn't aware of being capable of even deeper levels of sarcasm, but found I was. "I can handle different. I just can't handle stupid."

"Oh, fuck you, Rae."

"Fuck you more."

We stand, breathing fast, staring angrily at each other. Then I think about the damn roses and how nice he'd been to Torey. I remember all the crap he goes through to date me and feel ashamed. Still I'm unable to do much but stand and glare at him. He seems to be locked into a similar position. I realize how utterly stupid we both are, throw up my hands and sit on the couch. "I'm sorry. I'm the one who's stupid." I put my head in my hands and rock back into the cushions.

He sits next to me. "We've got to be more careful. Two people with tempers like ours need to think about what they're saying or it could get ugly."

"Yeah, we came real close to ugly tonight, didn't we?"

John chuckles. "I have to hand it to you, you got some mouth on you."

"You're right about that." We are quiet for a bit, and then I smile. "Fuck you."

"Fuck you more." He's smiling, too.

"Okay." I grin.

I stand up and began to disrobe, dropping articles of clothing on my way to the forward berth. It takes him a while to catch up. He's always doing mysterious things to the boat. By the time he gets back to me, I'm naked and under the covers. He's carrying my clothes.

"I'm sorry about all that." He lies on top of the covers and puts his hands behind his head.

"Me too."

"Hate me if you have to, but I don't want to know about your past."

"Why not?"

John puts his arm around me. "'Cause if you tell me yours, I'll have to tell you mine, and I don't want to."

"How come? Have you done something terrible?"

"No, I just don't want to."

"So what's the big deal?"

"I like not knowing everything about you."

"I don't get it."

"You don't understand what it's like growing up in a small town, where everybody knows everything. Most of the women I dated had mothers who knew everything about me." His voice takes on a hopeless note. "And my mother knew everything about them, and so did I."

"Are you saying you like it that we didn't grow up together, that my people don't know your people, that kind of thing?"

"Yeah." John brightens. "But it's more than that. It's finding out about you, Rae. I'm getting to know you without knowing anything about you, and it's exciting as hell for me. It's like I can be freer, if I don't know you. No, that's not right. I don't mean it that way." He looks away, frustrated, and then into my eyes. "It feels new. It all feels new with you, and I dig that."

I consider his words. He's a different sort of person for me too, and I had to admit it might one of the reasons for his strong appeal. Since he didn't like to talk, I kiss him.

"I don't know if we can keep up the newness forever," I whisper.

"Maybe not, but I'm sure going to give it a hell of a shot." John pulls down my blanket and rolls on top of me.

His wool sweater is scratchy on my breasts, so I pull it and his T-shirt up. Our naked chests touch and we groan. I roll on top of him and sit up. I put an index finger alongside my nose and tap him on the chest with the index finger of my other hand. "Pig," I say softly.

"For you I am," he says, and I'm smiling again.

Jailhouse Chili

Start with:
- at least a pound each of two different kinds of ground meat: Turkey, sausage, pork or hamburger is good. If you can get ahold of venison, even better. Recipe is easy to double or triple.
- two large chopped onions, sautéed with the meats.

Skim as much fat as can be easily accomplished from cooked meat, which means leave some fat.

Add in a slow cooker:
- two large cans tomatoes
- four regular-sized cans of beans, drained and rinsed (any kind, I prefer black and kidney)
- four cloves of garlic, minced
- one tablespoon of ground cumin
- four tablespoons Worcestershire sauce
- salt, pepper, Tabasco and/or red-pepper flakes to taste
- one ounce of bakers chocolate nestled in the top*

Cook overnight on low. Stir well in the morning. Let sit in cool garage or porch until dinner time and re-heat.

*I know, the chocolate sounds weird but trust me, it will make the meat meatier, the spices shine, and you won't taste anything remotely like chocolate.

December

As I drive my nieces to Lucy's, trying to figure out why I am among the doomed of this planet, among those with no luck at all, irritability creeps in like sand in a swimsuit. I used to believe I was… well, not exactly lucky, but at least responsible, able to take care of myself. Now I'm not so sure.

Torey's teaching Melissa how to clap to Miss Mary Mack and the giggling is driving me insane. I wonder if the judge and therapist are in cahoots. He orders people into therapy, and the only therapist in town gives him a kickback. That sounds reasonable. A tractor is ahead of me, an old one, top speed probably three miles an hour. I'm going to be really late if I don't pass it, even though it's a two-lane road and I can't see around the damned thing. Why do people think rural areas have no traffic problems? My heart's in my throat as I race by.

The therapist has a strange moniker. Sally Boom sounds like a stripper's name. Probably having an odd name like that screwed her up and now I have to go see a therapist who is a fruit loop. Even odder than the name was the Brooklyn twang emerging from the telephone when she called back to make the appointment. I'd never expected to hear that accent around here. How did a New Yorker find herself in this tiny corner of the world?

At *The Sea Witch*, we hear every kind of accent from people on their way to New York, the Caribbean, Florida or Mexico, but they are only stopping by in their yachts for supplies and drinks with other yachters. People like that don't live in Cornwallis.

It was a long phone call. Sally informed me Cornwallis Social Services had filled her in on the situation. *The situation*, my ass, I should warn people to never be Good Samaritans or take in children and then expect a judicial system to help or support them.

In addition to Torey's therapy with Dr. Boom, I'm ordered into Parenting Skills Training with this person. So, on top of working one and one-half jobs to support us, I get to have Ms. Boom all to myself, every Saturday morning, or until Judge Merrill and Ms. Boom decide I'm a fit guardian for my nieces.

Maybe I'm a victim of too much information. My degrees in criminal justice came with a lot of education in mental health topics. I'm no rookie in this arena. I know therapists might work from any number of theory bases, which could include anything from Freud to some vague notion about abuse from space aliens. I wonder what planet Ms. Boom is from.

I get to Lucy's driveway and pull up. The rain is pouring so hard we're forced to sit and wait for it to exhaust itself. If I'm late for the damned appointment, too bad, I can't fight nature. The slap-hands song has now morphed into a game of Tickle Melissa.

I can't stand any more noise so I tell them take the umbrella and go. I don't need it. Getting wet is at the end of my list of today's problems.

I watch them make their way towards Lucy's front door, giggling and jumping into puddles on purpose. It's good to see Torey playing with her sister, but I'm still grumpy as hell.

Because I had to get up so damn early this morning, to get the girls ready and take them to Lucy's, I didn't work last night.

I'm glad for the break yet sorry for the lost tips. I went to bed same time Torey did and slept ten hours straight, which I guess I needed. Still, it hasn't helped. I lean my forehead on the steering wheel and sigh. Where in the hell was this exhaustion coming from? I look up at the house. The girls must be inside. Lucy is waving to me from her doorway. I wave back and put the car into gear, every motion like moving through mud.

An irresponsible guardian wouldn't make sure her nieces had raincoats and boots. I see the kids at their schools. Most of them don't have raincoats, much less boots. I still can't believe I'm on my way to even more humiliation than our day in family court.

Judge Merrill seems to think I'm personally responsible for all of Torey's issues, and on top of everything, I have to come up with the dollars to pay for this unwanted intervention.

The rain stops and strong winds come bustling out of the clouds overhead, so strong they knock around my little station wagon. I get to the therapist's office, which isn't an office after all, but a house, with peeling light blue paint and white trim, barely off the little strip that is downtown Cornwallis. The leaves are so thick in her front yard I can barely find the walkway. Doesn't she know how to rake? I wade through the wet leaves to the steps.

I wonder if Sally lives here too. I smell the flowery scent of a dryer sheet venting from a wall nearby. I knock and Sally opens the door.

She's older than her voice led me to expect, very attractive with deep blue eyes ringed in black lashes. Her silver hair is braided and wrapped around the top of her head like a crown. She smiles and says, "Come in. Please call me Sally." Then she briskly walks back towards a glassed-in porch. I follow and am momentarily stunned by how beautiful it is.

The only homes I've been in lately are mine and Chip's. Places that, by necessity, are kid-friendly, which means shabby. And because both of us are broke, not chic in any sense of the word. Our homes' décors are made from mismatched polyester plaids surrounded by other almost cast-offs.

This room, with its plants, mountains of books, couches, overstuffed chairs, and art, looks like something out of a magazine. I'd actually forgotten a home could be this nice.

Sally sits on a couch next to some sort of huge spiky plant in an interestingly carved wooden planter. "I'm glad you made it on time. We've got a lot to cover today. Is it too bright in here? Because I could shut the curtains if you like."

It *is* bright, despite the overcast day. "It's fine," I say, looking around. "This is a great room."

"Thanks. I'm still working on the rest of the house, but I think I've got this room exactly the way I want it."

I sit in a suede chair directly across from her. A low-slung coffee table is between us. It's made of carved wood similar to the planter's, with a thick, transparent green glass top. More plants are grouped on one side, all in interesting containers. Sally is wearing a shawl made of some nubby-looking, gorgeous apricot yarns. It must be nice to have so much style.

Despite my misgivings about this appointment, it's a pleasure to simply sit and feel the distant remnants of sophistication I used to think I had.

She's flipping through some papers on a clipboard. I sigh and lean back in the chair. I hate doing it, but can't help comparing this place to our dilapidated, thoughtless home with its chipped tile flooring and two generations of semi-rejected furniture. For some reason, in the eight years I'd owned the cottage, it never crossed my mind to fix it up.

"How are things going at home?" Sally asks softly.

I sit up and look at her. "Better."

"Better than what?"

"Better than I thought it would be at this point."

"I have an appointment to see Torey after school next Tuesday. Her babysitter is bringing her, right?"

"Yes, that's right." Something else I get to pay for.

Sally looks at the clipboard, flipping through pages, her brow furrows and I wait. "I've spoken to Torey's pediatrician, two of her teachers, English and Spanish, and now it's your turn." She looks up and stares over red half-glasses that bring out the blue in her eyes.

I stare back, wondering what the hell she thinks I should say.

"I still have a lot of questions about Torey. It would help if I could fill in some of those gaps." She looks at me expectantly.

"Sure, I'm here to help Torey any way I can."

Sally asks me about Vicky, about us as kids and about our childhood. What I can't figure out is, if she wants to know about Torey, why isn't she asking questions about her?

Finally, after a very intrusive question as to the possibility of me and/or Vicky having an incestuous relationship with our father, I say, "I don't know why you need to ask these kinds of questions. Torey is the one with issues. I'm aware that Vicky has issues too, or else I wouldn't be here." I look at Sally with all the exasperation I'm feeling. "But Vicky isn't here and can't be treated by you, so what's the point?"

Sally's blue eyes stare intently for so long I become uncomfortable. Finally she says, "So, you and your sister come from a family of devils and angels."

"Pardon me?"

"Devils and angels, saints and sinners. In your family, people were good or bad, no in-betweens, right?"

"I have no idea what you're talking about." I'm moving from irritation to the world of the outright pissed off.

"It might have a lot to do with Torey trying to stay attached to her mom, trying to be a sinner like her." Sally looks like the epitome of a shrink, with her hand thoughtfully holding her chin as she regards me with that thousand-watt stare.

She'd spoken so softly, I had to strain to make out what she'd said. I think the large wooden cage across the room, filled with tiny birds making tiny noises, is somehow interfering with my hearing. "You think Torey does the things she does so she can feel connected to her mom?" I ask.

"A lot of kids come to me via the juvenile justice system, as well as family court. Did you ever look at the statistics about kids with incarcerated parents? I know you work in juvenile justice."

"I... ah, I guess so. I'm sure I did." What is that damned statistic? "I think it's over fifty percent of kids with an incarcerated parent having a juvenile offense record."

"More than that, it's seventy-eight percent. Adult arrest records are only slightly lower."

I rub my forehead, trying to wake up my brain. Where

was this fucking exhaustion coming from? So what? What's the big damned deal? Kids follow in their parents' footsteps. Big revelation. "So Torey is either behaving like the only role model in her life, or trying to maintain a connection to her. What's the difference? If Torey can't change her ways, she'll end up just like her mom. Who cares why?"

"Because maybe if you understand why, you'll help your girls understand, and then they won't have to repeat their mother's mistakes. Frankly, Rae, with your background, I'm surprised to find myself explaining this to you."

Through the fog encapsulating my brain, I search for the intelligence I've relied on my entire life and find it missing. "Torey's not coming to you as a juvie, she's here from family court," is all I can think to say.

"Juvenile Justice, Social Services—are the kids so different, Rae?"

She makes a point. Some days I see more social workers than probation officers. But kids that get into trouble, kids acting like their idiot parents, I'd never considered these kids as doing anything more than repeating their parents' stupid mistakes. I'd never thought of it as a way of keeping a connection alive.

Was it true? Was Torey trying to maintain some sort of solidarity with her mother?

The loneliness of that envelops me. What feel like pinpricks of electricity seem to penetrate my skull like needles. I massage my temples, trying to ward them off.

Most nights she still wakes up shouting something, crying or screaming, so she sleeps with me to not wake up Melissa, we say. But what we are really doing is trying to protect her from something, and the problem is, I don't know what the monster looks like or how to kill it.

I try to get her talking, and every now and then something slips out. It's not enough. She doesn't say it, but I know she's terrified she will do it again—be attracted to the wrong guy, attracted to the wrong situation, unable to stand the routine of school and home and me.

I tell her she knows better now, that there's no possibility she would do anything like that again. I don't think it's working. I'm terrified for her too.

"Was your mom a saint or a sinner?" Sally asks.

I'm startled. "My mom?"

"And your dad. Which was the saint and which the sinner?" Sally sounds a bit impatient.

Even though I've asked for an explanation and she still hasn't explained why I need to talk about my parents, I give it a shot, try to be compliant, even if Dr. Boom isn't. "I guess Mom must have been the saint, even though I never thought so, and Daddy had to be the sinner."

"What do you mean, even though you never thought so?"

"I mean I never thought of her as a saint, even though she probably thought of herself that way."

"Your mother thought she was a saint?"

"Yeah, but she wasn't. She only used that as an excuse."

"An excuse for what?"

"For being passive, for being a victim and never doing anything." My voice is almost a whisper, but Sally seems to hear me.

"Your mom went along."

"With everything. Daddy was charming, but he could be abusive, too, verbally abusive."

"Who was his target?"

"Mostly Mom, more than us, and even with her, only occasionally. He wasn't home all that much. It was more the three of us there, doing what we wanted."

"Your mom was easygoing?" She makes a note on her clipboard.

"When he wasn't around."

"Who were you closest to?" She is scribbling away, legs crossed like a yoga master.

"I was close to both of them." The rapid-fire questions are making me feel jumbled.

"Did your dad drink?"

That's a shocker. Sally looks up to see why I don't answer. "How did you know?"

"It kind of goes along with being a sinner. What else did he do?"

"What do you mean, what else?"

"What other sins did your father commit?" Sally looks at me expectantly. "That sounds almost biblical." She smiles.

I try and clear my head, think of an answer. "I caught him kissing a neighbor's wife at a party they had when I was around twelve, I think. Anyway, he saw me and acted like it was a big joke, but they were in the basement, and it didn't look very innocent, even to a twelve-year-old."

"So, you think he was unfaithful to your mother?"

"Probably. He had plenty of opportunities. He traveled a lot, owned his own business. She never questioned him, of course."

"So as you were growing up, were you suspicious?" It was a question but she says it like a statement.

I think about those days. "Yeah, I was. It was after that I began my Friday-night inquisition of Daddy. He got home most Friday evenings after being gone most of the week. I wanted him to know I was watching him. I think I read too many kid detective books and thought I could fix anything. I'm pretty sure that's the reason I was sent to boarding school."

"Because you were suspicious of your father?"

"Because I made his life such a misery with my questions. I wanted to know exactly who he had seen, where he had stayed, even what he ate for dinner. I wanted to know what he watched on TV. I actually watched shows I thought he might watch so that I could quiz him about them. I was a weird kid."

"So they put you in boarding school."

"Yes."

"Did you want to go?"

"Not at first. At first I felt like it was a punishment and cried to stay home. But they said I had to go because I was smart. I always knew that wasn't the real reason. It was because I had turned myself into such a pain in the ass."

"Even your mother wanted to you to go?"

"Yeah, Momma was always closer to Vicky than me. I think she liked the idea of having Vicky all to herself."

"I thought you said you were close to both parents?"

"Well." I feel myself blushing. "That's not actually the truth. I was always closer to Daddy and I don't know why I didn't want to admit to it."

"Maybe saying 'both' was a more politically correct answer."

"Probably."

"Will you try to avoid being politically correct here? I need all the honesty I can get if we're going to help Torey."

"Sure." I feel sweat pour from my armpits. If I get any more uncomfortable, there's going to be a flood.

"Was it a good experience?"

"What?"

"Was boarding school a good experience?"

"Oh, yeah, it was, once I got used to it. It was the best, actually, the high point of my life, even though I had to leave in the middle of my junior year. I'm still in touch with a few friends from then."

Sally takes off her glasses. "I have to talk to you about something, but you have to promise me beforehand that if what I say makes you angry or hurt, you will discuss your feelings with me."

This sounds strange and a little scary. "Okay."

"Why haven't you gotten any help for yourself and the girls before now?"

I squirm in the chair. "I don't know." Sally waits for me to come up with a better answer. "I guess I can see now I should have. I knew the girls have problems."

"So why didn't you?" Sally has an odd-looking smile on her face, almost a grimace.

"Lots of reasons. Money for one. Since I've gotten them, it's been one financial disaster after the other. A little over a year ago, I was earning three times what I'm making now. But I was out of work for a while. My sister's lawyer cost a fortune. Even this, this therapy. Are you aware my insurance only covers seventy percent of five visits with you? After that, I get to pay seventy percent. I'm fairly sure the girls, especially Torey, will need more than five or six therapeutic interventions." I'm heavy on the sarcasm. "Of course, you know I work an additional job to the full-time one, because I can't get their support straightened out."

"Torey's father pays support? I thought he was

deceased." Sally has her glasses on and is flipping through the papers on her clipboard.

"He is. It's her Social Security check I can't get straightened out. Melissa's father took a more routine way to duck his responsibilities. He disappeared."

Sally looks amused. "Before you lost that good-paying job, were you ever in therapy?"

"For myself?"

"Yes."

I feel cornered. "I really don't think my past is something I have to discuss with you." I believe I'm being upfront with Dr. Boom, telling the truth.

"Oh, great, you're going to be one of those fun ones. I honestly expected more sophistication from someone with your education and background."

I don't think I'd ever had a compliment inserted into such a smack-in-the-face insult before. I could think of no response.

"I know you are aware of your court order to be here." Sally ducks her head and peers intently.

I wait to see what else she'll say.

"I can't help the way you got here, can I?" she asks, giving me another intense, therapeutic kind of stare.

"No."

"And I can accept your disliking the situation, but I can't understand your reticence in talking to me. Can you explain it?"

I can't for a minute. I can't decide if I'm feeling angry or guilty. There seems to be some sort of war going on inside.

I decide to feel nothing and continue the conversation. "I'm not sure how to say this, but I think I've done all right with my life, and I know I did it completely on my own. I don't think I'm better than Vicky or our parents, I just think I was luckier. A lot luckier. And because I was lucky, I'm not like them. I don't have their issues and I resent the intrusive questions." I'm feeling embarrassed and don't know why. I'm only telling the truth.

"So you're part of the saint contingent of the family."

"That is so wrong." My voice rises. "I've never thought

of myself as a damned saint, but I'm sure no sinner either. I'm not the one who messed up those girls. I'm the one who has always tried to help them."

"You're how old?" She flips through the papers on her clipboard. "Thirty-six? Divorced, rocky finances, dysfunctional family, yet you never thought you needed help?"

I stare at the floor, trying to hold in my anger. I can't believe the crap I'm listening to.

"Rae, you are not my colleague in this situation, like you're attempting to be. You have been court-ordered into therapy, you and the girls."

Was she right? Was I acting superior? With my brains feeling like scrambled eggs, making it difficult to think or speak, I couldn't see how.

"What I'm trying to do right now is address your resistance to the therapeutic process." Dr. Boom smiles. "Maybe even save you a few bucks. Who knows?"

She waits for me to say something. I feel like a deer in headlights, frozen.

Sally sighs, deeply, and stares out the sliding glass door to her right. She turns back to me, trying again, "I know you want to do good a job with the girls. No one thinks you don't care about them. The problem is as long as you are locked into certain behaviors and beliefs, you force Torey into the same behaviors that got you both here."

The little birds sound like water in the background. I focus on Sally's words and try to figure out what in the hell I'm missing.

"It truly doesn't matter how responsible or caring you might be in the interim if you can't see how troubled your nieces are."

"I don't understand. I've always seen how troubled they are. I have always seen *why* too. My sister was an incompetent, drugged up mess."

"It's not just your sister's behavior causing this problem. It's your family patterns coming into play that you don't see. That's my job, to help you see those patterns."

Still frozen, I look at her with what has to be abject fear.

I don't know the rules to this game or what to say. Somehow everything has shifted.

Her voice softens. "I'm not trying to frighten you, Rae. I do admire your dedication to both girls. It can't have been an easy year and a half, but you hung in there."

I hate it when I'm wrong. I hate, hate, hate it. "I'm sorry for..." I can't think of what I'm sorry for. Maybe I'm not. I don't feel sorry. I don't feel much of anything. I look at my watch to see how much longer I have to endure this conversation.

"You're still angry about being here, aren't you?" Sally sighs and leans back on the couch.

"Yes, I am. I am so insulted I can hardly breathe." I hear my remark the same moment Sally does.

There's silence. I guess I'll be frozen in ice forever. After a pause Sally says, with way too much kindness, "I have a suspicion you've been working very hard your entire life." I look up. On the other side of the tears filling my eyes is a blur of apricot and silver on a deep green background. Anger, exhaustion, and damned fear begin coalescing. Crying begins.

"Oh, screw this." I bend over as sobs rip from my belly.

Sally leans over and slides a box of tissues towards me over the coffee table. I grab a bunch and bury my face in them while great, large sounds come up and don't stop. Along with the pain in my gut, I'm aware of feeling horrified of acting this way, being out of control to this degree. When finally there's a break in the sobbing, my first thought is, why put myself through this? I can't think of any reason to continue this humiliation. "I have to go," I say, and stumble towards the front door.

"What's wrong?"

It's Tuesday night. John's sitting on the sofa, drinking coffee and playing his part in our twice-weekly dinner theatre production we put on for the girls. The play is about two middle-aged people. They eat dinner and then talk about their day while the male lead drinks coffee. The moment

Torey goes to bed, we drop our roles and sneak out to the boat where we act out the sort of things you're not supposed to do around kids.

I'd just finished washing up. I sigh and wipe my hands on a dishtowel.

"What's wrong?" he asks me again.

What's wrong? I don't want to discuss it. I hear Torey talking on the phone in my room and I yell, "It's time to go to bed. Tell Jennifer good night." Melissa's been asleep for a while. She passed out the moment I put her down, like a stone into deep, still waters.

Even though Torey seems to have the phone permanently preempted, it's good she finally has a friend, a miracle named Jennifer. Jennifer was an afterthought in her family. I'd met her retired professor mother when I took Torey over to spend the day Saturday. Both parents are retired professionals, recently moved to Cornwallis. Thirteen-year-old Jennifer's next oldest sibling is a twenty-eight-year-old physician.

I walk over to the couch and plop next to John, almost spilling his coffee.

"What is up with you tonight?"

"I'm worried about the damned therapist."

"Did Torey have some sort of problem with her?"

"Torey? No, not Torey. Torey thinks Dr. Boom is terrific. I'm the one with the problem. Torey told me the doctor said I needed to call her."

"How long has it been?"

"Two weeks."

"Damn it, Rae, when're you going to fix this?"

"I don't know." I resolve every morning to call, and every day my resolve fails me.

"You can call her tomorrow morning before you go to work. Just do it and get it over with."

"I would, except I don't know what to say." I hate the whine in my voice.

"You don't have to say anything, just make an appointment and talk to her when you get there. You're too smart to be pulling this shit." He's right, I have to make the damned call.

"I will, I promise." I groan and snuggle under his arm. I want to quit thinking about it. I want Judge Merrill, the stupid therapist, my job, all of the crap I don't want, to please get the hell out of my life.

"You're gonna call me tomorrow after you make the appointment. Otherwise I'll call her myself and make it for you."

I can't decide if he's serious or not.

"Wait a minute!" He sits up, getting untangled from me. He looks around, then dramatically sticks a finger in his mouth and holds it up like he's checking which direction the wind is blowing. He bends down and whispers, "I think they're asleep."

I listen. He's right. Silence comes from the bedrooms. She's either asleep or close to it. Torey sleeps with me most nights, so is probably in my bed. We subscribe to the "don't ask, don't tell" policy on the subject of my sex life. She pretends not to notice me sneak out and come to bed later on in a much better mood.

John and I run out the back door, giggling like kids. I unbutton my shirt and flash him, laughing and running away. He chases me, tackling me at the bottom of the slope and we fall. I don't care about the cold or the dry leaves crackling underneath me. The only thing concerning me is the smell of him and the wonderful weight of his body covering mine. He needs a shave, and the bristles on his face are rough. I predict a rash on my face in the morning from this beard, but don't give a damn about that either. I don't care about anything except the heat coming off his body and this insane, delirious state of mind I fall into when I'm with him.

"Come on." He stands up and pulls me after him. We walk to the pier holding hands, like high-school kids. His boat is rocking in the gentle waves and I can hear the creak of cold ropes and metal clanging rhythmically in the night.

We go on board and don't even bother to turn on lights or heat. We've got plenty of our own.

Something's different, something I can't put my finger on. Every note the wind plays is clearly audible, yet stillness is here, too, either inside or out of me, I can't tell.

He's outlined from the moon and lights on the pier. I like him so much. He's the boy next door. My best friend, the guy I can count on for just about anything. He walks towards me and takes my hand again, bending down and kissing me. I wonder if this is love, if he knows I would follow him anywhere right now. We move toward the front of the boat, the bow, the bed.

Moonlight reflecting off the water is all the illumination I need. Besides, I could walk this blind. I am delighted to experience myself completely without fear. What is the opposite of afraid — is it courageous? But that doesn't sound right. Accepting, that's it. That's what I feel.

Yet the word doesn't seem big enough to encompass the depth and breadth of this, this boundlessness. Does he feel it too?

Intimacy, this must be what it means, boundaries between me and everything else melting into soft, gluey substances. Fear, I now understand, once accompanying me everywhere, suddenly absent. Gone, vamoosed.

What delight, this freedom. I become naked in a patch of moonlight, drunk on something far better than any intoxicating substance I know of.

I remember reading about a time in pre-history when women were worshipped, and know it's no theory but the absolute truth. There's power in me. I am so happy.

"What are you doing?"

"Dancing for you." I twirl around in my moonlight spotlight, arms upraised.

The cold is terrible, but so is the moment that I stop and lock eyes with him. The moon reveals us in shades of gray, alabaster and charcoal.

Sex will require courage, which seems odd. I don't know why this is true, only that it is. I wonder if I will be brave enough to consummate this encounter.

He's still dressed.

I smile. "Take off your clothes."

He does, and an invisible, sexual spirit in me crawls across the bed, sniffs him, strokes his back, tastes his neck and belly. Then crawls back and shocks me with her intensity.

He looks at me. "If we don't get under these covers, my balls are going to freeze and fall off."

I laugh, scrambling under the cold covers. "Maybe you should turn on the heat."

"I'm trying to," he says, climbing in and grabbing my icy butt.

The cold has nothing to do with where I live. I'm detached and free of concerns. I kiss his chilly lips and lay along the length of him. Touching is pleasure bordering on pain.

"I'm so cold, I can't feel a damn thing," he complains.

"I'll warm you up." I sense the creature who stalked him within me. I entwine my body with his and am so excited I can barely breathe.

John moans and grabs me, but his hands are rough, his mouth hard. Yet worse, much worse, is the startled sense of being pinned down by a stranger who clenches my wrists and jams them into the bed.

Excitement vanishes, replaced by terror. I struggle against him, but he mashes my head into the pillow, kissing becoming an attack, his whiskers rough, assaulting.

I get my hands free, push him away, then scoot up, pulling the covers with me, and scream, "Wait a god-damned fucking minute."

His face is angry. "What's wrong?"

"That's what I'm asking you." I'm still breathing heavy, so is he.

"What the fuck did I do?"

Get defensive as hell, for one thing. I get discarded and he gets defensive. There's no point in arguing. If he doesn't want to admit to what happened, then it's over anyway. How many times had I been involved in something like this and never noticed?

The memories come unbidden, all the times I'd been open and available to some version of this intimacy, yet left alone. I never took care of myself. I saw my acceptance of those lonely couplings as if it was all I deserved. When did I change?

And I see it was Dennis, with all his cruelty, who'd given me this, this need to care for myself and never compromise my truth again. After everything it took to extricate myself from him, I was, finally and at last, important to me.

I see this and am un-wounded.

I look in John's face, disappointed in his unwillingness to join me, yet feel no sense of loss. No rage, no pain even. The wild freedom I found with him is still mine and not bound to any other creature.

It's amazing how, in an instant, everything changes. I move from him.

"Are you all right?"

"I am. I feel wonderful." I think about getting up and going back to the house, but it doesn't seem to matter where I am. There is so much pleasure everywhere. All possibilities hold eons of pleasure for me. I sigh deeply and stretch out in the rough cotton sheets.

"Come over here."

"No. I'm fine where I am."

"Did I do something wrong?"

I look at this man, so recently the love of my life, and accept the ridiculousness of explaining to him what he'd done.

"You're ruining the moment, you know." John's voice holds anger.

I think about his words and see for him it's true. "You're right, I'm sorry." Some instinct nudges me to get up and start dressing.

"Where are you going?"

I stop, look at him and smile. "I'm not sure yet."

"Get back in bed."

"No." I lean down and kiss him. "But I love that you want me to." I continue dressing.

"Don't go... please."

I get still, unsure of where my life will take me next. I wait for his words. They might help me find out.

He looks uncomfortable. "Listen, Rae, I don't know what's gotten into me tonight. It's me, not you."

This sounds interesting. I sit and wait for more.

"I know you've been having a tough time financially."

I'm unable to make a connection between my finances and his bailing on us.

"The thing is," he says, shifting so he's sitting up, pulling the blankets up to his chest, "I'm having a tough time, too. Charters are down, diesel is up, local fishing is shot to hell. I can't even get rockfish charters, and I used to be able to always count on them." He looks at me as if this explanation is complete.

"I don't get what you're saying." I feel my wildness slipping away and a headache coming on. Talk of diesel and rock fishing is killing any sense of life and joy. There has to be some place on this planet where it's safe to feel this good and be this open. If I have to be alone to have me, I'll take it.

"I'm strapped. More than strapped, and I wish I weren't and had a little extra to help you out. I feel like hell that I don't. And then tonight, here you are dealing with Torey and the therapist and all that stuff and I go and pull some crap. I'm really sorry."

"What sort of crap do you think you pulled?" This is the real question.

"I… umm." He looks at me. I can tell it's going to be one of his long introductions to some sort of a statement. He coughs and stumbles around for a while without actually saying anything. But me, I don't react like I usually do, impatient for his words. This time I sit quietly and wait for him to get it out. "I got into my head there for a minute," he finally admits.

"What exactly does getting into your head mean?"

John sighs and looks away. "It means I get into thinking about the act of sex in a certain way and forget to be here." He glances at me and looks away again. "Or at least that's what my wife used to say, and I think… I think she was probably right."

I notice he doesn't say ex-wife. "What does thinking about sex a certain way mean?"

"Rae, this is embarrassing. I know it was wrong, isn't that enough?"

I think for a minute. "No, it isn't. I can't have this kind of thing secret between us if we're going to continue as a couple." I sound so reasonable I'm proud of myself. You'd think I'd been in healthy relationships my entire life.

He cups his chin in his hand, glaring at me. I can see he's

angry and the most remarkable thing is, it doesn't bother me at all. I actually smile.

He gives up. He throws up his hands and scoots down until he's lying flat on his back, staring at the porthole in the ceiling which still has moonlight pouring through. Like a small boy he says, "When I'm pissed off about something, like work, or anything, it doesn't matter what it is, I sometimes take it out on women by turning them into objects. Okay? I'm not pleased with myself, and I haven't pulled this shit in years."

"So that's what you did? You turned me into an object to fuck?"

"Basically, yes. You've got to be cold. Don't you want to get under the covers?"

"I'm fine right here. You know what? I believe you, because that's exactly what it felt like, like all of a sudden we were no longer lovers, not even people. It was empty and scary."

"Rae, I *am* sorry."

What did I need to know? "Why did this happen tonight?"

He sits up, keeping the covers up to his neck. "I didn't want to tell you but I'm going through a rough patch. I've got to decide if I'm going to take out another loan and keep things going. What scares me is between pollution killing off the fish, cost of diesel…"

"What do you mean, pollution killing off fish?"

"Oh, you know. Algae blooms, red tides, dead zones. Things in the bay are getting worse, and the charter industry is going to hell fast. I might be better off selling while there's still some interest in commercial fishing boats like this, get out of the whole deal. But if I do, I don't know what I'm going to do with myself. It's the only thing I know how to do besides hunt, and I can't make a living off that. Things are fucked up and I didn't want you to know."

"John, this is insane. You want to protect me by seeing me as some sort of object to fuck?"

"You're right. You're right. Because the person I'm really trying to protect is me. I want to be a big shot in your eyes, and I'm scared I'm not gonna be for long."

"Do you honestly think I'd think less of you?" The answer is, of course, yes, even though he doesn't say it. "So rather than tell me what's bothering you, you turn me into a fuck doll?"

He's quiet for a minute. "Well, yeah. I wouldn't have put it those words, but yeah, that's what I did."

"Can you not do that?"

"Can I not do what?"

"Can you not take your crap out on me?"

He sighs. "I can try. I can say I'm sorry as hell and mean it. I could say it will never happen again, but I didn't see it coming tonight and wouldn't if you hadn't called me on it." He seems older, tired. He props himself up on an elbow, weariness all over him. "I'm trying hard to keep it together. I don't know if I can make promises right now, Rae."

I get under the covers, nearly shivering. John scoots close and pulls the blankets around us. "Back in the old days I would have promised it would never happen again. Back in the old days I lied about nearly everything and never knew it."

He's still next to me, afraid, I think, to touch me.

I snuggle closer and nudge his arm around me. "Here's a radical notion. Maybe if you talked to someone—who knows, maybe even me—about things bothering you, maybe they wouldn't be such a burden. What do you think?"

"That would probably be a better idea than keeping everything under wraps." I hear his smile.

In my mind's eye, I see this great-hearted man with my girls tonight, being courtly with Torey, letting her know she is safe with him. Teasing Melissa. She is totally enamored, just like her aunt. I almost laugh but know he'd never understand if I did. He's a good man, misguided like all of them, but good. I lean up to kiss him, and something snaps. We are back in Eden and it's a good thing we are still mostly naked.

We've visited this place before, for delicious moments. This time we move in. John holds me and things like heat and cold are no longer factors. I sense he will kiss me, and when he does, a groan I've never heard issues from his chest.

I answer with a release of any boundaries between us, and we are no longer two people.

We discover sensations more powerful than movement. But sensation, touching, none of it matters because it's all outside our individual and mutual control. Movement is orchestrated by an entity much wiser and more ardent than either of us. Biology happens, or nature perhaps. I don't know what to call it. Whatever it is, it's wonderful, and it isn't sex.

When the right moment arrives, he enters me and every sense organ I have locks into this. Organic orgasm occurs, our choreographed dance ending gently, and with great emotion.

Maybe it was mating. No one ever warned me this could happen. I'm sweating and breathing hard. I profoundly love every inch of his body and every square inch of mine. I sense he is as deeply satisfied as I am, and we are both complete in our exhaustion. John rolls on his side and puts his arm over me. Right before going to sleep he says, easily, gently, yet sounding like he means every word, "Rae, I think this is love."

I think maybe we should have been warned.

Scalloped Oysters

- one quart of oysters
- RITZ Crackers
- butter
- heavy whipping cream
- Worcestershire sauce
- one lemon
- part of a small onion

Crumble a sleeve of Ritz Crackers. Mix with half a stick of melted butter, some freshly ground black pepper, some grated onion, dried oregano, garlic and onion powder to taste.

Drain raw oysters and reserve liquor.

In a shallow baking dish, layer:
- raw oysters
- a layer of cracker mix
- a layer of oysters, and
- ending with cracker mix

Stir reserved oyster liquor with:
- half cup heavy cream
- one tablespoon Worcestershire sauce
- the juice of half a lemon and
- a few drops of hot sauce.

Pour over top until coming to the top but not covering the top layer of cracker crumbs. Use more or less cream as needed.

Bake in 350-degree oven for about 45 minutes. Top will be brown and crusty.

STILL DECEMBER

I hope my old clunker makes it. I hope it's up to this trip, which I don't think I am. My gloominess doesn't fit with the gorgeous scenery of dramatic mountain ranges. Our station wagon is on its way to Ohio for Christmas; to Mother's penitentiary we go.

I'm apprehensive. Vicky hasn't had much to say to me since I let her know what happened to Torey. I can't blame her for being angry. Yet the fact I'm raising her children might be a mitigating factor if she'd stop and think about it. This trip was arranged courtesy of Torey Green, who Vicky still speaks to.

There's also the other mitigating factor of leaving John on our first Christmas together. Neither of us is happy about it. He told me we'd miss the boat parade. It sounds like a good time. They decorate the fishing fleet with lights. Usually some yachts join in. It begins at the marina next to *The Sea Witch* and ends at the nature preserve past us. John said it'd been a tradition for years, but I never knew about it. The whole procession parades past our dock, and he promises it's quite a sight.

Looks like I'll miss it again this year. In the rear-view mirror, I see both sleeping girls. I've got on some moody classical music that, since they are asleep, I can enjoy, if "enjoy" is the right word. At least I don't have to listen to damned rap.

It's late afternoon in West Virginia, and I'm driving into the last rays of the setting sun. Soon, I'll have to think about dinner and a motel, but for now I can just drive.

I miss John like crazy. I understand the tug of war that goes on between wanting to be someone's lover and wanting to be there for the kids. I wish it wasn't such a stretch between lover and parent. I chuckle, remembering my last day at work.

I was pretending to read a psychological report but was in reality looking at the same page while indulging in my latest obsession, the sex we'd had that Tuesday night. Or the mating, as I now referred to it. I was remembering every delicious moment when the receptionist buzzed and said, "Torey's on line five for you."

I said, "Who?" Torey and Melissa being people far removed from the realm I resided in that moment, but the world has a way of crashing through beautiful clouds and getting people back into reality.

In addition to not wanting to leave John, I'd had a heck of a time getting on the road this morning because I kept feeling like I was forgetting something important. I blame last night's dream about Torey and me on some sort of ship, like an ocean liner or a spacecraft. We had almost reached our destination when I remembered I'd forgotten Melissa.

In the dream I was frantically trying to tell Torey I'd forgotten her sister, but the words were stuck and I couldn't get across what I was trying to say. I woke up in a sweat, frantic, making *k-k-k* sounds in the back of my throat, and on the verge of tears. It was a crappy way to begin the day.

Thinking of crappy things brings me to the topic of Ms. Boom, Ph.D.

I wish I knew what the hell I was going to do about the homework she's assigned me. It's my penance for not contacting her after our first appointment. I have to show "good effort" in order not to get a bad report sent to the judge.

I can see her in my mind, red half-glasses perched on the end of her nose. "Rae, while you are on this trip, I want you to use the time away from your normal routines to become more aware of your personal history, especially childhood memories."

So my penance is to keep a journal and each day look for an incident that reminds me of my childhood. I'm supposed to write what happened, how it relates to something in my childhood, and my feelings about it. Today is the first day of our trip and so far zilch. I have no idea what I'm going to write. The whole idea is stupid. I don't know why I bother worrying about it. I have my hands full with kids and driving. I decide to write down anything, make something up if I have to. What a relief to figure it out.

I look in the rear-view mirror. Torey's pointy chin rests on her chest. Her pillow is crammed against the window while Melissa sprawls out in her car seat. I guess Vicky and I looked something like that once. I am eight years older than Vicky, a little over the age difference between my nieces — Vicky, who loved and hated me with such intensity, she made us all laugh at times.

I can write that down. Vicky and I probably once looked like Torey and Melissa do right now. After all, Sally didn't say how much I had to write, just write something.

How do I feel? I think if I have anything to do with it, my nieces will be a whole lot closer to each other as adults than Vicky and I are, or ever were. Good, one chore completed. Now all I have to do is write it down.

My homework has me remembering when Vicky was Torey's age. She seemed to change overnight. She stopped fighting with me, stopped accusing me of not loving her enough, and her involvement with the whole family evaporated. Yet no one seemed to notice, except me, and I had no idea what to do.

Momma and Daddy were too caught up in money problems and their private war to have energy to direct her way. Even after I tried to tell them something was wrong.

Later on, Vicky began acting out and she finally got noticed. But I still had nothing to offer. I was consumed with keeping myself from drowning in a sea of my own demons.

Boarding school had been a temporary savior and I knew it. Funny, Sally brought that up again at our last session. Between friends and teachers there, I'd been happy and had done well. I was horrified when my parents wouldn't let me stay and terrified of losing something I couldn't identify. But even though I couldn't identify it, when I came home, it vanished.

By the time Vicky turned thirteen, I was trying my damnedest to win an academic scholarship to Italy for my last year of graduate school. Somehow I believed if I won, I'd recapture the joy I'd lost. I desperately wanted it back before having to enter the real world of work and full-fledged adulthood.

I didn't get it, despite sleepless nights and the desperate grind I engaged in. Then Vicky's pregnant and I'm hoping like hell to find whatever was missing from my life in the career I'd begun. Nobody in our family got what they wanted, and I wonder if I should write about that.

My mind drifts to more positive topics. Finally I have Torey's Social Security straight. After nearly a year and a half of dealing with the mind-numbing bureaucracy that is our federal government, I'm due a very large check in a month or so. A much smaller check will continue to come every month until Torey turns eighteen or finishes college, whichever comes first. I'm going to be able to quit my part-time job, yet the thought doesn't make me happy. I wish I could quit the one that pays the bills.

Oh, well, it's fun to consider changes we can make when I get the check. After paying off the credit cards, I'm considering an addition to the cottage, maybe a room and bath for myself. What luxury that would be, to have some privacy. The girls could each have their own room, and we could paint and decorate them. Melissa wants a princess bedroom, and Torey wants to paint her walls black and get purple curtains and bedspread.

An updated kitchen would be nice, too, but more necessary than any of those things is our need for insulation, new windows, and a better way to heat the cottage. Our list is a lot bigger than the money coming in, but fun to think about.

"Arae, I'm hungry. When can we stop for dinner?" Melissa is awake.

"Soon, baby, soon." I switch off the radio.

The next day, we almost don't make it to the prison on time. On Christmas Eve and Christmas Day, longer than usual visitations are offered. Visitors are divided into two groups and assigned times. I'd filled out forms and applied for spots both days. We were assigned the first visiting time slot from ten a.m. to two p.m. on Christmas Eve, and the second one, from three to seven p.m. on Christmas Day. The problem is we'd overslept because Melissa, who always wakes up at the crack of dawn, didn't.

I'd made a mistake counting on her to be our wake-up call. So we ended up rushing over, finding a parking spot and racing through remnants of dirty snow for what felt like miles in bitter, bitter cold, to the glare of fluorescent lights off yellowed, cinder block walls. The inside of the building is almost as cold as out, although other visitors tell us it warms up quickly.

I'm worrying about Torey. She's getting the pinched look she gets when stressed. I work hard to keep that look off her face, but our trip here is taking more of a toll than I'd anticipated.

Melissa's so young, she seems immune to the oppression of cinder block walls and metal-barred doors. She's zooming around on the roller-skate/sneakers she'd begged from Santa that'd cost me way too much and which she will outgrow very soon if she keeps shooting up the way she is.

Santa came to our house early this year, I explained to Melissa, so we could come here and not miss it.

Torey notices the harshness of this place way, way too much. "It's not as bad as it looks," I whisper so Melissa can't hear. "It's always a shock. I remember the first time I inspected a detention center, I almost freaked out, but I had to act cool."

Torey gives me a hopeful look. "Really?" she asks.

"Yeah, it's just a shock when you're new to it." I hope she believes me.

I'd never been in a correctional institution outside of a professional capacity before. After her arrest, I saw Vicky before her court dates with the lawyer, but we met in a room in the court building.

Being here outside a professional capacity is so different. Some of the guards are okay, but most are demeaning. It surprises me how condescending they are to the smallest, most innocent request. Like a woman asking where the bathrooms are for her children.

The group standing in this hallway is nervous as a result of a rule I'd been unaware of. Coming here condemns the visitor along with the prisoner. I find myself carrying a vague sense of shame and don't know how to counteract it. It's scary to see how quickly my perceptions of myself are erased. I guess Torey isn't the only one affected by our surroundings.

We wait for over an hour to be inspected and let in which made the rush to get here feel stupid. The girls and I get through quicker than other families because we don't have food or packages.

All around us, people carry buckets of fried chicken, covered dishes, desserts, brightly decorated packages and things in plastic bags, all of which have to be inspected and scanned.

I hope Vicky doesn't mind we came empty-handed. The kids wanted to bring their presents, but I said, "Let's wait until tomorrow for that. It's enough excitement for today just to see each other." I never even considered food.

The visitation takes place in the gym where tables are set up. They are filling fast, so I grab the first unoccupied one I see. The girls stand near me and look around apprehensively. Melissa zooms off on her skates, circling the table like a shark and saying, "Hi," as she approaches me and her sister, and "Bye," when she passes by.

Double doors on the far wall open and a few prisoners in navy blue jump suits enter with guards.

A moan-like sound comes from the crowd of children rushing up to them, and it takes a while to recognize the words—Mommieeee, Mommy, Mommy, Mommy."

I don't recognize the skinny, muscular blonde with spiked hair at first, but the girls do and run to her with outstretched arms. I follow, not sure of my reception.

"Hey, Vicky," I say, but nobody notices. When Vicky looks up, her eyes are laughing. That's what Momma used to say when she looked like this, eyes shining with happiness.

"Hey there, sis," she says, pulling the girls closer. "Thank you. Thank you so much for this."

"You are very welcome." And that's the last thing I say for the next hour. It becomes evident my role here is a courier's. I deliver expected goods and am not needed until time to take them away.

I'm angry first, then insulted, then hurt, because it isn't just Vicky. It's the girls, too.

I fall into the background of their lives as if I'd never existed. I watch them paint nails, chatter, and laugh as if they were teenagers. Melissa feigns a prissy attitude I haven't seen in a while, and Torey's voice regains the rough, arrogant sound that used to trigger fights between us. Tomorrow I'm bringing a book.

Around eleven-thirty, Melissa begins to get hungry. For some insane reason, I can go out for food and it can be brought in, but I can't come back into visitation. Actually, I don't mind, anything is better than watching everything I worked to create with the girls disappearing before my eyes.

"So burgers are okay with everyone?" I ask as we settle where and what I should get.

"Wait a minute, before you leave..." Vicky looks around the room. "Girls, how about going to the vending machines and getting a snack? I need to talk to my sister for a minute."

She smiles her Mona Lisa smile at them. I swear she practiced the exact same look when she was twelve. They take some money from me and leave.

"How're things going?"

Wow, she's finally speaking to lucky me. "Okay." Irritation leaks out with the word.

"Oh, Rae, I'm sorry. I wasn't ignoring you. It's just been so long since I could see them, touch them."

Which was true. I cringe at my own insensitivity. "It's all right, don't worry. What do you want to talk about?"

"Is Torey okay? I mean, I wanted to talk to her about what happened, but I wasn't sure how to begin... and I didn't want to say anything in front of Melissa. Do you think Torey is disappointed I didn't ask her about it?"

"Torey's getting better, and you're right not to involve Melissa. Melissa thinks if you run away, you catch a bad cold and have to go to the hospital. I think she senses there's more to it, and I answer any questions if she asks. So far she hasn't wanted to know a whole lot."

"Well, do you think I should say something to her?"

"To Torey?" I smile. "I'm never sure what to say to Torey, so don't ask me. But if you want to talk to her alone, I can take Melissa with me. She could probably use a nap."

"No, don't do that. I want to see them both. But you think I did okay with them today?"

"I'm sure you were fine." I wait a beat. "She's told you she's in therapy, right?"

"Yeah, and you are, too." Vicky's laughing. I guess Torey says more than I realize during their phone conversations.

"Yeah, I am," I say, chagrined.

"How's it going?"

"I hate it." No point in denying it.

"Well, I feel sorry for the therapist."

I look to see if she's teasing or being serious, I can't tell.

"Rae?"

"What?"

"If I wanted to ask the therapist something about Torey through you, do you think that would be all right?"

"Sure. Like what?"

"Oh, I don't know. Like if I'm worried Torey isn't doing well, or she tells me something I'm not too sure about, maybe I could tell you and you could ask the therapist, keep me in the loop… this time."

I deserved that, so I don't say anything. "Sure, sounds like a good idea." But something in me gets suspicious. "Did Torey say something to you before she ran away?" I keep my voice even and light.

"Nothing definite. She was bored at school and thinks everyone there is a redneck, a wannabe gangster, or a Jesus freak."

"Did she say anything specific?"

"She told me about that Fisher guy."

She told Vicky more than she told me. "Do you think she might run off again?"

"Yeah, I do. She's the same age as me when I started."

I'm stunned. She's right, and I'd completely forgotten. Once, Momma called me at college with the faint hope Vicky had somehow made her way to me.

"I need to know—did she tell you Fisher wanted her to go away with him?"

"Not exactly, but in so many words, yeah." Vicky's face looks bored, expressionless, as she glances at her nails and bites a hangnail. I can't believe her casualness. It's unnerving.

"Why didn't you tell me?"

"Tell you what?" Vicky seems honestly confused.

"Tell me she might run away."

"I didn't want to go breaking the kid's confidentiality."

"Vicky, she could have died."

"Well, yeah." Vicky looks at the floor, then back to me. "Still, I didn't want to turn her in. She'd stop talking to me if I did."

"She'll stop talking to you for sure if she's dead." Anger roils in me and I stamp it down. Vicky still doesn't have a clue how to be a parent.

"Let's not argue. You're right. Next time I have some concerns, I'll let you know, okay? I mean, that's what I'm saying here. I want to be a better mom, that's why I want to communicate with Torey's therapist."

I look at her and suddenly feel tired. Beyond tired. I'm exhausted. It must have been a longer trip than I realized.

"Rae." Vicky's smiling at me. "Hey, I'm your friend here. I'm your sister. I'm trying to do better. I wanted to be alone with you so I could get some feedback, see if you think I'm acting right around them." She motions toward the vending machines where the girls sit on the floor like fawns, waiting to be told it's all right to return. "Do you think I'm doing okay? Saying the right things?"

"Yeah, sure. I mean, you all are just chitchatting. Nothing wrong with that. I'd better get lunch." I stand up.

"Well, wait a minute." Vicky gets a faraway look in her

eyes. There's something else she wants to discuss and she's working her way up to it. I know this look. I sit and wait.

When you grow up with someone it's impossible not to know certain looks and what they mean. I can write about that tonight for Sally. Good, day two taken care of. I wait for whatever it is, because I know she wants something.

She turns toward me almost exactly as if she just remembered something. "Did you get the Social Security straight?"

"Yeah, I'll be able to quit my part-time job as soon as it gets here."

"Did they say when it would be sent?"

"Probably January, maybe February."

Vicky gets a smile so artificial I can't believe she thinks I'm falling for it. "What are you going to do with all that money?"

"For one, finish paying off your legal bills," I say angrily. I don't like the direction this conversation is taking.

"There couldn't be that much left."

"You're right, Vicky, after selling my home and wiping out my savings, it's not too bad now." I hate the anxiety in my voice.

"You know I appreciate it. I only wish he could have helped more."

"And I wish I'd listened to people telling me not to waste my money on your lawyer. They knew you didn't have a chance, but I was bull-headed, as usual."

"I already said thanks. I don't know what else to say."

"You don't have to say anything. Are we done?"

"Almost. So anyway, you're getting a year and a half's support?"

"Yeah, that's what they said, but I'll believe it when I see it." If she insists we go here, I will, but I'm coming prepared.

"Well, that's great. I know you can use the cash, what with the bills and all. What do you plan to do with it?" Vicky seems interested, so I stupidly tell her about my dreams to fix up the cottage.

"You know, the money's for Torey's upkeep."

"What?" I feel suspicious again. Being around Vicky

seems to turn me into a breeding ground for paranoia.

"Only that it's Torey's money and probably should be earmarked for her care."

"Like you did?" I'm shouting. I look at the guards who are already staring back, cool and direct. I flush and calm down. "Listen, Vic," I hiss, "the money will be used to make us all more comfortable, which is a lot more than you can say you did with it. As far as I can tell, all the money you got for them went up your nose."

"Still judging me." Vicky conjures tears. Even here she is by far the prettier sister, but I'm immune to her looks and ways. Her beauty will rot here for the next eight years, no matter who she charms—and it won't be me. "All I'm saying is, it's Torey's money, and I've been thinking about things like college, things like that."

"Oh." I guess she's being a mother after all. I'm getting a headache from trying to carry on this conversation. "Shit, Vicky, I'm sorry for getting pissed off. I didn't mean to yell at you. Besides, what's done is done. I'm sorry for bringing it up."

"It's all right, Rae. My track record sucks."

"I guess I'm tired of being criticized about how I'm raising the girls. I'm doing my best. It's a lot of work."

"I know," Vicky says with emphasis. "I know how hard it is to raise kids. I'm sorry I can't do it anymore, and that when I had the chance, I blew it."

Now there are more tears that don't seem so artificial, and I feel unwelcome twinges of guilt. Is there an end to this emotional roller coaster?

"I'm not trying to sound critical. They owe you their lives, and I tell them that all the time."

I narrow my eyes, trying to bore into Vicky's skull where I might find something like the truth. It doesn't sound like anything she would say to them, and even if she did, I'm not sure I'd want her to.

"Listen, Vic, I guess we could keep part of it for that. It's not a bad idea. The problem with the cottage is, it's cold. It wasn't built for winters and to get it winterized will be expensive." I want her to understand I'm not planning to be irresponsible or selfish. "I've talked to a few contractors who come to the restaurant about it and…"

Vicky interrupts me. "Well, maybe once you see what it will cost, you could send me what's left." She's haughty and knows she's stepping over the line, but for some reason can't seem to stop herself. "As Torey's mother, I can't help but feel some of it belongs to me."

She has a hardness about her that's new, or at least new to me. I stand up. A stupid fear clouds my mind and I stammer, "Vicky, what do *you* want money for here?" I already sent the maximum fifty dollars a month for canteen privileges.

"I have needs too! Just because I'm locked up doesn't mean I've stopped living. Listen, Rae, I talked to Torey about it and…"

She begins to say something but I put my finger on her lips and hush her exactly like I did when she was little. "Stop, stop it, Vicky. Shhh. I don't want to know about this little scheme of yours. It'll never happen. The only thing that's going to happen is I'm going to raise your daughters the best way I see fit." I back up, away from the evil in front of me. "And right now, all I can think of, is they are a whole lot better off with me than they ever were, or ever could be, with you. You know that, don't you? You know you're incapable of caring for them, or anyone for real?"

She doesn't bother to respond. Her eyes blink and that's it. She tried and failed in her attempt to get what she wanted. I'm no longer standing in front of her. For Vicky, I no longer exist.

I turn and leave, sorry I can't hide the tears dripping down my face.

Ice Pie

Take freshly fallen snow, mix with sugar and a package of flavored Kool Aid. Pack it into a pie plate and freeze.

January

"Thanks for seeing me, I appreciate it."

Because Torey's still on winter break, her usual Tuesday afternoon appointment was changed to Tuesday morning, and I moved heaven and earth at work to take her place this morning.

"I have to tell you, Rae. I was surprised when you called."

"I can imagine." I'm embarrassed, but desperation rules.

"What's up?"

How to begin? "I'm freaking out," I say, beginning to cry.

"What happened?" Her concern is instantaneous, which is nice. I like that about Sally.

"I couldn't see her on Saturday."

"Who? Vicky? On Christmas Day? Why not?"

"I couldn't make myself go near her again." I'm crying hard, but this time I don't give a shit. Sally brings me a box of tissues and sits next to me on the couch with her hand on my shoulder. Maybe she wants to hold on to me in case I try to run away again, or maybe she's just being nice.

It all comes out in a jumble. I don't know how Sally follows what I'm saying. Telling her about seeing what my sister became, watching my nieces turn the clock back and become the exact people they'd been a year and half before. Finally, I told Sally about the fear I couldn't get away from, no matter how hard I tried.

"Vicky said she asked Torey about the money. Has Torey mentioned this? Do you think it upset her?"

"Torey never mentioned it, but honestly, I didn't ask either. It took everything in me just to get us home."

Sally sits up straighter, brushes invisible lint off her slacks. "So, Vicky's still a mess, big surprise there, and you drove fifteen hours straight, trying to get away from something you can't name. Do I have it right?"

"Yeah, that's pretty much it." God, I feel stupid.

"How was the trip home?"

"Okay."

"Okay?"

"Nothing happened. I drove, they mostly slept."

"They didn't ask how you were?"

"Maybe I was so quiet, they thought I really was sick with something."

"Because that's what you told them, that you were ill and wanted to go back to the motel on Saturday."

"Yeah."

Sally sighs, "I'm not getting this, Rae. Your sister's impact on the girls is understandable. *Anything* can throw them back into old behavior, and seeing their mother would certainly qualify as a big deal."

"I know." The damp wad of tissue in my hand still grows.

"What happened when you got home?"

"The damned jumpiness didn't go away, and I haven't slept but a few hours since we got back. The girls are worried about me. So am I. I'm afraid I'm not going to be able to keep it together much longer."

"Who's your doctor?" Sally smiles.

"What?"

"Who is your primary physician?" she repeats.

I tell her and she writes it down. "Why do you want to know?" I ask, even though I have a suspicion.

"Because, with your permission, I am going to call this person and ask for three prescriptions—a mild tranquilizer and a sleeping aid, just short-term, and some anti-depressants for the long-term."

"I figured that's what you'd say." I sigh, feeling more

like a failure than ever. I put my head in my hands. *Oh shit.*

"You're not crazy." Sally laughs gently and gives me one-armed hug. "I'm not saying that. I'm saying you need help right now, and pharmacology is just one of the tools that might help." She places a finger on my chin and turns my face towards hers. "You are worth this," she says, looking me in the eyes.

"I'm worth drugs?" I wail like a child and hate myself for it.

"No, no, no, you are worth getting some help. You have a lot on you, Rae. Two troubled children. I know finances are an issue as well. It's a lot for anyone, even an experienced mother which," Sally pauses, and pats my back, "you aren't."

"I know I'm not doing a good job. I don't have any patience. I can't stand the way they are acting."

"You're doing an excellent job."

"I am?"

"Yes, of course."

"Then why do I have to come here?"

"Because for some reason, you couldn't see how unhappy your nieces were, couldn't see they needed help. And that inability shows some sort of family pathology," she adds softly.

I think about it. She's right, I *had* expected them to function without therapy, without any supports. I expected what I gave them to be enough. I'd demanded it to be enough. I feel confused. "How come?"

Sally chuckles. "Maybe because your way of dealing with bad things is to shut down and keep on keeping on. Isn't that what happened when you saw your sister is still the person she's always been?"

I'm startled. Sally's right, that's all that happened. So why the panic? What in the hell did I expect? I look back over the past few days. "I don't seem to have another way," I say, feeling stupid, thick-headed.

"Well, Rae, there are other options and this time, you came to see me. That's different."

"Yes, it is." But if it wasn't for John and the girls' worry and concern, would I? I don't think so.

"So, this time, you're getting some help and I see this as a big step forward for you."

Sally's smiling like she actually means this. Like she's happy for me and the part of me who's always looking for that damned gold star relaxes a little. I guess I'll always be a sucker for approval.

I'm able to smile back. Exhaustion creeps in and I wonder how I'll make the drive back home. "I guess you're right."

"No matter what happens in therapy, Rae, these girls are going to challenge you like nobody's business." Sally has on what I call her "pilgrim" look, a sort of stern, foreboding attitude. I hate it when she's optimistic this way.

"No shit."

She smiles again. "The thing is, it doesn't have to be quite as hard as you make it."

"What do I need to do?"

"Allow assistance into your life. Let me help you look at things differently, let the drugs help you sleep, let anyone who wants to help you, help you."

I think about Chip, who offers to keep the girls so John and I can get away for a long weekend. I believed the girls weren't ready. It never occurred to me to ask them and see what they thought. Maybe they would be nice and offer to stay with Chip. They often are nice.

John, Chip, Lucy, and I guess, Sally. That's it. My family has dwindled down to two children and me, plus these four people to help us. All in all, maybe not too bad a deal. "I'll try."

"Good, Rae. Now you have to make a decision. We can go in one of two ways."

"What do you mean?"

"Well, we could talk about safe stuff, like things you could do right now to help you cope with the anxiety you are experiencing."

"What's the unsafe stuff?"

"We can talk about whatever it is that is creating all this anxiety for you."

I feel sweat break out on my forehead and nausea begins to grab my guts. "I can't even think about it without feeling sick."

"Then let's stick to the safe stuff. Maybe it would be better to talk about the other stuff after you've had a chance to recuperate." She waits for my answer. "It looks like you've been though something fairly traumatic."

"No," I say, surprising myself. I sit up straighter. "It'll be good to sleep, but I'm tired of running. I want to know what the hell is going on with me."

"Good for you." Sally sits back on the couch, no longer patting me on the arm. One distinctive thing about Sally is how comfortable she is in her own skin. Somehow this gives me confidence. "It won't be as hard as you think," she says.

Fear grips my belly again. I breathe through it. "How do you know?"

"How about trusting me? What could it hurt?"

I can't think of a reason not to. "Okay."

"Go back to the moment things fell apart for you."

I think about it. I'd been sitting alone with Vicky, who was putting on a hell of a show. "We'd been there all morning when Vicky finally acknowledged my presence."

"You said she ignored you."

"Yeah, she did, but so did the girls. It was like they went into their own little world. It wasn't that I was excluded so much as I simply didn't exist."

"Then what happened?"

"Well, after Vicky sent the girls away to talk to me, she got into saying a bunch of things I couldn't follow to save my ass."

"Like?"

"I don't know. She wanted to be able to communicate with you through me, or something like that."

"Vicky rarely responds to my reports."

"You send her reports?"

"Of course. I let her know what I'm working on with the girls, ask questions about their childhood, which she's not too forthcoming about."

"Then why did she want me to carry messages to you?"

"Probably she doesn't. What else can you remember?"

"She asked about how Torey was doing, my opinion of

how she was handling everything. I don't know." I put my head in my hands, feeling a headache coming on.

"Is your memory foggy?" she asks.

I turn and see the expression on Sally's face is concern—plain and clear, concern for me—and I realize I don't have to feel criticized by it. I understand that in the past, I have.

Shaken, I continue. "Not exactly, it was more like I couldn't get a handle on where she was coming from. I kept feeling like there was some sort of hidden agenda going on, but she kept saying things that would throw me off, so I was never sure. You know what I mean?"

"You were getting mixed messages." Sally says it like a statement, like a fact.

"I guess so. What exactly is a mixed message?"

"When someone has an agenda different from the one they present." I must look confused, because Sally continues. "When someone is trying to manipulate you, you sense the manipulative attempt. It's a mixed message."

I think about it and it makes sense. "Oh, she was definitely into manipulating, that's for sure."

"Because she wanted Torey's money?"

"Yeah, isn't that enough?" My question is sincere and I whisper it.

Sally sighs. "It's what I'd expect from a narcissist, which is what I suspect your sister is. What did you expect?"

"I expected her to be human." I'm still whispering, staring at the leaves of a plant on the table. They are fat, furry, and a deep, ugly green, on twisting thick stems.

"There's a moment here, Rae," Sally says quietly, almost hypnotically, "when something happens, a moment when it all changes. When is that moment?"

It comes to me in an instant—the moment I stood up to leave. "When I knew she was evil, and when I saw my nieces were poisoned by her and how she did it."

"How, Rae?"

I'm staring, seeing nothing. "The girls have to believe she cares about them, no matter what." I'm crying again. "She bribes and bullies them into it with lies and presents and no rules. She pays them off to not notice. The girls are purposely blind to it—to the fiction of it. She's not a mother. She never tucked them in bed or went to school meetings. I don't think she even cared if they had clean clothes."

I begin shaking.

Sally says, "It's okay, Rae. It's not going to hurt you this time." She begins patting my back again. "You know what happened," she says, urgency underlining each word.

"They're supposed to never confront her about any of this. It's all supposed to be all right. They have a cool mom, not a bad one, and in return..." I have to stop talking for a minute and grab some more tissues from the box.

"In return what, Rae?"

"In return, they get to do anything they want, stay up late, not do homework, watch anything they want on TV. No one cares if it's appropriate or not. They can become total shits, just like her, as long as they don't get in her way."

I take a deep breath and look at Sally. I need verification for the next part. "I don't think Vicky cares about them at all. She only cares about how she looks to them. She only wants to protect herself and she's willing to sacrifice their futures to that end. She's completely corrupt." I feel empty and cold inside. If anti-depressants can help me with this, I'm all for them.

Sally is nodding. "A parent is a powerful creature, Rae." Sally is patting me on the shoulder again. I feel a tiny piece of calmness.

She leans in and whispers. "I bet you know another mother like that, someone who put on a show because they didn't know how to love. Someone else who was unwilling to be honest or to learn how to become an involved, competent parent."

I watch Sally's lips move as she speaks. Her words register in some far-off land. I wait for the message to be translated.

She looks at me intently. "I bet you are intimately familiar with someone who can't be criticized. Someone selfish, so selfish maybe they appeared monstrous."

Momma. Momma and Vicky. Vicky and Momma. Were they the same?

Is that right? My brains feel like rags tied in knots. Momma went to a few PTA meetings when I was in elementary school, I think, maybe once a year for a couple of years. I bet Vicky's teachers never saw her.

When they had to let go of the maid and the cook, the house went to hell. Most of their arguments were about Momma's lack of effort around the place. Was she taking drugs? Momma took "nerve pills" and had a glass of wine in her hand every night from five p.m. on, but she didn't get noticed behind Daddy's drunken rages. I think she liked it that way. She was cold, too, just like Vicky. In a flash, I understand a terror dogging me my entire life.

And I notice in a vague, hazy way how the word—weary—can suddenly have new meaning for you.

"I'm going to miss working with you," Chip says late Thursday as we are setting up for tomorrow's breakfast.

"Thanks, but you may not get rid of me after all," I reply. My efforts to act friendly are not working. It's been a long, fucking night and I only want to go home. "I might be asking Marie to let me stay on."

"How come?" Chip smiles but looks concerned.

"Sally's talking about putting Torey in St. Ursula's."

"The ritzy girls' school?"

"That's the one."

"But why?"

"Because her friend, Jennifer, is going to go there and Torey wants to go, and Torey's therapist thinks it's a good idea, that's why." I stop folding napkins and look at Chip. "I guess it's a good idea."

"Does she have to stay overnight? I think they have a day school."

"I don't know. We haven't gotten that far with it. I have an emergency appointment with the headmistress tomorrow afternoon."

"It's expensive."

"I know. Maybe I can work out a deal. Our therapist is

on the board, imagine that."

"If it helps Torey, it will be good." Chip nudges me and laughs. "What in the world is up with you?"

"Do you ever find yourself living for some day or some time to happen?"

"Yeah, every July I begin yearning for the first day of school." Chip snorts when she laughs. When she notices I'm not smiling, she asks, "Are you waiting for something?"

"I hate January. I'm waiting for spring, I wish it was spring. I'm tired of being cold. I'm tired of my job, my car, my lousy paycheck. I'm tired of my whole damned life right now."

"Where's John tonight?"

"An overnight charter."

"So no quickie?" She's giggling.

"No, no quickie tonight." I sigh and go to the next table and began to bus plates and silverware. We are the last ones here.

"Rae, is that what you're in the dumps about?"

"John? No, I'm glad he's got a job tonight. I know they've been few and far between lately. I'm just thinking about stuff I guess."

"What's it like, being in therapy?"

"Okay, I guess. Sometimes it's weird, like she's psychic."

"Really, that's so cool. What's she psychic about, if you don't mind me asking?"

"You can ask. We were talking about something, what was it? Oh, we were talking about my family, or lack of family, that is."

"You don't have any people?"

I had to laugh. *People*. "I barely have a person. Outside of my nieces, my last living relative is my sister, and now it's like she's dead, too." Chip already knew what happened.

"You have every right to feel that way. Some people are just plain bad, and it's a blessing those kids have someone who's going to raise them right." I love it when Chip is outraged for me. I'm tired of being outraged for myself.

"You know what? I'm beginning to think Vicky's not as bad as she looks. I think she's exactly like our mom. Only difference is she never had the money Mom did to cover her tracks."

Chip hesitates. "That's sad, Rae."

"Yes, it is."

"Does Vicky know how you feel?"

"Yeah, I sent her a letter. I spelled it out pretty clearly. How Mom was, how I see her now. I said I forgave her and there's absolutely nothing she can possibly get from me ever again. Fifty dollars a month until she gets out is it."

"I'm so sorry."

"It's okay. I'm not even sure it's her fault." Chip is frowning, concern for me all over her face. I wish I was in a better place. I'm not happy at all. The pills either don't help or haven't kicked in yet, but at least I'm sleeping.

Chip carries a tub full of dirty dishes back to the kitchen.

Everything in *The Sea Witch* is dark red, and in the dimmed lights of the restaurant, the whole place looks covered in old blood. After everyone leaves we usually switch on the lights so we can see to finish up.

But Chip doesn't switch them on like I expect. Instead she comes back and says, "Let's leave everything for Hazel and go on home."

"Hazel will raise holy hell."

"Hazel is a lazy old bitch who will not be hurt by a little extra work."

That's a surprise. Chip "avoids profanity," to quote her.

"How about coming home with me? Your kids are spending the night at Lucy's anyways. We can sit up in the family room and talk 'til the cows come home."

"That sounds great, but I have to work tomorrow."

"You can wear one of my nightgowns, and I'll wash what you have on and let you borrow a top of mine."

I look down at my black pants and red T-shirt. I have a sweater in my locker. It might work. I don't think anyone would notice. I sure as hell didn't care.

"Please, I want to know more about your psychic therapist." Chip puts her hands together like she's praying. She looks funny.

"Okay." I'm not sure why I'm agreeing to this, except the

drive home to an empty, cold house does not appeal. At least her place is insulated.

By midnight, Chip and I are ensconced in the family room with popcorn and diet drinks. She has dragged the quilt off her bed and brought in pillows and blankets. I hope her husband is all right with this. I feel like an intruder.

"I haven't had a pajama party in fifteen years. This is exactly what I need." She looks like an excited teenager. I wish I could be that happy.

"I'm glad you can enjoy yourself."

"Oh, lighten up. Tell me some more about that brunch thing you were talking about earlier."

"It's probably a stupid idea, but I wonder why Marie doesn't stay open on Sundays."

"Probably because, around here, most places close on Sundays."

"Even restaurants? It doesn't make any sense. That place could be a gold mine if it did a Sunday brunch, or even their normal breakfast."

"Marie wouldn't have the first idea how to put together a brunch. She hasn't changed the menu once in the twenty years they've owned the place."

"I would."

"Really?"

"Yeah, I used to work for a caterer when I was in college. I started doing some catering on my own and I liked it. Buffets were my specialty."

"John says you're a great cook. How about asking us over for dinner one night?"

"Sure, you could bring your whole family to my place Saturday night. John doesn't have a charter this weekend. Does your husband?"

"I don't think so. Wrong time of year for them to be busy. Won't John mind us butting into your romantic time?" Chip giggles again. She loves talking about my love life.

"It's not John asking you."

She looks at me the way she does when I'm blunt. "Okay, yeah. That would be great. You know my youngest is sweet on Melissa."

"No, you're kidding. Is she sweet on him?"

"I don't think she knows he's alive. I only figured it out last week. I help out on Tuesdays. I read to the class at snacktime so the teacher can get a break."

"Melissa told me."

"I noticed my little man scootching over to sit closer to Melissa. He has stars in his eyes when he looks at her. It's so cute."

"It would be fun to watch them together." I eat some popcorn and think about what I could make for a crowd. I hadn't had anyone but John over since we moved in.

Chip is asking me something I don't get. "What did you say?"

"I'm worried about you. You've been really down for a while now."

"I know. I can't seem to shake it. I feel sad all the time.

"Are the kids still acting up?"

"Not so much. Actually, they're doing pretty good. I don't know what my problem is. John's been incredibly patient with me, and with the girls."

"Rae, I don't think you understand something about being a parent."

"What do you mean?" I actually feel the compassion oozing from her and it scares me a little. I'm not in the mood for deep sharing tonight.

"Being a parent is the most emotionally exhausting thing anyone can undertake."

"Then why does anyone do it?"

"Well, I don't want to sound like a greeting card or anything, but it's also the most rewarding thing you can do."

"Sorry, you sound like a greeting card."

She smiles. "Being a parent takes everything you've got and more. You will always find yourself overextended from time to time."

"Well, this is really cheering me up."

"You're not hearing me. You have to cut yourself some slack every now and then. Do something to take care of yourself, like this." She perks up and looks around with her arms extended.

It is nice to be here, warm and nice. I feel myself relax.

"I'm so glad you're back in my life. I used to be so bored."

I can't tell if she's teasing or serious.

"Tell me more about your psychic therapist."

"Okay. Well, there was this time when Sally asked me if I liked older men. I almost fell through the floor."

"Did you used to date older guys?"

"I still do. John's older than me."

"Not that much older. What is he, six years older?"

"Yeah."

"That's not much."

"You're right, but my husband was about twelve years older, and after him, I dated a guy a lot older, for a long time."

Chip asks, "How much older?"

I didn't want to say. "About 25 years."

"That sounds really weird. How old were you then?"

"I was twenty-nine when we started."

"And he was what? Fifty-four?"

"Yeah."

"How long did you date him?"

"Six years."

"Until he was sixty?"

"Yeah."

"Don't get mad at me, but that sounds gross."

"You have no idea." I sigh. "It was great in the beginning but absolutely awful at the end. And when I broke up with him, he was scary."

"Scary how?"

"He thought he could make me come back to him, and when I didn't he punished me."

"You mean physically?"

"No, but nearly as bad, he fired me." It was the first time I'd said it out loud. Hot shame ran through me.

"Did you like, work for him?"

"Yeah, I was his assistant. He was, *is*, head of Juvenile Justice for the State."

"He was your boss?"

"Yeah, and I was an asshole."

Chip chewed some popcorn and took a sip of her soda.

"So he took advantage of the situation."

"And I let him." I sigh.

"So what happened?"

"He sabotaged every interview I could set up for myself and I got desperate. I ended up crawling back to him, begging him to let me have the job I've got now."

"What a bastard. You really have been through it. I don't know how you kept it together."

Not sure about the next part, I hesitate, "I've never told anyone, but he told me if I gave him a blow job, right there in the office, I could have the crappy job I've got."

"You're kidding."

"I wish I was."

"What did you do?"

"I did it. I was scared to death I'd never be employed again. He knew I had the girls, the money issues with them and didn't give a shit. I can't believe I was with such a cold bastard for so long."

"God, Rae, I'm sorry."

"So was I." I look at her. "Something happened to me when it was over. I got so pissed off, I opened my mouth and spit his semen on my blouse, on purpose, right in front of him. I told him if he ever came after me again I'd tell his wife and I had proof. It's the only thing I'm proud of."

"He was married?"

I looked down. "Yes, and I knew it was wrong. I knew the whole time he was married and allowed it to happen anyway. I guess I was desperate."

"But why, Rae? You're pretty, educated, you could have had anyone. Why him?"

"I don't know. I didn't know why the entire time we were together."

"Did he stay away? Did it work?"

"So far it has."

We were both quiet while I hoped I hadn't shocked Chip to the point of never looking at me the same way again.

"Good for you, you didn't let the bastard win." Chip says firmly.

Gratitude for this friend floods me. "I guess not."

"I'm glad."

"Between Dennis and the girls, it was the worst time in my life. Even worse than when my parents died."

"So your therapist is psychic because she guessed you had a thing for older guys?"

"Yeah, that and other stuff. I'm always surprised by what she says."

"How did she know about the older guy stuff?"

"I don't really know. My dad was a lot older than my mom, so maybe that's part of it."

"So what did she say?"

I look up at the ceiling and think. "She said people in conflicted relationships with an opposite sex parent will often live out those conflicts in their romantic relationships."

Chip looks at me for a full minute, then says, "Does she really talk like that?"

"Yeah."

Chip starts to giggle. She's sort of funny-looking, sitting with her hand over her mouth, laughing like a little kid.

I think about some of the words that come from Sally's mouth and start to giggle, too. Then we howl with laughter and I'm feeling better.

Mournful Stew

My nana made this stew for grieving friends. She called it 'Mournful Stew' because she was always sad when she made it. She'd take a stewing hen and fill her stew pot with cold, salted water, throw in the hen and heat it to a low boil for an entire day, with the outside stalks of a package of celery, two unpeeled onions cut in fours, and a few unpeeled, cut-up carrots. The next morning, after it had cooled, she'd strain the broth and remove the meat from the chicken bones and chop it, throwing out the bones and used-up vegetables, refrigerate the broth and remove the fat, which she used in other recipes.

Some of the fat was put back in the stew pot, and she'd add slices of peeled carrots, the rest of the celery chopped up and sautéed with more chopped onions. Once the vegetables were cooked soft and slightly browned, she'd add parsley leaves, minced, if she had some, and the cooled broth. This would cook for an hour or so, then she'd add back the meat and some homemade noodles and boil for fifteen minutes or so. Add salt and pepper to taste.

Very good right away, even better later on.

FEBRUARY

"I'm having trouble getting through to Torey."

"Join the club." I like Sally a whole lot better than I used to but still resent coming here every damn week.

She's not the only one having trouble getting through to Torey, who now resides in some inaccessible place, like a princess in a tower.

Melissa and I are left to share the empty place Torey created. Yesterday morning while I was driving to work, an old Beatles song came on the radio, the one about a girl who leaves home, and I cried the entire commute. Even on the rare weekends we can lure her away from St. Ursula's, she's not really there.

Melissa is permanently sad, unable to handle the loss of her sister. She bit a kid at school and stole another child's crayons and probably some money, though she denies it. The problem is she's such a good liar I can't tell when she's being truthful. The school suspended her for two days. Lucy's response was to enroll her in Sunday school which hurts my Jewish soul, but at this point I'll do anything. I take her to weekly therapy with Dr. Boom. Sally tells me what she does with Melissa is called play therapy.

Melissa does seem a little happier when I pick her up after her sessions with Sally and after church too. Sally told me to structure more play time with her. Melissa likes board games, as long as they have a cartoon character she recognizes, and we play every night before bed. I think it's as therapeutic for me as her, the wonderful mindlessness of it. Sometimes I talk her into coloring in coloring books, which I enjoy even more.

Sally's red glasses slide down a centimeter. Only a client would know this to be a bad sign. "What am I supposed to be dealing with here?"

"What do you mean?"

"Where is the list of things that have happened to Torey? Does anyone know?"

"I still don't know what you're asking me."

"Was she sexually abused before the rape? Did her mother introduce her to drugs? To boyfriends?"

"Oh, that. I don't know for sure. I'm no fan of Vicky's, but I'd have a hard time believing she'd purposely harm Torey. I can't see what Vicky would get out of that. It would blow her cover as a cool mom."

"So far, Vicky still hasn't responded to my last request for information."

"I'll write her and let her know if she doesn't, I'll tell Torey what a crappy mother she's being."

"Will that work?"

"Yeah, probably. It's one of the few things I can hold over her head. She wants to look good in front of the kids."

"Rae, the problem here isn't only lack of information. It's that I'm very good at what I do and Torey is becoming a nut I can't crack. It's not a good sign."

"Why? What do you mean?" A shiver goes down my spine.

"It says something about the level of insults she's sustained."

Another chill runs down my back. *Level of insults*? I don't have a clue what that means. What if Torey had been raped before?

She's still close to her friend Jennifer, who lives at home and is driven to St. Ursula's every day. Jennifer's parents offered to transport Torey as well, but she opted to board.

It seems to take a lot out of Torey to be friendly with me and Melissa. It hurts to watch how carefully she speaks to us, to see the fierceness I've always associated with her dimmed down to the point of being extinguished. Her rare weekends with us seem to cost her and I feel guilty for coveting more. "Is she okay there?"

"At St. Ursula's?"

I nod.

"I think so, as okay as she'd be anywhere. Why do you ask?" Sally gives me a sharp look.

"No reason."

Sally notices when I'm less than forthcoming. She sighs, sort of disgustedly. "I need more family background. Maybe it would give me some clues as to how to approach Torey. I know this was a problem for you before. Would it be okay to ask some questions today?"

"Sure." I'm embarrassed as hell by her reference to the time I lost it. I will tell her any damn thing she ever wanted to know about us and more, just to prove how okay it is.

"When did your parents die?" She pulls out the infamous yellow notepad. I'm beginning to hate the color yellow.

"About nine years ago."

"You were still fairly young to become an orphan, weren't you?" She makes notes on her clipboard then gives me her unsettlingly direct stare.

"I was twenty-seven."

"Not very old to face the world by yourself."

"I was married."

"How long did the marriage last?" Sally flips back some pages on her clipboard. Her eyebrows shoot up almost to her hairline. I wonder what she's looking for. I want to say I'm still married, just to shake her up.

"The marriage fell apart shortly afterwards." I hate that I still feel awkward about it.

"So a lot happened to you in a very short time."

"I guess so." I'm beginning to feel antsy. Maybe this is the way John feels when I want to talk about his past.

"So how did your parents die?"

"I've always considered it a murder/suicide."

Good, that stops her. Sally looks over her glasses, her ice-crystal blue eyes a little more penetrating than I'm comfortable with.

"What did the police consider it?" she asks after a moment.

"An accident with two fatalities caused by a drunk driver," I respond in flat tones.

"Your dad was driving." It isn't a question.

"Yes."

"And your mother was the passenger?"

"Yes, and there were no other vehicles involved, just Momma, Daddy and a bridge abutment, outside of Richmond on a country road they had no business being on. At least I never could find out why they were there."

"How old were your sister and Torey when this happened?"

I have to think. "Torey was four and Vicky nineteen. They'd moved to North Carolina with a guy Vicky married the year before. I think taking Torey from them was the worst thing she ever did to them. I will always wonder what might have happened if she hadn't left."

"Your parents were close to Torey?" Sally is scribbling away.

"Torey was the only happy spot in their lives by then. Vicky was only fifteen when Torey was born, and they lived with my parents until she met Richard, married him, and moved away. I don't think my parents ever got over losing Torey."

"How was Richard with Torey?"

"Distant. He was distant from everyone. Even Vicky who probably realized right away she'd made a mistake, but she wouldn't admit to it."

"Was Richard into drugs?"

"Oh, yes. Nearly everyone Vicky dated shared her hobby."

"How long did the marriage last?"

"Until a few months after my parents died."

Sally smiles. "So you both lost your parents and husbands. Interesting, how did Torey take their deaths?"

"Torey didn't seem like herself at the funeral. She was very withdrawn. I remember trying to talk to her and not getting very far. I kept her after the funeral, at my parents' house while I got things ready to sell. I got a leave of absence from work and Vicky let her stay. I think even she was worried about Torey."

The eyebrows shoot back up while Sally waits for me to finish.

"You know what? I'm realizing something as I'm sitting here. This feeling I've got?"

Sally nods.

"It feels exactly like when my parents died. I'm grieving Torey, aren't I?" My eyes fill.

Sally nods again. Her eyes are kind instead of sharp and icy. It doesn't change a damn thing, but sometimes it's good to understand a few things.

"After we buried our parents, Vicky took her inheritance and lost any restraint she'd ever had. She moved on from Richard, who was bad, to a crowd that was horrible. I hated the thought of Torey exposed to people like that."

"Did you ever try to get Torey?"

"Always. I drove to North Carolina almost every weekend to get her while Vicky was partying and blowing her money. I tried to get custody, but Vicky wouldn't go that far. She knew she'd lose her power over me if she gave up Torey."

"What happened next?"

"It took a while before Vicky crashed. The summer Torey was six Vicky went into rehab. She was so ill it took her longer to detox than normal and then she did a thirty-day program. I was probably crazy, but I believed with my whole heart she was going to make it. That whole summer I was on some sort of insane cloud nine. I don't remember being happier."

"I never knew Torey lived with you. How did that go?"

"Like I said, great. I think part of the high I was on was having a family again. You know, when Vicky and I were growing up, I was so much older I was more like an aunt than a sister. But all of a sudden we were sisters, united in giving Torey this wonderful life. And Torey bloomed that summer. I had her in swimming lessons, art camp, all sorts of things. We visited Vicky nearly every weekend, went on little trips. I remember a great weekend we had in the Smoky Mountains.

I was proud of Vicky then." I say the last part with a crack in my voice. It had been a long, long time since I visited those days.

"What happened?"

"Vicky got back on her feet, Torey went home, Vicky met another guy."

"Another drug addict?"

"Actually, no. Billy was a regular guy, sort of low rent."

"Low rent?" Sally looks confused.

"I mean sort of a redneck, but okay. Sometimes he drank too much beer, but wasn't a drunk or anything. He was a mechanic, a car mechanic, and he spent a lot of time with his buddies. Like I said, he was a good ol' boy. I only worried about him with Torey because of the race thing."

"Was he racist?"

"Not so much, but his family was, and probably most of his friends."

"Badly racist?"

"Yeah. It's bad everywhere. Torey told me about it, some of the remarks. It sounded fairly rough."

Sally is writing. I wait for her to catch up.

Sally peers at me over her glasses. "Wait a minute. Billy is Billy Ames, Melissa's father, right?"

"Yeah, but Vicky kicked him out when Melissa was six or seven weeks old. She wouldn't tell me why, which was when I got suspicious.

"Vicky was using again?"

"I think so. By the time Melissa was a few months old, Vicky was openly back into the men who would supply her with drugs. Torey was eight and basically raising an infant by herself, unless Billy or his mother had Melissa. I was back going down there every weekend to get Torey and sometimes the baby."

"So then what happened?"

"I confronted my sister and asked her to go back into rehab."

"I take it she didn't."

"Nope, said she'd never do that again. She told me I was to never stick my nose into her business again if I wanted to see my nieces. She also told me to quit coming down so often."

"Then what happened?"

"I didn't know what to do so I left them alone for a while." I watch Sally to see her response to what I'm about to say. "I was losing it. I was so frantic about the girls I nearly got us all in an accident, and that woke me up, so when Vicky told me to stay away I did—for the girls' sake as well as mine."

"Were you having panic attacks?"

"No, although I was close to it. I was a basket case and then after a month of calming down and getting my act back together, I stopped by. The place was a mess, and when I say mess, I mean a nightmare. Unsanitary. Melissa was six months old and had sores from dirty diapers. There was no electricity and they'd been alone for a while. Torey was obviously hungry, and they were eating from a huge jar of peanut butter. That was pretty much all the food in the house. I turned Vicky in to Social Services. I didn't see the girls again until last year when Vicky was arrested."

"Did Social Services do anything?"

"Torey told me Vicky cleaned up her act for a while. She was charged with neglect and had to make some court appearances and random drug screens for a year, but as soon as she got the court off her back, she was back into her old ways."

"What happened with your nieces?"

"I don't know. I didn't see them or have contact with them. Vicky wouldn't allow it. She even got a restraining order against me. I tried talking to the social worker assigned to their case, but there was nothing she could do."

"So you were alone again."

"Yep, I had my job and was in a relationship, but I didn't have any family anymore, that's for sure."

Sally sighs. She starts flipping pages on her clipboard again, looking for something. I excuse myself and ask for directions to the bathroom. I go through glass doors that glide open easily, and follow Sally's directions down the hall to the bathroom. It's old-fashioned with tired-looking flowered wallpaper and cracked baby blue ceramic tiles. I guess she hasn't gotten this far in her decorating. On my way back to the sunroom, I find Sally in the kitchen.

"Would you like some tea?" she asks. She already has two mugs out.

"That would be nice." I wonder if I should go back out on the porch or wait for Sally to finish making it. I feel awkward standing here, waiting.

"It seems everyone in your family had severe behavioral problems, except for you. Even with your divorce, you were the different one." She hands me a mug, and I follow her out to the sunroom.

"How do you mean?"

"Meaning you got out, didn't hang around for the abuse. How come? Do you know?"

"I've thought about that a lot, actually." I sit back in my place on the sofa. It's funny how I do that, find a spot and claim it. "I think it's because I learned to get good grades."

Sally laughs. "That's an interesting response. What do you mean?"

"I think I learned to work hard and get positive feedback from teachers and stuff, and it carried over into my adult life."

"You think that made the difference?"

"Maybe, I'm not sure."

"Did you ever get positive responses from your family?"

"Not much, mostly outside the family."

"So your sources of hope and inspiration came from teachers, employers, things like that?"

I'd never thought of it that way, but it's exactly where I got whatever it was that made me think it was possible to save myself. "Yes, and my grandmother."

"Maternal or paternal?"

"Daddy's mom, the Jewish side. I always felt more at home on that side, than my mother's family."

"So that's a nice tradition to come from, and I take it your bubbeh was a positive influence."

I smile at the Yiddish term for grandmother. No one had said the word to me in years. "Yes, my bubbeh was a wonderful influence."

"So how did all that play itself out in adulthood?"

"Oh, I was hard-working, smart, and excellent at

sucking up. When you work for the state, there are endless opportunities to suck up. And I was very good at it. It's all who you know and how to play the game, and I was very good at appearing competent. You know, acting."

"Rae." Sally's giving me her kindly, stop-being-hard-on-yourself look. "I think a lot of people do that. It's not the worst coping mechanism to adopt."

"I'm not putting myself down. I'm glad I've got a professional persona. I don't think I'd be nearly as effective at work without it. I'm also glad hard work never scared me. I wasn't afraid to try for scholarships. I got some, too. I worked my ass off at school and with the catering business, and I started to pay for things my scholarship didn't cover. My parents had no money to help by then."

"So that's a positive outcome."

"It was. I'm glad I went to college, grateful I could find a way to make it work, but afterwards I…"

"What?"

"My job became my entire life. And like I said, it was important for to me to do well, better than well." I remembered my exhaustion and coming home to an empty condo after ten or eleven hours at work, the scared feeling of knowing I was losing ground and not knowing why.

"Earlier you said you lost your job?"

"Yeah, I was the assistant deputy director for the Department of Juvenile Justice."

"Sounds like an important position."

"It was."

"Did the girls cause you to lose it?"

"No, I did that all by myself a few months before I got them."

"You lost your job before you got them?" Sally looks confused and scans her legal pad sheets.

"Not exactly."

"Can you tell me what happened?" She has that damned clipboard ready in her lap.

"I ended an affair with someone who had a lot of power, the older guy I told you about." I can feel myself blush.

"How did that cost you your job?" Sally sounds confused.

"Because he could do what he wanted. After he figured out I wasn't coming back to him, after I got the girls, he got rid of me. He called it a budget cut, but it wasn't. It was my punishment for dumping him. Everyone knew it, too."

"That must have been difficult."

"It was. It was difficult, scary, and a whole lot of things, but I knew going back to him wasn't an option."

"Then what happened?"

"At first, I wasn't too worried about getting another job, but then, when I had a hard time getting interviews, much less another job, I did get scared. I only found out what was going on when an old boss took pity on me and told me Dennis Rielly, the rat bastard, was behind it."

"Dennis Rielly?"

"Yeah, have you heard of him?"

"His name sounds vaguely familiar. Who is he?"

"He was my boss, the director of Juvenile Justice."

"Yes, I've heard of him. Why'd you end the affair?"

I take a deep breath. This is the hard part. "Because he was too old for me, and too married, and when I found out he had another mistress in the department besides me, it became very clear I'd wasted six years of my life." The silence fills with my shame.

"So you woke up?" Sally says.

"Yeah, I guess so. For a saint, I haven't been very saintly, have I?"

"Well, I think you're on the way to making up for it." She sits back on the couch and gives me her direct stare.

I'm nervous. I want to say something, but it's hard to get it out. "I wish I could believe I'm making up for my mistakes."

"You don't?" Sally's patient. I'll give her that. She'll sit and wait until I spill the beans on my own.

"No, I don't. I've… I've been wondering about something, and I'd like if you'd tell me the truth."

"I usually do, don't I?"

"I think so." God, I feel stupid. "The truth is even though I worked very hard at my job, I was too blind to see I was alienating everyone in the department for being, basically, a slut."

"So you didn't see it until when?"

"When I realized I was supposed to put up with his newest slut, the same way his wife put up with me."

"So that's when you broke off the relationship."

"Yes."

"I'm not seeing a question here."

"Afterwards, when I lost my job to Dennis's phony budget cut, I saw how nearly everyone hated me. At the time it was an even more mind-blowing revelation than finding out about Dennis's vengefulness. What I finally understood was, even though I worked really hard, I never deserved any position I'd ever had with the department. And everybody knew it but me."

"I'm still not hearing a question."

"That's when I began to think that maybe Vicky and I were flawed, just basically flawed in some way that makes us unable to tell right from wrong."

Sally sighs and sits back. I feel her eyes on me and am unable to look back. "It sounds to me like you paid for your mistake and it would be all right to forgive yourself now."

"Really?"

"Yes, really. Honestly, Rae. A lot of women fall for the powerful father figure routine. You're hardly the first."

It feels bad to have it labeled that way. I feel bad. "You're right, I'm not the first."

"You know, for a smart person, you don't allow yourself to mess up much, do you? Do you think smart people aren't supposed to make mistakes? Is that part of being smart?"

She's being sarcastic and I'm not sure what to say.

"Everybody messes up. It is how humanity learns. I can't change that for you, Rae. You really need to forgive yourself and learn from your mistakes. That's all they are good for, learning."

Some shame leaks out. I can feel it leaving like a punctured balloon. I take the first deep breath I can remember in a while. "I still don't understand."

"Think about it, Rae. You knew it was wrong, but you did it anyway. It's the control thing. When you are involved in controlling everything outside you, then you aren't paying too much attention to the insides, are you?"

"I guess not."

"So the neglected insides go crazy, and you start doing stupid things like sabotaging your job with risky behavior."

"Risky?"

"Yeah, like dating the boss."

"Oh. So what's the alternative?"

"Begin by paying attention to your feelings and letting go of the control thing. It's a journey, not something you're going to accomplish overnight, but you could start by cutting yourself a little slack. Compassion starts at home."

I think about my self-inflicted blindness and how painful it was to wake up to, but I *did* accept responsibility and make some difficult changes. It *had* been a lesson. "Okay. You're right, and beating myself up for things over and done with doesn't do any good. It's just I feel so damn guilty. I can't seem to let go of it."

"Why? What are you feeling so guilty about?"

It comes out in a rush. "Do you think if I'd bothered to get Torey the help she needed when I got custody of her, maybe none of this would have happened? Maybe she wouldn't have run off and all the crap that happened wouldn't have. Sometimes I look at her and feel like I destroyed something beautiful. She used to be so alive, you know? She's not like that anymore." I hang my head. This sadness seems to have no end.

"I remember a child with an obvious oppositional-defiant disorder." Sally speaks softly.

"I bet you didn't know I headed up a committee that designed programs for kids coming from substance-abusing parents. I'm actually well versed on the subject." I look at Sally with some defiance of my own.

"Most people can't see issues in their own families. That's why therapists never treat family members; you need some detachment to see the issues driving a situation."

"I've worried for years that Torey might have been sexually abused by some bottom-feeder boyfriend of Vicky's. I've asked her and she says no, but I'm not sure I believe her."

"So why didn't you get her some help?"

I don't want to tell her I'm a stinking coward. I sit in this beautiful room and wait for something brave to speak. "I didn't because of the bad experience I had in my one and only attempt at therapy."

No response.

"I went to a therapist to save a marriage to a man so insensitive I couldn't stand to be in the same room with him."

"What did he do?"

"Who? The therapist or the husband?"

"Either, both."

"My husband fucked around on me the entire time we were together, even before we got married, only he did it online, you know, computer porn."

"What did the therapist do?"

"He wanted me to *investigate* myself as a woman."

Sally's quiet for a moment. "Sounds like you had two assholes on your hands."

"Three, counting myself." I look to see Sally's reaction, but there isn't any. "The thing is I tried to do what the therapist said and got into a very bad place, emotionally. I got to believing our problems were my fault. I can't tell you how difficult it was to get out of that marriage and put myself back together. Now I'm thinking about when Torey tried to tell me how tough her life was." My head sinks down. "All I did was talk to her about moving somewhere. I didn't take her problems seriously. I think I've had a bad taste in my mouth since my experience with the marriage counselor and now Torey is paying for it."

"Sounds reasonable. Besides, why would you?" Sally's peering over her glasses.

"Why would I what?"

"Why would you take Torey seriously?"

"What do you mean?"

"No one ever took your pain seriously. You had addicted parents and their problems were always more important than you. You probably had the same expectations for Torey that they had for you—do well no matter what the circumstances were. After all, you managed, and managed quite well."

"Are you serious?"

"Very." Sally responds as if I'm insulting her.

"I don't think I've managed all that well. And Torey's childhood was hell compared to mine."

"How do you know?"

"It's pretty obvious, isn't it?"

"Not really. And even if you'd gotten her into therapy right away, there's no guarantee that the exact same thing wouldn't have happened."

"Are you sure?"

"Rae."

"What?"

"You are being way too hard on yourself. All any of us can do is try. If she was sexually abused before you got her, we can try to help her with it, along with the rapes, and the loss of her mother, father, grandparents, and everything else she has lost. We can try and help her and Melissa sort through all the things they've experienced, and maybe put some of it behind them, maybe not."

Sally seems to be waiting for me to say something. I don't know what.

"Therapy is a crap shoot, just like life." Sally's looking hard at me.

I stare back, wondering what she's trying to get across.

"Sometimes a kid can be too damaged to be helped," she says.

"God, I hope not," I whisper.

"Me too, but Torey's a wild card at this point. Maybe she's able to get better, but then again, maybe she's seen too much, been through too much. I don't know."

"I want her to win."

"So do I. What I need from you right now is to understand two things—what to expect, which isn't a miracle, and that you aren't to blame for Torey's problems. We have to start where we are."

"I'm not sure I'm following."

"Okay, first of all, I need you to be committed to this process. Whatever happened to you with the marriage counselor sounds like a bad experience."

"It was. It took me a long time to get over it."

"I'm sorry, Rae. For all therapists everywhere, I apologize, deeply and profoundly. I wish things like that never happened. Unfortunately they do all the time. Luckily though, one bad therapist doesn't have to spoil the rest for you."

"I know." I pull at a thread in my jacket. A patch of sunlight has crept over my feet and feels good. "Torey is…" I can't think of how to put this. "She's so important to me. I can't distance from her anymore. I think I used to." Tears well in my eyes.

"When did that start?" Sally's expression changes, now she looks almost maternal.

"I'm not sure." When *did* it start? I don't remember. We were so close once. "Since before Vicky was locked up."

"How come?"

"After I turned Vicky in, the few times I spoke to Torey on the phone, things were different."

"Different how?"

"Torey was never herself with me again, like I was cut off or something."

"So Torey put up a wall and you did, too."

"Yeah, I guess, at least until the rape and then everything changed. That's when the wall fell for me."

"Torey's a kid who has been lied to, neglected, abandoned in every way imaginable. It's not like she's able to respond right away." Sally's voice holds a concerned note.

"I know. I don't expect her to."

"Then what?"

"Since then…" I wave my hand in the air, trying to encompass it all, whatever in the hell *it* is.

Sally fills in. "All the stuff that's happened."

"Yeah." I blow my nose. "But now she's shutting me out all over again." I'm so sick of crying all the damned time.

"She needs some time now, Rae," Sally says gently.

"I know, I know. I wish I didn't feel so left out or so scared."

"Look, you have some loss issues, too. Try not to let them leak into this situation, and understand, she's always cared for other people, her mother, Melissa. This is the first time she's had the opportunity to think only of herself."

"Is that good?"

"It's good, but remember, she's very depressed. Maybe that's upsetting you, too."

"How come her medications aren't helping?"

"They are, Rae. You have to understand, it goes deep. I'm worried, too."

"Do you think things will ever resemble anything normal for her?"

Sally smiles. "I don't have the foggiest notion what normal is. If you ever find out, please tell me." She smiles. "You know what? You are really touching my heart today."

"How come?"

"This caring, this love for Torey. I'm very impressed."

That feels nice.

"I'm going to tell you something that I hadn't planned to say. I believe Torey is in crisis right now, and your fears for her are accurate as hell."

I'm oddly comforted and take a deep breath.

"Torey's restlessness is increasing, and if I can't get her to open up I'm afraid she'll run again or do something to get herself thrown out of school."

Which states, clearly and out-loud, all the fears dogging my heels. "And you don't know how many more failures Torey can take."

"Exactly. I want to try something radical with Torey, soon. Torey is the primary focus of this therapy, and I have to get her involved somehow. I think I'm going to try and use Melissa as bait to get to Torey's heart and mind."

"I have no idea what you are talking about." It sounds like Sally is speaking to herself. She seems distracted and far away, very unlike her.

"Oh, sorry, I'm still thinking some things through. I was saying the process will be painful for her and for you too, at times. You can count on being a target, a substitute for her mother's sins."

"Oh, great."

"Well, you're the one who wants things to get normal." She smiles again. "I will protect you as much as I can, but sometimes I won't be able to and it won't be easy. I want you to take the hit if Torey says or does something ugly to you when we do this, no matter what."

"I don't understand, do what?"

"Oh, this thing I'm thinking about. I'll coach you before we get to it."

"It sounds tricky."

"You have no idea." Sally stands up and brushes invisible crumbs off her black slacks. "The thing I want to do? I'd like to have Lucy here for that session as well, and we'll need to set aside at least three hours for it."

"Lucy? Why?"

"Another perspective on the girls. I'll use her to check in about Melissa's progress. It's how I'm going to involve Torey, plus I need two adults to pull this off.

"Pull what off?"

"This radical thing I'm telling you about."

"What is it?"

"It's called holding therapy, I'm going to try and box her in, so I can lure her out." Sally smiles like I know exactly what she means. "I'll need a couple of sessions to prepare Torey."

"So when will it happen?"

"A few weeks, maybe a month, I'm going to have to play this by ear, timing can be everything."

"I hope it works."

"So do I."

Driving to pick up Melissa, I realize I'm feeling better. I'm working tonight, so we only have time for pizza before she goes back to Lucy's for the night. She wanted John to come, too, but he's busy with something, so it will be only us. For some reason, I'm glad. I can't wait to see her.

Sweet Potato Corn Bread Muffins

Two cups cooked mashed sweet potato, mixed well, with one cup buttermilk and one-half cup of brown sugar, packed.

One cup flour and one cup corn meal, sifted with two teaspoons salt and one tablespoon of baking powder.

Mix wet into dry, adding half a stick of melted butter at the end, and if needed, more buttermilk to make a very wet batter.

Put in paper-lined muffin tins, and bake at 400 degrees until done, approximately ten to twelve minutes.

March

I'm finishing up my shiny new brunch at *The Sea Witch*. Our brunches are so slammed we are lucky to get out of there before four p.m. It's time to think about hiring more help.

If I was willing to stay open, we could probably stay busy until eight or so. At least that's what Chip thinks, but I'm pushing my physical limits as it is.

Today is the second Sunday in March. We've been doing the brunch thing since the end of February, three Sundays, and we've done well.

Chip says April is when the yachts start their migrations and that's when businesses around here begin to pick up with summer people coming around to check on their cottages, see how things fared over the winter.

If we get any busier, we might end up with a line outside the front door. That would be wild, a business in Cornwallis with a line waiting to get in. Of course, we'll have to wait and see what happens once the novelty dies down.

Chip comes over. "Any chance I can talk you into making more pies?"

I knew she's joking, so I only have to glare.

"So sue me, I enjoy being part of a huge success." Chip's eyes sparkle like she's falling in love. I've never seen her so happy, and despite my misgivings about this venture, part of me feels proud as hell that we seem to be pulling it off.

"I wish I could be as relaxed and happy about it as you

are."

"Well, see, you're the artist. I'm only the artist's manager. All the pressure is on you."

"I need more help back there."

"I've been telling you that since we started. I think you could use two more people."

"I thought Torey would be here more than she is." I'm unhappy about that, and not looking forward to cleaning up. We have to get the kitchen and dining room in the exact shape it was when Marie closed on Saturday night. Marie likes this arrangement. She makes money without even getting out of bed.

"If you were thirteen and had to choose between being a kitchen wench or hanging out with your friends, which would you choose?"

"I would choose to be a responsible person and help my aunt."

"Liar."

"Where am I going to get good help? I don't want another goofball who doesn't even bother showing up."

"Why not ask Emmaline? After all, she didn't kill you for taking over her kitchen on Sundays. She even seems to like you." Chip laughs.

I laugh, too. Last Sunday Emmaline came in for brunch. Chip told me later her blood froze when she saw Emmaline come up the steps.

Emmaline is hard to miss. She's tall, strong, a mountain of a woman, and the primary cook at *The Sea Witch* for as long as anyone can remember. She's the backbone of the restaurant and carries its weight as lightly as the extra-large, man's winter coat resting on her shoulders and exposing her wrists. She rarely speaks. Somehow her silence translated into a reputation of someone who never forgot any transgression committed against her, ever.

Even Marie keeps her distance. I guess she knows her temper would be a dangerous commodity if she pissed off the giant.

Emmaline never hesitated at the register near the sign saying, "Please wait for Hostess to seat you." Chip reported a moment of confusion when Emmaline sat down at a booth and looked around for service. Luckily, Chip got her wits about her and went over before any of our teenage wait staff attempted to correct Emmaline's error.

Evidently, Emmaline had never been to a brunch before and didn't understand the protocols involved. Chip coolly went to the buffet and filled a plate for her. She did this a number of times and told Emmaline it was free of charge and we hoped she would give us some pointers on how to make it better.

According to Chip, Emmaline took her time and ate every scrap. People seated in the restaurant seemed nervous. No one had actually seen her eat in public before, and it was anyone's guess what to expect, including Chip's.

When Emmaline finished, she heaved her bulk out of the booth and, in her size thirteen work boots, stomped towards the kitchen.

Chip had been so busy watching Emmaline she'd forgotten to tell me what was going on. Then it was too late. She said she stood helplessly watching the large dark shape move towards unsuspecting me, praying for a good outcome.

I had Torey helping in the kitchen because the girl I hired hadn't shown up. I saw terror in Torey's eyes and looked in the doorway to see what was causing it.

I have to admit I was startled, too. But I knew Emmaline from working here and had always liked her. I never understood why everyone was so intimidated, because once you got past her size, she was a very nice person.

We said hi to each other, and then Emmaline made the longest speech anyone had ever heard. I was glad I had Torey as a witness, because no one would've believed me.

She said, "Dat ol' bitch Marie wouldn't know a good thang if it spit in her face. I tole her it was time to do new stuff around here, but she don't listen to me, naw sir."

I already knew Emmaline ended most of her brief sentences with "naw sir," so I understood she wasn't saying "no sir" to me.

She went on, "I tried to get her to let me try new stuff, but she got real nervous-acting and said she didn't like no changes." Then Emmaline reached in her purse. Torey later told me she was afraid Emmaline was going to pull out a gun.

I remember thinking how silly it looked, the little, black, old-lady handbag, hanging like a doll's purse from her ham hock of an arm. She found a card with writing on it and handed it to me.

In beautiful, old-fashioned copperplate script, Emmaline had written out her recipe for Sweet Potato Corn Bread Muffins.

"Dat ol' bitch don't want nothing I had, so I'm giving it to you."

And before I could say much more than "Thanks, Emmaline" to her back, she clomped away.

Chip said the entire restaurant went quiet when Emmaline went into the kitchen. People had been like statues, waiting to see what she planned to do to me. I guess it was real anti-climactic when all she did was leave.

Chip and I were laughing, but I noticed Emmaline's recipe was a hit. Next week I'd have to make double what I'd made this time if it was going to last. I thought about what Chip said. "That's not a bad idea. I bet old Emmaline could tell me who would be a good worker and who I couldn't count on."

"She sure could."

Chip is scanning the buffet table. She hates to see it half-gone like it is, but it's after two, time for these people to get going.

This happens every Sunday after we lock the doors. Everyone still left inside seems to hunker down for the real eating. I think they feel they needed to finish up the buffet for us before they leave, like it's bad manners or something to leave a drop.

Chip starts two more pots of coffee and breaks up a gabfest with two of our wait staff. She comes back to where I am standing.

"Is Ronnie interested in Fortuna?" I point to the kids she got back to work.

"I think so. He's done everything but turn green to get her attention today."

"Ah, young love."

"Speaking of romance, how is the hottest couple in town?"

"Are you speaking of Jonathan and I?" I ask archly.

"Who else?"

"Will people around here ever get tired of talking about us?"

"Probably not. People in this town never get tired of talking about anything." Chip folds her arms and leans toward me, speaking in a whisper, as if sharing good gossip. "Why people in this town still talk about the time Wendell Jackson was caught with Kaiser Blight's widow, and him a married man."

"Who in the world is Wendell Jackson?"

She points to an old man sitting at a booth near the corner.

"Who's he sitting with?"

"His wife."

Conspiratorially behind my hand, I ask, "How long ago did the Widow Blight affair occur?" It's difficult imagining the elderly gentleman I'm looking at in a compromising position.

"Maybe forty years ago, maybe longer, I don't know."

It's always fun to laugh with Chip, but this damned exhaustion will not go away. "I'm too tired to move. I need to go back there and clean up."

"How about I get Ronnie and Fortuna to go back and start washing up?"

"Good idea. Tell Ronnie if he doesn't do a good job, we won't leave them alone again."

"I will. How about you pour us two coffees and we can sit for a minute?"

She goes off and gets the cleaning started. I pour coffee in white mugs and am grateful to sit. Chip comes back and sits across from me in the booth.

"We need to think about staying open longer." The woman has a one-track mind. I should know by now she isn't concerned about me. She's only concerned with promoting her agenda, which includes working me to death.

"*You* think about it," I say. "I told you, I can't do what

I'm doing now."

"We could make so much money you could quit your probation job. Admit it, that's what you want to do."

We'd just worked thirteen hours straight and she looks like she could do it all over again. "Where in the hell are you getting your energy?"

"It's going to be big, Rae, real big." She's looking around the room, eyes sparkling.

"Glad you think so. But I'm waiting to see if this lasts. Then maybe, just maybe, I'll work for the City of Williamsburg part-time and keep *The Sea Witch* open longer on Sundays."

"That would be great. We could stay open until nine or ten in the summer. Summer people like to eat late." Then she's off and running, chattering about hiring shifts, food purchases, getting into the waffle business. When I hear John's name, I tune back in.

"So why is he acting like that?" she asks.

"Acting like what?"

"Like I was saying. Michael said he got into a big argument with his charter yesterday. The guy was a jerk, but Michael said John nearly cold-cocked him."

"John? My John nearly in a fight? I don't believe it."

"Michael isn't the only one. Somebody else was asking about him. Who was it?" Chip stares out the window next to us, trying to remember.

"Now that I think about it, he's been weird around me, too. His mom called and invited us to his dad's birthday party. I said we'd come, but John hasn't said a thing about it to me. I wonder if he knows she's asked us? I'm not sure how to handle it."

"That sounds uncomfortable."

"It is."

"Are you seeing him tonight?"

My relationship with John is about the only topic Chip will allow to interrupt conversations about our business.

"No, he's putting up some cabinets for his mom and doing some other stuff around the house for her. I've got Lucy keeping Melissa tonight and I'm taking off tomorrow."

I stretch my arms over my head.

"This is the first time I will be alone for twenty-four hours straight in..." I can't remember. I'd had the girls how long? "In a year and a half." I look at Chip. I'm startled to realize it *had* been that long.

She chuckles. "Welcome to the trenches of motherhood, but I'm glad you're taking some time for yourself. Good for you."

Back in the kitchen, it looks like Ronnie and Fortuna are doing a decent job. Ronnie is scraping and rinsing, and Fortuna is loading the washer.

"Ronnie, you missed all this," she says in a soft Latin accent. She's handing a bowl back to him. They both look at me as I get nearer.

"Everything okay here?"

"Yes, Mrs. Green," Fortuna answers.

"Fortuna, you look like you know what you're doing. I'm putting you in charge, all right?"

She gives me a big smile. "Yes, Mrs. Green."

I'm too tired to tell her, again, to call me Rae. I go back to the food locker and pull out some bacon for the morning. I do a few things to help out Hazel, the breakfast cook. I want to stay on her good side.

Suddenly John's behind me, kissing my neck. I melt, turn and put my arms around his neck. "What are you doing here?" I ask in his ear.

"I did everything Mumma had on her list, and she didn't even feed me."

"You poor, poor man." I sympathize, hugging him.

He holds me at arm's length and asks, "What's up? You look awful."

"I'm tired. I'm overtired. This is how I get when I overdo it."

"You want me to pick up Melissa for you?"

He's concerned. I like that so much. "No, you don't have to. She's spending the night."

"At Lucy's?" John's waggling his eyebrows at me. It's his silly version of a leer.

"Yes, at Lucy's, but you can forget any funny stuff tonight. I'm going home by myself. I need some time to veg."

"You want to be alone?"

He follows me to the dining room, but I notice he gets tense the minute we walk in. Maybe it's my imagination. It's a quarter to four, and we still have a few diners in the back of the restaurant. Chip looks at me and holds up her hands as if saying, "What can I do?"

The buffet is worn down to a nub, but there's enough left for one more plate. He gets what's left and I carry some empty bowls back to the kitchen to finish cleaning up. At four, I tell Fortuna and Ronnie to go on home. I know Chip will have everything out front done up soon. A little later, she comes in the kitchen with John. He's carrying his coffee cup and plates.

"Everyone's finally left and I'm leaving too. Are you going to be all right with this monster that gets into fights with his customers?" She shoves John, laughing.

"Yeah, go. I'm almost done here. I'll call you Tuesday."

"Okay, bye."

John's washing his stuff at the sink. He looks tired, too. "What's up with the fighting?" I can't resist finding out.

"Oh, you heard, huh?"

I smile. "Yeah, I did. It's today's big story."

"The guy was an asshole, Rae, didn't want to pay for the charter because we didn't get any tuna, and of course he reminded me, he specifically asked for tuna. I mean, what do they think? I'm gonna call up God and order something? He's not the first one this week, either. It just gets worse and worse. All some guys need is a pocketful of money, and man, they think they rule the fucking universe. You should have seen this one, a class-A shithole."

"You want to sit down and talk a while?"

"We could go upstairs." He waggles his eyebrows again.

"I'm serious, John. I'm too tired for the cure. Keep it in your pants tonight."

"What the fuck is up with you?"

"I'm tired, I told you. Shit, look at me, don't I look tired?"

"Yeah, but I am, too. So what's the big deal?"

I try to tell myself I'm overtired and should kiss him goodnight and go home. A smart woman would have done that. I realize I'm not a smart woman. "The big deal? I don't know. What *is* the big deal?"

John's startled. I can tell by the startled look on his face. For a worn-out person, I catch on quick. "Tell me what the big deal is, John. I can't figure it out." Maybe, since Torey's not willing to fight with me anymore, I need another outlet. John's still standing there doing a great imitation of a wooden post. "Say something, damn it."

"I don't know what you want me to say, Rae."

"Oh, God!" I stomp to the other side of the room. I see him standing there, looking so stupid. "I would like to know if there is a male entity in the universe who never, ever says that. I bet male space aliens say that to their females."

"What the hell are you talking about?"

"I bet dude aliens say crap like, 'What do you want me to say?' I'm so sick of that shit!"

"Are you okay, Rae?"

"Me! Am I okay? Explain something to me, why would I ask you anything, ever, if I was planning on telling you what to say?"

"What the fuck are you talking about?"

"See, John, let me explain what talking is. First, I say something, then you say something. It's not, I say something, tell you what to say, and then you say what I tell you. That's not a conversation."

I stand, glaring at him. I'm getting energized. I can see him struggling with not asking me some form of "what do you want me to say," and I feel like a boxer, itching to throw another punch.

"Rae, did something piss you off today?"

"As a matter of fact, yes. You did."

"What?"

"You don't want me around your family." I hadn't expected to say this, but am glad it's out in the open. I am so sick of all the damned unclear things in my life.

"That is not true."

"Bullshit fucking liar!" I scream and throw a clean bowl at him. I know it's wrong to throw things, but God it feels good. I wonder exactly how long I've been this pissed off at him, and not known it.

He ducks. It's a lightweight aluminum bowl, but now I'm going to have to wash it all over again. He stares at me like I'm a crazy person, which I guess I am. I start to cry, walk over and pick up the damned bowl.

I go to the sink and turn on the water. My hands are cracking from spending all day in soap and water.

"What's going on?" He walks toward me.

"Don't get within firing range. I'm warning you." I hold up the dripping bowl.

"Okay, okay." He takes a step back. "Calm down."

"How come you didn't tell me about your father's birthday party?" Now I have sniffles, along with cracked hands and probably bloodshot eyes.

That stops him, and I'm glad. His voice goes down about ten octaves. "You've been talking to Mumma," he says in his new baritone.

"No, John, she's been talking to me. I guess she knows you're trying to keep me a secret or something, but she called and asked me anyway."

He doesn't respond. He stands there, a damned post again, and looks at the floor.

"Why would it be so bad for me to go?"

"I told you, I don't like people knowing my business." He has the gruff tone he uses to warn me away, like some sort of disgusting, growling dog.

"This is like talking to a stone wall and I'm sick of it. I'm not doing this again, John."

"What do you mean, 'again'?"

"Every relationship I've ever had was about what the guy wants. I'm not signing up for that again. Besides, I feel like I'm still dating a married man. Why do you want to keep us a secret?"

"I'm not."

"Yes, you are. That's the problem, and you don't want to admit it. There are just too many damned secrets between us. We can't talk about our past because you don't want to. We can't be seen together in town because it makes you uncomfortable." I hadn't realized that part before, but it was true, too.

He knows I'm right and says nothing.

"How many times have I asked you to come to Dino's with me and Melissa?"

He answers, but in a defensive tone. "A few times."

"Well?"

I wait. He doesn't say anything. I clear my throat.

"Well, what?" He's being belligerent. He isn't going to discuss it.

I look at him and know my happiness is in no one's hands but my own. Damn him, damn him to hell for making it like this. "Fuck you."

"What?"

"You heard me, fuck you. Fuck you, fuck you, infinity times infinity."

"What the hell are you saying, Rae?" His voice is so low, he's growling.

I almost back down and then know I can't do that to me. It makes me sad. "I love you with all my heart." I'm crying again. I can't believe this is happening here, now, and that there is nothing I will do to stop it. "And until you agree that there is something wrong with the rules you put around us…"

I look to see if he will make eye contact. He does but stays silent.

"…and stop this shit—"

"Then what, Rae?"

"Then fuck you and fuck this."

He turns and leaves. And a little while later, so do I.

"You still haven't heard from him?"

"Nope."

I cradle the phone on my shoulder while washing dishes. Chip calls every evening to get the latest update on John. So far there isn't one.

"I can't believe he's acting like this. How're you doing?"

"I don't know, sad more than anything else. I think I'm going to bed soon."

"You do that. I'll talk to you tomorrow."

I look at the end of my pier, wishing his boat was tied up there, gleaming in the moonlight which now only reflects inky black water.

Oh, well. I go back to my bedroom and turn off the lights as I go. There's a dull ache between my eyes. It's been there for a while. At first I thought it was the result of crying and then understood it's from missing him. I drag through my days and wait for this hurt to leave. It's so unfair. I've lost too many people already.

Melissa is still sleeping with me. She says my room is warmer than hers, which isn't true, but I let her anyway. I can use the company. Moonlight streaming through the window is so bright I can see to hang up my clothes. Melissa's body makes a warm patch in the bed, and I go to sleep curled up next to her, dreaming of elephants walking through a forest.

I think it's the cold waking me up but my eyes are barely open when a shadow looming in front of the window scares the crap out of me. Whatever it is, it's making muffled noises that sound, to my half-asleep brain, like elephants breathing. "Who's there!" I holler and sit up, pulling the covers with me.

"It's me. John. It's only me," he says. But he sounds weird and I'm still afraid.

The commotion wakes Melissa up. I guess she senses my fear. John is saying something about windows I don't understand, and Melissa grabs me around the middle.

"Who's here, Arae?"

"Shhh, Melissa," I say, hugging her. "It's only John." I'm awake now and have figured out the only elephants in the room are ones of uncompleted conversations.

"Yeah, it's me. I told you those damn windows were no good. You got to let me replace them." The bedroom window is wide open.

"Would you close it, please? It's cold."

He shuffles over and closes it.

I'm afraid to ask, but have to know. "Are you drunk?"

"No. I thought about it for about one second is all."

"So you haven't had anything to drink?"

"No."

I turn on the small lamp beside me. Melissa sits up as

close to me as she can get, blinking like a little owl. We both watch John.

He's standing by the window and looks a mess. I think his face is wet. Is he crying? "Is everything okay?" I ask gently.

"Do I look like everything is okay?"

"Is your mom all right? Your dad?

"Oh, yeah, everyone's fine. Nobody's hurt but me."

Melissa's getting more alert and worried looking.

"This is scaring somebody," I say, hugging Melissa.

John looks at me, wipes his eyes on his jacket, and sits on the floor next to the bed.

"Hey there, little bud," he says to her.

"Hey there, Mr. Clements. Why are you crying? Did you get hurt?"

"No. Yes. Yes, I did. I hurt myself."

"Where?"

John tries to smile but it comes out like a grimace. "On my finger here. How about you kiss it, make it better?"

She does. Melissa takes boo-boos very seriously.

"Arae, can I get up now?"

"No, not yet." I get up and tuck her in. She makes me smile. She's still half-asleep. "We have a ways to go before morning." I get another blanket and cover her, kiss her and snap off the light. She doesn't argue.

I get my robe and pull John to his feet. Melissa is asleep before we leave the room.

"Want coffee?" I look at him, wondering what is up.

"Sure."

We go into the family room/kitchen area. I put a pot on the stove and look at the clock. It's four. I'm going to be hating work today. But I'm grateful he's here. Or maybe it's more like intense relief. "What's going on?"

He's sitting at the table and tears begin to leak from his tightly clenched eyes. He acts like it's physically painful to cry. I walk over and cradle his head against me. He grabs me around the waist, hard. I've never seen him like this. You'd think his mom actually did die, the way he's acting.

"It's all right for a man to cry, John." I say softly into his ear. Why do they always have to be told?

"I haven't cried since the day my daddy went into the home."

"I want you to tell me what's going on." I pull away and get him some paper towels. He takes them and I stand waiting. He blows his nose.

"You were right about me, Rae. You were right about everything, but I don't know why. I don't know what's wrong with me."

"You admit you've been treating me like I'm some sort of a bad secret?"

"No, I'd never say that. I've been a son of a bitch to you, but I was never ashamed of you or anything remotely like that."

"You aren't?"

"Hell, no."

"Well?" I'm confused and sit in the chair next to his, "Were you worried that your family wouldn't like me? Or that they wouldn't like Torey 'cause she's biracial? Is that it?"

"No! If my family said anything against any of you, I'd never speak to them again, and they know it."

He looks at me with such intensity I have to smile. I know he's a good person, so what the hell's the problem? He seems to relax a little. I fix our coffee and sit next to him at the table.

"I've got some questions."

"Shoot."

"Why can't we go to your dad's birthday party?"

"I want you and the girls, both girls, to come out to the home on Saturday. My whole family will be there, and it will be a good time to meet everyone."

"But why didn't you want us to go before?"

He gets up and walks with his hands jammed into his jeans. "I don't know. Mumma accused me of being ashamed of my family and maybe she's right. Some of my kin can be rough at times, and Daddy takes getting used to with the Alzheimer's and all."

"That wouldn't bother me, and your mom and I get along fine. She's been to the restaurant and introduced herself. I think she likes me."

"She does." He stops pacing and looks at me. "Sometimes

when you ask me questions, it's like I freeze up. I feel like I'm back in school and someone's calling on me and I don't know the answer. I hate that feeling."

I don't know what to say. I'm too tired to get up and chase him around the room. I want to get this settled soon because being apart from him is exhausting me. "How about sitting down?"

He does and rocks his chair on its back legs. When we were kids, Momma used to yell at us about denting the floors when we did that. I feel a faint sense of guilt that I don't make him put the chair back down but then think it's stupid to allow myself to be bossed around by ghosts.

"What do I do to make you feel that way?"

"It's nothing you do. It's just you being you, I guess." The chair comes back down and a sense of relief washes through me. "You are so different from any female I ever dated. I could never in a million years predict what'll come out of your mouth next."

I laugh. "Sometimes, neither can I, but is that bad?"

"No. No, no. It's one of the things I love about you."

"I'm confused." And tired and unable to comprehend a damned thing.

"You're so damned smart. You've got what? Two college degrees? Jesus, Rae, I barely made it through high school."

"So what? Am I too smart for you or too educated?"

"No." The gruff tone is back in his voice.

"Then what?"

"That's what I mean. I don't know."

God, I'm frustrated. I think he is too. I decide to try logic. It usually works with men. "You're right, I've got some college degrees, but it seems lately I'm making my living as a cook. Does that bother you?"

"Shit, yes. Everyone in town is talking about this Sunday deal of yours. People around here aren't used to eating like that. Here you are taking over some dinky restaurant, and it's taking off while my business tanks."

"I don't understand. You said you were happy for me."

"Listen, Rae, you're smarter than me, younger than me, richer than me, and…"

"Richer? How the hell do you figure that? I had to borrow money from you not too long ago."

"I'm not talking about money. I'm talking about how you are. I see you with the yacht people; you fit right in. What in the world are you doing with me?"

"Are you saying the reason you don't go out in public with me is because I don't fit in?"

He stands up again. Somehow he seems taller and bigger. His face has gone an ugly red shade. "You know, I don't know what the fuck I mean, and I sure as shit don't feel like talking anymore."

"What did I do to piss you off this time?"

"I don't know. I know this conversation is over."

He's pacing the length of the room, and I feel despair trying to ambush my spirit. This time I'm not letting it. In a warning tone I say, "I'm not going back to your damned rules, John." My heart is racing. I identify panic and paralyzing fear. But I refuse to cave, or to agree to live like this. I say it out loud. "I refuse to live like this. If you can't finish this conversation, then we're both better off if you go on home." I sound a lot more sure of myself than I feel.

I watch him wrestle with it, whatever it is. I figure if he doesn't leave the room, then he's still trying to find his way back to me. It takes a while.

"I'm afraid you're making a fool out of me."

"You're joking. Where did that come from?"

"It's nothing you do. It's just when we're together, here, in this stupid town, I always feel like people are saying things about me."

"Things like what?"

"Oh, stupid shit, like, John better pay off his boat before he goes trolling for a trophy wife."

I'm quiet. Either I pick John or pick me, and from past experience, I know where picking him would get me— nowhere I want to be again. John stands behind his chair, holding the back of it in some sort of death grip.

"Excuse me. I'll be back in a minute." I go to the bathroom, lock the door and pee. The light over the sink is a horrible green florescent fixture, but I flick it on anyway and look at myself in the mirror.

I look like hell. I'd make a sorry trophy wife, trophy girlfriend, or trophy anything else right now. The dark circles under my eyes are turning brown, a sure sign of doing too much, coping with too much, or getting ready to come down with the flu. Even my hair looks dull. I know the greenish fluorescent light doesn't help, but I swear my skin is mottled.

I've got to start caring more about myself. Talking to Sally has changed some things—like I no longer have a job that's more important than me for the first time in my life.

It's easier to be at work now, any work. My responsibilities with the girls don't kill me anymore with the relentless pressure I used to feel, and outside of my concern about Torey, the girls have become the best part of my life.

If I ever expect to be important to anyone else, I better start being important to me. I need to think about myself with at least as much consideration and concern I routinely give Melissa and Torey. What's the right thing for me here? I go back to the family room.

John's sitting at the table. He looks worried. I walk behind him, bend down and put my arms around his neck. I nuzzle his neck. I've missed the smell of him so much.

"I'm sorry you feel insecure, and I'm not going to live in some crazy way to keep you from facing it."

"I don't blame you, Rae." He turns to face me.

"So what's it going to be, Bub?"

"I'm agreeing with you. Why the hell should you put up with this shit? Wilson used to call me on it all the time. I don't know why I didn't listen to him."

"Who's Wilson?"

"I don't think I ever told you about him. Wilson was my sponsor in AA."

I sit down. "No, I don't think you have."

"Wilson was a great old guy. He was a bum. A real honest-to-God bum and I loved him."

I was surprised to hear John say he loved Wilson. He's told me he loved me. He's comfortable with the word, unlike some men I've known, but I'd never heard him say he loved anyone else. It was like catching a glimpse of the good child he'd once been, and I'm touched by the sweetness still in him.

"Wilson never owned a goddamned thing in his life. He told me it was a lot easier for him to feel good with nothing, than it ever was for me with all the stuff I owned. He was right, too."

"How was he right?"

"I let *things* get in the way a lot. Like some asshole that doesn't tip the bait-boy after a good day's fishing, shit like that, stuff I'm doing again," he adds, almost to himself.

"Why was he your sponsor?"

"I asked him to be. He said I had to ask him if I wanted his help. I was new at AA, trying to get sober, and man, I needed somebody's help. That was like six years ago."

"Why did you do it, go to AA?" Silence, and I wait. "Are you going to tell me?"

"I want to tell you. It's just hard getting started is all." He clears his throat. "My first wife was a diabetic, the kind that has to test their blood all the time and take shots. She'd been diabetic since she was a kid. Her mother, especially, worried about her health."

"Did you?"

His eyes held pain. "Me? Hell no. I figured Sharon and her mom worried enough so I didn't have to. One night, I got home real late, drunk as usual, and fell asleep on the couch. I didn't go back to the bedroom because she hated the smell of me when I got like that."

He looks at me, I guess to see my reaction, which is to raise my eyebrows. He continues, "When I woke up, it was late. The sun was up and that surprised me 'cause Sharon, she always got up at the crack of dawn and usually would have cussed me out like I deserved. But this time she didn't and I almost let her die."

I hold his hand.

"She was in a coma, diabetic shock. They took her to the hospital. Everyone was scared shitless that we'd lost her, that I'd let us lose her. So when she got well, her mumma took her back to their house. I guess they talked her out of staying married to a man who would have let her die."

"I am so sorry. Where's Sharon now?"

"She lives in Hampton, does something with computers. She's married again, but my ex-mother-in-law will still cross the street to avoid me to this day, and I can't say I blame her."

"So you decided to get sober, and Wilson said to ask him to be your sponsor."

"Well, not right away, but that was when I started having serious doubts about myself. Then I married the whore, just to prove to everyone I was fine." He laughs bitterly. "I already told you about that. It was after her and all that crap I finally wised up."

"I remember. So what about Wilson?"

"Wilson. That old dude probably saved my life."

"How?"

"It wasn't easy, I can tell you." John chuckles, and his eyes crinkle in the corners the way I love. "He had the worst apartment in Norfolk, but he made good coffee and we would sit there and talk for hours, sometimes two or three times a week."

"You know, John, it's hard for me to imagine you involved in a conversation lasting that long, or that often either."

"Are you being sarcastic?"

I duck my head. "Yeah, a little."

"How about not doing that? This is hard enough."

"Okay." I'm immediately ashamed. I guess this discussion isn't about me.

"It was a group of us that got together at Wilson's. He had a shot liver. All sorts of medical problems, but he was a happy old fart. Said he'd always been happy but hadn't known it. It took me a few years to understand what he meant by that."

"And you figured it out?"

"Yes, or at least I had until I met you."

"So I messed you up?"

"It looks that way. Listen, can we sit on the couch?"

After getting the pillows fixed right, I curl up next to him. It's that moment before dawn when you can barely see the outline of trees distinct from the skyline through the windows. I'm glad the old comforter is here. I wrap it around us.

"A few years after I met Wilson, he was in the hospital and he called me, wanted me to go by his apartment and get him some things. I said I would, but I couldn't get there for a couple of days. He said to come when I could."

John leans back on the cushions.

"What happened?" I ask.

"I'll never forget walking into that room. He went to the VA hospital. It was all run down then, and I hated going there. But that time was worse than usual because Wilson had tubes and things running all over. I found out his kidneys were shot, and they were putting him on dialysis."

John takes a deep breath. An owl screeches so close by we both jump. It must have been getting a last meal before sleep. I wait for John to go on.

"But before I knew about all that, I had this minute that hit me right between the eyes. I was standing next to his bed. He was asleep, and I was standing there and thinking about this old guy. I mean, you have to understand. He always smiled. Always. Always giving to people. It didn't matter who you were. Wilson had a smile and a good word for everyone.

"It would have been easy for him to give up, get bitter, start drinking and using again. It's not like his life turned out so great. But Wilson decided to get sober and take responsibility for his own happiness. He decided he wasn't going to rely on a drink or anything else to make him happy, and he didn't. And that's when I got it, Rae. Got what he had been telling me for however long it had been."

"That's it? That's the big mystique behind AA?"

"It was for Wilson, and he taught it to me."

"Just be happy? No matter what?"

"Try it."

I'd always wondered how AA worked. Vicky had been involved in AA's twelve steps at her rehab center. When I'd read them, they didn't translate to anything I understood. As far as I can remember, AA is about being honest and letting a higher power take over.

I think about being happy no matter what. No way could I pull that off. "You can do that?"

"Not at the time, but Wilson could. When I found out about the dialysis, I was more upset than he was. At first I thought it was because it had always been Sharon's biggest fear. Diabetics have to worry about their kidneys going bad, and she was terrified of the possibility. I figured Wilson didn't know what to expect, so I read him the brochures and stuff they had left about it."

"What happened?"

"When I got through, old Wilson said, "Yep, sounds like it hadn't changed much since Bubba was on it." Turns out he had a friend, some old drinking buddy that was on dialysis. Wilson used to go and sit with him during his treatments until the guy died. He knew exactly what happened in a dialysis unit, and the thing was it didn't bother him at all."

John stretches out his legs. The sound of his voice is soothing and I feel myself warm up and relax.

"Wilson was at peace with himself and his world, and nothing shook him from it. Later on when his liver started to go, he refused the dialysis treatments and he died."

"When did that happen?"

"A couple of years ago."

"I'm sorry. I guess you miss him."

"Yeah, I do. It was hard when he went. Afterwards I made the decision to sink everything I had into getting *The Clemency*. I'm sure Wilson would have approved because that's the other thing he taught me. If I was going to take responsibility for my own happiness, I had to be all right with the outcome of my decisions, no matter what, even if I lost everything. And you know what? When you think like that, it's hard to not go after your dreams. That's what Wilson taught me."

"Do I fit into your dreams?"

A few birds are beginning to make their morning noises. John pulls me close. A mourning dove is making her lonesome calls over on the water.

"Not really." He knows this isn't what I want to hear, so grabs me around the shoulders so I won't get up. "Hear me out, please. I never expected you, so how could you fit into any dream I had?" He waits like I had the answer to that.

I look at him like he's crazy. "You never expected to be in a relationship again?"

He laughs. "Naw, I expected that all right. I was dating someone before you came to town, you didn't know?"

"No." I'm going to get Chip for this. She said he hadn't dated anyone for a while. "Who?"

"No one important. I've dated lots of women, but I never got serious about any of them the way I have with you."

"How come?"

"I used to think it was the pattern."

"What pattern?"

"I was afraid that if I got involved with someone again, the pattern would get me to drinking again."

"What's the pattern?"

"The pattern of men and women always ending up on opposite sides of things. Maybe it's the way people are around here, I don't know. Sharon hated it when I got tore up, but I did it, went out drinking with the guys. Just like my daddy did."

"Were you screwing around?"

"No. Well, I might have once, but the details are too foggy to count it, even if I did manage to do anything."

"Why did you do it, go out drinking like that?"

"The biggest reason is I'm an alcoholic. The other reason is the pattern, being on different sides of the fence."

"What side was she on?"

"The right side, to hear her tell it. She wanted me to go to things to show me off. Things like church and church suppers, stuff like that."

"Why wouldn't you?"

"I did, not all the time, but I went sometimes. I never enjoyed it though."

"But she wanted to show you off. That doesn't sound bad."

"It's not the way you're thinking. She wanted to show that she had turned me into what she wanted, that she was in charge."

"Are you sure about that? Maybe she just wanted to spend time with you."

"It's hard to explain. Maybe you're right, maybe Sharon had a heart of gold and I never saw it, but that wasn't our problem. My drinking was the problem. But even if it hadn't been, it still wouldn't have ever occurred to either of us that we could have been friends."

"You guys weren't friends?"

"No. It was like we were in some sort of competition to see who was in charge of me, and I could always be counted on to act the fool."

"Sinners and saints."

"What?"

"Something Sally, my therapist, told me. She said everyone in my family was divided up into being either a saint or a sinner and I think she's on to something."

"You must be a saint, taking in your nieces and all, right?"

"No, I'm no saint. Well, actually I was, but not when I took them on. My sainthood involved achieving. That was my whole deal. I started off achieving grades and then moved on to scholarships and then achieving at work. I was into being perfect, but no matter how hard I pushed myself, it was never enough. I was a typical successful female, doing great at work and horrible at relationships."

"You're doing pretty good with me."

"Not yet I'm not." The sun will be up soon. I shift to get more comfortable. "But you and I are more alike than you realize. I was as locked into my crap as you were with Sharon. If I hadn't lost my job, I'd still be there—uptight, perfect as hell, and always alone. I'd even figured out how to be in a relationship and still manage to be by myself."

"You've said that before, but I swear I can't see you being that way."

"Thank God. You know, when I lost that job, I thought my life was over, and it was, but it was a life that needed to be over. You know what else?"

He hugs me. "What?"

"Getting those girls helped a lot, too."

"How's that?"

"If they hadn't ruined my life even more, it would have

taken me years to get out of that crap, if I ever did manage to."

John laughs, but I'm amazed at the truth of it. Everything I'd seen as a negative had actually saved me from a living hell.

"I think you and Sharon were caught up in the same patterns as my family—devils and angels, sinners and saints. Sally says those roles are life-killers."

"Sounds to me like Sally knows her stuff."

"I think she does. John, do you remember that night on your boat?" I'm almost whispering. "When it was so cold and the moonlight was real bright and we had that incredible sex?"

He's quiet for a while. "Yeah, I remember. It was the first time I said I loved you, I remember that. You said you loved me too."

"I didn't say I loved you. I said I felt like we'd been touched by love."

"Well, whatever, you said 'love' and 'you' in the same sentence. It was good enough for me."

"It sort of scared me. I never told you. Did it scare you too?"

John's quiet. So quiet I begin to wonder if he's gone silent again. "It scared me I couldn't remember what happened very well." He sounds sad and I wonder why. "It was all a blur the next day, sort of like the times I drank too much and couldn't remember exactly what happened the night before, something like that. It shook me up is all, which is why I didn't want to talk about it."

"It shook me up, too, and I needed to talk about it. My feelings were hurt when you acted like it was bad manners to mention it."

"I understand that now." He takes a deep breath. "I want you to know I love you. I've never been with anyone like you before and I'm scared shitless is all. Scared once you figure out I'm not much more than some dumb, good ol' boy, you'll get tired of me."

I start to say something, but he hushes me. "Let me get this out. I came here to tell you something and I still haven't gotten it out. It's tough enough without you interrupting all the damned time."

I sit in my mother's old ratty robe, waiting.

"I want you to know I'm yours. I will do anything to keep you, even go into therapy if you want. If you want to get married, I'm glad to do that, too. There's been nothing holding us back but my stupidity. I just love you and that's all there is to it."

I guess offering to go into therapy or get married was like throwing himself onto a flaming pyre for me. He has no idea how much I love him right now.

"Can I talk?"

"Sure." He sounds nervous.

"I don't want to split up," I say emphatically.

"Good."

"I love you. That night you never want to talk about did something to me."

"It did? What?"

"I'm not sure. I know I'm connected to you in ways I can't seem to undo."

"Well, that's good, isn't it?"

"I guess, but I'm not going to eat shit because of it though."

"You shouldn't."

"I couldn't breathe while you were gone. And don't get all cocky about this, but I don't think you are in any danger of losing me."

"You sure about that?"

"As sure as anyone ever is. Who knows about all this love stuff, but yeah, I'm sure I love your face." I think of all the ways I love him and sit up. "I love the way you smell and how you gave Torey flowers after she was hurt. I get turned on by looking at the back of your neck, do you know that?"

I think he's blushing. I can't tell in the gloom, but I can see him shake his head no.

"I love how gentle you are with Melissa's crush on you. You feel like home to me. You're where I fall apart. I never did that before."

He looks relieved and tired and happy. He laughs, stands up and pulls the ratty robe and me up into his arms and hugs us. He says, "Do you understand being with you is a whole different sort of ballgame for me? Maybe that's why I've been acting like such an asshole."

"We do more than ball."

He laughs. "Jesus, Rae, who put the toilet in your mouth?"

I'm laughing, too. He's leaning back, looking into my eyes and grinning.

"I only talk that way around you."

"I know. How come?"

"To throw you off."

"Why are you always wanting to do that?"

"Oh." I grin. "Maybe just to get your attention."

"You got it, lady. You got it."

Melissa's Favorite Meal

Boil some egg noodles in salted water until done and drain. Add some heavy cream and salt to taste. That's it!

APRIL

If this is family therapy, then I'm in one of the weirdest families ever. Today my "family" consists of Torey, Lucy, and me. We're all nervous, and despite the coaching, I still wonder what Sally is up to.

The only one not on edge is Sally. Torey's face has that pinched look I hate. If Lucy and I get any more phony polite towards each other, I'm going to puke. I have no idea why I'm feeling this way. I like Lucy. Most days I thank God for Lucy.

"All right, I'm glad we could all make it on time, this is going to be an especially lengthy session and I'd like to get started." Sally's grim smile would better suit a corporate CEO. I can't shake the feeling I'm about to get fired.

"Lucy?" I swear she jumps a foot when Sally calls on her. "Yes?"

"I especially appreciate your presence here today."

"Thank you." Poor delicate Lucy looks miserably uncomfortable. She's wearing one of her church dresses and high heels. I guess she's figured out she overdressed for the occasion. Even Sally is wearing jeans.

"Do you have any questions before we begin?"

Lucy is holding her lips in a prissy way I find particularly unappealing. "I still don't understand why I'm here, what you want me to do." She's nearly whispering.

"You don't need to do anything in particular. I told you we needed two adults who are attached to Torey, and you are the only other person I could think of." Sally smiles sweetly but I know not to trust it.

"But why two adults?"

"Because Torey needs to know that she has more than one person to turn to, and that you two are united in a plan for her welfare. But of course, we wouldn't want her to become too dependent on one particular person." Sally makes these remarks with the optimistic look and smile of the simple-minded.

I know Lucy's feeling confusion, fear, and discomfort. It's rather exciting to watch someone else be the victim. I don't think she's noticed yet that Torey and I, who actually know Sally, haven't said so much as "boo" yet.

We know what Lucy is in the middle of learning. On the surface Sally's comments will seem fine, but scratch the surface and be blinded by an avalanche of questions and contradictions that leave you dazed and trembling. I wonder if Lucy will go ahead and collapse right now or put up a fight.

"I don't know that I have much to offer Torey." She looks apologetically at Torey. "I mean, I like her and all. It's just that we aren't really close or anything."

She did it. She put her head in the noose. I'm home free.

"I'm aware you have a limited connection to Torey, but I need another adult here, like I said."

"Why didn't you ask John?"

Oh, no.

"John, who?" Sally asks.

"You don't know about John?" Lucy casts me a sideways glance that lets me know the gloves are off. "Rae's paramour?"

I didn't know the woman even knew words like "paramour."

"Obviously, I don't, and perhaps we can shelve that issue for another time."

Sally is pissed, and I'm fairly sure, at me.

"I also wanted you here today to get an update on Melissa. She is our other concern." Sally's cold smile circles the room like a shark. "Melissa also needs to know that the people she considers significant adults in her life, are united in a plan for her welfare. You are part of Melissa's team, too,

Torey, and the same thing goes for you. Melissa needs to guard her own dependency."

None of us, of course, have a clue as to what that means, but by now even Lucy has figured out not to try and clarify anything.

"Lucy, where do you see Melissa now? What are your concerns?"

"I don't know. I think Rae should say, after all she's the child's aunt."

Lucy is trying to make herself look smaller by huddling up on the couch. Good luck. I'm surprised to see behind the church-going, good-girl façade is someone with real skills. But she doesn't have a chance around me. "Oh, Lucy, don't act like you're not the one closest to Melissa. After all, she spends more time with you nowadays than she does me."

"Even though I'm not around a lot, I think I'm the one closest to Melissa!"

A flash of the old Torey flares up, and it's a wonderful thing to see. Maybe this thing is going to work after all. We all go quiet, more in appreciation than anything else.

"Does anyone hear what I'm saying?"

"Of course, Torey, and you're right. No one here is closer to Melissa than you. I wasn't trying to imply anything else." It's amazing to watch Sally's facial expressions change as she whips her head toward Lucy. "I wasn't aware that Melissa was spending more time with you than Rae. When did this start?"

"When Rae and Chip began their Sunday brunch at *The Sea Witch*, Melissa began spending weekends with me and Bob. Then for the past two months or so, she stays over on Thursday nights too."

"She's there three nights a week?" Torey is pissed.

"Thursday nights? Why?" Sally looks from Lucy to me, and I sort of blush and shrug.

"That's when she sees her paramour." Lucy answers for me.

"What the hell is a paramour?" asks Torey. "Is that like a boyfriend or something?"

"Honey, your aunt's a little old for boyfriends, so we call

them paramours instead." Lucy is just full of information.

Torey spins in her seat to face me. "Why are you letting her stay there so much? What's wrong with you?" Then she dissolves into tears.

"Is that bad?" I ask Sally, who is looking around the room with an impatient expression.

"You, Torey, look at me," Sally says.

Torey raises her dripping face from her hands. I bring her a box of tissues.

"We're going to get to those issues later on, I promise you." She's gazing intently into Torey's eyes. Torey nods her head like she understands.

"You, Lucy."

Lucy is trained now. She snaps that head around like a private to a general. "Yes, ma'am?"

"How do you feel about Melissa spending so much time with you?"

"Well, it's fine. Bob and I don't mind at all." Lucy's perfect red curls toss back and forth as she looks anxiously between Sally and me. I know exactly what she's doing. Lucy is looking for the absolute correct answer. I could have saved her the time. It doesn't exist. Hesitantly she continues, "Rae and I have worked out a deal where she pays me a flat rate each week no matter how much Melissa's there. It works out fine."

Sally sighs. I'm not sure what's coming, but I'm beginning to feel sorry for Lucy. "You keep a few kids, right?"

"Not so many anymore. My mother's sick and needs more attention right now."

"Have you ever kept a child who spends as much time with you as Melissa does?"

Lucy is instantly nervous, and I wonder what secret she's trying to keep. It doesn't matter though. Sally's caught the scent of it and is tracking it down. It's only a matter of time now. I've been in this exact position too many times not to know exactly what is happening.

"No."

"So why Melissa?"

"Rae needs me." She glances my way for backup.

I can't betray her on this. I do need her. "Lucy is my right arm with these girls, Sally. She brings Torey here for her therapy, even took Melissa to the dentist for me last week. I know Melissa's happy with Lucy, but even so, I feel guilty about the amount of time she's there and try to make it up to her when I can."

Sally's staring at me in a way that teaches what a python's victim must feel like. I shut up. "So you feel Lucy loves Melissa as much as you do?"

I'm trying to see where I'm going to trap myself and can't figure it out. Taking a deep breath, I say, "Yes, I do." I sneak a peek at Torey, to see how she's taking this. From her expression, not well.

Sally whips back to Lucy. "Rae tells me you don't have any children of your own, is that right?"

Lucy gasps. We all watch to see if she intends to breathe again. Finally, she exhales and takes a deep breath. "I find your question insulting."

Mentally, I tried to throw Lucy a lifesaver. *Shut up.*

"Why?" Sally is all smiles and charm.

"Because it's so…" Lucy is obviously trying to think of a word strong enough to hold the amount of rage she's feeling. "Rude!"

That invincible Southern standby—the highest insult. I know in Lucy's mind, Sally, this pushy, uncouth Yankee, had sent her over the edge. Lucy didn't want to be so blunt, but she is not responsible for Sally's uncivilized behavior. Lucy sits in outraged indignation, nearly shaking.

Someday I'll tell Lucy how I'd tried to help her and had gone unnoticed. Mentally, I wish her well, but she's on her own.

Sally is all warmth and kindness. I've seen this before too, and it's rather fascinating to observe as long as I'm not the target. "Do you find being childless insulting?" she asks in dulcet tones.

Lucy's eyes grow wild around the edges. "Of course not!"

"I'm trying to ascertain how you feel about the bond that is developing between you and a young girl in my therapeutic care. That you are childless could be a factor here."

"I don't see how!" Lucy's outrage is a nice note to the drama unfolding in front of us.

Sally looks perplexed, and I know she's doing it on purpose. "Is it your choice that you're childless?"

Lucy is barely thirty and was born and raised here. She's no match for Sally. Any tiny shred of sophistication she ever acquired is of no help. She starts crying.

"See? I'm right! She's trying to take Melissa from us, and you're letting her!" Torey stands up. For a moment, I think she's going to lean over and hit me. Then she looks at Sally and sits back down.

Lucy is red. The word "red" doesn't do Lucy's face justice. Fiery red, maybe, or volcano red might be more accurate. The bottom line is, right now Lucy is hard to miss. Torey is glaring at her, but Lucy doesn't know because her hands cover her eyes while tears drip onto her dress.

It strikes me with sudden unwelcome force that Lucy doesn't deserve to be treated this way. She has accomplished so much in the way of instilling manners and kindness in a child who possessed neither that I will be forever in her debt. Lucy probably saved me as well. The only reason I do as well with Melissa as I do is by sharing the load with Lucy.

Lucy loves Melissa like the sun and the moon, and everyone knows it. Me too, I count on it. I wrestle with trying to not feel like I'm taking advantage of a person who is probably the kindest woman I'll ever know. Maybe someday if I work real hard I might achieve a remote resemblance to her. I speak up. This might be my finest hour.

"I need to say something." I hear a noise coming from my niece and turn towards her. "Torey, give me a minute, please. I know you're angry but give me a chance to say something." Before she can respond, I take a deep breath and sit up straighter. "Lucy, I've been feeling guilty about something. I worry that I take advantage of your situation." Lucy starts to say something but I interrupt her. "I want to get this out, please."

The room is silent. Even Torey seems to be waiting to hear what I have to say. "You're one of those people who was made to be a mother. It's sort of like the town tragedy that you can't have kids. Is it all right if I tell Sally why?"

Lucy nods behind her hands, which are back over her face. "She had cancer, ovarian cancer, real young. What were you, twenty-two?" I ask.

"Yes." Her voice comes out muffled behind the hands.

"And because of her medical history, adoption is out."

Sally smiles at me. I'll never figure out where Sally's coming from, but at least I do know where I'm coming from.

I turn to Lucy. "Maybe you can't have kids, but you've got something I'll never have."

"What's that?" She looks at me and nods a thank you as I hand her some tissues.

"The way you are with kids, with Melissa. I'm not like you, I'm not very maternal." I turn in my seat to look at Torey while I say the next part. "I think I'm a pretty good aunt. I love you guys, and I think I'm a good caretaker. I'm responsible, pay the bills on time, make your doctor appointments and even have fun with you. I've learned to not yell so much. I've come a long way and I'm proud of myself. It's just that I'm not very motherly, and I know it." I turn back to Lucy. "But you are. I saw you and Bob with Melissa last Sunday. You guys were coming into the restaurant after church. You looked like a family."

Lucy's flush, the one that had been receding, now resurfaces. What is it about redheads that makes them flame rather than blush?

"I bet anyone who didn't know better would think she's Bob's child. She's blonde and sturdy like him, you know?"

"Yes." The scarlet on her cheeks intensifies.

I laugh. "They both look like Vikings or something." The next part is hard to begin. I clear my throat. "When I saw you-all together, I was happy for Melissa. I saw her laughing and walking between you guys. Then I noticed it wasn't happiness I was feeling, it was relief." I look at Lucy to see her response. She's staring me straight in the eyes, unafraid, so I continue. "Then I felt guilty for feeling relieved, like I was getting out of my responsibility towards Melissa or something. I guess if I'm really honest, if I was a better aunt, I would be jealous of seeing her with you and Bob. On Sunday, I got so mixed up I ducked back into the kitchen before you could see me. I've been thinking about that all week."

"I had no idea, Rae. You seemed fine when we saw you later on."

"I had time to regroup by then."

"Oh."

I glance around the room wondering what Sally is thinking. She's being unusually quiet. I sense thunderclouds over Torey's head and feel awkward and embarrassed but trudge on. "I feel bad about that and something else. I see how things are between you and Melissa, and I didn't tell you something you deserve to know. Melissa's mother is scheduled to get out in a little over seven years."

"Certainly you're not going to let Melissa go back to her, are you?" Lucy's voice is indignant.

"If Vicky wants her back, I might have to. Melissa might be lost to both of us in the end."

"Why would a judge do that? I mean, your sister will be a convicted felon on top of everything else."

"I know. The thing is, it may not be up to me, and I didn't want to tell you because I didn't want to mess up the situation I have with you. I think I need you as much as Melissa does."

Lucy smiles through her tears. Sometimes she's such a picky perfectionist, I find it easy to get irritated with her, but then she's always so damn nice, it's impossible to hold a grudge.

The thunderclouds around Torey are darkening. I wonder if I'm the only one who notices.

I look at Sally. "I see what you mean about being united in Melissa's welfare. There's a lot Lucy and I need to talk about."

"I've been feeling badly, too." Lucy gets up and fetches her pocketbook from the table by the doorway. She pulls out an honest-to-God hankie. I haven't seen one of them since my Nana Green died. She always kept a few in her mammoth bra. "I *have* been jealous, Rae." She shyly glances my way. She has to see the surprise on my face.

"I'm the last person in the world anyone should be

jealous of."

"That's not true," Sally interjects. "You've got two children. Some women would give anything for that."

True, but everyone wanted the adorable blond baby, not the disturbed, exotic looking teenager.

"I try not to feel this way. It's not right and I know it. I take this very seriously, Rae. Jealousy of this nature is against my principles—"

"Geez, Lucy," I interrupt, "quit being so damned hard on yourself. If love requires occasional jealousy, then thank you for being jealous. Because of you, I don't feel so damned alone raising Melissa. You have no idea how scared I was before you got involved. I even sleep better, and I know she's probably better cared for when she's with you than when she's with me."

"I don't know if 'better off' is the correct term, but maybe between the two of you, Melissa's needs get fulfilled—"

Sally's lecture on parenting is cut off by Torey's scream. "She's my sister! She belongs in my fucking family! God damn you, Rae!" Before I'm able to react, she's fallen on me and starts hitting me with clenched fists.

Torey gets in a couple of good blows before Sally tackles her and wrestles her to the ground. I'm in shock. I've seen her hateful but never violent. My head hurts. The sun goes behind a cloud and the room darkens. A buzzing sound begins in my ears.

"Rae! Get her legs!" Sally yells over the garbled sounds issuing from my niece. "Rae!"

I focus on what's happening. Lucy is white-faced and standing by the doorway. I wonder if she's going to run away.

Torey's flailing around, kicking and trying to grab Sally with her legs. Sally has Torey's hands pinned to the floor. I scoot to the floor and get hit in the jaw by one of Torey's flying sneaker-clad feet. That motivates me to get it together. Soon we have her pinned to the floor like a butterfly on a board.

Sally's at her head. I'm holding her feet. Sally shouts orders, "Lucy, get Torey's feet from Rae and *don't let go*." Torey's cranking it out now. For such a tiny person, she's a lot stronger than anyone could have guessed. Her entire body arches like an electric shock is running through it. Torey's communication is reduced to a vile salad of hate, mostly directed at me. Lucy secures her feet.

"Rae, sit on her. Not hard, just straddle her middle."

I do as instructed. I'm afraid of the hate pouring from my niece. Her eyes seem to have turned into black holes, sucking the life out of everything around them. She's trying to spit on me. I lean back to get out of range.

Sally's yelling, bent down close to her ear but out of biting range. "So you hate your fucking aunt? Say it, Torey. We can't hear you."

The screams and raw verbiage coming from Torey meld into a stew of malevolence. She seems barely human.

Sally continues to match Torey's volume and intensity. It feels wrong to notice Sally's surprisingly strong voice. The whole tableau feels surreal.

"Rae's the bitch? Rae's the cunt? Yeah, right! That's right! Rae's the stupid bitch. You tell her, Torey. You tell her now. Don't you leave out one damned thing."

It takes a long time, but I see it's like landing a big fish. Like the time I watched Daddy pull in a huge sailfish.

Sally matches Torey word for word, tone for tone. It's obvious when the dialogue of rage slows. Torey wears herself out just like that old sailfish did.

I can tell it makes her mad at first, when she gets tired, it cranks her up again, but even that doesn't last very long. Sally shows no signs of wearing out, and I wonder how she stays so fit.

Torey goes from cussing me out to cussing out Lucy, then Sally. Sally plays the line, watching the moves, anticipating the tricks. By the time Torey is still, she's crying and saying how much she hates Melissa.

"You can get off her, Rae. Go take her feet from Lucy.

"Luce?" Sally yells.

"Yeah." The church dress is shot. She'd dumped the heels somewhere and her hair is a mess.

"Are you all right?"

"Yeah. Whew. For a little kid, she sure can put up a fuss." Lucy stands up and stretches her back.

I can tell Torey is embarrassed. She's so embarrassed, she's in no danger of doing anything remotely like what she'd just done, which is why I have no intention of letting go of her feet. In my book, she can use some embarrassment right now.

"Rae? I'm all right now." The first intelligible thing she's said in over an hour. She's lifting her head from the floor, trying to sit up.

"I don't think so." Sally has a firm grip on Torey's shoulders. "Repeat that last bit about Melissa."

Torey squirms. "I don't remember."

"I can stay right here forever."

"I didn't mean it."

"Until you repeat it, you'll stay where you are."

We wait patiently for what feels like a very long time. My hands are beginning to ache from gripping Torey's ankles, and I want to scratch my nose. I look up at Lucy, who seems both curious and concerned.

"I said I hated Melissa. Now let me go." She tries to yank her feet from my hands and almost succeeds.

"You're not going anywhere until you tell me why you said it." Sally wrestles her back into position, her knees on Torey's shoulders, Torey's arms outstretched and pinned at the wrists.

"I don't know." Where does she get the energy? She's beginning to thrash around again. I hold on.

Sally's ratcheting it up a notch, too. She repeatedly yells, "Why do you hate your sister?" Torey tries to fight, but now she simply doesn't have the energy. I see it in her face when she gives up for real this time, and the unexpected pain of this almost makes me let go and hug her. Sally's warning glare disabuses the notion.

Torey's crying now, saying, "I don't hate my sister, I don't hate my sister," and rocking her head back and forth.

Sally seems to be gathering her attention, waiting for something. She continues to match Torey's volume and intonation perfectly, but now whatever Torey says, Sally says the opposite.

After a while, Torey stops arguing. She blinks back some tears. Her eyelashes are wet and spiky. She looks around the room, at all of us, and is quiet. Then she asks Sally what seems an honest question, "Why would I hate my sister?"

"That's the real question here." Sally lets go of Torey's hands and stands up in such quick, fluid movements that she's sitting on the couch before I let go of Torey's feet.

"You can let go of me, Rae. It's all right. I'm all right. Let go!"

She sort of shakes me off and sits up. I'm still out of it, unable to keep up with the pace of things transpiring here.

Sally says, "Why are you living at school?"

Torey is still pinned to the floor, only this time under Sally's intense stare.

"Um, I don't know. Maybe it's because I like being around Jennifer and the other girls. You said it was okay for me to live there." She looks scared, and I don't blame her.

"I know I said that, but why is it okay for you? What about Melissa?"

Torey doesn't answer. She looks at the floor and twirls a strand of hair. I never knew how to handle it when she shut down like this. I'm real curious to see what Sally does.

"Torey, look around. We all know what you did and what you said. You attacked Rae for letting Melissa get attached to Lucy. Then you accused Lucy of trying to steal Melissa away from the family. Come on out, chicken-girl."

A little of my old niece shows in the fire in her eyes. She hates to be called chicken. "I don't like her liking everybody else." An echo of the old defiance lingers behind the exhaustion in her voice.

"Well, of course not. Why would you?" Sally seems indignant for her.

Torey is wise to Sally, though. She knows better than to ask what she means. "It's not her fault," she says instead.

"That she likes other people like Rae and Lucy? How about her teacher and kids at school? Rae tells me she has a little boy in her class who's sweet on her, what about those people?"

"What about them?"

"Does it bother you, her liking them?"

"Her teacher and stuff?"

"Yeah."

Torey cocks her head, I guess to see if Sally is insane. "Hello? I don't think sooo," the long, sarcastic adolescent negative.

"Then why Lucy? Why is it so bad for Melissa to have Lucy?"

"She's not family."

"What's so bad about Lucy caring for Melissa? Are you saying only blood relatives can love her?"

"Yeah, that's what I'm saying!"

"Then why aren't you staying home to help take care of her? Rae can't work all her jobs and be there for Melissa, too. Come on, quit hiding behind your hair. Come on out and speak up."

But she doesn't come out, she goes further in. "I'm tired of it."

"Tired of what, Torey? Come on, you're almost there."

Torey tosses the mane out of her face and, with eyes blazing, screams at Sally. "I don't want to take care of her, damn you! Are you satisfied? I don't want to take care of her. I'm sick of taking care of her. I hate her all the time and I can't stop."

Sally's eyes are warm with what looks to me like compassion. She's looked at me that way before and it always feels nice. After a pause, Sally asks, "You hate how young she is? How easy it would be to hurt her?"

Torey nods and looks at the floor. I feel the buzzing back in my ears.

"You hate how much you want to hurt her?"

Torey looks up, shocked, and nods again. I guess Sally has ferreted out the truth. I'm stunned. I didn't have the faintest notion Torey actually felt like hurting her sister. No wonder she left home. No wonder she's so quiet and withdrawn when she's there.

"That's a very good reason not to be there, Torey. So since you can't help out right now, what's so wrong with Lucy?"

Torey appears exhausted. Lucy is sitting on the couch now and Torey doesn't look in her direction. She seems too tired to fend off any more questions. "I don't know. I'm sorry

I said it, I take it back. Okay?"

"Not okay. I'm surprised at you, Torey, trying to play a game like that. I thought you hated games."

"I do."

"Then you'd better not play them, or you won't think much of yourself. I don't think you're sorry, and I don't think you want to take it back."

I have to admit, Sally's good. I watch my niece wrestle with that little piece of logic and fail to conquer it. She sighs and glances at Sally as if asking, 'What next?'

"How about challenging yourself to the truth here?" Sally's voice goes up, getting louder and richer. "You remember the truth, don't you, the truth about how you feel?"

Torey's looking nervous and I don't blame her. I'm nervous and I'm not even in the line of fire.

"Why," Sally thunders, "can't Lucy love Melissa? Why do you want to stop her? What's wrong with Melissa being loved? Why would you keep that kind of love out of her life?"

Nothing happens. We are frozen statues waiting for Torey to say something, set us free.

"Do you remember when we identified the reason you ran away?"

Sally's telling secrets. I had no idea a reason had even been identified. Still there's no movement from Torey.

"You said the sight of Rae giving Melissa a bubble bath did it. She was happy without you."

That's the reason? I'm confused. That's the reason for Torey's rage? Then I see it. Ugly, raw and impossible to miss. Torey's jealous. Jealous? Yes, I guess she is. And that's probably only the tip of the iceberg.

Lucy and I lock eyes over Torey, who's back to hiding under her hair. I think it hits us at the same time. Poor Torey, poor lonely scared little kid. Not comfortable watching Melissa getting mothered or loved. Wanting to be happy for her but finding out instead she's filled with jealousy.

Torey, with the rage of never having that sort of concern for her when she was little, all those feelings coming up inside like an unwanted guest. Hating a sister who can go places she cannot follow. A sister she sacrificed for.

We three adults are quiet. Torey must have been curious, but when she looks up and sees us gazing at her with such compassion, I guess it scares her. Tears flood her eyes, yet it's clear to me she doesn't understand what we know. So painfully obvious, the mothering Torey never got and never will get from Vicky. Yet still waiting for her mother and unable to let us, any of us, love her. Torey looks at us with widening eyes and growing apprehension.

I'm still on the floor and Sally stands up, directing me to go behind Torey, not quite touching her, yet get very close. My legs are stretched out on either side of her.

"If you want to, Torey, you can lean back against Rae, but only if you want to." While saying this, Sally gets Lucy back on the rug on one side of us, and Sally sits on the other side. "Don't worry, no one will touch you unless you want us to."

Torey's face is hiding behind her curtain of hair again. Her shoulders are shaking as if she's crying, but she's quiet as a stone.

Sally starts, "You are a marvelous gift from the universe. You, Torey are a beautiful bright light." She motions to me like an orchestra conductor. I have no idea what she wants me to do.

Lucy does, though. "Torey is such a good sister. Melissa has always been lucky to have you to watch over her and protect her. Even now, you are still protecting her." She says this softly yet is firm, sincere. Lucy sounds as if she's speaking God's own truth.

I'm bewildered. What am I supposed to say? How come Lucy knows what to do and I don't? I feel on the verge of tears myself. I'm exhausted and tired of feeling so damned useless around Torey. This is my niece. I'm it, all she has. I can see the back of her head and her beautiful curls. I lean towards her. "I love you," I say fiercely in her ear. "I love you and I know you're wonderful. I always have. Thank you for surviving, thank you for making it, for being here." I'm crying for real.

Torey makes a sound, sort of like a gurgle. I know she's getting this, all the love I've always had for her. She leans back onto me and I wrap myself around her, holding on. Sally and

Lucy murmur words of encouragement. Suddenly Torey rocks us both with a scream that my muscles answer as I hold her tight. I feel the scream emerge more than hear it. It's like birth, good, honest and real as hell, or maybe heaven.

Afterwards we keep telling her she is blessing, to us, to Melissa, to anyone who ever met her. All of us crying freely, even Sally who smiles between the tears running down her face.

We sit on Sally's rug, doing that for a long time. It's an extraordinary thing to witness, and I will always be grateful to have been there both times Torey was born.

I'm running late for my session with Sally. She always sees "issues" going on when I'm late, so I like to get there early.

After our session, I'm getting Melissa and then we'll get Torey. Melissa loves going to Torey's school, the girls fuss over her to the point she's nearly bursting. Sometimes Melissa's fans make it difficult for us to leave, but I always enjoy seeing that little girl so happy. Torey will be with us until Sunday, and I'm looking forward to having the long weekend with her, even if most of it will be at work.

I don't have one reason to be late. I'd arranged to get off early and nothing happened to make me late. I simply lost track of the time and it pisses me off. It's four-ten when I pull up and run to Sally's front door.

She's all smiles and pleasantries, though. I'm surprised my tardiness isn't mentioned, and a little confused. Sally doesn't seem to be herself, she seems unfocused and like this is a social occasion or something. We go back to the sunroom.

"I'm glad to report my last session with Torey was absolutely terrific."

"That's good. Last weekend went well, too. We didn't talk about anything that happened during the therapy, but it was more comfortable than it's been in a long, long time. Even Melissa seems happier, more content, and that's lasted all week."

"Wonderful!"

We're sitting in our usual places. I need to get this over with. "I wanted to talk to you about John today."

"Who?"

"You know." This is embarrassing. "John, my paramour?"

"Oh, him. What about him?"

My suspicious nature is alerted. By now I know Sally and her ways. Why is she acting so nonchalant? "I'm sorry I didn't tell you about him."

"You aren't obligated to tell me anything, Rae, except where the girls are concerned. I take it John has been a positive influence on them. Torey seems to like him."

"I don't know why I never told you. It wasn't like he was a secret or anything."

"I think your instincts were correct. Your paramour didn't need to be brought up." She smiles with more friendliness than I'm used to. "And guess what, I have good news for you. You are released from therapy."

I glare back at her. "What do you mean, released?"

"I mean, you no longer have to come here every other week. We will probably need a few more family meetings and include Melissa in some of them, maybe even Lucy once more, but you don't have to worry about any of that right away." She is absolutely beaming.

I'm sure this is Sally's way of paying me back for not telling her about John. "How come?" I can't hide the distrustful tone in my voice.

"Because Torey is finally able to start taking advantage of all her situation offers her."

I'm confused. "You mean an education?"

"Only partly. The main reason I thought living at school would be a good idea was it offered her the opportunity to focus on only herself. Torey's childhood was preempted by everyone else's needs. When I realized she wasn't able to center on herself and was only getting restless and evasive, I was concerned that maybe she couldn't be helped. The therapy we did two weeks ago was a gamble, a big one, and I'm really glad it paid off."

"So what does that have to do with me?"

"Rae, you were court-ordered to be here for the girls, remember?"

She sounds kind, but I feel upset. "But as their guardian, don't you think I still need some help?"

Sally has an odd look on her face, kind of stiff, like she's trying not to sneeze. This is becoming one of the oddest sessions I've had with this woman, and considering some of the stuff that happens here, that's saying something.

"As their guardian, are you having some problems I don't know about?"

Sally sure is acting weird. When she speaks, it sounds like she's talking with a mouth full of marbles. I wonder if maybe she's trying not to laugh, and the thought pisses me off.

"Well, I think the kids would be better off if I got a little more help from you."

I never knew I was such a comedian. Sally explodes into laughter and has to excuse herself.

I hate being laughed at. I sit and fume. I need to talk about some stuff, damn it. Why is she trying to get rid of me?

"Oh, Rae, thank you." Sally breezes back through the doorway. "I needed a good laugh."

"Glad I could be of service."

"Don't be angry, I'm sorry. If you could've seen your face... Rae, this is a good thing, don't you see? You've graduated. Be happy. Most people don't do this well. You did. It's a wonderful thing, and you should be proud."

"Are you saying Torey's cured, we're all fine, and we can just go live our lives?" I ask, still angry, but feeling like an idiot.

She chuckles and then stops. "Sorry. No, Torey is not cured. Trust me on this, Rae. No one is ever cured."

I can't figure out how I'm so hilarious. Sally has another fit of laughter and I feel even more insulted. "I need to ask you something." I try to not sound pissed, but it doesn't work. Sally is still snickering.

"Go ahead," she gets out.

I'm afraid to ask her what's so damned funny. She'll probably fall out all over again. Instead I ask her about Torey.

"I'm still worried about Torey. I want to know what you think will happen now."

"Oh, Rae." She's wiping her eyes. "I'm sorry, but I needed this today. And you're right. Torey is still capable of becoming self-destructive. But it's like I said, I see her able to utilize this time now. She's got a lot of issues coming up from our family session. You saw her release a lot of the guilt and anger she'd been carrying around towards Melissa. Plus she's acknowledged her grief over Vicky. She can begin to look at this stuff now. The real work with her is beginning."

I can't help myself. The words leak out through my mouth despite my efforts to stop them. "But what about me?"

I'm looking at the floor, but I can hear her chuckle. "What about you, Rae?"

"What about the real work with me?"

"You aren't here for you. You were here for the girls, and you have done exceedingly well with both of them. I hope you realize that." She sounds sincere and kind. I dare to peek and see if she can keep a straight face. She can.

"Why were you laughing?"

"Oh, Rae." She starts giggling again, but then stops. "I'm sorry, I hope I didn't hurt your feelings. You caught me off guard is all. Here I thought I had some good news for you, and you act like I'd cooked up some sort of scheme to get rid of you or something. Please forgive me. That was very unprofessional." She's still wiping her eyes.

Since that's exactly what I had been thinking, I didn't find it funny. I wonder what to say next. The quiet stretches out a while before I realize I'm going to have to say what I want. "I need some help."

I guess the laughing helped. She looks relaxed yet thoughtful as she considers me. She takes a deep breath. "Paramour problems?" she finally guesses.

"Yes." This doesn't get any easier.

"What's the problem?"

"He wants to marry me, and he won't even live with me until I say yes."

She starts chuckling again. I can't believe it. Here I am, exposing my innermost feelings to this woman, this supposed therapist, and she's laughing at me. I feel humiliated, embarrassed, and ashamed all at once.

"Oh, Rae. It seems to me all your problems are good things." Sally blows her nose into a tissue. "If you knew all the women who sit in front of me, wishing some guy wanted to marry them... unless you don't want to. Is that it?"

I feel too hurt to answer. She must sense it. Sally comes and sits next to me. "Rae, I'm sorry. I didn't mean to hurt your feelings again, and I can tell I did."

I can't think of what to say.

"I had some good news this morning. A friend of mine is moving here and going into practice with me. What do you think of that?"

"From where?"

"New York, where I'm from."

"What made you come here?"

"I liked the area and was ready for a new adventure, so I moved here. It's worked out well. I can be semi-retired and still involved in things I care about." She gives me an encouraging nod. "Why don't you want to marry John?"

"I kinda do. I mean, in the abstract, it sounds fine. I would like to wear a diamond and have everyone get excited and make a fuss over me. The problem is, I get cold all over at the thought of actually doing it."

"Well then, don't! Be engaged forever. People do that."

"He won't go for it. I already tried." I feel the panic creep over me, the same one I always feel when I try and imagine marrying John.

"Why not?"

"He says he won't live with me because of the kids. It doesn't feel right to him if we aren't married."

"He sounds like a good guy."

"I know, but I don't think it's the truth. I think it's an excuse and that he actually believes in marriage for some weird reason. I think he believes in marrying me." I pluck a leaf from one of the plants on the table. I'd always wanted to see what this one felt like, and it's exactly as I'd imagined, a thick leathery leaf shining back at me. I look up from my leaf murder. "How come I'm like this? I love him more than anything. I don't understand." Something that's been threatening for a while breaks through. I begin shaking and feel stupid. Why am I acting this way? What the hell is going on with me?

Sally has her beautiful shawl on the back of the chair she usually sits in, shades of apricot and peach with long lunar-moth fringe. She gets up and wraps it around me. It feels as I'd imagined, too, soft and warm yet light as a feather. Sally sits next to me and pats me on the back. She's murmuring something soothing, but I don't make out what she's saying. It's not cold in here, yet I'm shaking like I'm freezing or something. I want to pull the shawl over my head and disappear, blend into the background of Sally's house and become dust, fade into the carpet and drapes.

"Rae! What's going on?" Sally's shaking my arm, bringing me back. I don't want to come.

"I don't know. I think I'm losing it."

"You don't have to marry him if you don't want to."

"I know!"

"Then what's the problem?"

"I don't know!"

I start rocking back and forth. I can't stop. Embarrassment is replacing fear.

"You said that when you thought about marrying John, you felt cold all over, right?"

"Yeah." It comes out all shaky, but I can talk. "It's like my brains are thrown into a bucket of ice water. They shut down and I can't think."

"Emotionally, what's going on?"

"I feel like I want to die. I feel horrible." My rocking is slowing down. Good, maybe I can make it out of here and never, ever come back. I feel a deep shame and feel my face burning.

More silence as Sally considers me. "Are you okay with looking at those feelings of wanting to die and feeling horrible?"

Can I look at them? I don't know. "How? I mean, horrible is horrible, isn't it? What else is there?" I feel bitter saying it and blame Sally for making me feel worse.

"Focus on the birds, Rae." She takes a deep breath, "Let me know when they have your whole attention."

She'd said this before when I'd been agitated by something. I didn't want to listen to the stupid birds, but had and surprisingly had become relaxed and calmed down. I hope it works again.

The large, ornate cage in the corner of the sunroom holds tiny birds making a constant background noise of warbles and bleeps. Yet their voices are so tiny you have to concentrate to hear.

I shut my eyes and listen. A truck roars down the street, but finally I'm able to pick out their sounds from others. "Okay," I say.

"John wants to marry you, and your brain goes cold…"

"Fear," I say before she finishes the sentence.

"How much fear?"

"Tons and tons of it." I hate seeing this. Hate admitting to it.

"It's okay, Rae. It's okay to feel this. You've never been committed to anyone who had the slightest option of being able to commit back. Anyone would be afraid. Do you understand that?" She moves closer and puts her arm around me. Sally's rocking next to me, or maybe she's rocking me, I don't know. It feels good.

"When you were married, your husband was emotionally unavailable, right?"

"Right."

"And when you were with that Dennis guy…"

"The rat-bastard."

"Yes, he certainly was. He was emotionally unavailable, and unavailable every other way, right?"

"Well, yeah, he was married."

"You dated a married man for over six years, if I remember right."

"That's true."

"Did you ever want to marry him?"

"No." The force behind the "no" surprises me. I understand in an instant I'd never believed my relationship with Dennis was anything but temporary. The depth of the lies I told myself depresses me.

Sally's right. I'd never been in a relationship with anyone who had something to give back. I'd been caught up in images. I wanted to look like I was part of a couple without risking anything. If I was the only one giving, then I was in control of what happened.

Even in my horrible, dreadful marriage I have to see I picked him and Dennis for the same reason. They were unattainable, for different reasons, but unattainable still. "Outside of the kids, John is the first person I ever loved who loves me back."

"There's a very good reason for this."

"Because of things at home? How estranged we all were from each other?"

"I'm sure that's why. You learned it wasn't safe to love, because love was not going to come back to you."

"But my parents weren't terrible people. They never beat us or did all the things that I see happening to kids on my caseload."

"I'm sure they looked very normal and that they did their best."

There are those words again, "looked normal." She didn't say they *were* normal. "So how did I end up like this?"

"Because you can't fake love. Children always sense it. It's an emotional lie, the kind that does the most damage."

"An emotional lie does the most damage?"

"It's the worst kind of lie for a child. Children can forgive their parents for lies, because after all, they lie, too. But emotional lying and violence to a child cause damage. They can't comprehend doing that to their parents. Pretending to love is not possible for them. Purposely inflicting pain on a loved one isn't possible, either. You learn how to do those things and only older children can accomplish it."

"So I learned how to fake it?"

"I guess that's as good a way to put it as any, but Rae, in the short time I've known you, I've seen a lot of changes."

My tears are gone and I'm no longer shaking from some internal storm. I take off Sally's shawl and hand it back to her. We smile at each other, me sheepishly.

"I can see I was faking it all these years." I sigh and feel old. "But I'm still terrified at the thought of getting married."

"Then date. Let your life happen. Come see me when you want to, and we'll talk about it some more. I truly believe that if you let it, healing will happen."

"I let it!" I say, rather dramatically, and raise my arms to the ceiling.

Sally laughs, only this time my feelings aren't hurt. "I mean if you want to deal with this you will, but you can't force it. Maybe you'll end up deciding to never get married. Maybe you won't. I can't predict the outcome, only the process."

"What do you mean?"

"Some therapists believe that when an issue is paramount in a patient's mind, small, usually unnoticed circumstances get attention, and the patient is led to a resolution by their subconscious."

"Is that what you believe?"

"You know, Rae, to most people I would say yes, but I'm going to tell you the truth."

I wait.

"I think we are all drawn into healing situations by our own wish to re-connect with our authentic selves. I think these situations happen almost magically. The funny thing about healing situations is most people are horrified when they find themselves in one."

"I know exactly what you mean. I was telling John how all the things I thought were so awful ended up getting me out of a truly rotten existence, and into good place with the kids, with him, the restaurant, a bunch of good things."

"You mean like losing your old job?"

"Yeah, that and getting the girls."

"You once told me that you were tired of the illicit nature of your relationship with Dennis and that's why you broke it off with him."

"Well, that and his other girlfriend."

"You said you had a strong urge to do the right thing, if I remember right."

"Yes, I felt like I wanted to be clean. That's the best way I can put it."

Her voice goes kind and soft. "Well, sometimes, Rae, if you try and get right with your world, you end up getting right with yourself, too."

"So you think trying to do the right thing was what caused everything else to happen?"

"I'm saying that I have no idea how the universe works, but I've seen enough to know and respect the power of emotional truth. I know that I respect the journey you're on."

I think she means it. I look in her eyes and make sure.

Shrimp Fajitas

Between two flour tortillas, place cut-up cooked shrimp, sautéed onions and peppers, spiced feta cheese and shredded mozzarella.

Cook in oiled pan until brown on both sides, turning once.

Remove from pan and cut into triangles, like a pie, to make appetizers or use a single, folded-over tortilla to make individual servings for main dish.

MAY

Thursday night. Date night. I'm bored with being appalled by how much I wait for this each week. Fuck feminism, I live for the moment I do him.

Do him good.

It's my reward for the rest of my week. I'm sick of arguing and fighting to get services for kids who desperately need it. I don't know if all administrators are as corrupt as Connie, but I can barely keep the lack of respect I have for her out of the few conversations we can't avoid.

The world disgusts me. Everything is money, money, money, politics, and apathy. I grow tired of being involved in things that don't work. Date night is my reward for making it through another week.

I love spring, though. Peepers singing in the wet woods make me feel hopeful in the small hidden places of my heart, despite everything. My hope must have been hibernating too because I feel it waking up and rejoicing in this glorious spring. It's been so long, but like riding a bike I remember who I am when happy, even if only one night a week.

I'm naked and waiting for him in his bed, on his boat, out in the Chesapeake Bay. My hands are behind my head, and I like the smell of spring in the brisk breeze blowing through the cracked open porthole above. We are anchored to a tiny, empty, remote island. And unless it's raining in the morning, we will wake up and have coffee and breakfast on the deck while watching birds flutter and sing in the trees.

He comes into the cabin and I smile, unashamed. I pull down the sheet with my toes so he can appreciate me better. I hope he won't say a word and somehow my telepathy is working. John smiles and begins stripping naked for me, my fine-looking man. John's teeth flash white next to the dark stubble of his two-day-old beard.

He's going gray on his chest. A source of constant annoyance to him, but I love his grizzled looks and the gray beginning to show in the curls above his neck when he needs a haircut.

We have perfected a dance of sorts. Licks and kisses. The sheer joy of him makes me laugh. Every time is different, sometimes wild, sometimes sweet. When did I learn to trust?

I wish I had a real sister, one I could love and talk to, or girl cousins to call up. I'd gossip until three a.m. and paint my toenails pink one night and red the next. I wish I had older relatives to talk to. I could use advice from an aunt or a grandmother. I don't dare talk to Chip because all she does is try to badger me into marrying him.

I don't want to get married. I want to live together in front of the whole community and my nieces. Me, the straight-arrow egghead, gone wild at age thirty-seven. John says no, but I'm working on him.

That's why I wish for female relatives. I could be as weird and strange as I actually am, and they'd have to accept me because we are related and they couldn't get rid of me.

I wish for relatives while John loses his. He lost Jack.

John found him, behind the bar. They said it was a stroke and the whole town went to the funeral. Marie looks old all of a sudden, all the fire in her gone with Jack. I understand her grief and want to comfort her, but she is walled off and unable to hear me or anyone else.

The restaurant was closed for a week. Chip and I catered the wake and opened the restaurant again last Sunday for brunch, but it was still a wake. People from town needed to come by and speak to each other, talk about Jack and miss him some more.

John's moved out of his room over the restaurant and is

living on the boat full-time. He didn't feel comfortable with Jack gone.

I doubt if Marie's even noticed he's left. He's stored some things at our cottage, giving into my scheme of slowly moving him in, but he still refuses to live there.

We live together Thursdays, most of them out here, somewhere on the water in his big boat, and he says he doesn't give a rat's ass who knows it.

He makes a point of taking me and Melissa to Dino's on Tuesdays after work. We went to the parade in town last week. They have one after a Catholic priest blesses the boats for a season of good fishing. John put Melissa on his shoulders so she could see the parade pass by. We are beginning to feel like a family.

On Thursdays, I usually find a moment to check in with myself, take the temperature of my pain. I guess it's the only time of the week I feel safe enough to do that. John is napping beside me, worn out from our lovemaking.

Jack's death comes to mind and how it had impacted so many people. The whole town seems to have suffered a blow, a true loss.

I feel it, too, but not as deeply as the others. John's sadness I understand. Jack had been a favorite uncle. But so many people are so sincerely saddened by Jack's death that it seems odd to me. I try not thinking about my parents' double funeral, two dead people summoning up barely twenty mourners.

Something in my belly grips with fear. I hear Sally's voice in my head—"Just go with it."

An answer floods in. Emptiness. Barely twenty people huddled against the emptiness of that big room in the funeral parlor, my dominant emotion that day embarrassment and never understanding why. Mortified and feeling somehow responsible for giving my parents such a poor send-off, incompetent failure that I was.

I cry quietly but he wakes up anyway. I don't want to talk about it. I say, "It's not you, not you, don't worry." The water around us doesn't care if I cry. It absorbs everything.

John rocks me exactly the way he did the night we met.

But now he's not a stranger. And I'm not a stranger to myself anymore either.

I stop crying after a while, and am glad to be done with it. "I was crying about Jack's funeral. I actually enjoyed it."

"You're not making sense, Rae."

"I know and I don't mean it that way. I'm saying I'd never been to a funeral as... I don't know, comfortable as his."

"Sorry, Rae, you're still out there in the ozone. I have no idea what you're talking about."

I'm starving but too lazy to get up. "How about making us some sandwiches?"

"Not until you explain yourself."

Motivated, I search for a better explanation. "I enjoyed finding out how people felt about Jack. So many people felt exactly the way I did, and it just amazed me. At the funeral, people getting up and spontaneously just coming out and saying what a terrific guy he was. I mean, people were laughing and crying. It was great. I enjoyed the funeral tremendously."

"You're weird."

"Whatever."

"So why were you crying?"

"I'm beginning to understand how horrible my parents' funeral was."

"Oh."

He doesn't seem to know what to say, which is fine. I don't care. It's only important I hear me.

The nicest part about date night is it doesn't have to end any particular time. We eat, sleep, and make love in any old order. And like most Friday mornings, I wake up anchored somewhere in the Chesapeake Bay, rocking in my Johnny's arms.

Walnut Salad

Gently heat a cup of walnuts in a pan with some olive oil and seasoning salt until fragrant and slightly darker in color.

Make a green salad and add dried fruit (I like cranberries), sliced red onion and half the walnuts.

Make the dressing in a food processor or blender. Use:
  - a cup of olive oil
  - one-third cup of balsamic vinegar
  - two or three cloves of garlic
  - some of the dried fruit
  - seasoning salt
  - pepper
  - a few drops Tabasco sauce
  - a tablespoon of sugar
  - the rest of the toasted walnuts

Blend and put over the salad. Any leftover dressing keeps well, refrigerated.

June Again

"Marie is selling the business?" I ask Maggie. I'd just gotten back from taking Torey to Jennifer's. Our deal is that Torey helps in the morning and gets out of here before we open, which will be in half an hour.

Chip hired Maggie to help, a decision I wasn't too sure about. She's putting out pitchers of juice and looking at me like I'm crazy. "You didn't know? Where the hell have you been? You know Marie can't run this place without Jack."

"When did this happen?"

"It's been happening for a while. Marie is supposed to be meeting some family from Maryland around noon. They have a couple of restaurants up there and want to expand. She told me to tell you to expect them and keep a table free."

"How much is Marie selling the place for?"

"How the hell would I know? I just hope they let me keep on working here and that I can stand them. Marie can be a bear but at least you knew where you stood with her."

Maggie is by nature pessimistic, and she irritates me. I will be glad when Chip gets here to handle her and the rest of the staff. Chip and I have come up with a scheme where I take the early, cooking shift and she takes the late, cleaning-up one.

"Is Marie upstairs?" Her car was parked out front when I came back, and I wondered about it then. She's never here on Sunday.

"I think so. I think she's up in her office."

I go into the kitchen and sit, wondering if I have the guts to go through with this.

Fortuna comes in after the early Mass set up for migrant workers. As soon as she changes, I tell her I need to talk to Marie, and show her what needs to get done. My mind is racing as I climb up the back steps.

I look around. We store dry goods and cleaning supplies in the big room next to Marie's office. The back rooms are filled with old tables, chairs, and broken kitchen equipment. I'm intimately acquainted with the large bedroom and bath on the other side. I know Marie and Jack used to live here when they first owned the place. I see outlines of a home, underneath all the junk. Marie never could throw away a damn thing.

The girls wouldn't mind. I can see us here, I see this working. Taking a deep breath and with knocking knees, I walk into Marie's office.

"Marie?"

She looks up from the desk. "Yeah?"

It had been a while since I'd looked in those eyes, usually sharp or calculating, but now only empty and old. I cleared my throat, feeling embarrassed and like I should apologize for interrupting her pain. "I, um, I wanted to talk to you about *The Sea Witch*."

"What about it?" It seems to take effort for her to speak.

"I was wondering, how much are you asking for it?"

"Why would you want to know?"

I almost cave. I feel myself waver. "Because," clearing the throat trying to close up on me again, I continue, "I might want to buy it."

"How in the hell could you do that?"

The woman is outright pissed. I remind myself of her loss. "I own all that property beside Tinker's Creek, remember?"

She remembers, and looks at me with interest. Then shakes her head and laughs a sound with no laughter in it. "How in the hell do you expect a young woman, by herself, with two kids to raise, to run this place? My God, you don't have any idea what it takes to keep a restaurant this size going smoothly."

"I wouldn't be by myself."

"You wouldn't?"

I gulped. "No, Chip will be my right arm, like she is now with the brunch stuff."

Marie scowls. I'd used the wrong approach, our success with the brunch trade apparently didn't sit well. But the way Marie is right now, nothing would sit well. "A restaurant is an every-day job." She glares at me and thunders, "Every damn day."

"I know that Marie. I'm not afraid of hard work, and besides, John would be here too," I blurt out.

"John Clements?"

I nod yes, appalled by the lengths I will go to get her on my side.

"Why in the hell would John be involved in this place?"

"Didn't you know me and John are getting married?"

"You are?" Her surprise knocks away the anger.

"Yes." I say, and nod, affirming the notion while hoping God doesn't strike me dead for my lies.

"First I've heard of it."

She's pissed again, she's so pissed she's glowering. I've read the word before but don't think I've ever seen it displayed quite so clearly before.

"Well, he's asked me." I faced the glower as if it wasn't there. "Actually he's asked me a bunch of times." At least that part wasn't a lie.

"I heard you two were dating."

She's still glowering. My brain scrambles for a way to turn this around. An idea comes. "Well, John and I have talked about it," Dear God, forgive me, "and John's ready to give up charters. It's a losing proposition anymore. He wants to run the bar."

It's working, her eyes stare off in the distance, remembering and seeing. She speaks softly. "Like Jack did."

"Yes." I lie, not caring it's a lie.

An hour later, after negotiating a price I can live with, I go down the steps, the new owner of *The Sea Witch Saloon and Grill*. I will own the building and the property up to the marina, including approximately 30 feet of waterfront and an acre of parking. Walking back down the steps is an exercise in maintaining balance.

The kitchen is in full swing and Fortuna smiles at me. "How is Marie?"

"Marie is great." I get started on more of Emmaline's sweet-potato corn-bread muffins.

Driving home I come out of my clouds long enough to realize that if I don't get groceries, the girls are going to cite me for neglect. I'm greasy from working in a kitchen without good ventilation, something else I'm going to change.

My heart is beating so fast blood is pounding in my ears. I've had so many ideas flying around I've stuck note cards in my pockets to keep track of them. Chip is thrilled. That's the only word for it, but I've sworn her to secrecy until everything is signed, filed and paid for.

Pulling into the grocery store, I get out a card and write, "new ventilation" underneath "enclose outside deck," "new menus," "change front counter," "get rid of gift shop." My cards are getting full.

I'm thankful for the shock of damp, air-conditioned coldness after the thick humidity outside. The ancient grocery store smells of old wood, ice, fish, and tired raw vegetables, like places my Nana Green used to take me to in Baltimore.

I attempt to picture the grocery list on the refrigerator at home. Bread and milk are a given and peanut butter will never go bad at my house. I can't remember a damn thing, so walk the aisles and get anything that look familiar.

As I pass fellow shoppers, I wonder how people will react to the news I'd bought *The Sea Witch* and feel shy and happy all at once.

In the checkout line I begin to feel antsy. Screw that, I'm not going to back out so I might just as well go home and forget about it, get some rest. I've got to quit my job tomorrow! Oh, my God—quit my job, look into getting insurance. Tell John and the girls what I did. I wonder what they will say?

It occurs to me John might enjoy running the bar. Maybe I wasn't lying after all?

The girls will be fine once we get settled. Transitions for them are difficult, so we will go through that. But it will be okay. And the best part is we have lifetime rights to the cottage, clear thorough Melissa's lifetime. I sold the property to the Chesapeake Bay Foundation and got that as part of the deal. It will never be developed into condos, McMansions, or a high-rise, and I am so glad. Our place will always stay exactly as it is.

In town the girls will be able to have friends over, not be so isolated. I really think it's going to work. I stifle my excitement as I lug groceries to the car. All I want to do is get home and tell them. John's supposed to pick up the girls and meet me there.

When I arrive the place is its usual chaotic self. Toys, clothes, mail piled on the table with cereal from sometime yesterday—the usual weekend mess. Something juicy and good is bubbling inside me. The radio is on and I turn it off. I go back out for more groceries.

I feel something in my chest, an odd sensation like bubbles bubbling. It feels nice and I have no wish to stop, even if stopping had been an option, which somehow I know it isn't.

I go back for the last load, feeling somewhat wobbly and uncertain of my footing. The sun is setting, and the stillness I once found with John is back.

Closing the back of the station wagon, I look around at a world bathed in the golds and pinks of a setting sun. Is it my imagination, or is there something unusually beautiful about this afternoon?

Juggling groceries I reluctantly go back inside. The chaos I saw earlier is unchanged, but somehow it's been transformed into a place of great beauty. Dirty, crumpled socks lying on the floor are major artworks expressing the fragility and tenderness of youth.

Still holding the groceries, I stare at them for a full minute while joy seeps in. I turn and notice spilled orange juice on the counter, gleaming beautifully in the reflected pink light of sunset, making it rosy. The entire room shimmers in pink-golden light.

I wonder if I'm experiencing a full-blown psychosis and then think, who cares? If a full-blown psychosis feels this good, I'll take two. I float around the house straightening and putting things away as if involved in a profound, joyful, and sacred religious observance.

I guess the girls and John are on the dock, which is fine with me. This spell might be broken by human voices. Maybe John took them out in the Whaler which he recently brought back.

I slowly unpack groceries, cherishing the chicken breasts in a wonderful marinade before putting them in the fridge. The lettuce that pissed me off for being too expensive now regards me from its deep green, serene loveliness. I make a walnut salad to die for, with new thyme and chives from my tiny kitchen garden in pots on the porch.

Finally, it's simply time to move on. I hesitate. I don't want to risk losing whatever it is I've stumbled into. But it's time, and I leave by the back door and walk towards the pier. I see them checking crab pots suspended by ropes tied to the dock. Melissa's obsession returned with the summer, and my fingers are raw from picking meat from shells.

They are talking, bits and pieces of words—like murmurs blending with wind, waves, and birds—float towards me. Everything is bathed in the last strong blaze of the late afternoon sun, the tall grasses beside me gleaming red-orange.

I'm consumed by love. it happens suddenly and there is nothing I can do to prevent it or change it in any way. I sink to my knees in the sand and watch my family on the pier. They haven't noticed me. I lay on the sand, with bits of shell poking into me and try to grasp what's happening.

A part of me is dying. For one terrifying moment I think all of me will succumb to death, then I understand, it's only a part.

The voices wafting to me from the pier change. I hear concern but it's already too late and I'm saddened I can't say goodbye. I loved improperly, often incorrectly, yet my care and concern were genuine and the person who felt this will not be here when they reach me, no matter how fast they run.

Like an oyster shell, the crusty old part of me will sink in this sand and be gone. It's heartbreakingly sad. She was everything when I had nothing, and it seems unfair to kick her out now, but there's no choice in the matter—death of a thing is always out of our hands.

They are almost on me. I hear the pounding of their feet up the bank and feel love. Just love, so easy, and I'm so completely unable to feel anything else. For a moment I wonder how I'm going to explain what happened and feel mute, tongue-tied. But already I understand; I don't have to explain anything. They already know who I am. They always have.

Emmaline's Apple Butter Cake with
Carmel-Apple-Butter Frosting

An easy cake to make, it looks deceptively fancy when done. Everyone loves the spicy-apple flavor, and the cake is moist and keeps well. It's actually better the next day, and is a great way to use up last year's apple butter when you accidentally purchase too much of it.

Cake:
- one stick of butter, soft
- one cup of firmly packed brown sugar
- three eggs
- one cup apple butter
- two and one-half cups flour
- three teaspoons baking powder
- one-half teaspoon each baking soda, cinnamon and nutmeg
- one cup buttermilk or sour milk.

Cream butter and sugar until light and fluffy, add eggs, beating well after each, add apple butter and alternate all dry ingredients sifted together, with milk.

Bake in two pans, greased and floured with parchment or wax paper liners. Bake at 350 degrees for half an hour. Test doneness with a toothpick inserted in the center; no crumbs should adhere to it. Remove paper liners from cakes.

Cool cakes on racks. When cool, frost.

Frosting:
- two tablespoons butter
- one-third cup heavy whipping cream

- two-thirds cup firmly packed brown sugar
- two dashes of salt
- three cups confectioners' sugar
- one-half teaspoon vanilla
- three-quarters cup apple butter (not for frosting, use after frosting is made)

Place butter, cream, sugar, and salt in a saucepan and bring it to boil, stirring constantly. Remove from heat and put in a mixing bowl, add vanilla, then confectioners' sugar in small doses, using electric mixer or whisk to incorporate to right spreading consistency (which means use more or less confectioners' sugar as required).

Assembly:

Cut each cake layer into two layers. Be careful to place tops so that you can put them back together exactly as they came apart. (This means you want to take off the layer and put it back where it had been, so there are no dips or hikes when put back together.) A long, serrated edged knife is good for cutting, but fine wire, held taut, and sliced through the middle of the cake, does a better job.

Between the individual cake layers, frost with one-quarter cup apple butter and re-assemble into original two layers.

Frost top of one cake, put other cake on top, frost top and sides of cake. Using last of the apple butter, glop it with a spoon on top of caramel frosting and swirl with a knife to create a marbled effect.

AND YET ANOTHER JUNE

"He's crying again."

I look up from the cake batter I'd been desperately trying to finish before this moment arrived. "Shit."

Torey comes near, her hair now down to her hips, and peers at the ingredients in my bowl. "Are you making cake?"

Jonah is fussing, but not pitching a fit yet. I wipe my brow with the back of one hand. "Yeah, apple butter cake. It's almost done." The commercial mixer is loud and, as usual, the noise quiets Jonah for the moment. "Let me finish, then will you put it in those pans, over there?" I'm nearly screaming and waving at the row of cake pans, greased and floured, with parchment paper bottoms. She nods but I'm already cracking the rest of the eggs and adding them, two at a time, and then flour alternating with buttermilk.

"When you're done with this, the big oven is already pre-heating. Will you call Melissa for me? See if she's ready to come home yet?"

"Where is she?" Torey yells, watching my progress.

"At Madison's house." I yell back. Torey smiles and nods. Having another set of hands around here is a lifesaver at times.

"Scrape it down good after one minute, and let it go another two minutes, okay?" I yell in Torey's ear as she passes Jonah to me. "And put your hair up."

Torey smiles, loops her hair into a knot and wraps a scarf

she fishes out of her shorts pocket, around her head. She goes to wash her hands and I take Jonah the Whale back to the storage room. I'm ready for the break, and for the baby.

John's built a screen, three pieces of plywood connected by hinges, but it gives me some privacy and a place to nurse our Whale. His mother surprised us with a rocker that has a foot-rest that rocks too—really neat, and comfortable too. It's perfect back here, a little paradise for me and the Whale.

At three months old, he still nurses every three, sometimes two hours; ergo the "Whale" addition to his name. At least he now sleeps through the night, or at least most nights, and I take all the sleep I can get.

I have to juggle him, pull up my shirt and bra, and then let the greedy monster have a go at me.

I have so much milk, I keep a stack of washcloths back here for whatever breast he isn't nursing on. Otherwise I'd drip through my shirt and embarrass yet again everyone who works here with my milk-spotted T-shirt. Since it doesn't look like the Whale intends to stop this anytime soon, I wish everyone would just get over themselves about this nursing stuff.

Jonah latches on. There's that moment, almost painful, yet not—not painful at all. I guess it's a sharp sort of feeling, and then my milk lets down and we relax. I put up my feet and begin rocking.

Outside the windows, all kinds of boats rock too. Seagulls, ducks, herons, and wrens fly through the air, screaming, quacking, and chirping.

The antique radio John dug up somewhere can sometimes pick up Williamsburg's NPR. Not today though, as I try fiddling the dial.

Instead of the radio, I hum some tune, suckle my son and keep an ear out for any unusual sounds from the kitchen.

A storage area in this part of the building is outright stupid. Why someone put a storage area fronting the water, I'll never know. I'm itching for a re-do, to expand the dining area into here, put in new windows, and add on out back for the kitchen. A new refrigerated room would cost hardly nothing to run. New grills, new oven.

But John says, "Not now, please."

Every time I bring up the subject—"Not now, please." Like last night, he stood with his hands on my shoulders like he was pushing me down, closing his eyes, leaning back and saying, "Woman, will you give it a rest?"

When we talked about it before, he said he'd never faced so many changes in one year and it would be a while before he was ready to take on any more.

I understood, and he's probably right when he tells me our plates are full right now, and that I don't need any more distractions.

But I'm still itching.

I bend down and kiss Jonah's head. My little boy has perfect brown ringlets.

Jonah is getting out of the frantic stage of nursing and slows his rhythm. Our son is a small mass of strong emotions—starvation, exhaustion, intense rage, or great joy.

He has the oddest, deepest chuckle whenever something in his world causes him to laugh. It's such a funny sound, the rest of us crack up. He's gotten the entire kitchen laughing to the point of wiping their eyes.

Torey is, surprisingly, such a help. The amount of stuff she remembers from when Melissa was a baby is amazing.

I bet Melissa is the one who lined the window sills with oyster shells. Probably her way of sprucing up the place. I keep meaning to ask her, so I can thank her. I make another mental note.

They aren't the prettiest shells in the world, that's for sure. Rough, uneven, barnacled and broken, yet still, they make a nice statement, there in the window, piled up exactly the way Melissa would—balanced one atop another in small towers.

I think the statement they make is about indestructibility.

I could take those shells and throw them off the marina's dock, and tiny oyster spats would attach themselves and begin building shells of their own. It would take years for them to get as large as the ones on my sills, but what else were oysters supposed to do but become oysters?

I smile at the things that go through my head when I

feed Jonah and rock us both. I'm turning into a crazy woman. A very happy, very crazy woman, and I kiss Jonah's ringlets.

A small boat rides the waves, heading west. Probably some guys off work for the day, going fishing. I silently wish them good luck and hope whatever they're after is hungry for their bait.

Why wouldn't I? After all, I've got plenty of luck to spare.

About the Author

Elvy Howard lives with her husband, three dogs and one cat in Midlothian, Virginia. Happily, the couple's grown children, and still-growing grandchildren, live nearby.

Love on a Half Shell is Elvy's first novel.

Thank you for purchasing *Love on a Half Shell*. We hope you enjoyed Rae's story!

For our most up-to-date news, including author events and upcoming releases, please visit us at www.EdwardAllenPublishing.com.

CPSIA information can be obtained at www.ICGtesting.com
Printed in the USA
LVOW081924030413

327512LV00001B/3/P